The Ofsted Murders

Gary Sargent

THE OFSTED MURDERS

A Lulu Book ISBN 978-1-4452-1573-0

Published in the UK by lulu.com
This edition published 2009

www.lulu.com

For Emma

I - Friday

George Anthony Loatheworthy cupped one hand around the luminous face of his wristwatch, squinted at it through the darkness, and allowed himself a thin smile.

It was five-thirty-five: time for a break-in.

Everything was running to plan. At dusk he had coasted slowly into Rymers Lane, his headlights off, enjoying the stealthy sound of frosted mud and gravel clinking and spitting under the BMW's tyres. In his mind the car was stalking the school, as if it were a grey shark nosing up to the scent of a flabby and asthmatic non-swimmer who was paddling too far from the shore. He had parked in the shadow of an ancient gorse hedge which screened him from view and waited, leaning back against the car's bonnet with his arms folded, watching darkness come on through the thorns.

From this angle Hornby County Infants School *did* resemble a swimmer, stretching long classroomed arms companionably outwards across the edge of a pool-like cinder playground and a large oval field which had been officially out of bounds for the children since mid-October. Loatheworthy watched through the tangled greenery as a row of lights winked out across the back of the building like a count-down. Eventually, only the staffroom (which faced away from him), cast out a pool of yellow light onto the ground before it. The final staff-meeting of the year had begun and the rest of the school would now be empty.

Narrowing his eyes and hunching his shoulders, Loatheworthy stood up from his car and moved slowly to the lowest point of the hedge. He could not help but imagine two low notes from a cello repeated over and over and see a fin cresting dark water. Now they would learn that the school's splashing had drawn in an especially wily and dangerous predator.

Two minutes later he emerged on the other side of the hedge, wild-eyed and frightened, pinwheeling his arms as if to ward off an unseen enemy, and cursing lightly under his breath. The hedge had dragged his coat from one shoulder, filled its hood with brackish water, and taken one of his shoes. He pivoted clumsily on one leg and then spotted it, lodged deep in a deposit left by some local wildlife - possibly a colony of yak or rhino.

Loatheworthy lurked by the hedge-side, wiping his shoe carefully, emptying his anorak, and getting his breath back. Eyeing it balefully, he swore revenge on the swaying foliage, then turned to face the school again.

The playground was still empty. A small climbing frame, shaped to look like an elephant, glared at him, resenting his intrusion. He ducked low and trotted across the yard towards the building, ignoring the dampness in his shoe and the fact that every second step now emitted a low and dreadful squelch.

Each classroom had a door opening out to the yard, and Helen Haversham's was last in the row. Loatheworthy reached the door and peered in through the glass. The room was dark and empty, and the only one to which he had not yet managed a clandestine visit. Helen Haversham had proved to be a most inconvenient woman; until today she had been ever present, or had left the room locked.

Was it locked now?

Loatheworthy hesitated, his hand on the door handle, his reddish moustache twitching nervously. He had drafted a proposal for night-time covert surveillance of schools, but it had not yet gained approval from his superiors at the Inspectorate, and so being caught here might prove inconvenient. Haversham would surely *make* it inconvenient. Her face rose up before him: a measuring gaze so like her father's, and his hand convulsed on the handle and pulled the door outward.

After a moment's hesitation he crept inside and stood in the hanging shadows of the children's bizarre Christmas decorations, peering carefully into the corners of the room and trying to familiarise himself with its layout. Her desk was the place to start. Where was it?

On the windowsills there was a cityscape of cartons of sharpened pencils, long-handled paint brushes, trays of paints, and tubs of crayons. They cast firmer, more jagged shadows into the room, reminding him uneasily of child-like grasping fingers. He followed their points, past a sign written in wobbly pink lettering almost a foot high, made bloody maroon in the half-light: 'Junk Modelling is Fun!' The exclamation point had been crafted from one half of a detergent bottle and part of an egg-carton coloured-in which resembled a large unblinking eye.

He spotted her desk, nestling content below a poster showing famous landmarks: the palace of Westminster, the Statue of Liberty, the Eiffel Tower. He went to it.

The classroom's art tables had been covered with fresh newspapers ready for Monday, and Loatheworthy trailed his hand along them as he walked, relishing their crispness. In the centre of the second table his fingertips snagged on an edge, and he looked down to see that someone had clipped a photograph from this particular edition of the *Daily Mail*.

He stooped and read the headline: *Ofsted Murderer Kills Again*.

Loatheworthy straightened up and glanced quickly around the classroom and out to the playground over his shoulder as if he might see a spectre lurking there, but there was nothing. A frisson of nervous energy ran through him at this mention of the murders, and then he looked down at the table again, frowning slightly.

This piece of newspaper was central, as if it had it been deliberately placed here, centre-stage as it were, to provide a message for the first inspector to arrive on Monday. He picked it up and gazed out through the hole, putting his face where the photo would be. Had the clipping simply been removed to spare the children a gruesome sight? Or did it now form a part of someone's private collection? Was this Haversham's idea of a joke?

Was it a warning?

He pondered these questions in the darkness until some sound - perhaps a note of protest, perhaps laughter - muted and indecipherable, washed in from the other end of the school, then he carefully replaced the page, and with renewed determination made his way towards Haversham's desk.

At that moment, Lady Helen D'Haversham was returning the favour and thinking of Loatheworthy. She strode purposefully across an unnaturally green and healthy lawn, beneath an unnaturally blue and cloudless sky. She was dressed entirely in tweed, except for a monocle, mud-spattered boots, and a large shotgun broken and draped casually across her forearm. As she reached the lawn's centre, a bizarre tableau came into view. An over-large clay pigeon launcher sat waiting beside a bending butler. Atop the fragile trembling disk, crouching and gripping its edges, there sat a small school inspector. As Helen reached the machine, she made her gun whole, and seated it at her shoulder with one sweeping and fluid movement.

"Pull, Hedges!" she cried.

"Very good ma'am," Hedges replied, and did just that. Helen traced a high wide arc as the pigeon flew, her finger secure on the gun's trigger…

" …to add?" Hedges asked, inconveniently.

Helen blinked, and the field, the sky, and the gun disappeared and were replaced by the questioning expression of Rosemary Fairport, Headteacher of Hornby County Infants.

"Anything to add to that, Helen?"

Helen shifted in her seat, nodding sagely-

"No," she said. "Spot on. I quite agree."

"Excellent. Excellent. If I could just run through the lunch-duty roster once again so that there are no nasty surprises next week, then I… "

The Head's voice faded again, but this time Helen resisted her daydream and glanced up and down the long staffroom table at her colleagues. The inspection was changing them.

When she had first met Kim Ewing, who took point duty and welcomed Reception classes into her floral-print-clad bosom, Helen had been impressed by Kim's unshakeable, almost glacial calm, and her gentleness in word and deed. Now Kim had given up yoga, tofu, and wheat-grass juice, and instead put all of her energy into an unusually vicious strand of karate which she used to administer savage beatings to a life-sized bean doll known only as 'Inspector Bobby'.

During their first full year of schooling at Hornby, children passed through either Helen's, or Alison Green's care. Helen eyed her friend (who sat to her right, taking the minutes for the meeting) carefully. There was a little more grey in the black bob-cut, and she looked tired, but otherwise she seemed unscathed. Alison caught her looking, screwed up her face, and poked out her tongue like a six-year-old.

Miriam Fitzpatrick, A.K.A. Manic Miriam, and occasionally these days, Medicated Miriam, sat closest to the Head. She was the younger of their Year Two teachers, and was also, at first glance, the closest thing they had to a stereotypical schoolmistress. Miriam was fifty, unmarried, wore enormous plastic-rimmed glasses which magnified her eyes until they resembled lightly fried eggs, and lived alone with her cactuses and cats. She also, thanks largely to Ofsted, now exhibited the most alarmingly theatrical mood-swings of anyone Helen had ever met, and her mood was indicated by her choice of clothing: black for her black days, and sparkling royal blue for her sparkling royal blue days. When the Head had asked for suggestions for the spring school trip Miriam had, on alternate days, suggested a local theme park ("It would be so jolly!") and Meadow Green, the local cemetery ("they're *six* now, they need to know, to learn the futility of it all, the hopelessness, the black earth... the *end*...")

Miriam was also, Helen had been reliably informed, conducting a frantically impassioned, immoderately pleasurable, and as far as she was concerned *secret* affair with Oliver Crodd, the school's only male educator, and guardian of the other Year Two class. Helen had been amazed that Crodd was up to the job. He was a wildly enthusiastic hypochondriac, who now sat slumped in a hard plastic staffroom chair facing Miriam as if he might have just died. Crodd and Miriam were the perfect foils for one another's neuroses, which in the last few weeks had begun to spiral out of control. Miriam had been wearing black for almost two weeks solid, and Crodd had become convinced that he was developing a bewildering variety of fungal infections.

The Head, herself responding by becoming yet more brusque and odd, brought a loose-leaf file up onto the long table.

"Now, to other business. I'm afraid that I have had to make the decision to refuse Miss Wilson's kind offer to bring her collection of rare ethnic arts in for the children to view."

Kim Ewing's gaze cleared-

"Why? I thought we'd agreed it would be good for the children, culturally I mean."

"Well," the Head replied, "firstly, I'm not convinced that Ms Wilson's collection of artefacts is either rare or ethnic, or even, for that matter, art. When I visited her at her workshop, she gave me the impression that she was making her artefacts from plaster-of-Paris in the back garden."

Kim looked at the Head over steepled fingers. "Authenticity," she said, in a tone which suggested that this comment might boggle their minds, "is in the eye of the beholder."

The Head sat back. "Have you actually *seen* her collection?"

"Well, er, no. But I've heard that it's very good."

"Did you know that Ms Wilson has a particular interest in totemic fertility objects?"

"Well, yes, but... "

The Head removed a series of glossy photos, several of which were in panoramic letterbox format, from the file, laid them out in front of her, shook her head, and then began to slide them along the desk so that they could be seen by all. Kimberly paled. There was a long and careful silence.

"What am I looking at?" Miriam asked, adjusting her glasses. Alison reached over her shoulder, grasped one elongated photograph by a corner and turned it right way up. Miriam raised one hand to her lips. "But it's so... Extraordinary," she said.

Kimberly apologised.

Alison glanced up at the Head. "Should I minute this, do you think?"

"Of course."

Helen watched over Alison's shoulder as, with an expression of sublime glee, she wrote-

Here the Headteacher took her opportunity to display a series of obscene images to the staff.

Helen leant towards her. "Better make that 'artistic', do you think? You don't know who might read that."

Pouting, Alison changed the entry.

Loatheworthy tried both desk drawers, and found that both were locked. He glanced around again. Yes - there - a coat peg holding an oversized brown anorak. He felt irresistibly drawn to it. During a similar prowl, three inspections before this one, he had found an intimate note signed by a married school governor in a teacher's coat pocket, a discovery which had brightened up that inspection no end.

He searched the coat's outer pockets carefully and found nothing but tissues, confiscated sweets, and a headless action figure. Then his hand brushed against something more substantial suspended in the garment's lining.

It was a capacious inside pocked. He reached in carefully, frowning with concentration. His fingers touched cold metal, perhaps something wooden, and then closed around a small rectangular object. He drew it out and it glinted mysteriously in the half-light. Another confiscation? No, it seemed far too expensive for that.

It was a small wooden box, about the size of a matchbox, highly polished and inlaid with fantastically detailed marquetry. He held it up to catch the ambient light. The design was of a cat, sitting primly and staring out at him with over-large eyes. The corneas were amazingly detailed, a series of dark and light woods sandwiched together to give the effect of a rich and knowing gaze. He shook it, something inside rattled, and he smiled an unpleasant smile as the idea struck him that this might be a pillbox - drugs! A definite sacking offence. He slid his thumbnail under the lid and exerted some upward pressure but nothing happened; it was locked somehow. He put it down on the desk and, sitting in the teacher's chair, took out his pocket knife. Eventually he was able to slide the thin blade under the box's lid, yet still some mechanism resisted as he tried to turn it. He applied more force, pushing the blade inwards and turning it clockwise, and suddenly the box sprang open, spilling tiny black and white fragments across the desk.

Loatheworthy blinked in the darkness, waiting to see whether the noise would bring a response, and when it did not he reached down, picked up one of the objects, and laid it in the palm of his hand. Cautiously he sniffed it; there was a subtly familiar aroma that he associated with the kitchen, with apples. The white objects were harder to identify, and it was not until he found a larger rounded fragment with a jagged edge and two identically shaped holes in one end, that he realised that he was holding a selection of mouse bones in his hand. He dropped them onto the desk again.

The woman was carrying around a box filled with cloves and the skeletal remains of a small rodent. He shook his head; this was odder than he had expected. It was evidence that she was at best a New Age type, obsessed with auras and spells and the motions of the stars, or at worst she was deranged, an exponent of the popular art of rodenticide, *spiced* rodenticide; neither case was useful to him.

With a new reverence he carefully swept the debris from the edge of the desk back into their tiny prison, closed the lid, and as an afterthought wiped its surfaces with his handkerchief.

On the underside of the box, in wedges of dark wood, he could make out the simple legend - 'cat and mouse?'. He stared at that for a moment then dropped the box back into Haversham's pocket where it clanked against some other objects. Time was running out.

The meeting moved on to the arrangements for next Thursday's carol concert, a 'one-off' this year, thanks to Ofsted. Yes, the paper lanterns were ready (and *not* flammable). Yes, they had chosen reliable children with a limited blasphemy vocabulary to introduce each carol, and yes, all parts in the Nativity scenes had been taken by non-vomiters. Meticulous planning was considered to be an issue of both personal and national security in the school, since the spring fête of two years before (referred to obliquely in the staffroom as 'the May Day thing'). On that fateful day a country-dancing volunteer had missed her footing and become hopelessly entangled in the mechanism of the maypole. She was only discovered four hours later when her weak cries were heard during the clean-up operation. It was a calamity overshadowed when several of the smaller children had gone hog-wild, seized the 'throw a wet sponge at teacher' stand by force, and laid waste to large areas of the school field using guerrilla tactics which would have shamed the Viet Cong. When the stand was finally recaptured, it was discovered that the children had been in the process of creating a soap-filled 'flame-thrower' from the school tuba. Helen still sometimes awoke, smelling wet sponges on the morning air, and hearing Miriam screaming "Charlie's out on the wire... Incoming... *Incoming.*"

"As you know," the Head said, "the money for the costumes for this year's concert, along with a very generous donation to school funds, came to us from an anonymous patron."

A gentle ripple of conversation spread down the table. Along with the Ofsted murders and their own inspection, this had been a hot topic for staffroom gossip in recent weeks. Who was the school's guardian angel? Helen had developed the theory that some ex-pupil with fond memories of the place had had a lottery win. Alison had developed the theory that the Headteacher had signed a secret (but very lucrative) deal with Satan.

The Head smiled warmly. "Well you'll all be glad to know that the mystery will soon be solved. He, or she, will be attending the concert on Thursday."

Helen raised her eyebrows, there was another ripple of conversation, and Alison leaned towards her. "Ah," she said, "the smell of brimstone."

The meeting drifted on through discussions of the timetable and the school's 'special children' - a teacherly euphemism for students who were soldiering on through their education with special difficulties or gifts, or a tendency towards evil-genius - until Crodd took a roll of something out of his jacket pocket and offered them around. Alison absently took one and popped it into her mouth. Helen frowned-

"What are they Crodd, mint imperials?"

Crodd manoeuvred his to the front of his mouth, removed it, squinted at it and said, "Beta-Blockers, I think."

Alison spat hers out into her hand.

"For God's sake Crodd these things are prescription only. They're diuretics aren't they? I have to go enough as it is."

The Head frowned mightily, "As I'm sure you remember," she was saying, trying to override them, "during Loatheworthy's so-called orientation session."

Crodd snorted. "Is that what he called it?" he asked in an undertone. "More like a white-knuckle ride, strutting around. Thought I was going to have some kind of gastric spasm."

Sage nods around the table, and a faint moue of disgust from Helen. She looked to the darkened windows; night pressed against them and threw back their reflections. It might be time, she felt, to take a turn around the school.

"Whatever he called it, he expressed a... " the Head shuffled her papers, then found the note she was looking for, " ...yes, a concern over the school's 'ability to manage its special children within the remit of its policy documents and established best-practice' whatever that means."

Alison was wrapping the Beta-Blocker in a tissue, her face darkening to a shade just before purple. Helen recognised this: it meant that an outburst was coming.

"Manage? What does he mean - manage? I am not a manager, and this is not a factory."

The Head's frown deepened.

"Alison, if you would just... "

"What's next? Are the children 'units'? Am I a Headstuffing and Behaviour Modification Resource?"

A lengthy argument was brewing.

"Does anyone mind if I duck out to the loo?" Helen asked.

"No," the Head said, resigned to Alison's tirade, "it'll give us a chance for more tea. You may as well collect what's left of the children's party food; it's in your classroom."

Smiling faintly, Helen pushed open the staffroom door and made her way down the corridor.

"Ah Herr Oberstgruppenfuhrer," Alison was saying as she left, "the Learning Ram is in place and I have processed twenty units today. I have the piano wire ready in case they forget anything... "

Loatheworthy stood, and opening the anorak pocket with his left hand, carefully reached further into its depths. At the other end of the school the volume of background noise rose briefly, he heard voices and then the familiar 'k-chunk' of a closing door. He froze, looking around at the dark classroom. Should he duck down behind the desk and hide, or slip out undetected through the door and back across the playground? He flushed with indignation. This was simply not playing fair; he had found nothing of any use, certainly nothing which would give him an edge.

Footsteps approached the corridor on which this classroom lay. He stood transfixed, muscles trembling slightly with the effort of staying perfectly still, and then decided to flee.

Withdrawing, his outstretched fingers encountered something with a sharp corner, something folded - paper? A note?

What was it?

The person in the corridor seemed to be shuffling their feet, and something in the manner of the sound suggested to him that it was a woman out there, perhaps Haversham herself, doing something to the corridor's wall displays.

He groped in the darkness, trying to find the object's edge. In the corridor he heard the telltale gurgle of water running through the fountain as someone stopped for a drink - only seconds now. Again, he felt cold metal under his hand, something square, with weight, and something that could only be the edge of an envelope. As the sound of the fountain stopped, he grasped it, and by the time the metal bar of the mousetrap had snapped down upon his fingertips, footsteps were approaching the door.

The pain was so sudden and surprising that he uttered only a startled gasp, and two syllables- "Nung... *Nung!*"

With some effort Loatheworthy resisted the temptation to perform the universal dance of the squashed finger (contort face into grinning rictus of pain, bend knees slightly, stick out bottom, and caper lightly from one foot to the other). Instead, he drew his hand out and stared open-mouthed at the small square of wood and metal that was now attached to it. Even in the darkness, he could see that the ends of his fingers were taking on an angry purple cast. Wearing an expression of fear and amazement so exaggerated that he would have found it comical in another, he looked up as a shadow hesitated behind the classroom door.

With no time to remove the trap, he made a break for it, pushing open the door to the play yard and scrambling through. Once outside, he ducked below the level of the window sills, cradling his wounded hand to his chest with his back against the wall. Sweating with the effort of not making a sound, he watched the pneumatic door-closer do its job with agonising slowness. In frustration, he pushed at it with the side of his foot, but it refused to be hurried. The angle narrowed... narrowed... then, as the door snicked closed, he heard the classroom door open, and light spilled across the playground all around him.

Clammy in the cold night air, Loatheworthy's panic reached new heights. He was sure that there must be a call; she *must* have heard him. He became aware that his breath might be seen, rising into the air in frosted clouds, and so he held it. Across Rymers Lane were houses, maybe twenty upper-story windows, any of which might suddenly frame a curious face staring out at the stranger in the playground, crouching unwelcome in a pool of light. He closed his eyes against the possibility, but no shout came. Instead the lights simply flicked off, and as he heard the classroom door close once more, he was bathed in blessed darkness.

Loatheworthy discovered that there is no painless way to remove a mousetrap from one's own fingers, and he resorted to curling a thumb under the bar to ease the pressure and wriggling the swollen digits free.

Lucky for him that it hadn't been a larger trap, or he'd be dealing with breaks rather than bruises.

He waved his fingers, blowing on them.

Why did Haversham have a trap in her pocket?

He paused to consider the question properly. It was possible that the trap (and the mouse bones?) were part of some ghastly show-and-tell, a macabre teaching aid for Monday's class. Equally, there could be something in the pocket that she wished to protect - it was not rational behaviour, certainly, but she *was* a teacher. This was a disturbing possibility, but not quite as disturbing to Loatheworthy as the third option that came readily to mind. He held the trap up before narrowed eyes: maybe she had been expecting him.

The envelope lay in his lap. It was made, probably by hand, of thickly textured paper, and was sealed in the centre with a blob of crimson wax, indented with a gothic capital H. This leant more weight to option two: the trap was there to defend this envelope and its contents from tiny inquisitive fingers.

He glanced around himself. The playground was empty and quiet. The elephant climbing frame gazed at him vacantly. He gathered his nerve and stood, slinking back the way he had come, skirting the malevolent hedge with the envelope and the sprung trap tucked into his own pocket. His fingers throbbed in the darkness but he had a first aid kit in his car.

Safely installed behind the wheel, and overshadowed by greenery once more, Loatheworthy switched on the BMW's interior light and rummaged in the glove compartment. He came up with a can of spray-on antiseptic and liberally coated his fingers, cooling them.

Eventually he could stand the anticipation no longer and tore off the end of the envelope. He shook out a piece of notepaper, again thick and seemingly expensive. He lifted it to his nose - no perfume, but it might still be a good find.

The paper was folded in half four times, and as he opened each fold, he carefully smoothed out the crease against his thigh. The message, when it was finally revealed, was written in what he thought was called a glitter-pen, and the large jolly letters sparkled cheerily in green and gold. A single word, emphatic, underlined, followed by an exclamation mark, the point of which was a Mickey Mouse sticker. Mickey was dressed as the sorcerer's apprentice, wearing a long comedy robe and floppy wizard hat, holding his white-gloved hands out at the message, and presenting it as a conjurer would a particularly amusing trick.

It said- 'GOTCHA!'

Loatheworthy sat in his warm comfortable seat and stared at the expensive notepaper for what seemed to be a long time. He was faintly aware of the headlights of cars from the main road washing across the mouth of the lane with less and less frequency; the Friday night rush hour, such as it was in the town, was coming to an end.

Presently his eye was caught by the flick and glow of fluorescent lights shining again from the dark side of the school: someone in a classroom - in *the* classroom. He reached up to switch off the car's interior light and adjust the side mirror. A servo-motor hummed briefly in the quiet as he tracked the mirror from side to side, hunting in the darkness for the best view of the classroom through the evil hedge. It balked him again, and he settled on an angle where he could just make out a hazy figure, no more than a disturbance in the light, passing backwards and forwards by the window.

Its dance went on for five minutes by the dashboard clock, and then all was dark again. Loatheworthy looked down at the note in his lap, then, lifting it with exaggerated care by one corner, as if fearing that it might explode, he turned it over and examined the blank side. Nothing. After a moment's pause he placed it reverently on the passenger seat beside him, and looked into the rear-view mirror. He was wide-eyed and pale, his thin hair tousled, his fingers throbbed, and an unpleasant aroma was rising from his violated shoe. He began to feel yet more anger towards Haversham. There would be revenge. Not just the long-planned-for revenge that he had come here tonight to serve, but even more, an extra bit, just for Helen.

He nodded to himself in the mirror, to make sure that he understood, then started the car and slowly turned in the narrow lane. He kept his headlights off until he reached the lane's end, then turned out onto the main road and drove away from the school, towards his home and his study, where he might tend to his crushed fingers properly, burn his shoes, and make more appropriate plans.

#

Minutes passed, and the sound of Loatheworthy's car died away on the night breeze.

In the darkness of Rymers lane, an irregular-shaped patch of black unfolded itself from its resting place at the base of the gorse hedge, and grew into the shape of a man. He was tall, and wore a trench coat. He watched the mouth of the lane for a moment, and then peered over his shoulder at the school, seeing the view that Loatheworthy had enjoyed half an hour or so before. Eventually he nodded, deciding something internally, pulled a cell-phone from his pocket, and dialled. Its brief orange light flared and died as he put the phone to his ear.

"It's me," he said, after a short pause, "I'm certain. She has it."

#

Hours after the brake lights of Loatheworthy's car had glowed red and died, hidden snug in the depths of his two-car garage, someone else pushed open the door of yet another classroom and took a step inside.

This one was different. There were no Christmas decorations, no cheery messages, no Santa's footprints or Nativity scenes. This room was stark and functional, and yet still maintained an air of clutter. Long high desks, each joined to its neighbour, ran out in parallel lines from a wall with windows so narrow they resembled arrow-slits. Stools were spaced at regular intervals, wooden and angular, casting shadows like statuary on the white-tiled floor.

The desks here were thick and old, and even from the doorway it was possible to see scars and pits in their surface. Much of the marking was writing: graffiti - dates and names coasting gently into history, but some of it seemed to be chemical burns made deep in the grain. At the back of the room were three Butler sinks, each with an arched chrome mixer tap. At the front were two locked storeroom doors, blank, like closed and sleeping eyes. Between them stood another high bench, set up for demonstrations, and a large old-fashioned rolling blackboard.

Gloved fingers, glowing whitely in the scant security lighting that leaked in from a walled yard, hesitated by the light switch. They tapped the wall, moving like undersea creatures. The intruder was sure that there was no one in the school, and the walled yard meant there was little danger of being overlooked, but still...

Caution was best, and the figure slipped comfortably into the darkness and closed the classroom door behind it. Gloved fingers trailed along the hind desk which, being furthest from the watchful eye of teacher, bore the most marks. The fingers found a love heart, circling the words 'AL '93'. A pause, a quick calculation. If 'AL' were in his (or her?) final year when this had been carved, then they would be... thirty-something now, older, heavier, perhaps balder, and sitting in a living room somewhere preparing for the weekend. Almost certainly they would have forgotten this little piece of themselves, left behind to be polished away eventually by other peoples' elbows.

Gas taps dotted the desks, coming through on sturdy piping, but the Bunsen burners, little gods of science, were locked safely away in one or other of the cupboards. Fingers turned a tap and were rewarded with the narrow hiss of escaping gas, a sound which brought a faint smile. Quickly, the level was adjusted with an expert touch so that only a tiny amount of gas escaped into the room, and then it was shut off completely. A sniff: the heady smell of waiting combustion, undercut by a mix of foul school chemicals, cleaning fluids, and chalk dust.

It was time to go to work.

The intruder touched thumbs and forefingers together, to make a white plastic-coated finger-frame, and sighted through it. Yes. The photograph would be taken from - two steps to the right - *here*.

The room was pleasantly symmetrical. In the morning, light from the narrow windows would wash in and highlight the scene perfectly, or not quite.

In an excellent mood now, pleased with the choice of venue and the thrill of new work, the intruder bustled to the front of the room and pulled at the demonstration desk. After a short struggle it moved forward, grudgingly, scraping ruts in the tiles.

A look to the left. Yes. Now it would be in line with the window, and the newly created 'display' would be properly lit. The intruder hefted a sports bag onto the desk and climbed onto the stool. A zip was opened, equipment was laid out. A bizarre mix of familiar and esoteric items: a syringe, three-quarters full of some viscous yellow liquid; a wafer ice-cream cone; blue fabric; a single sheet of paper; an actor's crown covered with fake plush and paste jewels; a rubber mask of someone once famous - a jowly countenance, almost, but not quite jolly. Finally, a pair of flip-flop sandals, worn and battered, found on the street yesterday morning. The intruder liked to include such objects - something random - in each scene. It kept things fresh artistically.

The smell of chalk dust was stronger here, and the intruder turned towards the blackboard.

Almost forgot!

The heavy board fabric was pulled slowly around on its rollers in the search for a clear space. At the back, someone had written 'Mr Court is a Tosser!' in a hurried Friday-afternoon scrawl. The intruder laughed a little, almost in a reverie of the past. Though the message had a certain artistic merit, it could not be allowed to remain. It was rubbed away, replaced with eight carefully lettered words, and then the intruder climbed back on to the stool (which probably belonged to the erstwhile Mr Court) to wait.

It was forty minutes before there was a jangle of keys, the sound of hurriedly taken breaths, and then the heavy tread of footfalls in the corridor. The intruder smiled in the darkness. He was trying to be *quiet* - how sweet.

As the footfalls stopped by the classroom door, the smile faded, and one gloved hand groped for the syringe.

Showtime!

II - Sunday

By the time Helen reached the bottom of the stairs it was already too late; the hedgehog had left her a small and delicately sculpted present on the parquet flooring, near to the cat flap. She ignored it for now, scoonching into the kitchen, mule slippers scuffing on the lino, and headed for the kettle. She filled it, switched it on, and invested some time in staring into space, occasionally bringing one hand up from the warm pocket of her dressing gown to rub sleep from her eyes.

Yesterday's weekly postcard lay on the table. She picked it up, smiling faintly, and read it through again. It was written in her father's characteristically laconic, slanting hand. It said simply- 'Have Volkswagened past the Tanami dessert to the Bungle Bungles. Your mother wants to see Shark Bay. Blissfully happy as ever. Still wandering. Love you.' She flipped it over - another view of Uluru. Her father couldn't get enough of that big red rock.

When one corner of the kitchen began to fill with voluminous clouds of steam, she started the long search, up work surface and down, for an unused cup. Eventually, still squinting, reluctant to let in too much light, she faced the horrifying truth: she would have to select one from the precariously balanced pile of unwashed dishes on the drainer and wash it up herself.

Upstairs Marie's alarm sounded, and Helen heard her friend stir. She counted - one... two... three... and then tilted her head upwards. Yep, there was the double floorboard-shaking thump of Marie actually leaping from her bed and heading for the shower, a frightening blur of activity, her life one long goal-driven sprint. God, she could be hateful.

Helen was bringing a second cup of the blessed coffee to her lips, eyes closed, resting a hip against the kitchen table, when she felt something butt at her right big toe. It was unpleasantly warm and wet, a little like the rubber end of a pencil dipped in washing-up liquid. It butted again, more insistently, and she cracked open an eye and peered downwards. The hedgehog peered back up at her reproachfully.

Wastrel, it seemed to say. *Where the hell's m'damn breakfast?* And it butted her one more time for good measure.

Helen stooped and laid the back of her hand flat on the cold lino, and the creature scuttled onto her palm; its claws tickled. As ever, she was surprised by the animal's weight as she lifted it awkwardly up to eye level. The hedgehog made no attempt to curl up, and instead made itself comfortable, tucking its short legs beneath a decidedly portly body. It twitched its long snout up and down, sniffing the air, and refused to wither under her long sullen stare.

"Just one lie in," Helen whispered, "just *one*. It's not too much to ask for is it, on a Sunday morning? Just one lie in?"

She imagined the creature's obstinate old man reply-

It's always me, me, me, isn't it? I want a lie in... I don't want to find you sleeping in the tumble dryer any more... I don't want you tripping me on the stairs... but what about my *needs? Hmmm? My dreams? Indulging this narcissism is all very well, but it isn't putting any breakfast on the table for me now, is it?*

A muffled clatter of tennis shoes, a blinding flash of white, and Marie was gleaming in the hallway.

"Don't get too close," she said. "Those things are crawling with all kinds of horrible wildlife."

Marie was dressed, like a minor goddess of fitness, in a bright white track-top and tennis-skirt, and held a badminton racquet balanced on one shoulder. Internally Helen groaned. Where did she get this much energy?

"You know, I don't think this one has a single flea," she said.

The creature seemed to nod its agreement-

Clean... very clean... but hungry...

Marie peered curiously into the corner of the hall, then pointed with her racquet; the case-zip jingled merrily.

"Hedgehog poo?" she asked.

Helen considered, "Thank-you, but no. I think I'll stick with toast and marmalade."

"Hmmm. Deliberate misunderstanding for comic effect. I get it," Marie said. "Be a love and have a go at it though could you? I'm not dressed for poop-wrangling, and I really don't want to meet that on my way in tonight."

Helen looked accusingly at the beast in her hand, which didn't even have the decency to look shame-faced. There was only one word burning behind its bright gaze-

Breakfast?

Dismissing the matter, Marie zoomed into the kitchen, propped her racquet against the fridge, and poured an enormous fruit smoothie into a clean glass. Helen was convinced that she kept a supply of pristine tableware in some conjurer's limbo, and could produce such items at will.

"Sorry I'm rushing out," she said between gulps, ducking to see the street through the kitchen window, "I feel as if I'm abandoning you."

Helen smiled. Marie always rushed out, every morning. Lately she had begun to imagine that everywhere her friend passed she left a sonic boom, a swirl of litter, and a clutch of confused passers-by swearing and shielding their eyes.

"That's okay. I have lots to do. I have to see Alison, and I'm meeting David in the Welly, and there's always more work."

Sipping the last of her smoothie, Marie gazed out through the window.

"Hmmm. David, David, David. Who'd have thought it? How's that going?"

Helen nodded, trying to keep her face expressionless.

"Pretty good. I like him."

Marie grinned salaciously.

"Fantastic! Is he a stallion? An athlete? I knew it. *Knew* it! It's always the quiet ones, isn't it? Such a brilliant surprise."

Suddenly she was at the sink, rinsing her glass.

"He's writing some article about teaching and stress, that's all, so today he's interviewing me."

"Uh-huh. Interviewing you... yes... pumping you for information... of course he is... "

Helen glanced down at the hedgehog. It too seemed to be favouring her with a knowing smirk.

"Oh stop it, both of you!"

Marie's forehead crinkled into a frown.

"Both of you?" Then she looked at her watch.

"Look, I have to go. Let's do the Mantra."

"But I don't... "

"Let's do the Mantra. It's essential. You have to say it every morning. You know you want to."

"No, I really... "

Marie ignored her.

"Don't fight it. Concentrate. Now- who's the best, the absolute best teacher in the country?"

"Marie, I really don't need... "

"Say it."

Helen huffed, then repeated in a rapid monotone-

"I am. I'm the best, the absolute best teacher in the country."

"Good. Now - who'll still be the best, the absolute best teacher in the whole country, no matter what is written down or said by a bunch of hit-and-run inspector tossers?"

"Marie, I... "

"Say it."

"I don't... "

"SAY IT!"

Helen gave in-

"I will. I will still be the best, the absolute best teacher in the whole country, no matter what is written down or said by a bunch of hit-and-run inspector tossers."

"Brilliant. But next time say it like you mean it." She touched Helen's shoulder. "You are sure you're going to be okay? I don't want to come home and find that you've decided to end it all in some disturbing and grotesque manner."

"Well, that does sound attractive, but no. I'll be fine."

Outside a sleek black car stopped by their driveway. The horn beeped twice and Marie jumped.

"Bugger's *early*," she said, looking uncharacteristically embarrassed. The horn beeped again. "I really should train him out of doing that."

She gave Helen's shoulder a further squeeze, and then she was gone. The front door slammed, and Helen saw her ponytail bounce across the bottom of the kitchen window. There was a solid and expensive-sounding thunk as a car door closed, and then the low hungry rattle of an exhaust note as Marie's current beau revved the engine and pulled away at speed.

Helen glanced down at the hedgehog in her palm, which seemed to shake its head ruefully. She agreed. In all other aspects of her life, Marie seemed so in control, so self-possessed. She was like a god to most of Helen's other friends because she had done exactly what all teachers were always threatening to do (but never, ever did), and left pushing chemistry towards bored thirteen-year-olds for a job in the City. It was a job that Helen found incomprehensible, but which paid more than double her salary, and yet Marie entertained a seemingly endless stream of irritating boyfriends.

Irritation made her think of Loatheworthy, and suddenly Helen was wearing tartan trousers, one glove, a golfing cap, and a sublime grin. It was not a crisp December morning, but the eighteenth green on a gentle summer's day. A breeze ruffled her hair. Loatheworthy's shoes and the cuffs of his trousers were visible, peeking from the edge of an extremely large golf-bag. Beside her a policeman stood with his notebook open.

" ...and how many times did you hit him with the club Miss Haversham?"

She tested the good weight of a nine iron in her hand.

"Four, maybe five times... hmmm... let's say it was a four, okay?"

She snapped out of it. The hedgehog was looking at her hopefully-
Breakfast?

After a moment in the now quiet kitchen, Helen placed the creature carefully on the doormat, where, forcibly returned to the scene of its crime it shuffled its feet nervously. As she washed her hands at the sink and retrieved a half-empty tin of cat-food from the refrigerator, her sleep hangover began to melt into the bright winter sunlight. She spooned the brown gelid lumps (*mmm... delicious. Good for your cat, good for you - cue jingle*) onto a saucer, and, wincing at the less than delicate aroma, mashed them into manageable-sized pieces.

The hedgehog's nose followed the saucer down to floor level, and then it got stuck in. Helen stood with her arms folded, watching for as long as she could stand the small sticky noises of enjoyment.

"See," she said, "breakfast. I wouldn't let you down. But if you ever, *ever* do that in my hallway again, I'll nail up the bloody cat flap."

The creature raised its nose and looked up at her; she gave it a bright smile.

"Okay?"

It paused briefly, and then went back to its meal. Helen chose to believe that this demonstrated assent, and headed for the disinfectant and rubber gloves.

#

The *Duke of Wellington* was a pretty pub, sprawling in a hollow at the bottom of Combe hill. In the summertime the Welly's beer garden, with its flower baskets and parasols, was often full, and regular drinkers (Helen and Marie amongst them) would collect their pints and snacks and head off for the quiet shade of a tree in one of the surrounding fields, away from the tourists. Now though, most of the trees were stark and the fields were empty but for crows. The only remnant of summer that Helen could see through the dusty pub window was a forgotten glass wedged down by Atkinson's fence, and a faded crisp packet snagged by the long grass that twitched in the breeze.

Helen and David had a hefty bar-snack habit themselves, and a small pile of debris had accumulated between them. Now, coming to the end of his questions, David was slowly dealing out a series of glossy black and white crime-scene photographs, and placing them amongst the glasses and empty packaging, as if they were over-large playing cards.

Helen had seen them all before, of course, these murder shots, but they were still worrying. Her eyes flicked across them as he lay them down, taking in scattered details.

One classroom had high narrow windows, and sunshine streamed in and picked out a desk and a chair. The inspector sat there, ramrod straight, holding a class register out before his eyes. Perched on his head there was a large red floppy Santa hat, and hooked over his ears was a fake cotton-wool beard. Behind his right shoulder, on the classroom whiteboard, someone had written: 'Ho Ho Ho - Have a Satisfactory Christmas.' in jolly, multi-coloured magnetic letters.

The Ofsted murderer used a prescription drug called *Fermaxipan*, ordinarily a simple but effective laxative, safe, gentle, and harmless. The murderer, however, had discovered that if *Fermaxipan* was processed (using a method the details of which the press were oddly reluctant to reveal), and delivered intravenously in a high enough dose, it had a unique effect. Death was thought to be instantaneous, and quite painless. The inspectors' bodies could then be posed, waiting for a peculiar post-death rigor to freeze them into position, as if they were statuary. The police were baffled. Four murders in five months in the greater London area had provided little forensic data, and few leads. Great herds of teachers were arrested, questioned, and then freed. A PE teacher from Hounslow was even charged, then also released when another murder occurred whilst he languished in custody. There had been TV reconstructions, phone-ins, and appeals for witnesses, all to no avail.

The second classroom to be visited had undergone more embellishment. The teacher's desk had been made-up to resemble an old-fashioned bed, complete with a stack of fluffy white pillows and an intricate patchwork quilt. The inspector had been found propped against the pillows, wearing a pink winceyette nightgown and matching bonnet, trimmed with fading white lace which clashed fetchingly with his beard. He was frozen, primly and delicately, holding the bedclothes up to his chin with his thumbs and forefingers. A single white rose had been tucked into the banding of his bonnet. Flashing like a beacon on the classroom's interactive whiteboard, above the inspector's shoulder, was the legend- 'Why Grandma Ofsted! What big teeth you have!'

David laid down the third picture between two empty glasses. Helen winced. After the 'Grandma' inspector, the killer's sense of scene had become yet more bizarre. Two weeks later, a man who rejoiced in the name of Camberly Pickles, had been discovered standing astride two class desks like the Colossus of Rhodes. Over his suit he wore a baby-blue check pinafore apron, and one arm was raised in a salute towards the blackboard. His hair had been carefully teased into a Hitlerian forelock, and a tiny moustache completed the image (it was not clear whether the killer had clipped it, or if Pickles had always worn it that way). In his outstretched and saluting hand, he brandished what had later been identified as the upholstery attachment from an ancient Electrolux vacuum cleaner. An overhead projector put the legend- 'Ein Volk. Ein Reich. Ein Inspectorate!' on the wall behind him.

Fear had reduced Ofsted's numbers. Many inspectors demonstrated a surprising reluctance to risk their dignity and their lives in the cause of educational reform. The chief inspector of schools refused to be cowed, and had made a great rallying evangelical speech urging his teams to continue their work. Some did so, but inspections in the London area were now observed by undercover police, and across the country teachers about to undergo inspection were interviewed - Helen had been herself by two bored but spooky members of Thames Valley CID.

Though slightly less elaborate, the final picture, now dealt over a ghostly beer stain, was somehow far more disturbing. Here the inspector was posed beneath the blackboard, crouching, knees bent, arms outstretched, each encircled by a brightly coloured armband, as if he were about to make a shallow dive into a swimming pool. He wore goggles and a nose clip, and carefully stuck on the top of his bald head there was an industrial sized sink-plunger. The plunger's wooden handle stuck straight up in the air and pointed to the legend on the blackboard. It said, 'Join the Inspectorate - Take the Plunge!'

"Do you think they deserved this?"

Helen hesitated; something in her heart was saying *yes, yes... oh yes... and more...* but her eyes flicked down to the plunger - an absurd thing - and she realised that this was real, not some stress-induced fantasy, and felt a pang of guilt. David was studying her intently, though this was not unusual. She had noticed that David studied everything - people in their daily interaction, clouds, menus, spoons - with equal wide-eyed intensity, as if the world were a constant source of surprise and wonderment to him.

"No," she said firmly, "of course not."

Her conscience lent her words more vehemence than she had expected. "They're the bane of our lives, but no one deserves *that*." She tapped the picture with her fingertip.

David nodded slowly.

"Even after the revelations?"

Yes. The revelations. The Ofsted murderer's 'scenes' were not quite as random as they at first appeared, and the killer had chosen his (or her) victims with great care; all of them had secrets.

Open within the register that Morris, the first inspector to die, had been found holding, was a copy of an ancient police record, together with a deed poll certificate showing a change of name. Adrian Morris, eleven years before, had been Adrian Moor, and in the mid nineteen-eighties, Adrian Moor had narrowly escaped detention at Her Majesty's pleasure after being investigated for embezzling funds from a Christmas savings plan which had left thousands of families across the north of England turkeyless and enraged.

Tucked neatly into bed beside Grandma were a series of photographs, some of which would later appear in part-pixelated form in several tabloids, showing Grandma adopting a variety of uncomfortable-looking postures, whilst closely supervising (some would say too closely) a first year teacher-training undergraduate. For three weeks afterwards, worried young women contacted the police to inform them that they too had fallen prey to Grandma, whose *modus operandi* typically involved selecting the loneliest student, who was furthest away from home, and getting them drunk as a skunk before retiring to his apartment.

Pickles was a petty tyrant. On the desk before his brave saluting stance was a full record of his work for Ofsted. Fifty percent of his inspections resulted in an unresolved complaint from a staff member. Sixty percent resulted in some form of special measures for the school in question.

Whilst working for his local council, sink-plunger-man had lobbied hard for six schools to be forced to sell the land on which their swimming pools were situated, and have their young swimmers bussed in to the municipal pool. This seemed to make financial sense to the council, and, indeed to sink-plunger-man, since the land was sold at a knock down price to a building company owned by his brother-in-law, who promptly turned it into luxury housing. Two deposits of two hundred thousand pounds swelled sink-plunger-man's offshore bank account in the month that followed this deal. The Ofsted murderer left copies of the paperwork propped up before his outstretched fingertips.

"No. It doesn't matter what they did. They didn't deserve that."

David nodded earnestly.

"Are you sure? I've talked to other teachers and had some very weird reactions: smiling, helpless laughter, and I've had three separate requests for framed copies of the photographs."

Helen nodded sadly. "They bring out the worst in us. They put us under a great deal of stress."

And so they did. She had read a psychological profile in some glossy Sunday supplement, which theorised that the killer was almost certainly a teacher, a teacher's assistant, or a relative. The Ofsted murderer was someone with an extreme sense of powerlessness and persecution, who acted to right some real or imaginary wrong. It had struck Helen that the profile could have been describing the profession in general, and it had given her the idea that the murderer might be a phantom, a creature unconsciously conjured from the collective paranoia and myriad ill-wishes of an entire industry (her own included). Perhaps things would improve when the 'new style' inspections began.

"Yep. But there's stress," David fluttered his fingers up by his ears to suggest the rigours of a busy day, "and then there's *stress*." He indicated Grandma, sat for all eternity in bonnet and bedclothes.

Helen shrugged.

"They've just driven some poor soul over the edge, that's all." She thought of her fantasy earlier that morning.

"It's quite simple really. Even I've had… thoughts."

"Thoughts?"

"Well, imaginings. Little vignettes where one of the team inspecting our school comes to a sticky end. Daydreams, really - harmless enough, you know: Loatheworthy gets caught in a mantrap, Loatheworthy falls into an open sewer and dies, Loatheworthy's head is mounted on the wall in my bathroom and he looks *really* surprised." She smiled nervously, suddenly aware, with the grizzly photos on display below her, how odd that must sound. "That sort of thing. And I can't seem to stop; but I don't think that that's abnormal. Most teachers I know fantasise about the death of their inspectors at one time or another. Yes. It's normal. A perfectly normal reaction to stress. That-" her gaze flicked down to the images again, "-is an abnormal reaction to stress."

"What about one of your colleagues, then?"

Helen raised an eyebrow. "What was your thesis title again?"

"It's *Youdunnit: Crime Fiction and Society*. And yes, I am obsessed. But what about them?"

She shook her head. "No. I know them well, and they're slightly eccentric, but repeated homicide is way out of their league. Besides, the police have cleared them all. No," she said. "No loonies at Hornby."

David nodded slowly, as if in agreement, and behind him the pub door opened again and spilled in cold air and another group of patrons seeking lunch. It was getting on for midday, and Helen was due at Alison's. She looked at her watch, and reluctantly finished her drink.

"Well, time for me to be off. Did you get what you needed?"

David glanced down guiltily at his almost empty notebook.

"I think so."

"Are we still on for Tuesday evening?"

He closed the notebook with a decisive snap.

"You know it's poetry?"

"Hmmm - is this going to be culturally edifying?"

"No. No, certainly not." David thought for a while, "Well, it might be, I s'pose."

She gave him a sly look. "You're not trying to improve my mind are you?"

"Of course not. I resent that. If you feel in any way improved by the experience we can heckle him, or throw things."

"Or tell each other off-colour jokes in loud voices in the restaurant, after?"

"It's a deal."

David's smile died away, to be replaced by a carefully impassive and non-judgemental expression. He leaned forward slightly, and took Helen's hand.

"I have to ask you," he said, "er… you didn't do it, did you? You didn't kill them, I mean?"

Helen stood to leave and grinned wolfishly.

"Ah. Now, I didn't say that, did I? Everyone needs a hobby."

And with that she made her way to the door.

David glanced around, aware of several sets of male eyes following her with interest. She waved from the street, and he waved back, then turned and once more surveyed the photographs lying on the table before him. He put his head in his hands.

What on earth was he going to do?

#

"Another date? This is getting serious. Try to make these more blobby," Alison said.

Helen ignored the implied question, and kept her brush out of the way as Alison whisked her three paintings from the table, held them up to the light, squinted at them, and then added them to the pile she was making on the work surface. She replaced them with three more blanks.

Helen washed her brush in a large jar of cloudy water, and swirled the particles of paint around until they made a pattern that lasted for a few seconds when she took her brush away. They could all do with some more sun, she thought. That morning's early brightness had now faded, and been replaced by low-set clouds that looked as if they might hold snow. She picked up some yellow on her brush and blobbily blobbed three children's suns on the three blanks.

"No," Alison said, "you're thinking like an adult again. There's always at least one kid that'll do it in a weird colour - puce, or aubergine."

Helen picked up some blue and the third sun became an unearthly green. She looked sideways at her work and decided to put a big bowler hat on the sun, and to give it a lop-sided smile.

"Much better," Alison said. "If I were an inspector, I'd believe a six-year-old had perpetrated that."

They had decided late last week that they would have to fake much of the artwork in the lower classes. Glancing through the trays of children's paintings had revealed a parade of images that would have made Hieronymus Bosch weep. The children seemed to be picking up on staff tensions (or were being allowed to consume too much post-watershed programming), and were expressing this artistically.

Helen had come across one image that she felt demonstrated enough demented psychosis to haunt her dreams for the foreseeable future. To her eyes it seemed to show, in angry red lines, several human forms thoughtfully impaled from above on large stakes. In the background a river of blood flowed past, bringing with it a jolly slew of dismembered body parts.

After much deliberation, the child involved had been carefully questioned, and revealed in a candid whisper that the picture actually showed- 'me and Daddy at the seaside, flying my birthday kite.'

With Helen in the background pretending not to listen, Alison had pointed to the blood-river and asked slowly, in a deliberately calm tone-

"What are these people doing?"

The child had looked at her as if she might be simple, and replied- "backstroke" in an equally slow and careful tone.

Immediately, all became clear: the dismembered bits were simply swimmers ploughing their way through a sea that the child had decided should be red, rather than blue or green.

Perhaps worse still were those pictures that were unintentionally X-rated. Some children, it seemed, quite innocently reduced almost any image (tall buildings, rocket ships, cars, balloons, family members) to a few simple shapes, which they invariable chose to colour pink. Viewed by an adult these drawings often resulted in a long worried silence. Teachers came to expect such anomalies, but inspectors? No, it would be best to filter out the more deranged images - no matter how innocent they actually were - and replace them with more benign counterfeits.

"What's he like then?"

Helen drew in a stick person. Stick people, she knew, should always be brown and have one disproportionately long leg, six fingers on one hand, and four on the other. Another hat, and now it resembled a scarecrow.

"He's nice. Bright. I like him."

Alison rolled her eyes. "No," she said, affecting a mock Mediterranean accent and describing an exaggerated hour-glass figure in the air with the palms of her hands, "*whaat* ees he *like*."

"I said. He's nice. I like him."

Alison tried another tack. Presenting an unusually toothsome grin, she pressed her hands together-

"Good. When can we meet him, then?"

"Oh no. No way. I'm not going for that one again. Last time I brought a boyfriend here Robin bored him senseless with rugby stories, and you got drunk and threatened to show him your Caesarean scar."

Alison pouted. "Well, he was interested, love him."

"He was *not* interested. You frightened him so badly he didn't call me for nearly a week. Nope. Not doing that. Not yet, anyway."

Alison sighed.

"So what did you two crazy kids talk about anyhow?"

"School."

"You were dazzling him with the sheer breadth of your conversation then?"

"Uh huh." Helen smiled, "He's writing about the murders. Wanted to know about the staff, about how they're coping."

Alison huffed, slouching into her chair, her chin almost on her chest.

"Ofsted will probably have them all destroyed. It might be a kindness."

Nodding solemnly Helen began to fill in the grass of her painting, making sure that it was light brown, perfectly flat, and that it strayed well into the skyline.

"He had those photos, you know, of the murders."

Alison looked out through the window, into the middle distance. "Oh those," she said quietly, "I *love* those."

"Alison, that's twisted."

She huffed again, "I know. But this is your first go on the inspection roller coaster, isn't it? See how you feel by Thursday afternoon. By then you might find yourself wishing that Loatheworthy *would* get a visit." She considered, "Not to kill him, obviously, just to frighten him a bit."

"Hmmm. Maybe."

Helen stared downwards into the murky depths of her painting, at the simplistic rutted landscape and the single scarecrow, and her thoughts strayed to Friday night, to leaving her classroom door open, and her coat behind, to the

(*charm?*)

Yes, there was no other word for it - to the charm. Had she dealt with Loatheworthy? Had she frightened him enough?

The thought of the inspector brought with it an undeniable mental image of herself choking him and grinning, and then driving a fast red sports car over a cliff. She shook it off.

"I think he's going to be a problem," Alison was saying. "I think he'd *really* like to trip us up."

The certainty in her tone made Helen doubt the wisdom of her actions yet again, and she jumped as, without warning, the back door flew open and spilled the rest of Alison's family into the kitchen.

Robin, her husband, stepped in. He was burly and capped by a ridiculously tiny bobble-hat, and he herded the children before him like a small, blonde (but very friendly) avalanche. Chloe (four) took up her usual position by Helen's knee, studying her work with the thorough intensity of a nuclear physicist inspecting a chain reaction. The boys escaped into the hallway where James (eight) began laughing hysterically at Craig (four, and Chloe's twin) because he had become trapped in his jacket. Robin deposited three unfeasibly large buckets of fried chicken on the counter and turned to them, grinning.

"You were a long time. Where have you been?" Alison asked.

Robin nodded towards Chloe.

"Could you field this one for me please, darling?"

Chloe thought for a moment, then said in a careful and halting tone, suggestive of a certain amount of rehearsal-

"Nowhere. We certainly weren't buying mummy's Christmas present, or anything like that."

Her father nodded. "Job well done. Excellent."

Feigning disinterest, Alison began gathering cutlery and plates. A wail of pain arose from the hallway and Robin rolled his eyes.

"Chloe," he said, "go and sort out the boys for Daddy."

Chloe grinned and marched off purposefully towards the hallway. Alison held three fingers in the air and began a silent countdown. When she reached zero, another louder cry rang out, and then there was an ominous silence.

"It's great," she said, closing a drawer with her hip, "give her a blue hat and she'd be a UN peacekeeping force."

Robin leaned across the table and pushed the door to the hallway closed.

"Seen this yet?" he said, producing a late edition of that day's *Sunday Mail* from inside his jacket as if it were contraband.

"No. What's up now?" Alison asked.

Robin looked pained, the expression of concern sitting oddly on his usually cheerful face.

"Now," he said, "you promise not to freak out? You're going to see it anyway, so you might as well do it now and get it over with."

He unfolded the newspaper and laid it on the kitchen table beside the paintings, where it made a disturbing counterpoint. Helen blinked, reading the headline twice before taking it in:

Police Baffled by New Ofsted Slaying.

Her eye was drawn down to the photograph beneath, travelled up again to re-read the headline, and then settled on the full bizarreness of the image. The photographer had displayed an excellent sense of scene, and had taken his shot from low down at the back of a classroom, a science room, judging by the décor.

The inspector was framed by row upon row of desks, and caught in slanting light coming in, side-on, from a narrow window. He was dressed as the Statue of Liberty, holding aloft a square ice-cream cone. He wore open-toed sandals, a bed-sheet toga the exact blue of tarnished copper, a crown with points, and beneath that, a latex caricature mask of the late U.S. president Richard Milhous Nixon. The camera angle, peering slightly upwards, made him seem truly monumental. On the rolling blackboard, just over his left shoulder, barely legible from so low down, was scrawled the message, *'There can be no whitewash at the Inspectorate.'*

Helen skim-read the breathless accompanying story. His name was Wilfred Downey. He was fifty-five, single, and had gone missing from his hotel room some time after eleven on Friday night. Comments from a police source suggested that the killer had employed his (or her) usual care, and few clues had been discovered at the scene (an Upminster comprehensive). It was thought that Mr Downey had been lured to the school by threats of blackmail. Neatly tucked inside the ice-cream cone torch, which Downey held aloft in his final earthly pose, was a typed record of his actual education and work experience, along with a copy of the CV that Downey used. These two documents did not tally. Mr Downey was a liar of such monumental complexity that it was almost breathtaking. There was little he had achieved in his life, from a silver swimming certificate at age nine, to his appointment as head of an Ofsted team, that had not been gained by elaborate and painful (for others, at least) deception.

Robin shook his head, puffing out his cheeks slightly with an exaggerated sigh.

"It's like my old Dad used to say," he said. "If you've got to go, you might as well do it dressed as a foreign national monument."

Alison tapped the image with one finger. "Great photo though," she said, "very dramatic. Taken from just the right spot." Then she brightened.

"Hey, do you think this means they'll cancel *our* inspection?"

Helen felt a sudden flare of childish hope. Yes. That would be right. Something good must come out of all of this death and destruction, to make sense of poor Wilfred Downey's bizarre demise. One good thing shining like a bright poppy on a wasted battlefield, a star in the Christmas night, a...

"Oh, hang on... Nope, says there," Alison pointed again, "'Ofsted are expecting to carry on their current round of inspections into the new year, but inspectors, now immersed in a climate of fear, are again being warned to take extra care, and to meet no one after school hours.' Damn." Her grin persisted. "Still, 'climate of fear' eh! See how they like it, eh, eh?" She nudged Helen with her elbow.

Helen thought of what David had told her this morning, and wondered if Alison would keep the clipping.

"This is murder," she said, "a tragedy... probably."

Robin cleared his throat, and opened the paper to page four. "Yeah," he said, "then what do you think of this?"

Ofsted To Be Given Greater Powers.
Teaching Unions Say More Will Die.

Helen skim read again. It was a puff piece born of a Downing Street press release, sneaked out on a Sunday morning, and obviously written before news of the new murder had emerged. Ofsted, the article suggested, might be given the power to cut the salaries of, or even to fire, teachers it considered to be incompetent. The leader of the largest teaching union had responded by predicting strike action. The newspaper had responded by having its staff psychologist suggest that this might be the impetus needed to make the Ofsted murderer kill again. For good measure, they had reprinted photographs of the killer's previous crimes, and sure enough, there were Helen's favourites - Grandma and Mr sink-plunger - staring back at her for the second time that day.

Alison's expression darkened. "Bugger," she said. "Why not give the sods the authority to have us shot? I'm starting to see things from the Ofsted murderer's point of view."

"I still think actual murder is a bit strong," Helen said, again thinking of her own homicidal fantasies, "but if this happens, I'm leaving teaching and going down the garden to eat worms."

Alison nodded, "Maybe that's the aim, though."

"To get me to eat worms?"

"No." she grinned. "Perhaps the murderer's trying to put enough of them out of action to stop the inspections altogether, or to stop a *specific* inspection. Perhaps it's a really really violent non-violent protest."

They all nodded glumly, and as if to fill the silence the hall door crept open and Chloe wandered back in.

"All done Daddy," she said. Robin hastily gathered up the newspaper; Helen saw Grandma and sink-plunger-man crumple and disappear.

"I'm hungry. Whatcha doin'?" Chloe asked. The women looked at each other carefully.

"Painting," Helen replied. There was a long silence as Chloe slowly dipped her nose almost to the paper, and then looked up at them, frowning. "It's not very good, is it?" she asked.

Helen smiled and shook her head. "Of course not. But these are the last ones. Would you like to finish them for me? Mummy's going to need the table."

Chloe stamped out of her Wellingtons and coat and jumped into Helen's seat. Immediately she went for the black and began over-painting the sky of each picture in great darkening swirls. She added small figures on the horizon and some grey lumps that might have been rocks, and within seconds, Helen's sunny scarecrow-in-a-field scene grew wickedly sinister. When Chloe had finished all three paintings they joined the others on the pile, and they all sat down to lunch.

#

The fried chicken was delicious, and although the image of Wilfred Downey and his strange demise lingered in the minds of the adults, as their meal progressed he faded, and was reduced to the status of a dim spectre, revived only by the evening news. Afterwards they went through the annual pre-Christmas *Twister* tournament, a fiercely contested event which Alison and Robin had begun as students. Craig won, gaining the apparently wonderful (and to Helen, incomprehensible) prize of being allowed to stack the dishwasher.

Next came the ritual of helping the children to decorate the ancient Green family Christmas tree. It was Alison's one and only heirloom, a thing of tinsel and glitter. Whilst the other adults directed, Helen and the children covered it with yet more tinsel and glitter and paper-chains that the children had made, and then they placed a Bratz doll, inexpertly dressed as a fairy, on the top. When they were finished and the Christmas lights had been carelessly tossed over the plastic branches, Robin dimmed the house lights, they held a countdown, and the tree was switched on. It worked first time, glittering in the darkness, and putting fleeting, odd-coloured shadows onto their faces. Neither the school nor the inspection was mentioned again, and all in all Helen thought that it was an afternoon well spent.

When she left the house two hours later, waving to the family group in the doorway, with Robin holding a twin under each arm, Helen's sense of well-being left her momentarily, and she felt suddenly deflated, almost melancholic. None of their afternoon rituals could prevent tomorrow, and 'D' day - inspection day - was coming. She glanced up towards the low milky clouds and shivered, *something* was coming.

When she reached the corner of Pound Lane, the Green's hearty goodbyes fading behind her, she stopped and held one hand out in the breeze, her eyes closed. When she opened them again there was a light frosting of snow on her palm, like salt, which immediately began to melt into the air. She glanced around herself, up and down the street.

For now there were only tiny flakes: barely noticeable pin-pricks of ice hesitating in the air, barely settling on the pavements; but the street had a huddled, almost dormant look, and as she turned for home, Helen had the feeling that they would soon grow in strength and size, ready to blanket the town.

III - Monday

David turned left onto the High Street, pedalling hard through gritty slush and hunching over his handlebars as the street uncurled before him. Up ahead, seeming to glow in the sparse morning light, he could make out the spire of St Mary's. Bells were ringing, but the sound was corrupted by the grind of traffic, like a radio signal succumbing to static, fading as a bus splashed past him on the inside and he cut through a suicidally tiny gap onto Longwall Street. He zoomed past a fragment of ancient city wall, and rode on towards the faculty building.

Arriving in the half-deserted car park, flushed and out of breath, he coasted towards the bike racks still standing on one pedal. The building - a three-storied slab of glass and concrete which hid the smaller law library from the road - loomed above him; its steel clock said five past nine.

He had slept through his alarm, and now he was late. Worse than that, he had left no time to precision-plan his entry. There could be no stealth, no initial sweep to check that the coast was clear, he would have to rely on luck and a frontal assault. Frowning, he grabbed his briefcase and ran to the double-doors, pausing once to look over his shoulder and nervously survey the empty car park. There was no one lurking between the parked cars, or hunkering down in the shrubbery - this worried him further; everything looked far too normal.

Inside it was warm and dim and smelled of old books. David peered cautiously into the gloom of both corridors, then sprinted up the stairs, taking them two at a time. He almost overbalanced at the top of the second flight, but managed somehow to transfer his momentum to the right direction and skidded into the upper corridor, heading towards room C13.

As he reached the door his demeanour changed. He removed his coat and draped it over one arm, took a deep breath, straightened his jacket and ran a hand over his hair. Then, with the air of someone about to enter dangerous territory, he turned C13's handle, confidently pushed it open, and swept in-

"Sorry I'm late," he said, "I had a very important... "

The room was empty. David glanced around, feeling both relief and chagrin, stepped inside, and then peered behind the door, as if he suspected that someone might have secreted themselves there. When he was sure that he was alone, that his luck had held, he let out a sigh and began to relax. His students weren't here, but he had gotten away with it, he had managed to avoid Dr...

"Hello Barclay," a voice said quietly from a space only millimetres behind David's right ear.

David froze, trapping a panicky expletive by biting his tongue.

How could he possibly have crept along the corridor so quietly, and so fast? For a moment David entertained the creepy notion that thinking of *him* might have actually called him up.

"Hello Doctor Love," he said, his mind racing. "How are you?"

"Everything seems to be working just as it should, thank you."

David turned, and beheld Dr B. H. (Bernard Hilary he had discovered, after some considerable research) Love. Love lounged comfortably against the door frame, his arms folded. David knew how this game was played, and worked hard to show no outward sign of his surprise.

Dr Love was the senior tutor at St. Jude's college, and the most notorious person that David knew. Existing inside a perpetual cloud of speculation, Love was a rumour magnet and a black hole for myths, all of which he seemed to encourage with his mild gaze and his unwavering ironic smile.

There he stood, the smile already in place, refusing to blink. Clearly he was an ex-spy and assassin who had worked for the CIA, Mossad, and United Biscuits. Dr Love was a Dot-Com billionaire, insurance fraudster, and advisor to the treasury who had made his fortune racing speedboats and inventing new names for mushrooms. An opium fiend and part-time dentist, Love spoke twenty three languages and had ordered a network of tunnels dug beneath the college to house some dark unknown project. It was well known that Love had an aversion to silver and garlic, and that he appeared in several authentic Renaissance drawings. Also, Love did not find his name remotely funny. Behind his back, with grinding undergraduate originality, he was known as 'The Love Machine.' It was a nickname of which he was well aware, and it lurked behind his laconic outward manner as if he were continually daring you to believe that it might be true. Of course, Love drowned those he heard using this nickname in the college water butts, and then buried them in shallow graves beneath St Jude's tiny gravel car park.

Secretly David believed all of the rumours concerning his supervisor, and had come to suspect that Love was a retired timelord. Other students whispered his name in dread whilst peering over their shoulders; other members of the faculty simply forked the sign of the evil eye at his back, turned around three times and spat.

"You're not avoiding me, are you David?"

David grinned shamefacedly-

"No. Definitely not. Wouldn't do that. You know how it is right at the end of a degree, all work. No time to stop."

Love raised a thoughtful eyebrow. "Hmmm," he said. "I wouldn't know. I spent the latter part of my doctoral research on Peyote."

David's smile waned. "Really? Didn't that get in the way of things?"

Love considered this gravely. "No. Actually, it seemed to help. Now *I* think you've been avoiding me, hmmm?"

David shook his head.

Love's expression remained unreadable.

"Odd. I saw someone who looked *exactly* like you exit through the bathroom window of that Greek restaurant on George Street, and run off into the night." He stroked his chin, "Last Friday it was. Just after I arrived."

David thought that flat denial might be his best course-

"No. Nope. Definitely not. Couldn't have been me, I'd have been at home, working very hard."

For the first time David noticed that Love was carrying a slim valise made of very shiny brown leather. It glowed mellowly under the fluorescent lights, and its handles were bound together with a heavy padlock.

He stared at it, then glanced quickly up at Love. Love's smile seemed to have widened indulgently, and then he felt his gaze drawn back to the valise.

His luck had run out - it was the doomsday case!

David took an involuntary half-step backwards.

The doomsday case: the myth of myths, rumour of rumours - an object of true terror. He had heard other graduate students whisper of it and of its terrible but unknown cargo during drunken dorm-room horror stories. These stories often involved Love making deals with the Devil, or space aliens. Sometimes they told of mystical objects of unimaginable power retrieved from the rain-soaked jungles of South America during an anthropology field trip, which only Love survived. Often, they told of research students driven mad with terror, or of rival professors retiring into senility and incontinence.

Love was (probably) married to Lady Katherine Shaw, and it was said that during their courtship a spurned suitor had made unwelcome advances towards Lady Katherine at one of the College's May balls. Love had unleashed the terrible force that even then he had kept imprisoned in the valise, and the man had been found four hours later crouching high up in the branches of one of the College's oaks, looking for all the world like a large dinner-jacketed owl.

For months David had been expecting Love to mention it to him, but now he had *seen* it. He swallowed hard.

"How many theses do you think I have overseen here Barclay?" Love asked.

David dragged his eyes away from the case and tried to estimate the man's age. He could have been anywhere between thirty-five and fifty-five, say ten years, three doctorates or more a year.

"Forty?"

"You," Love pointed with one long index finger, "are the two-hundred and twenty seventh. And none of them have been late." He stroked the case with the same finger. "I am here to tell you - Barclay - that *yours* will not be late."

David realised that Love had still not yet blinked, and felt his own eyes begin to water in sympathy.

"I've seen all this," Love waved his free hand in the air, "this pointlessness before. Students stop coming to my lectures, they duck into doorways when they see me, or they begin a complex series of rotations in the library so that they can never be found at the same desk twice. Nice, by the way, I liked that."

David shrugged.

"In the final days of their work, my students avoid me as if I have some new strain of plague. I have seen one hundred and eighty-eight different variants on climbing out of that restaurant window, David - *you* weren't even particularly original." He gazed briefly upwards towards the ceiling tiles. "I once had a student have herself flown as air-freight to Buenos Aires in order to avoid bumping into me. Now *she* was dedicated. Uh-huh. Oh yes."

He rocked back on his heels, his gaze snapping downwards again. "Where's the thesis Barclay? When will you finish it?"

David tried to think of a suitable answer, and the one that came unhelpfully to mind was "not *this* week." How could he tell Love that over the last month he had discovered a new and consuming project that had sapped his interest and drawn his attention away from his thesis? That his doctorate was almost complete, imprisoned in the three-hundred-and-sixty-odd pages piled neatly on his desk, and yet incomplete, lacking a final full stop on the final page.

"It's more or less in the bag. I mean weeks, not months. I'm neatening the final draft now, and you can see it by, oh... " he looked at his wrist for a watch that he wasn't wearing, "late February?"

Love studied him carefully.

"Your scholarship's up for review, isn't it?"

David nodded reluctantly.

"And that means I'll have to make a recommendation to the committee?"

David nodded again.

"Hmmm. Well I'll be keeping a special eye on you David." Slowly Love pointed to his right eye. "This one, in fact."

"I'm flattered."

"Please, let me finish. I'll be keeping a special eye on you, and do you know why?"

David thought carefully. "Because you find my work intrinsically fascinating, and you wish to encourage original lines of inquiry?"

"What? God no. Don't be facetious."

"Because I'm secretly your son, and you're trying to win me over to the dark side of the force?"

"No. Not quite. It's because I sense that there is a quality of *lateness* about you, David. Hmm-mmm, saw it from the start. Disorganisation I can stand, it could be creative. Even showing me no work for more than nine months - fine, perhaps you were worried that I might plagiarise you, it does happen. But I think you might be stalling. Worse - I think you might be planning to be *late*."

Love leaned in slightly closer; David could smell expensive cologne.

"It seems to me that you have been writing up for far too long - so *finish* it, or you might be my first late student, and then the committee will be the least of your worries."

David could feel a drop of cold sweat trickling between his shoulder blades.

"Late?" He laughed weakly, "Me? No, no. Honestly... "

Love raised the valise to chest level, caressing its slick surface with his free hand. To David it looked as if it might be bulging slightly on one side, as if something had shifted position in there.

"No more excuses. I'll have that final draft on my desk by January first."

David paled.

"And if you're late... " Love inclined his head slightly towards the case, and raised his eyebrows.

David tried to resist asking, but found that he could not.

"What's..? " Too quiet. He licked his lips and tried again.

"What's *in* there?"

Love flashed a quick and sunless grin-

"Ah, David. You don't need to know... yet. You might *never* need to know. It's something I picked up abroad, back in the 'sixties, something *useful*."

He let the sentence hang in the air between them, his faint smile not changing. Then, at the precise moment when David felt that he might actually go insane, Love looked at his own watch.

"Well, I have to be elsewhere now, people to unsettle, you know how it is. Those half-wits down in the computer lab won't inconvenience themselves, now, will they? Hmmm? I take it you have tickets for the Dasch thing on Tuesday evening?"

He looked at David expectantly, and David nodded.

"Good. Good. I'm encouraging everyone to go. He's a poet of great subtlety and sensitivity... almost Swinburnian. An ex-student of mine. Quite brilliant; poet for our age; needs our support. Well, enjoy your class... " he glanced around vaguely, "wherever they are. And remember... "

Dr Love stepped out of the doorway, and the door swung closed behind him. Through the glass panel David saw him walk swiftly to the stairwell, and then, knowing that David would watch him go, Love turned on his heel and raised the valise again. The leather gleamed unpleasantly. David stared, fascinated.

"I don't want to open it David, but I will, so don't be late."

And then, without waiting for a response, he was gone.

Halfway to the ground floor, when he knew that he was well out of David's line of sight, Bernard Love paused by the stairway window

and took his keys from his trouser pocket. He removed the padlock from the top of his valise, snapped the case open, and then dropped it inside, where it landed on top of something, making a hollow thocking sound.

Love peered into his case, smiling gently, then looked out through the window at the wintry scene before him. He shot a furtive glance over his shoulder, then, standing on tiptoe, craned over the railing to peer down the stairwell. When he was sure that he was alone, he reached into the valise and took out the object he had placed in there that morning, along with his lecture notes and a pile of banana sandwiches. It was a large sphere of polished glass, chipped in places, and flattened slightly at its bottom edge - a snow-globe paperweight. The scene inside was of the New York skyline, and it bore the faintly engraved legend, "NY, 1968, Kat 'n' Bernie."

That ought to do it, Love thought. Students were easier to scare now than they had been in his day.

He held the paperweight up to the light, viewing the Oxford landscape through the vista of tiny alien skyscrapers, little streets and yellow taxis, and when he had the view just right, he shook the ball once. A million tiny flakes of snow swirled languidly upwards and began to fall on the Chrysler building, the Statue of Liberty, and the Empire State. Behind them, distorted in the glass, the Oxford hills and towers caught some of the snow, and Love's smile widened.

Thinking that he would enjoy a white Christmas very much this year, Dr Love dropped the globe back into his bag, where the snow kept swirling, and went on his way, singing gently under his breath.

Behind him David, who had withdrawn to the safety of his desk, listened with mild astonishment to Love's retreating voice singing-

"Let it snow, let it snow, let it snow-oo-woe... "

#

Like many of the general rooms of the University, C13 was disappointingly prosaic. Inside there were no chandeliers, no chained books, and no antique furniture. There *was* a glass-fronted bookcase, but it contained only a few reference works, and stood alongside a tatty notice board covered with sign-up sheets, pamphlets, and reminders. The Dangerous Sports Society would be snake-handling whilst hurling each other through the windows of fast-moving lorries in the second week of the spring term, and student bands *Killer Breath* and *CatFlop* would play various pub back rooms throughout January.

David sat at his desk, and opened his own bag. Inside were his notes for this final seminar of the year, and the reason why he had not yet managed to complete his doctorate.

After a moment's hesitation he drew it out and unfolded it. It lay flat, apparently harmless and inert, covering most of the desk before him.

It was a home-made wall chart of bewildering complexity, the kind that he would ordinarily pretend to use to organise his thinking about some aspect of his work. It showed a spider's web of increasingly sweaty and worried thinking; a record of a month-long, gradually deepening obsession. It was a tracery of how a gentle, speculative thought had grown, until it had forced him to watch hours of TV coverage, read thousands of column inches of newsprint, and had quietly ruined his life.

Around the outer edges of the chart were the deranged images he had shown to Helen on Sunday morning. These were newspaper copies, grainy and letting out print. Around them, attached to pointing arrows, were cramped sets of notes. He traced a fingertip over Santa, moved clockwise over Grandma, the inspector with the vacuum cleaner attachment, the man with the sink-plunger on his head, and now, freshly pasted, Wilfred Downey, holding aloft his ice-cream-cone torch.

Directly beneath each image, he had noted in an almost unreadable scrawl, a police estimate of the date and time of each murder. Beneath each date and time, he had written the hopeful query 'Alibi?'

In various colours of pen, reluctantly added after various apparently casual questions, were four negatives, and beneath Downey's image, a gap. Running out from each negative was a thick red line, each leading, like lethal spaghetti, through more panels of notes, towards the chart's centre.

David's eyes flicked over some of these notes, laying out suppositions and conclusions, some his own, some that he had picked up elsewhere-

Murders becoming more frequent and much, much loonier-pressure of some upcoming event?

Placement of objects around bodies suggests that killer is left-handed.

Use of schools as setting.
Unusually cunning use of seemingly innocuous resources.
Lethal deployment of withering irony-
Killer is a teacher?

Hoover?

Aimée Vibert *rose?*

Inevitably, his gaze was drawn to the centre of his diagram, where all the red lines met in a tangle. There he had pasted a picture of Helen, taken on the night that they had met at a mutual friend's thirtieth birthday party. She had taken her own photo with his phone, and entered her number.

Helen had no alibi for any of the times of the Ofsted murders. So what? Who did?

Helen was under pressure from the upcoming inspection at her own school. So what? Life was pressure.

Like fifteen percent of the population, Helen was left-handed. Also, like a considerably smaller percentage, she was a teacher.

All of this, so far, must apply to thousands of people.

But then there was the Hoover, and the rose.

The third time that David had gone to Helen's house he had noticed an ageing Electrolux, lazily coiled and sitting ready in her hallway. It was the kind that had its attachments stowed inside a plastic cavity at the back of the machine. They were all missing.

Again- so what?

But a seed had been planted. The idea itself was fun... at first. David felt that he lived in an age of increasing uniformity, and a girlfriend with an unusual quirk was therefore a bonus. Helen did not like to garden, she was not a foodie, and she did not have a passion for glugging oddly named vino. She did not chat online or belong to a book group. No. Helen Jane Haversham apparently enjoyed dispatching school inspectors with nasty secrets, and posing their bodies in a variety of bizarre ways.

He became obsessed, gradually spending more and more time reading news reports and endless speculation, investigating as best he could. He created the chart, and began to add things to it, diverting energy from his work.

The idea that Helen might actually *be* the killer gained a worrying and horrible persuasiveness.

He had berated himself (which is less fun than it sounds). Why was he doing this? Was he trying to provoke Dr Love and sabotage his chances of gaining his doctorate? Worse, was he trying to ruin the best relationship he had been in for years? Was he losing his mind?

Or worst of all, was he right?

A week ago he had walked Helen home after a movie, a slow and comfortable walk, the most pleasant he could remember, hand-in-hand through the early-December evening. It was crisp, and frost sparkled, and houses glowed mellowly with winter lights around them.

The walk was so perfect that it left him still smiling as he stepped from Helen's front door into her sideway, calling some absurdly cheery and carefree goodbye.

His smile had lingered like something forgotten as he glanced into Helen's back yard and saw an object gleaming there, then his mind had dismantled it piece by piece, and swept it away.

Aimée Vibert. It was the flower discovered peeking absurdly from Grandma's bonnet. And the flower which grew in a small, thorned and twining shrub along a simple trellis, nailed years before to Helen's fence. It was amazing that the shrub was flowering at all this late in the year; he could only guess that the fence shielded it from the worst of the weather but kept it in the sun. Even so, there were only two small blooms, self contained, wrapped around themselves, pearls in the gloom.

And between them, a single stem where another bloom should be, expertly cut slantwise above two thorns.

He had rushed home. Examined the images he had of Grandma. Hoping that some detail - size, pigmentation, would rule out Helen's missing rose, but it did not.

Eventually he calmed down. His discovery proved nothing. The *Aimée Vibert* rose was relatively common. He had looked it up. There might be twenty or thirty examples growing in gardens between Hornby and Oxford.

Relieved, he had met Helen yesterday seeking reassurance, but instead got an apparently casual admission that she often lapsed into murderous fantasies.

It was too much.

He turned to the window. Below him, traffic passed on Longwall Street, generating a distant hum. In the long, foreboding (and, of course, phallic) shadow of the Psychology department, some college team had run out, and were practising line-outs and passing and scrums on their playing field. Their shouts drifted up to C13's window, thinned and made cartoonish by distance.

David faced a terrible fact. After many years of diligent searching, he had at last found the perfect woman for him, physically and mentally, and it seemed that she might be a homicidal maniac.

Should he try to turn her in?

He imagined Helen's bright gaze, weary and betrayed, searching him out from a crowd as blue lights played across some dreary street scene, and knew that that was not an option. He was far from sure, after all. He knew that his own obsessive reasoning could lead him astray. Once, many years before, he had come to believe quite sincerely that his local refuse collectors were trying to kill him, and with his thesis imminent, he was under not a little pressure himself.

Behind him, there was a grumpy and ill-timed knock on the door. Hillman. It had to be Hillman. Tim and Rachel, who completed his complement of students, had paired up at the start of the term with unseemly haste and great enthusiasm. Usually, David became aware of their presence only when he noticed a low passionate moaning emanating from the corridor. On opening C13's door to investigate, Tim and Rachel would tumble into the room locked in some fabulously complicated embrace. He had found it to be almost impossible to interrupt their foreplay with any education.

With a surly shove of the door, Hillman slouched into the room, hidden beneath his greasy hair and the faint aroma of BO. David hurriedly folded the chart, and slipped it back into his bag. With barely a glance at this curious behaviour, Hillman slumped into the chair opposite him, and slapped his latest essay onto the desk. It was crumpled, and there was a coffee stain on one corner.

Few things in life were as essentially prosaic and rational as Hillman, and suddenly David felt a little better. Surely a world which had spawned Hillman, would not, *could* not also have supplied him with a murderous girlfriend.

#

Lunchtime was coming to an end at Hornby Infants, and Helen sat beside her classroom's carpet area, running her eyes over the room in an idle search for her desk stapler, whilst pretending to go over a lesson plan that she knew by heart.

The inspection was underway at last. Theirs was one of the last of the old-style audits, and so the school as a whole had been preparing for this day for four months or more. Teaching on bright sunny Mondays, photocopying on dull Friday evenings as rain ticked against the windows, and pretending not to bicker at interminable, panic-inducing staff meetings, it had been the undercurrent of all of their thoughts; now it was finally here. Part of her, Helen realised, had focused on this week with such intensity that she had half expected to expire when it finally arrived, and now she felt a gentle surprise that she had survived.

Her morning's teaching had been watched, picked over, and approved by an inspector from the office for standards in education. At the end of the Literacy Hour, as the children ferreted out the necessary art equipment for their next lesson (they had rehearsed this countless times and knew that mistakes were punishable by death, or at least a hard stare), the inspector, a Mr Alan Godfrey, approached her with his clipboard and asked if she would like some immediate feedback. Helen's pressured mind had considered several answers, some of which included extreme profanity, but in the end she had simply nodded.

"Great lesson," Godfrey had said. He was small and neat and rounded, and in that moment she loved him. He radiated enthusiasm, and placed stress in his sentences not only with his tone, but also with a slight bend at the waist, as if he were bowing, making obeisance to the fickle gods of educational admin.

"You successfully implemented *all* of the Literacy Hour guidelines, and it looked to me as if the children did two *crucial,* (bow) *crucial* things."

He put one chubby pink finger in the air. She gazed at it, almost mesmerised.

"*One*, they *learned*." He said the word slowly, as if it might be an exotic piece of technical jargon that a mere teacher would be unlikely to have come across in the ordinary course of her duties.

"And *two* - they had *fun*!" He grinned broadly, as if he had just successfully pulled off a particularly difficult piece of conjuring. "If all of your work is of this standard, I don't think you'll have any problems."

Somehow, Helen did not share his confidence.

She sat back in her chair, letting the ebb and flow of tiny (but at the same time incredibly loud) voices in the playground wash over her. There was something ever cheery about children playing in the cold. They were all bundled up, their cheeks red, their breath puffing out in clouds as they played games that were simple, and yet unfathomable to anyone over the age of ten; it was a glad and festive image.

Not everything had gone her way that morning though, and she had had a few tricky moments. It was the unpredictable nature of children, no matter how well trained you thought they were, that made inspections so unnerving. Young children were like some rare and newly developed radioactive material, and if you didn't handle them correctly, they would leave you sitting, blinking dazedly at the centre of a large smoking crater.

This morning, for example, just before break-time, Ollie Rease had returned from the bathroom and approached her with the sort of solemn, inquisitive expression that she knew meant some kind of trouble, and one trouser leg rolled jauntily, even Masonically up above his knee. Helen had bent almost to his level, feeling Godfrey's attention, and sensing his pen poised over his clipboard.

"Yes, Oliver?"

Huge dark soulful eyes that girls would someday find utterly irresistible peered up at her.

"My knee Miss Hav'sham."

She examined it carefully, "Now Oliver, you scraped that knee last Wednesday, it can't *still* hurt, can it?"

It seemed impossible, but Oliver's eyes widened still further-

"Well... Miss," he stage-whispered with great urgency (and not a little pride), "I've... I've *widdled* on it."

Ollie nodded slowly, a nod gravid with meaning and conspiratorial dignity, as if he had achieved this difficult undertaking solely for the purpose of furthering mankind's understanding of such things, and was favouring Helen with a secret of enormous scientific merit-

"An' ... An' it *stings.*"

Carefully expressionless, Helen had sent him back to the bathroom to rinse the offended knee, trying not to wonder how he had managed such a feat in the first place, and also trying to see if Godfrey might be noting anything of the encounter down on his clipboard, to use against her at a later date.

She put down her lesson plan as her eye came to rest on the familiar shape of her stapler. There it was, now sitting brazenly on the edge of her desk, exactly where she wanted it to be. Had it been there before? She frowned, rose, and prodded at it suspiciously with the edge of her lesson plan.

"Where did you come from?" she muttered under her breath. "Are you *you*, or something else?"

Outside the hand-bell was rung with high glee by whoever Alison (whose 'voluntary' lunchtime duty fell on a Monday) had given the honour to that day. Children took any such opportunity to repress their peers very seriously, and so the distribution of the hand-bell represented yet another weapon in the teacher's armoury of mind-control. Weak sunlight caught the bell as it passed by her windows, throwing faint golden glints onto the walls. Lines began to form by the classroom doors. Helen heard Alison say-

"Wait for it. Wait - for - it... "

She glanced up, and saw a shadow lingering by her classroom door - a stray. Quietly, she left her desk and approached it, wondering what further delights the children had in store for her this afternoon-

(*Miss... Russell's constructing anti-personnel devices in the playground again... Miss... iron filings taste like chicken... Miyiss... the guinea pig's gone on dirty protest again...*)

But it wasn't a child, it was Loatheworthy, hovering by the door and peering in through the tiny gap. Helen felt an unpleasant jolt of apprehension, though in a way she had been waiting for him all morning. She blinked, and this time she was crouching down behind her desk wearing hunter's gear and a chain of crocodile teeth slung around her neck. She was clutching a crossbow to her chest, and she knew that the bolts in the bow were tipped with a rare and fabulous poison which would induce a week and a half of chronic and perpetual malodorous flatulence, followed by certain death. Loatheworthy pushed her classroom door open, she levelled the weapon and aimed it at his chest.

Then she was back. How long had he stood there, watching her? Had he heard her talking to herself?

When she pulled the door all the way open, the inspector tried to pretend that he had been reading something on the wall display. Helen favoured him with a look which suggested that she knew better.

"Hello," she said. "What can I do for you?" Her voice was bright, but she could not keep a slight edge of coldness from her tone.

Loatheworthy met her gaze evenly, but, she noticed, his cheeks had reddened slightly.

"I was just, just er... " He pointed down the corridor with his clipboard, then waved it impatiently, as if there were something there which would immediately explain his behaviour.

Helen leaned around the door-jamb, and peered down towards the office, then looked back at him, eyebrows raised, refusing to let him off the hook.

Loatheworthy seemed confused by this, then cleared his throat.

"Miss Haversham, isn't it?"

The inspector's reddish brown moustache twitched, and Helen was seized by the idea that he was receiving a radio signal from Ofsted's central command through its filaments. He nodded, as if confirming something to himself - *message received Control, will begin spirit-crushing process ASAP.*

"Just here to let you know that I'll be in to... er... to properly assess you," he checked his paperwork, "either Wednesday, or Thursday, or both." He flashed the semblance of a smile. "Can't say which day yet, like to keep you on your toes, but I'm sure it will prove to be... informative." He tapped the clipboard with the end of one finger, and repeated, "Very informative," as if savouring the words.

Internally Helen sighed. If you managed to impress one inspector, then there was always another much meaner one standing right behind him.

Loatheworthy was still peering into her classroom over her shoulder. Gradually, Helen leaned to her left, cutting off his line of sight. For a moment he followed her, then caught himself leaning and straightened up. Helen felt a bright spark of anger kindle within her.

"You like your job, don't you Mister Loatheworthy?"

His expression became grave-

"Yes," he said, "yes I do. I like it very much." He glanced into the room again. "It often amazes me what one might find in a classroom."

Helen nodded, long and slow, keeping a steady poker-face. "Children, mostly," she said.

Loatheworthy seemed to be keeping the fingers of his right hand carefully shielded out of sight behind his clipboard.

"No, besides children, Miss Haversham. Do you have your planning for Wednesday available? Perhaps that will help me to decide on a day."

Helen retreated wordlessly to her desk, unlocked the bottom drawer, and removed a copy of her plans. Loatheworthy remained in the doorway, watching her carefully. As she offered the paperwork to him, he reached out to take it with his right hand; his index, middle, and ring fingers were covered in sticking plaster. *Gotcha,* Helen thought. She tried not let her glance linger, but he caught her, and so she nodded towards his hand, smiling brightly-

"That looks nasty."

He regarded her for a long moment.

"Yes," he said eventually, tucking her plans into his clipboard and raising his hand. "I trapped my fingers in something. The victim of someone else's carelessness, I'm afraid."

"That's too bad." Helen nodded in apparent sympathy, still smiling faintly.

He frowned. "Did I say something amusing?"

She shook her head. "No, not at all. It's just that you reminded me of the children then, you know, when they've been into something that they shouldn't have." She mimicked a high childlike voice- "'It wasn't me, it was so-and-so's fault.'"

Loatheworthy's eyes bulged slightly over his reddish moustache, and Helen could see tiny scarlet capillaries beating there. She took a half step backwards, wondering if she hadn't pushed things too far, if he might not be about to break cover. He took in a hurried breath, as if he were about to speak, but then the children began to come in, filling the school with noise and with the tail-end of lunchtime games that might be picked up later.

Loatheworthy seemed to get himself under control.

"I think it was a misguided prank," he said. "But such things do not go unnoticed." The slightest flicker of a cold and dangerous smile.

"Until Wednesday… or Thursday."

Then he turned on his heel and began to walk away, leaving his words like an implicit threat.

Helen lingered in the doorway, her arms still folded until he reached the corner and turned. It wasn't until he had passed the rising-fives unsettling visual interpretations of the little red riding hood story, now known in the school as 'the nursery-crime wall', that she began to relax; it was as if she were seeing him away from her territory.

This wasn't over yet, she realised glumly. He clearly saw her actions not as a warning, but as a challenge. His ego was bruised along with his fingers, and there was likely to be some kind of reprisal. In short, she should look out; he still had it in for her.

She stared blankly at the corridor walls, not seeing the sugar-paper and lettering and the flurry of mad woodcutters breaking down doors and fanged wolves under night-caps, tapping her cheek with one outstretched finger.

The question was: what would Loatheworthy's next move be?

#

At the northern edge of Hornby, roughly four miles as the crow flies from the school, the land rose to form a crown of hills that were softer than those to the south, but bare of woodland, and divided into ragged fields. The largest of these northern plots was known locally as Jackson's Acres, though the eponymous farmer Jackson had long since sold his land and moved into the Cotswolds. The plot had probably retained his name solely for its value as a double-entendre (*have you seen the state of Jackson's Acres? Yes, dreadful, you can get an ointment for that, you know*), but it now lay fallow, and more than two hours after full dark, showed occasional weeds and grasses through a moonscape of rutted and frost-silvered earth. To the west there was a lane, and a scraggy fence with a line of barbed wire stapled to its top meandered down its side, replacing the ancient hedgerow that had once stood there. Caught in the fence's barbs there was the occasional tuft of wiry animal hair, though the only beasts that passed this way now were owned by weekend pony-trekkers.

An old scarecrow, forgotten, leaning drunkenly with its straw-filled head resting on one shoulder, stood nearby. Loatheworthy squinted at it through his car window, trying to make out whether it was a human figure or not.

Eventually the inspector was forced to bring his car's slow progress to a halt, wind down the passenger-side window, and stick his head out into the cold to get a clear view. From outside it seemed obvious; not even Hall, the man he was here to meet, was that scruffy.

Still, the scarecrow unnerved him, waiting in the darkness as if it were evidence of some primitive agricultural ritual, or worse, a witness to what he was about to do.

He glanced at his watch. It was almost six. He had twenty minutes if Hall deigned to be on time, but that was unlikely. Hall had never been punctual as a pupil, why would he be as an adult?

When he was safely past the scarecrow, Loatheworthy brought his car to a halt and the engine's hum died away leaving him with the faint glow of the dashboard lights and the sound of the breeze. He pushed his head back in his seat and tried to relax, but it was difficult; he felt frustrated. Worse than that, he was beginning to feel thwarted, and when he felt thwarted it always raised the craven, grinning, ungodly spectre of Fly Day.

He held his bruised fingers up before his eyes. His moustache trembled.

Once again, his efforts were being checked, as if by some malign anti-Loatheworthy force. A pattern he knew all too well was being repeated. He would get so far with some scheme or dream, he would bring some plan to the point of fruition, and then an invisible barrier would seem to rise up before him, and his plans would go awry, his schemes would end in bizarre ruin.

Take Fly Day as an example. The yuppie decade had been kind to Loatheworthy, and he had spent the nineteen eighties steadily working his way to the top of a company called Argle Water and Sewerage Services Ltd. There he had found a climate of management in which he could flourish, a new ruthlessness that he adored.

By mid-decade Loatheworthy was one of four directors controlling the whole of Argle, and he was the front-runner to be chosen by the board to succeed the ailing Grangeforth Argle, and pilot the company through the difficult transition into the brave new world of full privatisation. His competition was all but beaten, and he had prepared the ground for a final dazzling meeting. Here he outlined the stock-options and bonuses, the enormous wealth that awaited the upper echelons of the company after privatisation, and laid out a mould-breaking scheme to take Argle into the financial sector; pensions and life-insurance were sure money-spinners.

It had been a great success. As old Argle's cheeks shone brighter and brighter with greed, his fellow directors sank lower and lower into their chairs. Loatheworthy had begun to sense triumph and strut by the side of his overhead projector.

Ten minutes from the presentation's end, as he dimmed the lights to show yet another set of fabulously large figures, a bluebottle had entered the office through a fan-light window. It had completed a single lazy circuit of the room as if on reconnaissance, and then flown with disturbing and flawless precision directly into Loatheworthy's open mouth. He had been mid-sentence, a gold-tipped pointer raised high in the air, and there had been nothing for it but to reflex-swallow noisily, and continue.

It was Fly Day.

When he had finished his sentence and glanced fearfully at his audience again, Loatheworthy had seen in each horror-glazed eye and twisted, repulsed grimace, the essence of his own downfall.

Fly Day was year zero of a new era. No one, it seemed, would take him seriously (or in most cases even meet his gaze) after that. Where he had once inspired fear and awe, he now found disdain and barely concealed mirth. A week after Fly Day he had been sitting in a stall in the executive washroom, quietly reading the financial pages when, unannounced, two high-pitched voices in cracked and off-key harmony had drifted stealthily under the stall door:

We don't know why,
He swallowed a fly,
Perhaps he'll die!

Then mad giggling, the sound of the outer door closing, and by some mystical transference the sidelining of his career at Argle.

His rivals began to treat him with open contempt. One had even beckoned him into the empty boardroom on a lonely Friday afternoon, and offered him 'a succulent earwig', which he had found in the corner of his office. Grinning widely, the man had opened his cupped palms before Loatheworthy's eyes (eyes which were bulging with indignation) nodded encouragingly, and said, "Go on. Treat yourself!"

Jokes followed him everywhere, haunting the corridors as he passed (*oh waiter, there's a fly in my soup. Oh I'm sorry sir, it's probably hiding from Loatheworthy*), and on one memorable Monday morning he had discovered, laid neatly on his desk, an immaculately typed menu of delicious cordon-bleu invertebrate-only dishes.

That one moment had ruined him at Argle. His meteoric float to the top had halted, a lesser man had been promoted above him to take charge of privatisation, and gradually he had become more and more marginalised. Now every grudge that had been held against him on his rise to power was settled. Every man whose face he had trodden on during his climb now kicked him on the way down.

If only he could have changed that one moment.

That one moment, and the fact that privatisation had actually led Argle into enormous debt. And the fact that expansion into the financial sector had led to fines for miss-selling financial products. And the fact that Argle had been swallowed up in a hostile takeover by a larger Belgian concern. He had been blamed for it all, and in the next round of streamlining it was decided that four directors was a horrible extravagance, and one of them had to go.

Loatheworthy had then turned to education. Large inner-city schools, the government of the day was sure, needed a new and vital management strategy. He retrained, and had been fast-tracked in as an area consultant. Then, with a minimum of teaching experience, he had become executive co-Head of three large comprehensives. From there, he had jumped ship to the Inspectorate, a natural move, forming his own highly profitable team, and bidding for inspections across the country.

In a way then, by thwarting him, Fly Day had brought him here. The invisible anti-Loatheworthy force had conjured up a bluebottle to disappoint him, and now he could almost feel it happening again, as if there were a buzzing in the air, drawing near.

Absently, he raised one hand and waved it by his ear, just in case.

Thwarted.

He said the word aloud in the confined space of the car.

George Anthony Thwarted Loatheworthy.

His luck was bad. He bought a car, a brand new BMW (the car before the one in which he now sat, in fact) and when it was delivered, showing less than a mile on the odometer, he had found a shovel, a tarpaulin, and a bag of quick-lime in the boot. The police had towed it away and disassembled it into tiny, tiny pieces. When it was dry his garden collapsed, and he fell into his own septic tank. He moved to a house by the river, and when it was wet, it flooded (with poisonous water). He travelled abroad on holiday and habitually experienced either hurricanes or coups, or sometimes both. His wife purchased a dog, a tiny tropical breed, which to Loatheworthy's way of thinking resembled nothing so much as a deep fried chicken nugget with great bulging eyes. The dog savaged him, kept him prisoner in the garden for hours, and then ran away with most of his trousers, his wallet, and his house keys. He had become an Ofsted inspector, and inspectors began to be murdered. It was as if he were somehow cursed.

He thumped his knee in frustration.

That was the keynote of his life. It was an undertone that had begun years before, and the whole thing was a circle. His entire career had an ironic circularity, because if Fly Day had led him here, to a showdown with Helen Haversham, then he had been led to Argle - and hence to Fly Day - by a similar wrangle with Haversham's father.

The irony of it! The sheer *fatedness* of it, stretching across all of his trials and disasters had suggested that here, at last, he was meant to have his vengeance. Imagine it - Jonathan Haversham's daughter living and working only a few miles from his home. She did not recognise him, and she was working as a teacher, developing a career that he was in the ideal position to ruin.

It would bring him ultimate satisfaction.

He smiled, opened his eyes, and glanced up at the windscreen.

A gaunt figure stood close to the car, leaning towards it. At the moment that Loatheworthy looked upwards, it leant forwards and rapped on the windscreen with two white knuckles. Inside the car, Loatheworthy jumped in his seat, screamed effeminately, and clasped his chest with one hand. The figure took three or four steps back from the car and grinned vacantly, as if pleased by this.

Disoriented, Loatheworthy opened the car door and stepped out into the breeze. The other man gestured towards him half-heartedly and said something, but it was too quiet, and Loatheworthy only caught half of it-

"...atch it, ..it!"

Too late he realised what the other man had said, and looked down to see that, for the second time in four days (and the one-hundred-and-thirty-ninth time this year) he had stepped straight into a small pile of manure. He extracted his foot, then tried with no great success to wipe it on the grass; yet another pair of ruined shoes. He had hoped to draw some authority from his clothes and car, his social status during this meeting, but now that seemed an unlikely prospect. Eventually he approached the other man, one hand outstretched to shake.

Martin Hall leaned against the low fence, surveying the desolate field, and drew deeply on a cigarette; its tip glowed balefully. He ignored Loatheworthy's hand until it was dropped back to his side.

Hall was twenty-two years old, and the nightmare apparition that haunts the consciousness of every parent with a daughter old enough to date. He was tall and dark but not handsome. His hair was long and lank, thinning slightly, and glinting with oil in the half-light. His right ear was pierced both through the lobe and the upper cartilage, and through the piercings was threaded a slim silver dagger. Those who met Hall found it difficult to decide whether this was ornamental, or the aftermath of a particularly vicious knife-fight that he had not yet bothered to clear away.

The earring, and a series of monochromatic tattoos (a spider-web stretching across his neck, and a list of girls' names on his lower arms) had been added since he had left school, but otherwise he looked the same as when Loatheworthy had expelled him almost seven years before.

"You have it?" Loatheworthy asked, trying to sound businesslike, but he was betrayed by a tremor in his voice.

Hall nodded, still not looking at him, then reached up and unzipped about a third of his jacket. With his cigarette still smouldering, he reached inside and drew a large clear plastic bag upwards so that it just caught the light. Loatheworthy saw a tangle of dark shredded foliage and pills, glinting in the moonlight.

"Is it all... real?"

"Some grass, no resin, but good grade stuff. It might be dusted. Some pills, mostly non-prescription." Hall closed his jacket again, and looked both ways along the fence. Their exposed position was clearly making him nervous. When he looked Loatheworthy full in the face his lip curled in a sneering, wolfish smile. "What do you want done with it?"

Loatheworthy told him, his voice gradually steadying as he counted the points off on his fingers. When he had finished there was an uncomfortable silence, and Loatheworthy tried not to squirm under Hall's vacant stare. Eventually the younger man spoke-

"I always knew there was something... something *wonky* about you," he said, and poked at Loatheworthy's chest with his index finger. He smelled of cigarette smoke and decay. "Even when I was a kid, I *knew* you weren't on the level."

He took a final drag from his cigarette and cast it away. It bounced off the cuff of Loatheworthy's right trouser leg, throwing out a spray of sparks. Loatheworthy took a quick hopping step backwards.

"Sorry," Hall said, grinning furiously and looking anything but. "Now, have *you* got what *I* want?"

Loatheworthy nodded, trying to quell the inner voice which was even now questioning the wisdom of standing here, in a deserted field shining with frost, which no one knew he had come to, with a convicted felon (possession, grievous bodily harm, aggravated assault, and burglary). He found that his hands were shaking slightly inside his coat pockets as he walked back to the car and opened the boot. Inside was a black briefcase, combination locked and empty except for a roll of money, again encased in a plastic bag. The roll was made up of low denomination bills which Loatheworthy had been careful not to handle. He took it out and turned around.

Hall had approached with distressing quietness and now stood immediately behind him, grinning again. Loatheworthy let out an involuntary squeak and leant backwards, then proffered the bundle.

"There you go," he said, sounding ridiculous even to himself.

By now, Hall had another cigarette burning. He puffed as he snatched the roll of money from Loatheworthy's hands.

"Want to count it," he said, turning away slightly, as if this act required privacy. With some relief, Loatheworthy gave it to him, and, after a few moments of quiet, turned to face the scattered lights of Hornby, spread out below him; he found them evocative.

Inevitably they reminded him of another dark night of dark deeds, more than thirty years before. On that night, which had changed his life irrevocably, strings of Japanese lanterns hanging from the ivied walls and windows of the great stone manor house had made very similar patterns. Gazing out at the hills, he could almost hear the murmur of many conversations from across the years. There was the clink of wineglasses, and in the distance he could hear the civilised growl of Sinatra asking who had the last laugh now, his voice blending uneasily with the harsher, guitar-driven whine of some rock band singing about the Garden of Eden.

Loatheworthy closed his eyes, lost in the memory, and to his left he heard laughter and panting as someone (probably a junior trader) chased their partner into the fragrant summer woodland.

This was where it all started, his tussle with the Havershams, the curse, the bad luck, the point to which he could trace all of his life's frustration and sourness.

It was August of 1976, and Loatheworthy's star was on the rise for the first time. Tonight, on the evening of the seventeenth, he had decided that it would emerge from the eclipsing shadow that was his employer - Holding Company Holdings - and shine for all to see.

It was quite a shadow. In less than half a decade HCH had become one of London's most profitable investment houses, quickly outstripping its more venerable rivals. Loatheworthy's uncle knew someone who knew someone who went to school with a director there, and a position had been snagged for him. Money flowed, and for the Company's employees there were profit-sharing schemes, generous pensions, interest free loans, and every August a staff party at the Old Man's mansion which was the envy of every other City firm; it all made for a happy work environment.

Loatheworthy was not happy, far from it.

Too much fun. He shook his head from the shadow of the corner of the big house. When he gained control, he would regulate fun.

The trimmer, younger Loatheworthy of 1976 had carefully hatched a plan to savage the hand that fed him. Client lists and accounts summaries, he knew, were kept inside the great house, locked in a safe on the second floor, the combination of which only the Old Man and Jonathan Haversham, who was nominally his boss, knew. Loatheworthy had been idly searching Haversham's office late one evening, and had found it scribbled carelessly on a memo, which Haversham had shredded and binned. Loatheworthy had pieced it together, and it now sat as a comforting weight in the inside pocket of his suit.

HCH's success was a mystery to its rivals; its ability to win in large-scale investments was legendary, and smacked of insider dealing. The competition would do almost anything to see its internal accounts, and such information would buy Loatheworthy wealth and power at a firm that would understand him better.

He stole through the shadows to the corner of the great house, feeling the heat of the day imprisoned in its stone, and then made his way through a side door. Three more right turns and a sweeping staircase later, and he was outside what he knew to be the Old Man's private office. He took a pair of leather driving gloves from his pocket and slipped them on with quiet deliberation. The sound of the party now seemed miles away. He opened the door and crept in, cutting a laugh from the party below him in two.

An odd room this. It had no windows, but there was a wide alcove in the centre of each long wood-panelled wall. A single tapered candle in a marble holder stood in each alcove, casting a shifting glow over an untidy desk, ancient patterned rugs, a high-backed chair in each corner, and a series of murky Renaissance portraits.

Squinting in the gloom, Loatheworthy felt for a light switch, but one did not meet his hand. No matter, he could see the wall-safe well enough. It was grey, metallic, and stood next to the alcove on the left-hand wall. Sweating now, he took out the combination and read it to himself.

Loatheworthy had the documents he needed safely in the inside pocket of his jacket, and was closing the safe door again, his breathing more regular now that the deed was done, when a voice spoke from behind him.

"Hello George."

He wheeled around, eyes wide in the gloom, excuses already forming on his lips, but they died there when he saw the figure sitting in the high-backed chair by the door: it was Haversham. Loatheworthy blinked. How had he missed him? He had passed within five feet of the man, why hadn't he looked around more carefully?

This was it then: the end of his career.

Jonathan Haversham was hidden deep in a pool of shadow and Loatheworthy could not read his expression, seeing only candle-glints on the frame of his glasses. He expected angry accusations, perhaps a little pointing of the finger of blame, but it did not come. Instead, Jonathan said in a low, apparently friendly tone-

"Doing a bit of after-hours work George?"

Loatheworthy didn't reply, interpreting this as sarcasm, and Jonathan continued, not moving in his seat.

"After tonight the combination will be changed, then even I won't have it."

Still Loatheworthy said nothing. Any self-justification seemed to melt away under that steady tone.

Haversham gripped the arms of his chair; his fingers seemed very white in the dim room.

"Here's the thing George," he said. "I've been meaning to get you alone for a while now, so that we could have a chat."

Loatheworthy frowned. What was this? Haversham was acting as if they had just met in the bathroom, or in a corridor; surely he knew what was going on here. Had he seen what Loatheworthy had taken from the safe? Was he drunk? Hope dawned; was Haversham stupid enough to let him get away with this?

At last, Jonathan shifted forward in his seat, massaging the bridge of his nose with one hand.

"Do you know Jane, Jane Yorke, George? She's a secretary, works on the second floor."

Loatheworthy's frown deepened. Yes, he knew her.

"Well, Jane and I are going to get married," Haversham said, "and I wondered if you'd... I'd like you to be best man, George. At the wedding. I think you'd be just right."

Loatheworthy looked on in fascination. Best man? Didn't the wretched man have any friends?

Haversham left his seat and crossed the room.

"The company needs you George," he said, "needs your... edge if you can just calm it down a bit. Come along to the wedding - it'll help you. Be best man. Make a witty speech - people always love that - then come back to the company and make lots of money."

Haversham nodded towards the safe - the first proper indication that he had seen what Loatheworthy had been up to.

"Forget about this," he said, touching Loatheworthy's elbow. "If you need a raise, just see the Old Man, you're due one, I won't say a word. But at midnight tonight the combination on that safe changes, and anything that's out, won't go back in again, and there are things in place. I've used... There's security... it would be bad... very bad."

Haversham's expression was still difficult to read in the gloom. Loatheworthy decided that he was definitely being mocked in some way, but how to respond?

Before he could, there was a noise in the hallway and the problem was resolved as the door burst open, spilling light and laughter around them. It was the Old Man, staggering, and carrying a bottle of whisky.

"There you are," he said, slurring decorously. "What're you doing skulking in the dark?"

Haversham spoke up quickly, confidently. "Just talking things over," he said.

The Old Man's smile faded briefly as he took in Loatheworthy and the proximity of the wall safe. Then his gaze snapped back to Jonathan Haversham, and he beamed a wide and foolish grin.

"Just bumped into Jane," the Old Man said. "Popped the question at last then, did you?"

Haversham's smile was more fleeting, and he nodded.

"Well come and have a drink with me, celebrate the year."

The Old Man glanced at Loatheworthy again, who placed his hands behind his back, hiding his driving gloves.

"Both of you!"

So he had endured an hour in some awful dining room on the ground floor of the house, toasting the health of a man he hated above all others, and expecting that at any second Haversham would announce his treachery and arrange for the ruination of his life. He had even posed for a photograph with the two other men - some society pages thing for one of the Old Man's pet newspapers - and they had not guessed that his twisted attempt at a smile was inspired more by panicky fear than by fellow feeling.

Two hours later, Loatheworthy had walked dazedly to his car, escaping, but not really understanding what had happened.

Next morning it had finally dawned on him: Haversham had been giving him a *chance*, his offer was genuine; he had offered Loatheworthy a chance to change his plans. Ludicrous. He had been seized by manic joy that he should be let off this way, that Haversham was too weak to deliver a killing blow.

Within two hours the client lists and accounts summaries were being analysed by lawyers acting for the largest of the HCH's competitors. An hour after that and HCH's larger clients had been informed of a pending investigation. Loatheworthy's success seemed assured.

But then there had been one of those mystical transformations *à la* Fly Day, and Haversham's and his own fortunes had not played out quite as he had hoped.

For one thing, the information was useless. HCH was as clean as a whistle and the investigation resulted in no action being taken against them. In fact, surviving such an audit intact actually boosted the company's reputation. Then, as HCH's fortunes increased, so Loatheworthy's own seemed to wither, and the curse took hold. His investments made only losses. He earned no trust from his new employers and they were rid of him as quickly as possible. He had been left to the slow grind of provincial executivism, had married a woman who disliked him and reminded him more and more as the years passed of a warthog, and eventually he had dedicated his life to sewerage, it seemed like the only thing to do.

Haversham, on the other hand, prospered. He married Jane Yorke and a relative took the role of best man. A mutual acquaintance had shown Loatheworthy a photo of them beaming from the steps of a small City registry office, looking genuinely happy. After that he had lost sight of Haversham in the real world, but the man had always been there in the background somehow. He was a capering, blissfully happy spectre in Loatheworthy's mind, mocking the subtle and growing ruination of his life with diffident decency, and the idea, secretly poisoning his every moment, that if he had acted differently on that hot August night, then the whole pattern of his life could have been altered, made better. Somewhere, in a parallel universe, there was a Loatheworthy who had snapshots of himself making that witty speech at the Haversham's wedding. He was uncursed. He had stayed at HCH, and for him there was no warthog-wife, no Argle, no tiny vicious dog, no murder incorporated BMW, no mousetrap, and he had never ingested even the teeniest tiniest invertebrate.

Haversham had given him the chance to change his life, and he hated him for it. Now there would be some recompense.

Loatheworthy blinked and saw the lights of Hornby again. Hall had turned towards him once more and was regarding him narrowly.

"You know what to do, then?"

The other man nodded in the darkness, exhaling smoke-

"Tomorrow night."

Loatheworthy edged past him, sank back into his car seat, and closed the door, grateful for its comforting bulk. Over by the tree-line a bird erupted into the air, squawking and squabbling, startling them both. Hall turned and rapped on the window again. Loatheworthy reached for the control, and the window hummed downwards.

As the gap opened, Hall turned on his heel, cat-quick, and leaned in, suddenly furious. His hair was hanging in his face, the dagger earring glinted, and he grasped Loatheworthy by the collar and hauled him to the window with surprising strength. Hall looked into Loatheworthy's eyes for a few seconds-

"If this is some kind of scam," he said, slowly, "I'll find you, and then I'll turn you inside out. Understood?"

Loatheworthy nodded, trying not to imagine how such a feat might be achieved.

Hall stared at him for a few seconds longer, and then released him and retreated from the car. Loatheworthy closed the window as soon as he was able, then watched Hall stalk, without another word, across the fields towards the rambling pathway that led eventually to the main road and the town.

As Hall's figure retreated into the dimness, Loatheworthy's fear began to be replaced by a wondrous anticipation. 'Gotcha!' Indeed. Let's see if Helen Haversham can get out of this one, he thought. There would be no flies this time, no bizarre coincidences of anticipation, just sweet revenge.

By the time he had completed a turn in the lane Loatheworthy was whistling to himself. He no longer felt thwarted.

IV - Tuesday

For David, Tuesday passed very slowly. Driven by the horrible spectre of what might lurk in Dr Love's valise, and by a need to be away from his rooms and the wall chart, he spent his day beneath the soft lights of the Bodleian library's upper reading room. He leafed through ancient periodicals, checking references that he had checked twice before, and by mid-afternoon had begun to draw disapproving looks from the librarians, and smirks from the sparse rows of other readers, as his head nodded lower and lower towards his desk, his nose falling closer into the musty book smell. By three o'clock, with his cheek resting lightly on textured paper and the comfort of elderly print, he had fallen into a light and troubled doze. He dreamed of Dr Love and his malign baggage chasing him through endless college corridors. When he awoke it had grown dark outside, Oxford lay alight around him, and he had a perfect newsprint image of some long-dead German poet neatly printed across one side of his face.

All in all, he was glad that the day was over.

Helen shared his mood, and her day also dragged. From dawn until dusk a heavy white covering of cloud did not lift from the sky. It seemed to enclose the school, and made it impossible to tell where the sun might be. Though no inspectors were scheduled to come to her classroom she felt an unpleasant and slow-growing sense of tension. Almost in defiance of her feelings, she spent her lunch hour in the school hall, which blazed with cheery yellow light, braving a swift rehearsal of the Nativity. She watched Miriam bash enthusiastically at the school's geriatric piano, and listened, smiling, to small groups of gleeful children committing grotesque and fiendish crimes against melody. They hurriedly tested the various backdrops, the spotlight high up in the final scene which would mimic the star of Bethlehem, and they awoke one of the four-and-a-half-year-old wise men, when he fell asleep behind a large Christmas tree, inexplicably present in a stable in first-century Palestine.

When not at work in the classrooms, the inspectors kept to the rooms set aside for them, as if chastened by the weekend's events, or perhaps by the carols. Only Loatheworthy prowled the corridors. As Miriam wrestled with the introduction of *Hark the Herald Angels Sing,* Helen turned in her seat to see him peering in through the closed glass doors, his hands clasped behind his back. When he saw that he had her attention he smiled a worryingly toothsome and satisfied smile. Helen did not think that his expression was prompted by enjoyment of their show. She turned back to the children quickly, and after a few moments, felt him leave.

It was the day's only excitement.

#

Robert Murco's Tuesday, on the other hand, was very exciting indeed. At Midday Murky stood, gazing impassively at a blackberry and two bells, and wondering sourly what he had done to deserve this. He fed in two more coins, his last two, and the slot-machine booped happily, almost smugly. *That's right*, it whispered, *I'm hungry, hungry! Feed me aaaall of your earth money.*

Leaning against the machine Murky gazed intently at the reels, then held the two bells. Each hold caused another beep (redolent of gratification and not a little disdain), which echoed slightly in the morning-empty pub, then he pushed the start button again. The third reel, the blackberry, flipped around at dizzying speed, then thunked into place.

Banana.

He let fly a great slurring stream of vivid and ingenious invective that raised dust from the Duke of Wellington's carpet and started a dog barking somewhere out on the street.

He pushed the start button one more time, but already knew what would happen. Now (one spin too late) the bell would appear on the outside reel, but with no others to match it.

Thunk, thunk, thunk.

There it was, fake light glinting on its rim, too late for the little bell soirée he had planned, bringing with it a strawberry and a grinning clown's face. That was his luck today. The machine booped again, three times, each one indicating with its tone a lower estimation of Murky's character and intelligence than the last.

He glanced around himself, slightly woozy, giving a long slow blink. In the distance he could hear the whine of a vacuum cleaner, and a thump-thump as someone butted it enthusiastically against a skirting-board. The thumps echoed his heartbeat.

Even by his own standards, and with diligent application, Murky had managed to consume a quite startling amount of alcohol. He began to grin with simple pride, imagining himself describing his state to his limited circle of friends that evening, but then he remembered his reason for being at *The Welly* in the first place, and his grin faded.

He stood straight, looking down at the fruit machine with something like contempt, as if it too were a friend that had betrayed him. The three reels stared back at him, the clown's merry grin taking on a sinister cast. *Where'sh our shtuff Robbie*, it lisped. *You were holding it for ush for a few daysh. Just a few daysh... Now we've come to collect.*

Abruptly Murky decided that it was time to weave his way uncertainly towards home. For all he knew, Hall might now have returned to the flat that they shared. Perhaps he had been out at a club, or at some friend's place - he often disappeared for a night - and now he was home, and the baggie was back under the loose floorboard, under the cupboard, under the sink. Murky imagined it there, fat and brownish and beautiful, come to save his skin, and fleetingly his smile returned, but he couldn't believe it. Hall was a scumbag, and had run off with Snoopy's valuable merchandise.

In Murky's mind the space under the sink was empty again, as it had been that morning, as empty as Hall's room and his unslept in but slightly rank bed.

Murky had staggered around the flat calling Hall's name, much as he now staggered across the empty bar towards the Gents, though this morning it had been shock and fear, rather than lager, that had ruined his balance and turned his legs to jelly. This was serious, he could get hurt, seriously hurt when Snoopy tracked him down.

As he shouldered open the door to the Gents, a coach or a truck stopped at the traffic lights outside, darkening the dusty windows slightly, a large silver Jaguar pulled purposefully into the pub car-park, and Murky had a vision.

He saw himself go back to the flat, check one more time under the sink, and then head for the bus garage and buy a ticket to somewhere, anywhere. London, Cambridge, Cornwall. *A single to Glasgow please, my good man...*

It didn't matter, as long as it was far away from here. He should have known he was out of his depth letting Hall mind stuff for Snoopy; sooner or later there would be trouble, and he had realised it just in time.

Outside the lights changed. He heard traffic noise as the pub door opened, and a gruff rev as the coach pulled away. Bugger it, he wouldn't even go back to the flat, he'd draw the last of his cash from the hole-in-the-wall in town, and go straight to the bus terminal. Whichever coach passed through next, that was the one he would be on.

Smiling again, feeling suddenly free, Murky entered the bathroom, not seeing the swift shadows which moved in behind him like hyenas on the scent of something limpy which has already wandered from the herd.

Murky waved one hand at a time under the asthmatic hand drier which wheezed tepid air at him reproachfully, leaning with the other on the cracked and crazied tiles above his head. He read a line of graffiti ('for big sex fun fone... ' and then a number, obliterated by angry marker lines) over and over, as if with diligent attention and careful research, he might discover some more profound sense in it. He was reading it for the twenty-third time when the quality of the artificial light before his half-closed eyes changed, and a large hand grasped the back of his head and pushed his face into the tiles, squashing his nose upwards and to the side. Another hand grabbed his arm (his hand was still, of course, wet), and twisted it expertly up behind his back. With his right eye he could still make out the words 'big sex' on the wall.

Someone - probably the person holding him - leaned in close behind his head and said, "Boo!"

Whoever it was had incredibly bad breath, and it washed over him like a stale garlicky tide, making his open eye water. Off to his left he heard a high-pitched gleeful giggle, and then a further voice, one he definitely recognised, said-

"Hello Robbie. I've caught you at home, how niysh."

Murky opened his mouth to speak, to tell Snoopy (that lisping nasal quality was unmistakable) that he had the stuff, he'd just go and get it for him if he'd wait right here, but the hand on his head simply increased its pressure slightly, mashing his lips against the tiles, and all he managed to say was "Unmkff!"

There was a brief silence in which adrenaline sobered him up in record time, and he felt his own heart-beat in his throat. All Murky could see were shadows cast by the unshaded bulb on the once white wall in front of him. Three, one almost indistinguishable from his own, but huge; another, slimmer, off to the left; and the third, Snoopy (with the new clarity of fear he felt he could make out the shadow of the fabled, unbelievably large nose which had earned Snoopy his nickname) pacing backwards and forwards behind him, his shoes squeaking on the lino. Rough hands searched first his jacket, then his jeans pockets. "Nothing there Boss."

Eventually Snoopy stopped pacing. "I'm a fair man," he said. "I'm willing to give democrashee a chansh. Shall we squash hish head now boysh, or let him live for another five minutesh."

"Squash him."

"Yeah, let's squish 'im now."

Murky actually *felt* his heart miss a beat. There was a bump, then a long, long pause whilst the world (or what he could see of it), began to take on an over-bright and grainy texture; then, finally, there was another bump, and the world jarred back into place.

"Sho much for the democratic proshesh. Give me dictatorship any day," Snoopy said. "The pub ish empty, we won't be dishturbed. I shay we ashk him a few queshtionsh firsht."

Murky was sweating now against the cold tiles. A drop ran down his forehead and into his open eye. He tried to blink it away.

"We trushted you with shomething very... important," Snoopy hissed, "and today wash the day when we were shupposhed to get it back. We waited, and waited, but you shtood ush up. When you and Hall didn't arrive at the meeting thish morning I became shushpishious that you might have done shomething shtupid, sho I tore Bob here away from hish dreshes and pumps and shent him to your horrible little flat sho that he could turn it over. What did you find there Bob?"

Bob's voice rumbled behind Murky's left ear, brimming with confidence that it knew the correct answer.

"Absholutely nothing Bosh."

There was a long, long silence. Snoopy's shadow paused in mid-stride on the wall, and then drew in towards them and became indistinct. Murky could almost feel the smile falling from his captor's face to be slowly replaced with a look of confusion.

"Are you taking the pish?" Snoopy hissed.

"Sher... er certainly not."

Another long pause. Murky guessed that Snoopy was debating with himself how to deal with this new complication. He seemed to come to the conclusion that Bob was too stupid to be mocking him.

"From now on," he said, speaking slowly, "you don't talk, ever. Not ever. Jusht nod, okay?"

"Yesh."

From slightly further away there was a sort of half snort, half squeak as the other henchman - the tall thin shadow - failed to suppress a traitorous snigger. Snoopy's shadow turned on the wall.

"Do you have shomething you'd like to share with the resht of us Donald?"

High-pitched, strained: "No."

The shadow whirled again.

"Shtop this *flipanshy*! I won't have thish happening *again.*"

The shadow head turned back and forth. Bob's hand (and presumably the rest of him) shook violently with suppressed mirth.

"Thish ish *sherious*. I *will* be taken *sheriously!*"

Open sniggering now, they seemed helpless to resist.

The shadow raised its arms and dropped them in a gesture of exasperation. In a lower voice Snoopy said, "I'm going to get the equipment, and when I return I exshpect a little more *dishiplin.*" He left the bathroom, the door banging behind him.

Equipment? *Equipment!* What did that mean?

Now Murky's heart began to race as more massive doses of adrenaline made their presence felt in his system. With the Boss gone the henchman's giggles quickly trailed off. Bob leaned in towards him once again.

"Shame," he said. "I quite liked you."

He considered for a while, seeming to debate telling Murky something, then, in a slightly lower tone, said-

"I should warn ya. The Boss - worl, ee's mad, an' I don't mean *angry* neeva. Ee's... " Bob's right hand briefly left the back of Murky's head, and he saw its shadow, index finger extended, twirl merrily around the big man's temple.

The other one - Donald - also closed in.

"Yeah," he said. "We're just stereotypical henchman, y'know; we just do what we're told. It's just a job for us. Home to the Moll after a hard day's corruptin' an' menacin' an' breakin' stuff. But the *Boss*, well he enjoys his work. Puts in overtime."

Another pause. Murky felt that both men were silently recalling terrible images from their past.

"I'd tell him what you've done with the stuff right away, save yourself a lot of aggro." Bob added, finally.

The door swung open again, hitting the tiled wall with a sound like a gunshot, and both henchman escaped whatever dreadful reverie had caught them and snapped back to attention. Murky's face was squashed into the tiles with renewed vigour.

"Donald," Snoopy said, "where *ish* Mishter Shticky?"

Murky squeaked involuntarily.

Donald sounded stricken again-

"Er… we lost him Boss, remember? About three menacin's ago? We left him in the bar, and when we came back, he was gone… Don't worry, I've been to B&Q and got another one. It's in a bag on the front seat."

Snoopy returned more quickly this time, and with his one unobscured eye staring at the shadow play on the tiles before him, Murky saw him approach, his heels clicking on the cold floor. He held his right hand out before him. He was brandishing something which looked slightly like the barrel of a gun with some dish-shaped contraption attached to its end.

Murky forced himself to calm down. *Don't panic,* he thought. *Don't panic. This is just nice cop/nasty cop; they won't do anything until they've got their stuff back, just in case you're holding out on them.*

Snoopy approached, brandishing the object.

"Do you shee thish?" He didn't wait for an answer.

"I pershonally have killed two men, and maimed sixsh with one jusht like it. It will enshure that you tell me everything I need to know."

He came closer still, and then Murky felt something which might be a gun barrel press against the back of his neck, through the material of his T-shirt. The skin there seemed to freeze, cold under a slick of sweat, and he twitched with an involuntary shiver. Snoopy's voice came from just behind his left ear.

"Theresh a way out for you though Robbie."

The pressure of the object on the back of his neck seemed enormous. "Do you want a way out?"

Murky nodded - the tiniest of movements - but Snoopy was close enough to see it.

"Now we both know that you are not the brainsh of your particular operashun, don't we?"

A pause, and then again an almost imperceptible nod.

"Do you know what I think? I think Hall ish the brainsh, and he'sh out there now, ishn't he, planning to shell our shtuff for hish own grubby profitsh?"

Snoopy seemed to like this last sentence, and he hissed it again, punctuating each word with a jab from whatever he held in his right hand.

"Hish Own Grubby Profitsh." Murky felt each prod as if it were a shovel-full of earth, falling onto his coffin. His neck started to go numb.

"I hope for your shake that you know where he ish, and what he'sh doing, *right now.*"

Murky's mind raced with almost sickly speed. Could he make something up that they would believe? He doubted it. Had Hall said anything that he could use? Where had he been going yesterday evening? If only he had more time to think. Slowly the grip was once again released from the back of his neck and he began to babble.

"I don't know, I don't know. He didn't come back last night, and I expected him to come back, but he didn't, often he doesn't, and I came here, and he wasn't here, so I had a drink and waited and waited and he didn't come... "

If only he listened more carefully to what people said to him. For years people had been telling him that he had a short attention span and a low tolerance for information. Ever since junior school he'd been meaning to change, but had never quite gotten around to it. Now he realised, he might never get the chance. Bob pressed his face into the tiles again, as if he might simply squeeze the knowledge that they wanted out of his head.

"Wash he on a job?"

Dimly, something in the back of Murky's mind stirred, a neuron fired, a connection was made. A job, yes. What was it? Something he had to do in town? Murky blinked sweat from his eyes again. Yes, yes! But that wasn't the important bit, that wasn't the bit that made the connection for him. Hall was always on a job, always doing something nasty to somebody.

After a while, perhaps realising that if the skittish and rather shallow conscious part of Murky were to suffer serious harm, then it might also, the deeper recesses of his mind decided to help him out a little: *school*, it whispered, *think about school*.

He did. *School... muddy football field... desks... bullying... bikesheds... exams... sportsday... teachers*. His eyes widened and a palpable, but probably premature feeling of relief spread throughout his body. Muscles that he hadn't realised he was tensing relaxed gratefully, and he let out a hitching sigh that was almost a laugh.

"Hmmshmm," he said. Snoopy signalled, and Bob released his grip a little more.

"Haversham." Murky said. "He said Haversham, or Haversack or Hoverpack or one of those names. And something about a school." The hitching sigh again, then, "Someone phoned him, and he said something about a school in Hornby."

"Shcool. *Shcool*?" There was a new tension in Snoopy's voice, and Murky saw the shadows of both henchmen turn towards each other, almost in dread. Bob raised his eyebrows in exasperation.

Snoopy had faded into some private dream-world.

"Shcool!" he said, clapping his unoccupied hand to his forehead and looking up at the ceiling as if it revealed some beautiful vision. "Ah... How I loved the exprelions on thowsh little childrensh fayshes when I shocked 'em with the Van de Graaff." He sighed. "Thrown out. Removed from the noble profeshun, and why? *Why?*"

Hesitantly, obviously wishing to redeem himself, Bob answered-

"Was it because you were makin' LSD on school grounds Boss, an' you accidentally took some, an' a party of HMI's found you climbing up the physics lab, naked apart from your safety goggles and a heat-proof glove?"

There was a moment's silence, then Snoopy nodded sadly. "Yesh Bob," he said, "yesh. That wash why."

Snoopy stared into space for a while, and neither henchman seemed minded to disturb him, then he turned back to Murky.

"What elsh?"

Murky thought quickly. "He told me he was going to see about a job, last night, and I thought it was this school job... But he might have been meeting a contact, y'know to sell the stuff, or spread it around anyway."

"Shure'?"

"Yes!"

The story obviously seemed plausible enough to Snoopy. Murky sensed meaningful glances passing between Boss and Henchmen. Eventually Snoopy spoke again.

"Thish ish whatsh going to happen, Robbie. You'll like thish." Another pause, "Well actually you probably won't like thish, but I will. Thish ish my favourite bit."

Movement behind him. Murky scrunched his eyes shut, as if this might ward of the expected bullet, and was surprised to hear Snoopy speak again.

"Thish ish my lucky coin." A grubby fifty-pence piece was thrust into Murky's line of sight.

"I am going to flip thish coin, and if it comesh up tailsh - I hate tailsh, *hate* it - I'm going to kill you now, right here. If it comesh up headsh, then you live. For a while anyway." Donald giggled again.

Before Murky could properly digest this wholly unwelcome information, he heard the unmistakable sound of a coin being flipped by a thumbnail, and then there was simple overload. Murky's mind, already overworked, simply could not cope. Realising that the usual trick of occupying the panicked body with a vision of all its past experiences would not work, since Murky's life experiences to date had been unremittingly dull, drab, and tedious beyond record, his mind sought a fitting metaphor that would allow his consciousness to cope with the temporary suspension of mental services. Murky's mind seized upon one supplied by the telephone networks and put him on hold. Whilst Snoopy's infernal coin turned and tumbled in the air, the harsh bathroom light glinting even on its dulled surfaces, Murky's mind played him a sickly, reedy version of the birdie song.

The coin landed on the bathroom floor with a tuneless ring, and there was a long pause. Bob's brow furrowed in confusion. Usually when the Boss did his little double-headed coin trick the scumbag he had hold of showed *extreme* interest in its results. This one, however, simply stared at the white bathroom wall. Bob shook him a little, knowing that if he kept the Boss waiting it would only lead to extra nastiness.

"Well Robbie, ish it headsh, or tailsh?"

Softly, under his breath, "*la la lalla la la laa, la la lalla la la laa. Laa laa laa laaa...*"

The henchmen shot each other a startled glance over Murky's (and the Boss's) heads. Bob shook him again and Murky's vision seemed to clear - normal mental services were restored. Finally he realised he had been asked a question, and opened his unobscured eye and looked down.

"Heads," he croaked; then, with more conviction, "heads!"

Donald stooped and picked up the coin.

"You are a very lucky shcumbag Robbie. Both lucky and shtupid, a dangerous combinashun. Heresh the deal. We are going to leave you now, to go and find Hall, and Mish or Mishter Hoverpack, or whatever, sho that we might organeysh the shafe return of our... merchandeysh. If you should happen to shee them in the meantime, you will shay nothing to them. You won't shee them in the meantime though Robbie, becaush you are leaving town."

Murky's knees sagged against the tiled wall with relief, and only Bob's grip on his arm kept him upright.

"Shoon we are going to leave." The object at Murky's neck was removed. "You will wait here until we are gone. But I am going to leave *thish* here Robbie, ash a reminder to you not to crosh ush in any way." The object was tapped on the back of his head.

"If you do crosh ush, or dishobey my instrukshuns in any way, we will find you, Robbie, and end you with one jusht like it." Donald made a strained noise of disgust.

"Now are you prepared to do exshactly ash I shay."

Murky nodded for a final time.

"Okay, now shit."

A confused silence. Murky felt Bob lean across towards Snoopy-

"I think he may have already done that Boss - that coin thing scared him quite badly."

"Oh for Godsh shake. Not shit, *shit*, on the floor."

Another silence, before Donald cleared his throat and piped up-

"Look Boss, we've done some pretty despicable things in our time, but I don't think I want to see *that*, do you know what I'm saying?"

Murky could practically feel the white heat of Snoopy's anger. He shouldered his way through his employees, stood behind Murky, and pushed down on his shoulder-blades. Bob released his grip on Murky's arm, and he collapsed onto the floor; dimly he heard Donald say, "Oh, *shit*."

"Count to sixshty now Robbie. Then leave. Forever. Come on moronsh, your bush is leaving."

Murky heard a wet plopping sound followed by a *sproiinng*, then the door swung back and hit the wall, making him wince as three sets of footsteps disappeared away.

Robert Murco counted under his breath, feeling unutterably tired, as if he could go to sleep right here with his forehead resting on the bathroom wall. By the time that he reached fifty, the toilets had been quiet for a while, and he could once again hear the sound of a vacuum cleaner bumping against the skirting board upstairs.

After a while, as he played the incident through in his mind, a new feeling came upon him, a kind of mental defence mechanism. Murky began to feel sure that their threats must have been empty, that they had come into the bathroom to heavy him - the way Hall was sometimes hired to heavy people - and they had done an expert job. A few idle threats, a little stage-managed pressure, and he had crumbled. Incredibly, with the adrenaline clearing from his system, Murky's beer-buzz was returning, and he began to feel foolish, as if they had tricked him. He took a deep breath, stood, and turned around, his mind filled with a vapid curiosity.

The bathroom was quiet, all seemed normal, and at first he had to search for whatever it was they had left behind. He had actually taken a few steps towards the exit before he saw it, stuck to the wall by the battered door, still vibrating gently. He approached it, feeling a combination of dread and levity, and reached out a hand to touch it, as you might to something you suspected of being very hot, or not quite dead.

Eventually a disturbing question dawned behind Murky's fascinated eyes: just how *did* you kill someone with an industrial-sized sink-plunger?

This question (and its many frightening answers) brought with it a whole new life for Robert Murco. He left the plunger stuck to the wall, where it would be discovered and wondered over twenty minutes later by two businessmen enjoying a liquid lunch. The first coach he came to was headed for Taunton, and he stepped onto it without a backward glance. Once there, he pursued his new found goals of a wife and children, a well-landscaped garden, pets, and a respectable job with vigour. He forgot his old life almost completely, and if there were any clouds which hovered silently over his new life of cosy domesticity, they dwelt solely in his dreams. Occasionally the memory of Mr Sticky would invade his sleeping consciousness, and he would awake fevered and staring, disturbing his new wife greatly, with the whispered cry-

"The plunger. The *plunger!*"

#

At six-thirty, David was standing hopelessly before the half-length oval mirror on his wardrobe door, and wondering whether the shirt he had selected was a good idea. He looked to his fish for inspiration, but he had forgotten to switch them on, and they huddled together in one corner of their artificial tank, staring sullenly out at him as if they were planning some dastardly crime. He reached for the switch and they began to bump dutifully against the glass. One of them, the blue one, turned more quickly than the others and began a dash for a clear space at the far end of the tank.

David sighed. It had seemed like a great idea when he had seen them in the shop: artificial pets that needed no feeding or cleaning. All you had to do was change their batteries every once in a while and the brightly-coloured fish would swim up and down for your entertainment all day long, twitching their tales in a jolly but eerily lifelike way. Deep down though, David was a tender soul, and after two days with the fish he had begun to worry that they might not have enough space in their ten-inch tank. After all, it took them very little time to swim from one end to the other, and the sound of their plastic noses bumping against the glass had begun to seem less a companionable noise, and more like a cry for attention. 'Let us out,' each bump seemed to say, 'we are prisoners of conscience.'

As he sat down on the bed the red one bumped up to the front of the glass and showed him first its left, then its right eye. The idea that it was inspecting him carefully was difficult to resist, and David opened his jacket at the lapels and raised his eyebrows. The fish offered no comment on his fashion sense other than to turn its back and swim with seeming sullenness towards some plastic weed.

David pointed at it. "Don't think I need your approval," he muttered, "I'm my own man. I've eaten bigger fish than you."

This veiled threat had little effect, and now the fishes seemed to be peering out through their plastic weed, looking over David's shoulder at an uneven stack of newspapers and notes spread across his battered desk, and whispering about him. He followed their gaze, seeing his unfinished thesis (now dusty), and the untidy pile of source materials that he had sifted through so feverishly in order to create his wall chart, then glanced back.

The red fish scowled at the pile reproachfully, and sitting on the edge of his bed, amongst the evening noises of the big house, with the pleasant anticipation of a date in the offing, David could see its point. Somehow, over the course of the day, and as the weekend faded from view, his suspicions had again become ridiculous; as absurd as a nightmare upon waking. Often, he reflected, some dream would spring him from sleep, sweating, a cry caught in his throat, paralysed by its terrifying portentousness. Later, he would try to explain to someone, to communicate to someone safe in the waking world, why the duck in his dream had had such an air of simmering hatred and menace, and why it was smoking a cigar, and why it had spoken to him in his mother's voice. Under analysis the dream's inner reality crumbled and its silliness was revealed. Thinking of Helen, of seeing her tonight, his suspicions began to crumble also.

He could see what was happening here quite clearly. The red fish nodded to him knowingly, and he could imagine it stroking its tiny fish chin with one fin and saying in faintly accented English-

"It is true. You are deliberately diverting energy away from your thesis, so that you will not complete your work and submit it, and you have chosen to do this thing in a way that will also ruin your relationship with Miss Haversham."

The analysis was correct. There was a loony brilliance to it, but it was still only a kind of self-destructive stage fright.

A traitorous, knowing part of his mind whispered- *yes, yes that's all true, but where* was *she on Friday night? You should at least find out. And what happened to those roses? And why...*

He killed it, deliberately and brutally, before it led him off towards more reasoning, perhaps another wall chart. He had known Helen for more than a month now, and she was no murderer; it could not be. He was not ready to convict her on the strength of a string of coincidences, a white rose, and a missing Hoover part. He resolved to destroy his notes, to wantonly crumple his absurd wall chart and throw it away. He would finish his studies and be happy.

The red fish nodded its approval.

He was moving to the desk when a staccato knock interrupted him. Superb - Dr Love and Mrs Gibble in the same week. He looked speculatively at the window and considered hurling himself through it, but if he did, his fish would then be orphans.

Mrs Gibble was a true rarity: a relic from the nineteen-fifties; a genuine twenty-four carat oppressive landlady. Nosy, absurdly judgmental, and supremely prejudiced, she had survived the permissive late twentieth century just as the crocodile had survived the meteor impact that had supposedly wiped out the dinosaurs.

Gibble had inherited this enormous Victorian house in the early seventies, and hers were now the cheapest clean rooms in a town awash with students from Oxford. For each room in the house there were probably ten eager applicants. Also (a definite bonus for those whose finances were more than a little shaky), she let her boarders pay weekly instead of monthly, probably because she liked the act of collection, of having a legitimate reason to enter her boarders' rooms for a good look around.

In exchange for low-cost and clean accommodation, Mrs Gibble's boarders put up with her moral policing. Most evenings she would do what she was doing now, and quietly prowl the hallways of the large house, a tall woman with her grey hair in a bun and a paperback romance clutched in her widow's hand, listening for anything suspicious. A bedspring which creaked with a little too much regularity perhaps, perhaps the clink of wineglasses, or the smell of smoke. The result of such transgressions would be a loud knock, a cry for entry, and if anything suspicious were found, immediate termination of the tenant's letting agreement, followed by swift egress into the street, sometimes assisted by Gibble's hulking and silent only child Peter. In his three years here, David had seen it happen twice, but Mrs Gibble was fallible. Geraldine Dawson, for example, who lived in the rooms across the hallway, showed remarkable respect for the traditions of farce, and had twice successfully hidden her lover under the bed.

Tonight was rent-run night, and Gibble knocked on each door in turn, collecting the right amount with gimlet-eyed zeal. Earlier in the year, almost on a whim, David had arranged for an Internet chemist to deliver one hundred tubes of maximum strength haemorrhoid ointment to Mrs Gibble's flat; interestingly they had not been returned. Gibble suspected him, largely because he had tried all summer to elbow the word 'pile' into every sentence they had shared, but she had no proof, and now played a waiting game which he suspected she rather enjoyed, trying to catch him out.

He gathered up his keys, and the rent, and took one last glance in the mirror, checking again that the newsprint image was gone from the side of his face. He would have to do. He switched off the light, wondering briefly if the fish minded the dark, and then answered the door.

There Gibble stood in all of her glory, wearing a claret-coloured housecoat, fringed with what seemed to be real muppet fur, grey slippers, and a hairnet. Geraldine's door was also open (she had already received her knock), and she now leaned against the frame in her baggy grey jogging gear, munching a bowl of cereal.

Gibble peered at him over the top of a pair of tiny gold-rimmed glasses, and tapped on his open door with the end of one spindly finger.

"Rent day."

In sudden rebellion David slammed his door behind him just as Gibble was about to peer in, almost catching her nose.

"Thank you Mrs Gibble," he said. "You know, if it weren't for your weekly visits, my money would just pile up."

Gibble eyed him suspiciously.

"Someone in your room?" It was part question, part statement.

David shook his head. "No, I was talking to the fish."

She ignored him. "You know I don't like people in the rooms after dark. I don't like people in the rooms *at all*." She turned and gave Geraldine a baleful glare. Geraldine waved her fingers cheerily, smiling around a mouthful of cornflakes.

David proffered a wad of notes. "See," he said, "all in a neat pile."

Gibble snatched the notes from his hand. "Don't like fish either," she said, "too noisy."

David glanced at Geraldine, who shrugged.

Gibble took a step backwards in the hallway and favoured David with a long glance.

"Fish are like *young* people. Too noisy, and too clever for their own good." She emphasised her words by stabbing the air before her with one bony outstretched finger, then paused, measuring his reaction. For a few beats, David could see himself reflected in the greedy sheen of her eyes, and then she nodded slowly to herself, seemingly satisfied. At last Gibble turned, and beginning to count the money, shuffled off in search of further victims.

David watched her go, shrugging into his coat, then with a wave to Geraldine made for the front door. When he reached the zone of still and chilly air that crept in around its ancient frame, he took in a deep breath and tried to leave any sense of suspicion or mistrust behind him.

Watching from the landing Geraldine mistook the gesture for one of Gibble-inspired frustration.

"Cheer up," she called cheerily, still clutching the cereal spoon, "you never know - she might die."

#

Hornby Infants' playing field was flooded with wide swathes of silver moonlight, and dotted with frozen puddles. With its low points pooling only the faintest of night-mists, it offered little cover for an intruder.

Martin Hall stuck to the ghoulish shadows afforded by the heavy foliage at its outskirts, and slunk through the dark until he reached the back of the school. The play-yard glittered with frost. He passed two classroom doors, and tried the third. *Far too warm*, he thought, *far too cold - ah, just right*. Unlocked - just as Loatheworthy had said it might be.

Breaking in to the school was easier than he could have imagined. He made a mental note to return one day, after all there had to be valuables here - computers, maybe even petty cash.

"Little pigs," he whispered under his breath, his teeth shining in the darkness, "little pigs... let me in."

He slipped inside, a darker shape amongst dark shapes, and looked back at the classroom door, smiling indulgently. The key was still in the lock, its twin dangling towards the floor, he reached out and turned it, and it made a satisfying click.

Like many adults, who in the normal course of their lives have no reason to re-enter the world of children, Hall now felt instantly out of place, or rather, out of size. The chairs were tiny, the largest barely reaching his thigh; the posters and pictures on the walls were set low down by little hands for little eyes; and had he wished, he could have stepped onto the work surfaces and tables and strode over this tiny world like a giant.

Following an obscure impulse, he drew out one of the chairs, which scraped on the tiled flooring, and gingerly sat on it. When he was sure that it would take his weight, he reached into the seemingly bottomless pockets of his coat, and laid out the tools of his trade: a crow bar, a large kitchen knife - its serrated edge lying uneasily against the table's surface, and his favourite - the sawn-off. Then he sat back, leaning again, hands behind his head.

"Fee, fie, fo, fum," he murmured, gazing impassively around himself; had he ever been this small?

Over in the corner, awakened by his voice, Mister Tribble, the ageing class guinea pig began to scrabble and gnaw frantically at the bars of his cage. Hall found the noise that the creature made irritating. It was a small insistent noise, perhaps the night-time ghost of the small insistent voices that ruled this classroom during the day. He rocked back on the chair and picked up the knife, gazing at its edge, following its tiny peaks and troughs with his eyes as the noise continued, and then stalked over to the cage.

Mister Tribble was cleverer than he looked, and as Hall bent low and pointed the knife at him between the bars, he retreated, his eyes shining.

When the animal had been quiet for at least a minute, Hall nodded his head slowly, as if this demonstrated something.

"I'll deal with you later," he whispered.

Perhaps Mister Tribble would simply disappear - a classroom mystery - or better yet, perhaps he would leave a present behind, a tiny guinea pig skin rug, set neatly on the teacher's desk for the children to discuss on a Wednesday morning.

The desk. Yes. To business.

He tried the top drawer first and like Loatheworthy before him, found that Helen had locked it securely. Unlike Loatheworthy, however, Hall knew how to get around this. He bent low, facing the lock, and fed the slim blade of his knife into the gap between the top of the drawer and the desk sill. Mister Tribble scrabbled weakly at his bars again.

Ignoring the noise this time, Hall slid the blade to the left until it hit the locking mechanism. He shook his head - typical council-supplied stuff - it was old and worn, badly made to start with, and the lock barely protruded into the sill. He wedged the end of his crowbar into the gap on the opposite side and exerted pressure - it creaked and widened considerably. The metal of the lock was softer than his blade, and it bit into it, giving him just enough purchase. Slowly, he twisted the knife. The keyhole moved before his eyes, slowly... slowly... and then it was enough. He slid his blade further to the right and pushed it downwards. The keyhole turned ninety degrees.

Not elegant, but effective. He pulled the drawer open.

Its contents were disappointing: incomprehensible paperwork, a half-eaten chocolate bar, paper clips and rubber bands, and some stickers, presumably confiscated from a child.

From his bottomless pockets, he produced the baggie he had shown Loatheworthy the day before, again smiling in the darkness. He disliked teachers; even halved, there was enough in the bag to make this teacher look like a dealer.

He would need light for this. He moved to the classroom windows and peered out. All was still and quiet, and so, made reckless by his apparent success, he flicked on the lights and returned to the desk to divide up the stuff. He had another bag, and began to fill it with half of the foliage and pills: extra profit. He would leave Hornby in style. Why go home? He could take this, and Loatheworthy's money, and that idiot Murky would have to deal with the fall out.

There were several hard objects in the centre of the bag, and Hall's smile faded. His brow furrowed as he pulled them out, and examined them. They were four foil-topped pill trays. He read the trade name *Fermaxipan* on the side. Some new prescription sweetness that he had not heard of? He kept some, and put the others in the top of the teacher's bag - share and share alike. Then he sealed his own baggie, pushed it inside his coat, and as Loatheworthy had instructed, laid its twin carefully in the desk drawer.

With the important work done he flicked off the lights again, and gathered up all of his tools, leaving out only the knife.

The crowbar had left a small indentation in the upper surface of the lip of the desk drawer. Hall ran one gloved finger over it... barely noticeable, fair wear and tear. He prized the tongue of the lock upwards again with the knife's tip, and found that he could slide the drawer closed and have it spring back into place, locking itself. Perfect. Again, exactly as Loatheworthy had ordered.

Business was over, now for pleasure.

The knife fitted perfectly into the palm of his hand, and cast a beautiful shadow. He made his way slowly to the back of the room, back towards Mister Tribble, watching that serrated shadow trail on the classroom floor.

Tribble regarded Hall's slow approach, his eyes glittering. When the man was three feet away, he began to dig frantically in the sawdust at the bottom of his cage, but it was no use, and he knew it. As Hall reached out for the hasp on the cage door, he turned to meet his fate.

Hall paused, his head on one side. Off to his left, footsteps were approaching, crunching in the play-yard frost, and there were voices. Mister Tribble blinked in triumph. The voices grew louder as Hall listened in the darkness: one male, one female, coming towards them.

Hall walked swiftly around the edge of the room, staying in shadow, then ducked beneath the windows and made towards the classroom door. He reached a hand out towards it, but it was too late. He froze as someone did as he had done not twenty minutes before, and tried the handle. With furrowed brow, hand still extended, he watched it rise up and down, and up and down again; but he had locked it. The voices faded away, moving around the side of the building.

After a moment's thought, Hall crawled slowly to the desk, passing behind it, thinking that he might find somewhere away from this room to hole up until whoever it was had gone. A familiar sound - the scrape of a window opening - stopped him in his tracks again.

It was a second break-in. He heard the woman's voice, clearer now, say- "Go."

Across the room he could see another door with yet another set of keys dangling from its lock. He crawled towards it and pulled it open. Inside he could dimly make out a narrow L-shaped room, shelves, reams of coloured paper, baskets of arcane equipment: a store cupboard. He slipped into it, taking his tools and the keys with him, and also locked the door from the inside.

After a moment of standing in the darkness, listening, he drew the shotgun from his pocket and ran one hand over the stock. Then, slowly, he began to smile again.

#

Inside the Town Hall's single conference room, it was full-to-bursting and dimly lit. It reminded Helen more of a pub gig by a popular local band than a poetry reading, but she liked it. As Christmas drew near, she found that all gatherings could gain a sheen of seasonal cheer in her mind. Even the High Street today, filled with curmudgeonly people deliberately bumping into each other and refusing to apologise, screaming feral children, and threatening gangs of avaricious loafing teenagers, had been cheered up no end by a liberal application of tinsel and twinkly lights. There was a companionship in midwinter crowds that she enjoyed.

David was glancing around, anxiously taking in the throng behind them and the temporary stage blocks before them, clearly not appreciating the crush. His mood had not been helped by a tour poster for Simon Dasch's one-man show, which they had seen thumb-tacked to the main noticeboard in the foyer. It had been formed from a photocopied review of one of Dasch's previous performances, enlarged to eight times its original size. David thought that he recognised the font as coming from either *The Telegraph* or *The Psychiatric Review*. Before it had been copied, someone had blanked out all of the text with a heavy black marker pen, except for the reviewer's name, and the words 'flailing', 'terrible', 'cleaver' and 'authentic madman'.

David had let out a pent-up breath, seemingly unable to tear his gaze away from the implied violence wreaked on the text before him.

"I should have guessed," he had muttered darkly, "Swinburnian, my backside."

"This is not *quite* what I had in mind," he said now, "I thought it would be more… sophisticated." Then he jumped slightly, and looked around with a startled expression-

"I think someone just pinched me!"

He looked around for the miscreant, but was thwarted as the few lights which cast a sickly glow over the stage blocks began to dim, and he was forced to turn back towards the stage. "Here we go," he said, with more than a touch of apprehension in his voice.

There was sporadic cheering and a few wolf-whistles from the back of the crowd. As the light died away it took the last of these noises with it, until there was silence and an irresistible feeling of building dramatic tension: the sensation of the audience focusing on the small stage area before them. When the darkness and silence had gone on for about as long as Helen thought it could safely last, a single spotlight shone down on to the stage from above, casting a neat pool of light, perhaps a metre across, and almost too bright to look at.

There was a further pause and a creaking sound, a sensation of movement from above them, a flash of colour, and then a despairing shriek as a human form crashed out of the rafters onto the stage. It hit with a bone-jarringly-loud thud, which they both heard, and also felt through the soles of their feet.

There was a weak cough in the stunned silence, apparently from the form on stage, and then, clearly audible, from way above them, someone said-

"Holy shit! That never happened before."

Quiet again, then bewildered murmurs. Helen started forwards to help, but the spotlight went out and they were plunged once more into confusing darkness. Then, over to their left a polite ripple of applause began, spreading through the audience like a disease until almost everyone had caught it and joined in. She glanced at David in disbelief, he shrugged his shoulders. Was this part of the performance?

The house lights gradually brightened to twilight levels, except those over the stage, which were brighter, and now revealed a tall man looming over the prone form, enjoying the crowd's fascination.

Helen looked at the body again, more carefully now, and her shoulders sagged with relief. It was a mannequin, well dressed and lifelike, but a mannequin. Its hairpiece had become detached, and lay forlornly on the stage like a bloodless road-kill. The man (Dasch, she supposed), smiled worryingly in the light.

Dasch was theatrically dressed, wearing a rumpled dark suit, black or wine - it was hard to tell in the dim light - over a white shirt open at the throat. Between the fingers of his left hand there dangled a lit (and now probably illegal) cigarette, gently wreathing his languid form in smoke. His sideburns were sculpted, and the ends of his moustache waxed into points, a trench coat was draped over his right arm.

Leaning in towards a stand-mike and a skinny lectern, Dasch spoke in a rich low monotone-

"That was 'Fall from Grace,'" he said. "Poetry is pain. Poetry is power. Thank you."

Applause swelled again, and from the back there were cheers. The poet's smile lingered.

"Silence!" he said, and the audience was so surprised that he got it. Helen began to like him.

"Before I go on I have a few thank-yous to say." He took a deep drag from the cigarette, as if drawing inspiration from it. "Firstly, I'd like to thank Bernard Love for promoting this debacle-"

Beside her, obeying some lightning quick instinct, David ducked below the level of the crowd as if pole-axed, and began glancing around wildly.

"-though he can't be here tonight."

There were more faint cheers from the back. Slowly David rose again, grinning sheepishly.

"I'd like to thank you all for not staying at home, and I'd like to thank the authorities here in Hornby for forcibly editing my performance." His smile widened slightly. "I love it when they do that, don't you?"

Light glinted on his lectern, then shifted, and for a moment Helen had the impression that he was looking straight at her over the front two rows, singling her out. She suppressed a ridiculous urge to answer him, and his gaze passed on.

"Yes. Ladies and gentlemen the art you have come here to witness tonight, and paid good money to see... well, miserably inadequate money if you want the truth, is being forcibly censored by your town authorities."

Dasch managed to imbue the word 'authorities' with the same qualities other speakers might have applied to terms such as 'Nazis', or, Helen thought, 'school inspectors'. There were a few spirited 'boos' from the back, reminding her of the pantomimes of her childhood. Dasch paused, emphasising the heinousness of the offence to his art, then lay his trench coat on the stage and raised his hand. In it, he held a gadget, which trailed a thick cable past the mannequin and over the stage's edge; it resembled the remote control stick for a slide projector.

"Not only have they discouraged me from employing most of my live animals on the stage... as if a costumed stoat would hurt anybody, but I have been instructed, in fact, I have been *ordered* by the town fathers... and mothers, as it were, not to use words which may be considered profane or obscene in my performance here tonight."

Another sound rippled through the crowd, an 'aww' of disappointment.

"I have reluctantly submitted to self-regulation," Dasch said, "and I will use this device for self-censorship." Here he waggled the stick before his face and pushed the button on its tip twice in rapid succession with his thumb. The P. A. system emitted first a quacking sound, then a long drawn out bleat: baaaa.

Helen glanced at David, and he nodded solemnly. "A poet for our age," he said

A woman behind them made a 'shushing' noise. Helen turned to glare at her, but her expression of exaggerated, almost constipated enjoyment, chin up, eyes wide, only made her smile. Dasch began to speak again-

"This, then, is for the town... mothers. It's called 'The Censor.'"

The crowd was silent once more as he went through his reading preparations. He flipped his long hair away from his face, and with an exaggerated motion cleared his throat, brought his notes up before his eyes, and began to read in slow opulent tones that suggested levels of profundity not previously experienced by humans-

Censors pretend
To be your friend
Their eyes are like the gentle caress
Of a white feather
In the hands of a lover.

The front rows of the crowd 'ahhh'd' in satisfaction, as if they were attending a fireworks display, and Dasch had just let off a particularly beautiful rocket.

They have a subtle, special insight
That allows them to judge.
But I hold a grudge.
And they're a bunch of F-quacking Baaa - Baaaaa's
*Who can F-*Baaahaha *off and die.*
Mired in the putrid swilling filth
Of their own degradation.

Thank-you.

He bowed low over the mike, feigning exhaustion in a great roar of applause, and cast the remote control device to the floor. David and Helen looked at each other sharply and both began to giggle until the poetry lover behind them shushed them again.

When all of the applause had died away to an expectant silence Dasch raised his head and swept the audience with his amused gaze, like a challenge. Once again, as he reached Helen their eyes seemed to meet, and the poet seemed to be examining her expression. This was quite a trick, Helen knew, something she cultivated in her classroom. She looked up and down the ragged front rows of the audience, everyone was facing forwards, and she wondered how many of these people were now convinced that Dasch was giving them his full and undivided attention. To create such an illusion, Dasch was clearly a natural performer.

When she glanced back at the stage the poet was still looking only at her. Dasch's smile widened slightly, as if he had caught the drift of her thoughts, and then quite deliberately, he inclined his head towards her as he turned a page in his notes, and dropped one eyelid in a solemn wink.

"Now, this next piece is the title poem from my new collection, it's called- 'Auto-Erotic Cannibalism for Fun and Profit: A Beginner's Guide.'" He turned to address someone standing in the darkness behind the stage- "Guido, if you would toss me the juggling equipment at the end of the second verse, that would be lovely."

From the darkness behind Dasch, there arose the unmistakable sound of someone firing up a chainsaw. The crowd, David and Helen amongst them, began to back away from the stage with a certain urgency.

Dasch rolled up his sleeves, all the while grinning unnervingly, moved centre-stage, and began to recite.

#

Afterwards, when it was all over - the screaming and crying, the moustache twirling, the fire eating, the apparently drunken haranguing of the audience, and of course the poetry - they walked home through the quietening town together, then out to what passed for the leafy suburbs of Hornby.

Eventually Helen broke their silence-

"Do you think that they were trained? The rats, I mean?"

David nodded, long and slow, reflective.

"Oh yes. Couldn't really be anything else. Unless they actually were responding to the pipes."

More silence; a few more steps on the gritty pathway through long fingers of moonlight, then-

"I'm no fan of the bagpipes, hate them in fact, but playing them like that, in that way, from *there* it seemed… wrong somehow, just… very wrong."

David also seemed to be solemnly contemplating Dasch's felonious piping.

"Yeah. But a virtuoso performance though, you have to give him that. Amazing control; but also, as you say, wrong… very wrong. Clearly a crime against God and nature. Probably an actual crime too… "

This seemed to set his mind to something else, a few more steps, then-

"Do you er… Do you ever have flowers in the house, cut from the garden?"

Unable fully to tear her thoughts away from Dasch's manic performance, Helen didn't track this apparent sudden left turn in the conversation too closely, and so after a few more steps, she simply answered-

"Sometimes. Marie's been known to cut a few roses and bring them in, or lupins, she had a thing about lupins for a while."

"And on Friday, Friday night, you were at the school?"

At last, what he was saying filtered through her mental image of Dasch and his trained rodents, and her brow creased in a small frown.

"The school?" she said, a little more carefully. "Yes. Until about nine. I was backing the last two boards in my classroom. Why?"

"Oh... no reason. Anyone else there?"

She stopped walking and turned to face him.

"Why do you ask?"

"Just curious. You know... about the life of a teacher, how it all works. What it takes to keep all the plates spinning."

She looked at him closely to see if she were being teased.

"I think Crodd might have been there," she said vaguely, " ...oh and Kim. I definitely said goodbye to Kim. But they were working at the other end of the school."

"And Kim saw you?"

Helen's frown deepened- "Yes. I assume so. Why are you?... "

She trailed off. Talk of the school had made her try to find its shape in the darkness, to seek the large dark space of the field and Rymers Lane spread out somewhere over David's shoulder, below them and to the left. As she did so, she was just in time to catch the after-image of something. At first she interpreted it as movement, but soon realised that it was a change in the structure of the shadows down there: a light being turned off. She replayed what she had seen in her mind - yes, it had been a light, and no one should be at the school now, no one who had a right to be there, anyway. David was still talking-

" ...don't know how relieved that makes me. I thought... well I," he laughed a little, "you won't believe this - but I thought you might be... "

Helen stopped him by backing away slightly.

"We have to go to the school."

"I *actually* thought that you were... The school? Why?"

She was already walking away from him, back down the hill.

"I just have to. I have to... to do something there. Err... set something up, something for tomorrow."

David also looked down the hill at the emptiness where the school should be.

"But it's late, and dark."

She was already walking further away.

"If we cut through the back of Thompson Terrace, we can go across that field and get into Rymers Lane that way. We'll be there in five minutes. I'll kill that little... "

Once again her voice trailed off.

David watched her go, a relieved smile gradually leaving his face.

The school. The dark, empty (probably, let's face it - creepy) school, where she apparently planned to do someone violence. A faint puff of cool breeze lifted the hair from his forehead.

"But," he said, too quiet to be heard, "but... "

Helen turned for a final time, a hint of exasperation in her voice-

"Are you coming, or not?"

He thought about it for what seemed like an age, and then his feet began to move.

Yes, apparently he was.

The school rose up out of the night to meet them, dark and lonely, like a ghostly steamer coming out of a fog bank. They rounded the hedge, passing the spot where Loatheworthy had parked his car several evenings before, and then came into the playground. Helen looked around herself - the yard was covered with footprints, most of them child-sized, and nothing seemed to be out of place. She moved to her classroom door and peered inside (over Martin Hall's head), but her view was restricted by the darkness and the children's Christmas drawings taped carefully to the windows. Again, everything seemed normal. She reached down and tried the door, twice, but it was, of course, locked. That was inconvenient; it meant she would have to break in.

David had been strangely quiet on their march to the school, and seemed even more so now; he was watching her in a curiously flat and evaluative way.

"David, you'll have to help me."

"O - kay."

"The school's locked and I don't have a key."

He nodded.

"I'm going to have to break in."

"Break in? You know, isn't that... Don't the police take sort of a dim view of that?"

"Well we're not going to steal anything, are we? I work here. I have a perfect right to go in and... and do stuff."

"Stuff?"

"Yes. Stuff."

She gestured impatiently towards the high window of the ladies staff toilets, which, she knew, had a broken catch. The window seemed much higher, and the gap to squeeze through much smaller than she had remembered, but it would have to do. David stood behind her, still hesitant.

"This really doesn't look good," he said, almost to himself.

"No one will see."

He continued in an undertone-

"Could be normal. Could be, could be. It's not really what I'd expect from a date. Conversation - yes. Pasta - yes. A kiss goodnight, coffee, maybe an invitation to stay over - yes. Breaking and entering - *nooo.*"

"Do you know you're still speaking out loud?" Helen asked, slipping off her shoes and handing them to him. She looked upwards; what was that, maybe six - seven feet? She could do that.

"Boost me up."

David gazed down at the shoes as if they might be a relic from another world.

"What?"

"Like this," she said impatiently, lacing her fingers together and bracing herself against the wall.

"This stuff you need to do must be really important. What is there… There's not, like… there's not, like, a body in there or anything, is there?"

"Ha ha. Please?"

Reluctantly David placed her shoes on the asphalt and took her place, leaning against the wall, crouching slightly, holding out his clasped hands.

Helen stepped into them, stretched upwards, and he felt her steady herself as she pushed at the window. It clearly wasn't used to such treatment, and at first it refused to budge.

"Hold on."

She dipped into the pocket of her coat, drew something out, and then let the coat slip from her shoulders. It fell in a heap at David's feet, and he glanced at it, before looking up at her again. She was reaching behind her head now, tying back her hair with a hair-band, and holding something between her teeth. He blinked - it was a Swiss army knife. As he watched she carefully unfolded one long slim blade and began to insert it beneath the window frame.

"Is that a knife?" he asked, trying to keep any sign of panic from his voice.

She didn't look down. "Oh yeah. This is all in teacher training. Basic knife skills is second term, after surveillance, poisoning, and crowd control. Hang on." She shifted her weight again, wobbling, trying to get some purchase on the frame. Then, just as David began to feel that this was taking too long, the window gave with a clearly audible pop, and Helen held it open with one hand.

"Okay," she said. "When I say 'go', can you give me a lift?"

"Absolutely," he said, though his arms were getting tired, and he wasn't sure. She tensed, preparing to stretch.

"One, two, three, *go!*"

She disappeared up to her waist through the window, kicking briefly at thin air, like a damsel in a 'B'-movie swallowed by a monster. For a few seconds the issue was in doubt, but then the school had her, her feet disappeared, and the window banged closed like a pistol shot in the night.

David looked around himself, dusting his hands in the sudden quiet. He heard a thump from inside and some muffled cursing and then silence. With nothing else to do, he picked up Helen's shoes and coat, getting a brief trace of her perfume, and wandered back towards her classroom door.

A knife? Poisoning? And kill someone... she had definitely said she wanted to kill someone.

He stared inwards, into the dark classroom, but his view was obscured, and he was not at all sure that he wanted to see what might be in there.

Thanks to judicious use of the dusty window sill and cistern Helen narrowly avoided a headlong dive straight into the toilet of the second stall. She climbed down on to the hard grey tiles, cold under her shoeless feet, and leaned against the flimsy cubicle wall, getting her breath back and listening for anything unusual in the stillness.

Nothing. What had she expected? The doors were locked; whoever had been here was probably long gone.

She opened the door of the Ladies and padded down the corridor, nevertheless moving as quietly as possible, unwilling to give away her position. She reached her classroom door and listened: again nothing.

Should it be a stealthy, or a sudden entrance?

Almost before she knew what she was going to do, she depressed the handle and flung the door open. Her eyes were well adjusted to the gloom, giving her an immediate view of most of the room. In the faint light the children's Christmas pictures spread long crazed shadows on the floor. In the far corner Mister Tribble gnawed frantically at the bars of his cage as if he were implementing some mad escape plan - *'through the bars at o-six-hundred, Charlie. Abseil from the edge the desk, then mingle with the crowd using your fake moustache and documents...'*

There was no craven inspector pawing through her things. All seemed normal, but...

In the centre of the classroom a single tiny chair stood, pulled way out from the orbit of its table and left there, stranded; it had certainly not been left out that afternoon. She went to it, arms folded, looking at it quizzically, wondering what it meant. After a few beats she knelt, gingerly reached out a hand, and placed her palm flat on the plastic seat. It was cold, its texture, grainy and unpleasant, gave nothing away. Nevertheless the little tableau convinced her that someone *had* been in her room, and recently.

The idea that it might not have been Loatheworthy skulking in the school, but someone else, someone worse, occurred to her, and suddenly she did not want to be alone there any more. It was the first time that she had ever felt uncomfortable in her own classroom, and she did not like it. She could see a shape outlined by the windows - David - and she padded to the door, and grasped the key; for an instant it felt warm in her hand. Looking at it, she was seized by an uncharacteristic moment of panic. She felt cool air stir on the back of her neck, and was filled with a childlike sureness that she would not be able to get the door open in time to deter some awful menace that was surely coalescing, rearing up in the darkness behind her.

With some effort, she got a hold of herself and slowly, deliberately, turned around.

For a third time: nothing. Tables, chairs, equipment, the blank white door of her storage cupboard. She was spooked by the dark. She turned again, twisted the key in its lock, and pushed the door open quickly.

David, who was standing close to it and looking in, jumped, and gave out a hitching little cry.

"That's not funny David."

She pulled him inside, took her coat and shoes, and then looked at him quizzically. He sidled sideways into the classroom, keeping a good distance between them, then began to glance around in the gloom, leaning, and peering under the desks.

"What are you doing?"

He straightened up. "I don't know. What are *you* doing?"

"I… it doesn't matter. Take a seat, I won't be long, I just have some… "

"Stuff?"

"That's right, yes, stuff to do. I won't be long."

She hesitated, then flicked on the lights, went to her desk, and began to shift piles of paperwork about.

David continued his oddly stilted tour of the class, his hands behind his back, as if he did not want to touch anything. The classroom seemed laudably normal: coat pegs, children's drawers, art tables...

No bodies.

Presently, he heard the jangling of keys, then a sharp intake of breath, and glanced towards the front of the room. Helen was now crouching by the side of her desk, where one drawer was open. When she had not moved for twenty seconds or more, he took a few hesitant steps towards her.

"Bloody Hell!"

Tweezed between her thumb and index finger Helen was holding a large bag of brownish foliage and lumpy indistinct objects up before her eyes.

"Is that... ?"

She nodded.

"Is it yours?"

This seemed to clear her mind and she looked up at him.

"Of course it's mine. All infants school teachers dole out narcotics. I'm the spliff monitor."

He took a step closer and peered at the package again. Through the bag, David could now clearly see two trays of larger pills. The green logo of *Fermaxipan* was unmistakable.

"*Fermaxipan*. That's it... that's the drug that the... that's the murderer's drug."

Helen pulled out her chair and sat down, still holding the bag away from herself. Neither of them could take their eyes from it; it was dangerous, almost hypnotic.

"I *know* that. He knows that too."

For a few seconds David seemed not to hear her-

"But no, that's okay. Don't worry. That's okay; don't get excited. It's all okay. I understand... the stress. I'll... I'll stand by you. We can get you help... therapy, something like that. It can't be too hard to cure, can it? I mean, in other ways you seem so normal. He? He who?"

"He. Him. Loatheworthy. The man who put this in my desk."

David's expression did not change, and Helen waved the bag in frustration.

"For the second, and hopefully the last time, this is not my bag. Someone's been here." In her mind, Helen saw Loatheworthy grinning at her through the double doors of the school hall. "I saw a light on," she pointed, "and that chair has been moved. I've been having a... well, a feud with somebody, one of the inspectors - Loatheworthy. He's snuck into my room before, on Friday, and this is obviously his latest surprise for me, only I wasn't supposed to find it, not now anyway, not until tomorrow. That foul, rat-hearted little... God!" she shook the bag to-and-fro, throttling it with one hand, "I didn't think he'd go this far."

Now David's expression showed a curious battle between anxiety and hope-

"An inspector?"

"Yes."

"Here, in your classroom?"

"Yes!"

"And he, and this Loatheworthy, he wants to frame you as a murdering drug fiend? That's not their usual remit, is it?"

Helen released her grip on the bag, and they both followed its progress as it dropped to her desk.

Whump.

David shuffled his feet-

"Let's call the police. They'll know how to deal with this."

Helen looked up at him again, a little frantic now-

"And how would that look? I'm a teacher undergoing an inspection who just happens to have the Ofsted murderer's drug of choice stashed in my desk." She shook her head. "And I touched it. Now it even has my fingerprints on it. Oh he's cleverer than I thought."

She felt suddenly exposed in the bright classroom, panicky, and fought an urge to go and switch off the lights.

"David, you have to help me."

David glanced around the classroom, as if seeking inspiration there, and tried to think. Everything pointed neatly in one direction: the rose, the fantasies, a worrying proficiency at breaking and entering, and now even the drug in her possession, but...

Helen was still looking at him, wide-eyed and earnest. She passed one hand across her forehead, and he noticed that it was shaking. Why did she have to make such a direct appeal; he was helpless, he could not resist it.

"Of course. Will there be anything else planted here, do you think?"

She glanced around the classroom-

"I don't know. There might be."

"Well, we'd better make sure."

In the darkness of the long storage cupboard Martin Hall heard their search. They checked the children's drawers, under the tables, in Helen's filing cabinets and amongst the toys. They were thorough, but found nothing more offensive than a piece of chewing gum wedged under one of the computer tables.

Hall heard them drawing near. He was still smiling, pressing against the door, leaning into it, feeling the texture of the paint cold against his cheek, willing it to be pulled open.

The sawn-off hung in his gloved right hand, suspended, like a phantom limb. The faintest light, creeping under the door, glinted on its shortened oily barrel. Like its owner, the gun was poorly made and had a defective trigger. Hall had developed a taste for pointing the gun at people, and telling them what to do; he had even tried it on Murky. He found that it worked like a great big remote control, but for people. He liked to use it.

Eventually, after the sound of much searching, the male voice stopped very near to the door, and said-

"What about in there?"

Hall held his breath so that they would not hear him. Slowly, he brought the gun up to his chest, his finger curled around its triggers, and then he fixed his gaze on the door handle, a faint shape in the darkness before him.

Outside, Helen frowned, then glanced thoughtfully at the out-of-place chair. Slowly, she approached the door, feeling that sense of childlike trepidation creep over her again, raising goose-bumps, as if the situation were about to slip from her control. She fought to find the same direct remedy she had used earlier, and marched stiffly up to the cupboard, and put out her hand.

Hall tensed, baring his teeth, ready to pop out like some malign jack-in-the-box.

The door handle depressed once, and then shook before his eyes. The door rattled back and forth, and a little more light fell in fitful strips across his face, illuminating his grimace of frustration.

Again, locked. He blinked. Of course, he had done it himself; the keys were in his pocket.

"Locked!" Helen confirmed, unable to keep relief from her tone. "It's locked. I usually do lock it at the end of the day. It stops pilfering. Teachers can't get enough backing paper. The key'll be in my other coat, at home."

David answered, from further away-

"Right, we should check out the rest of the school." And their footsteps retreated to the corridor.

Slowly, Hall reached down and felt for the keys. His big entrance was spoiled and he felt obscure humiliation, a blush crept out of his collar.

Teachers.

No matter what he did, teachers were always causing him trouble. He should slip out of the cupboard and wait for them. He should sit at this teacher's desk, and deal out a few lessons of his own.

He paused. In his mind, as far as he was able, Hall weighed the cost of being seen against the benefit of being able to point the shotgun. It was a brief struggle; he was more a creature of instinct than reason, and he heard and felt the decision being made for him, almost as if he were a bystander, as the tiniest click in the darkness.

Hall had almost brought the long key to the lock when he realised that the sound that he had heard was not purely internal; his grin froze.

Simultaneously he became aware of two things. He could feel something cool on the back of his neck; it was ticklish, like breath; yes, he could even *hear* someone breathing. Also, there was a sharp pain in his upper arm. He looked down at himself, and saw that there was something long and thin and empty sticking out from the ropy muscle there.

The sawn-off fell from Hall's hand and thumped, seemingly in slow motion, onto the lino. The keys fell also, tumbling and turning and giving out a faint ring as they struck the floor, causing Helen, now rifling through the filing cabinets in the school office, to glance up for a moment. Hall blinked again, his vision blurred, and he felt suddenly very hot, as if he had sweat in his eyes. With some effort he managed to focus on the object protruding from his arm: it was a syringe.

Martin Hall turned as he collapsed in the dark cupboard, coming around to face what was waiting behind him. Too late, he realised why breaking into the school had been so simple.

He fell into waiting arms, staring with surprise into waiting eyes.

"You?" he said, and then unconsciousness overtook him.

Through the gloomy corridors, Helen and David completed their brief search. The Head's office was locked, and they had found nothing suspicious in any of the other classrooms. They searched silently, and with escalating haste, working under an increasing sureness that at any moment they would hear the amplified voice of some armed policeman bellowing from the playground.

Eventually, Helen could stand it no longer.

"We need to get that stuff out of my class," she whispered, and David agreed.

They retreated, closing doors behind them, and when Helen pulled the bag from her desk again, it was no less disturbing. It hung from her hand like a stoner's dream, twirling slightly under its own weight. She stuffed it unceremoniously under her coat, and with one final quick glance around, they left by the classroom door. Helen locked it securely, and rattled it, then put the keys in her pocket.

Halfway to the climbers, with the thin polythene bag of foliage hidden beneath Helen's coat, they stopped and stood listening in the empty playground. David stood a little behind her, and she looked back, impatient now to be away. He could hear nothing but faint traffic noise and the hum of his own senses.

He surveyed the tree-line thoughtfully, then looked at the foot marks they had left in the frost.

"You'd better give it to me," he said.

Helen frowned. "Why I..?"

David glanced around himself again. "Because if someone is going to try to catch you with it, they could just as easily do that at your house as here, couldn't they? They could be waiting there now."

Helen thought about this. She imagined blue flashing lights sweeping lazily over a crowd of gawping neighbours, as the police, egged on by Loatheworthy and for some reason carrying pitch-forks and burning torches, battered at her front door.

"But what about you?"

"This Loatheworthy doesn't know me, does he? We'll split up - and I'll take it home and get rid of it."

Still she hesitated, trying to come up with a better option. The frost was reflecting light from the sky, making everything seem suddenly too bright to her, as if they were standing in the dying flare from a camera flash. At last she took the bag from inside her coat and David stuffed it into his. She gave a final glance to the school, unable to shake the feeling that they had missed something, then shook her head slightly, dismissing the feeling. They moved off towards Rymers Lane, where, in the shadows of the big gorse hedge, they parted, both surprised to feel the thrill of conspiracy.

For a while all was still and quiet behind them. Then, barely audible in the empty school, there was the stealthy sound of Martin Hall's heels scuffing, squeaking lightly on the lino, as someone dragged his now lifeless and cooling body deeper into the darkness.

#

Hours later - as midnight approached - both Hornby Infants' and Helen Haversham's dreams were disturbed, almost as if they were connected by the winter wind which now blew gently across the two or three miles of frozen pathways standing between them.

As the store-cupboard door in her classroom finally inched open, pushed not with the bullying show of force that Martin Hall had envisaged, but with stealth and determination, Helen moaned and turned in her sleep, and pushed one of her pillows from the bed to the rug-covered floor. Beneath the bed, the hedgehog with no name was rootling quietly in one of her slippers. He had once found a large spider nestling deep inside one sheepskin-lined moccasin - a snack made all the more wonderful by its unexpected crunchy nature - and now he always checked there on the off-chance. This time, despite extensive snuffling, he was disappointed. He retracted his nose back under the bed just in time as the pillow fell past him and landed with a 'whump'. He stared at it with some concern, as above him, Helen turned and whimpered again, twisting her duvet into a ball.

At that moment, David was sitting by the larger of the arched windows of his rooms, trying to see the street below him. The house's central heating system gurgled and creaked and rumbled; it was ancient, but just efficient enough to make heavy condensation on the window glass. Thousands of tiny beads of water diffused the street lighting, and gave off a pale yellow glow. He touched the cold glass and watched as a drop of liquid, released by his fingertip, made a lazy runnel through the droplets, and slowly trailed its way down to a pool on the sill where the trays of *Fermaxipan* stood guard before the bag of dope.

He had rehearsed that evening's roller coaster of emotions two or three times already. He moved rapidly up a clanking hill of dully increasing suspicion, then crested and ran downwards at enormous speed into a trough of great relief. This then twisted somehow into a high-speed corkscrew of extreme fear, then a hill of self-doubt, then a moment of dreaming blue, cresting again into the clouds as his attention wandered. Another dip into relief, which again faded as he circled back and began to climb that initial hill of suspicion once more.

It was maddening (and not a little nauseating).

So Helen definitely, obviously, and conclusively was not a murderer. She was simply the victim of a series of coincidences and half-chances, and a malicious school inspector.

That was certain. He nodded to himself, and over in their tank, the fish regarded him soberly.

Unless she really *was* the killer, guilty of five counts of inspectorcide, and everything that had happened that night was all an elaborate cover story designed to keep him quiet whilst she brought some dark and evil plan to fruition.

His heart said she was innocent, his mind still whispered that she might be guilty. He needed help to decide, not least because if she was guilty, he was now an accessory after the fact.

He smiled ruefully - drugs, breaking and entering, fitting someone up for a murder - it was as if he had finally managed to step inside the mechanism of one of the novels he had so efficiently picked apart for his forgotten thesis.

It was more exciting than he had thought it would be.

Behind him in the hallway there was the stealthy creak of a floorboard; not the central heating this time, but Gibble, prowling again. He glanced down at the drugs on his windowsill. If she knocked on the door now it would be inconvenient. He padded over to the light switch and flicked it off, then waited, holding his breath. The hall floorboards creaked again, and he felt Gibble move away.

With his own light extinguished, he could now see out into the street through the stripes he had made on his window. Down there the frost was still glistening, perfect for a December night. Unaware of his gaze, a couple walked past, hand in hand, back from a club or a Christmas party. As they drew almost level with the house, they stopped by the lamp-post to kiss. The woman was wearing matching knitted gloves and a bobble hat in colours that the streetlights made maroon and gold.

In the darkness, David picked up the bag and the trays of *Fermaxipan*, and moved to the bathroom. He could hear Gibble on the floor below him now. He upended the bag over the toilet, and when about half of its contents had fallen in, he flushed. When the cistern had refilled, he emptied the rest of the bag and the pill trays, and flushed again, hoping that this would not cause some kind of blockage in the house's ancient pipework. He doubted it, if there was one thing the Victorians had known how to do well (possibly for dietary reasons), it was build sewer pipes.

Back in the bedroom, he listened. Gibble did not return, and below his window, the couple were gone. It was time to turn in for the night; he knew what he was going to have to do.

Desperate situations called for desperate measures.

Tomorrow he would have to take his life in his hands and visit the Rat Hole and the Dead Presidents, and get some *real* information.

#

At the school, Martin Hall's heels dragged once again on the flooring, as, after a long wait, his body was at last moved through the darkness and into Helen's empty classroom. He was heavy, and his killer stopped to lean him against a wall and wipe a hand across a sweating brow. Sleepy Mister Tribble watched, taking careful note, his feet tucked under his plump body.

A toe tapped on the floor tiles, arms were folded. This was inconvenient - to be forced to kill this minion. And a gun! What to do with the gun?

The killer eyed it warily, as if it might be a rival, then scooped it up in one gloved hand and tucked it onto a shelf. Coloured paper was stacked in front of it, and it was given no more thought; the body was more important. A finger frame was made and sighted through - no, not a good scene, this room was far too cluttered.

The cupboard door was closed and locked, and Hall was propped against it, his final expression of puzzlement and shock staring out into the classroom, whilst the killer searched the school for an appropriately secluded hiding place.

Doors were tried, cupboards and classrooms and offices opened for the second time that night. A tour was taken through the empty and echoing hall. Tiny tickings and sighs, sounds which could be dismissed as meaningless in the quiet corridors, again moved in time with Helen Haversham's troubled sleep.

A final door was opened. This room was shabby, filled with plastic chairs and the residue of old staff-meetings, but inside it there was another door with yet another key, and beyond *that* a further tiny room: a disused bathroom.

Perfect.

Hall was dragged through the school, through both doors, and into the tiny bathroom, and the door was locked on his final expression of surprise.

Now it was time to decide on a theme. Inspiration, that's what was needed. The killer glanced around.

On the wall of the larger room there was a poster, photocopied onto light blue paper. It said-

Donkeys! Wise-Men!
Shepherds!
The Saviour of all mankind!
See them all at Hornby County Infants School Carol Concert
and Nativity (entrance 10p).

Of course! After all, it was Christmas time. What was needed was a Christmas scene, something filled with festive wonder. Yes, that was the way to go; think big! One last big effort. This one should be used as a prop; window dressing for the real target.

A frown creased the killer's brow, and then dissolved - necessity had forced the use of the last of the distilled *Fermaxipan* - but no matter, improvisation was good for the creative instincts.

Wandering back through the dark and empty school the killer stopped by the water fountain, bent low, took a drink, and then left.

Hall's shotgun stayed behind, forgotten on the cupboard shelf.

V - Wednesday

Wednesday's dawn was clear and cold. A silver-blue sky put down long straight shadows across the paths of Oxford, which kept strips of last night's frost safe from the sun. By the time David arrived in the city, the blue was beginning to fade into high white. Looking nervously at the sky, he locked his bicycle in the racks on Broad Street, and began the walk to St. Jude's.

Most of the undergraduates had gone down for the Christmas break, and at this time of the morning, going north and away from the shopping district and its bright crowds, the wide pavements of Oxford were almost empty. Leaves in russet drifts, relics uncleared from October, lay in sculpted heaps by the Victorian gateposts, and David could feel the year itself curling up and settling, getting ready to flatline.

St. Jude's, which squatted precariously on the edge of the University parks, was kept from the street by a long, carefully maintained gravel driveway, and a stout brick wall topped with ornamental spikes. The wall parted mid-way for a set of wrought-iron gates, and the College swung into full view only as this entrance was reached. Rising from the centre of a lawn, with its towers and crenellations and insane extensions, St Jude's resembled a lop-sided wedding cake.

These days the gates were padlocked to discourage tourists from wandering around the private (or dangerous) areas of the college. During his first year of living in the quad, David had drifted gently out of slumber one day to be greeted by a camera flash, and a brief musical burst of Japanese. He had opened his eyes, assuming that this was the tail end of some surrealistic dream, in time to see three smiling faces looking down at him and another poking through his stuff on the enormous ornate desk he shared with his roommate. The tourists had been startled and a little indignant to be shooed from the room, since, as far as they could see, it was part of the tour: Mediaeval ruin, gallery with Renaissance cartoons, candle-lit dining hall, and hungover student quietly drooling into his pillow in authentic Victorian study-room.

David glanced around the quad, then, before he could lose his nerve, ran as fast as he could towards the eastern part of St Jude's cellar, a section lovingly known to the computer-science fraternity as the Rat Hole. Three flights of whitewashed stone stairs taken at break-neck speed delivered him into the cool shadowed bowels of the College, an area where Dr Love was rarely seen. He passed the main computer laboratory, a long curving room set with banks of the very latest equipment (thanks to the Presidents). Three more steep steps and then a blank lime-green iron door which would have looked more at home in a prison. In a ragged hand from which the red paint had dripped and run, someone with a rudimentary sense of humour had written 'Abandon hope all who enter here'. David stretched up and tried to peep through the spy-hole, but could see nothing, then pushed the doorbell.

He was rewarded by an unexpectedly melodious ring, as if this might be the lair of some suburban housewife, rather than the Dead Presidents. There was a commotion inside. It sounded as if someone had fallen from a chair, there were whispered imprecations (he heard the word 'Love' spoken with some urgency), then a crackle, and a sinister voice, made reedy and thin by the electronics, issued from the doorbell speaker-

"Yesssss?"

David resisted the temptation to say 'Avon calling,' and instead plumped for, "It's me."

Another whispered conversation from inside, this one plainly audible.

"It's him, er... Barclay," then high-pitched giggling.

"Should we do it anyway? Maybe no one would miss him."

David stepped smartly away from the door up one of the steps; the Presidents had something of a reputation.

"Er, guys, shed-loads of people know where I am," he lied.

There was a long disappointed silence from inside, then David heard the enormous lock on the other side of the door draw back, and it popped open a crack. In the darkness beyond, he could just make out a pair of blue eyes behind tiny rose-tinted wire-rimmed glasses: it was Jonson.

"Are you alone?"

"Yes."

"Did anyone see you coming in here?"

"Yes."

"Have you had any dental work done recently?"

David considered asking why they needed to know that. Did they suspect that his teeth would be bugged? Did they believe that fillings attracted UFO's? Or did they just hate dentists? After a moment's thought he decided that it was best simply to answer. He had been through this kind of thing before, and the Presidents only did it to increase their mystique amongst impressionable young minds.

"No."

"Ever had colonic irrigation?"

"No."

"Do you want some?"

"Definitely not!"

He took another step backwards, looking around himself carefully. In the background, he heard another, deeper voice say, "Let him in, he's okay."

Jonson drew the door open just wide enough to allow him to slip through, then slammed it and drew the enormous bolt across again. David glanced around himself. No matter how often he came here, this part of the Rat Hole always fascinated him. It was a long L-shaped room, its walls festooned with ducts and pipes and prolapsed mechanics from the College's vital systems. There were several desks, each covered with mysterious and complex bits of technology, and computers, without their cases, hot-wired together and humming whilst they affected the Presidents' dark purposes.

In the toe of the 'L' sat Kennedy, looking at the monitor of another perfectly ordinary-seeming computer. David was startled to catch sight of his own face, in an enlargement of his passport photograph, staring back at him from the monitor, underscored by some dense panels of text. Kennedy hit a key and the image changed. His face disappeared and the screen darkened and began a slide show of what seemed to be views of space. David could read the legend 'Unusual and Irregular Galaxies from the Deep Survey'. He considered demanding to be told just how the hell Kennedy had managed to get hold of his passport records, but then thought better of it. The Presidents were, when it came to the world of computers and computer-stored information, like third-rate gods: more or less omnipotent, but secretive and too fond of practical jokes. Also, of course, it was exactly the reaction Kennedy was hoping for, and one that had absolutely no chance of a reasonable reply.

Kennedy sat before the screen, overhanging his swivel chair on either side. When he was sure that he had David's full attention, he swung around to face him. David half expected him to be stroking a large white cat, but his arms were empty, folded across his expansive chest.

"My apologies Mister Barclay. Jonson there is rather annoyed with Dr Love. Our blood feud has deepened and we thought you might be a messenger. You're not, are you?" Behind his large horn-rimmed glasses one bushy eyebrow rose and waggled comically in the air. David shook his head. Behind him, Jonson sighed.

"What can we do for you then?" he said, scooting around David on his own swivel chair so that now they both sat before him.

They were by a long way the oddest members of the College's small computing fraternity, and in that crew they had some stiff competition. David was struck by how physically different they were, like a cliché of partnership. Jonson stood six-foot-four in his stockinged feet, lanky and graceless, and wore a succession of ragged T-shirts (today's showed a caricature of Pacman with teeth, chasing a crowd of frightened cartoon people through a city street), always partnered with the same pair of off-brown jeans. David suspected that the jeans had not started their working life that colour, but had *become* that colour after months of diligent attention. Jonson's lank blonde hair was long, sometimes drawn back in a ponytail, and he always wore glasses with tinted pink lenses.

Kennedy was of medium height but large and graceful. His shock of black hair and moustache were always perfectly neat, and he always wore a suit and tie, sometimes a three-piece.

Like Dr Love, the pair held a special place in the College hierarchy. Undergraduates and high-table grandees alike whispered their names in awe, though probably for different reasons. Almost two years before, they had invented a nifty new file-transfer protocol, and had registered their invention partly in their own, and partly in the College's name. They were, reputedly, now both millionaires, and they had made Collins, the shrivelled College bursar, a very, very happy man. What stopped them from being the ultimate blue-eyed boys for the College authorities was their rampant paranoia, the suspicion that a lot of their activities might stray over the line into illegality, and a little incident at the Founders' Day garden party, just after their kind donation to the College.

David had been there to see Jonson, smiling widely, his eyes eager and earnest beneath the feral pink lenses of his glasses, trying to hand the college's only Professor Emeritus a tray of sandwiches. The Professor was a Classics don who had been heard to disparage the Presidents' work. His hand had hovered over the uppermost sandwich for several moments whilst Jonson smiled and gestured and nodded invitingly. Then the old man had noticed that, though its crusts were neatly cut off, the sandwich barely concealed a large bundle of electrical cable which trailed off across the College lawns and down into the cellar. To this day, nobody (except the Presidents) knew whether the cable had been live or not. The incident had been passed off as an odd joke; David wasn't so sure.

The Presidents, then, were thought important enough to have their own office whilst they conducted their research, but deranged enough for said office to be well away from visitors, other academics, and the light of day.

"I've come for some information," David said. He would have to be careful here, the Presidents would delight in misleading him if he didn't handle this correctly.

"Information?"

"Yes. About this."

He reached into his coat pocket for one of the Ofsted murder clippings, and, in that moment, the Presidents each scooted away on their chairs, their wheels rattling on the stone floor. Jonson fetched up behind a desk, ducking down and peeping over. Kennedy backed up to his workstation where he grabbed a brown paper bag by one edge and pointed its long form in David's direction.

"Whoa," Kennedy said. His hands were shaking, and the lumpy top corner of the bag swayed in the air before his eyes. "What are you reaching for, man?"

Startled David slowly brought the clipping out of his pocket, gripped between his middle and index fingers, and held it in the air between them.

After a long moment of silence, Kennedy shook his head in apparent disbelief and placed the brown paper-bag back on his desk where it made an ominously heavy thunk.

"Close," he said. "I wish you knew how close you had just come. We haven't even *tested* it yet. What is that?"

Gingerly, David handed the clipping over, still held between his fingers. The Presidents drew together and peered at it.

"The murders?"

David nodded.

"I need more information. I need to know what the police know. I need to know if there's any physical evidence, DNA or suchlike, that they haven't revealed to the press. You two are the only ones I could think of that might be able to help me with that."

Jonson scooted forward on his chair and peered up into David's face.

"If you think you might get us to do your foul bidding with flattery alone, you might be right, my friend."

Kennedy joined him.

"Yes. Yes... But flattery only gets you so far. If you goad us lightly with the sense of an almost insurmountable challenge, we might just bite."

"Well," David said, doubtfully, "police computers must be fairly secure... hard to get into; surely that's a challenge?"

Kennedy shook his head, dismissively. "Pah!" he said.

David blinked; he had never heard anyone actually say the word 'pah!' before.

"Can you do it? I bet you can't do it."

"We can. But we need to know why."

"You will never discover that."

The Presidents exchanged a glance.

"Your girlfriend – she's a teacher, isn't she Barclay?"

After a moment's struggle, he agreed; there was no point in denying it. Jonson whispered something in Kennedy's ear, then giggled.

"Yes," Kennedy said, almost to himself. "Yes, and he thinks... Interesting... interesting." He stroked his chin. "And he suspects that she... "

"I do not!" David said.

Kennedy looked suddenly innocent and startled-

"You do not what?"

David tried to keep from betraying anything with his expression. Kennedy smiled.

"Never mind, Barclay. We've all done it. Jonson here has done it twice. Homicidal maniacs are just irresistible, so attractive, so *lively*."

Kennedy returned to his workstation. "We'll help," he said, "but turn and face the wall. I can't let you to see me working."

David did as he was told, and turned to face a dartboard which had two photographs pinned to its surface with cheap plastic darts. One he recognised as Bill Gates, the ex-*Microsoft* supremo, clipped from a Sunday supplement. The other seemed to be a Polaroid of a suburban living room. A greying woman and a man with very dark glasses and mutton-chop sideburns smiled out from its depths. The man, who was cheerily holding a glass of wine out towards the photographer, had a dart through the centre of his forehead.

"Those are my parents," Jonson hissed in David's ear.

David didn't turn around. "Jonson, that is a computer enhanced image of the Queen, sitting next to Carlos the Jackal."

There was a brief pause, punctuated by the sound of keystrokes from Kennedy's terminal. "Well," Jonson said sulkily from further away, "they could have been."

"Okay. You may turn around."

David did so. Once again, Kennedy's terminal was showing the strange galaxies. David was sceptical.

"That quick?"

Kennedy nodded-

"That quick. We keep a line into Met. Central, and they keep a descriptive log of physical evidence which is searchable by keyword. No DNA has been recovered from any of the Ofsted murderer's crime scenes. That's one careful loony. Is your girlfriend the careful type?"

David ignored the question, but could not hide his disappointment. Kennedy raised one finger in the air-

"But, at scene number four there was a lamentably sloppy lapse in concentration. The Met. are very excited about it - he or she left behind a partial print, known as a latent left half-palm, on the shaft of the bog-plunger."

"I see."

Kennedy opened a drawer of his desk and took out a large brown envelope.

"I'm not sure that you do. This print has been digitised for comparison with those held on computer by other forces, though not many of them take palm-prints, so, if we wish to, we can see it."

He held out the envelope, and David took it. It was heavy, and he peered inside.

"Basic fingerprinting kit," Jonson said. "Powder, adhesive, fixing tape and instructions. If you have... someone in mind, simply get a print for us, left palm," he held up his own hand, fingers splayed. "Coffee cups are good for that - a good shiny surface. Then we can make a comparison."

David was still peering with interest into the envelope.

"Right, I can do that. I'll come back tomorrow... "

"No!" they chorused together. "No, It might not be, er... entirely wholesome here tomorrow."

David nodded as if he understood.

"No. Slip it under the door. We'll find you with the results."

Something else occurred to him, and he opened his mouth to speak and then checked himself, hesitating for a second. The Presidents were a serious bane to wish on a man, no matter how repellent you thought he might be; it was something that should not be done lightly.

"There's a name, as well, someone I'd like you to look in to, if you would."

Kennedy raised an eyebrow-

"A name? Curiouser and curiouser."

"He's called Loatheworthy. A school inspector - he's working at Hornby Infants, right now. I just need to know if there's anything... odd about him."

"Hmmm... Odd like he buys Barbie dolls on ebay, or odd like he has a cellar full of crack cocaine and a testicle collection?"

"Either would do."

This reply seemed to please Kennedy immensely, and with the prospect of nasty work ahead of him, he began to scoot back to his workstation.

"I tire of this foolishness," he said, over his shoulder. "Begone!"

He made a gesture towards the door, and Jonson stood and once again drew back the enormous iron bolt, but this time heaved the door wide. He ushered David through.

"Have a nice day!" he said, and then the door swung shut on any further questions, leaving David bemused and clutching the envelope on the whitewashed steps. When he wandered out into the weak winter sunlight a pair of tourists were haunting the college gates, looking jealously inwards, and he made towards them, glancing up at the clock, wondering exactly how Helen had fared at the school that morning.

#

At twenty-to-nine Helen sat at her desk, and struggled to connect this daylit classroom with the shadowed and uneasy world that she had moved through only hours before. Everything seemed so bright and safe now, her desk was wholly innocent but for the piles of work stacked upon it, and not a chair stood out of place.

Everything seemed normal - as normal as it could be at the start of another inspection day - and under the pressure of so many normal things, last night's exploits began to lose their credibility.

She heard voices in the corridor, and winced; a fragment of yesterday evening was about to reappear. She identified the Head's voice - somewhat conciliatory, and another, well-projected and hectoring: Loatheworthy. A low burning coal of last night's anger re-ignited at the sound with a seemingly audible pop, and she looked up at the door, her gaze bright and apparently mild.

Here he was, leading the Headteacher, wearing a brown wool suit with the jacket unbuttoned and a starched white shirt beneath. He was puffed-up like a toad and ready for confrontation.

Helen leaned forwards slightly, smiling, or at least showing her teeth. That was okay, so was she.

" ...more target-setting for your staff is clearly the only thing that will have an effect..." he was saying, " ...and there needs to be more order."

He bustled towards her with an indulgent smile which widened as Helen met his gaze. She blinked, and suddenly she was in a panelled drawing room clutching a brandy balloon, big enough to hold a shoal of bright tropical fish, in her hand. Mounted on the wall before her, occupying a lovely rosewood plinth, was Loatheworthy's head. The inspector's smile was mutated into a grinning rictus of surprise. "Ugly blighter isn't he?" she was saying to some guest or other whilst giving the brandy a languid swirl. "Caught him in the chicken coop, botherin' the hens, bagged him right there and then..."

Loatheworthy ignored the warning signs in her gentle gaze and ploughed on.

"Miss Haversham," he said, "do you have the Special Needs records for your class to hand? I understand that each teacher keeps their own paperwork?"

His eyes glittered with the prospect of triumph, and Helen felt a high, burning anger and a sense of unreality. This was it; if she hadn't happened upon the school last night, this was where he would ruin her. George Rowley, the head of the school governors, appeared in the doorway. *An impartial audience*, Helen thought wonderingly, *and right on cue*. When and how had the inspector managed to arrange that?

Wordlessly she rummaged in her handbag and withdrew her keys. She jangled them in her palm, sure that she could feel the intensity of Loatheworthy's gaze as her hand hovered by the side of her desk, then she moved it to the lower drawer. Now the inspector looked not amused, but startled. Helen kept her own expression neutral as she slid the drawer open and looked inside, then paused for as long as she felt was safe, enjoying every millisecond of his discomfort.

"Oops, wrong drawer," she said.

As she moved on to the top drawer, inserted and turned the key, then seized the handle, Helen felt that she could actually *see* Loatheworthy stretching forwards, his expression fierce, leaning towards her desk with every fibre of his being. She considered pretending that the drawer was stuck; but no, she didn't want him to have a coronary right here in her classroom.

She glanced up one final time and then yanked the drawer all the way open as quickly as she could. On top of her register and Special Needs files there was a plump clear plastic bag.

"My God," Loatheworthy hissed, pointing into the drawer. "What on earth is *that*?"

He turned an outraged face to Rowley.

"This is blatant deviancy," he said, "and in a classroom... it's... it's depravity... moral insanity. Criminal, that's what it is!" His jowls quivered slightly as he shook his head in mock indignation. "This is very serious. Very serious. I must ask - no, I'm afraid I must *demand* Miss Haversham's immediate suspension and the involvement of the police in this... "

As he spoke Helen brought the large plastic bag of pic-n-mix sweets out of her drawer and plopped them, with a studied lack of theatricality, onto the desk before her.

There was silence. Loatheworthy's jaw hung open and his hand still lingered in the air, then both his eyes and his pointing index finger dropped their aim slightly to consider the brightly coloured package before him. He looked first at the Head, then at Rowley, and then prodded the bag wonderingly with the tip of his finger, as if he suspected that it might waken and prove to be dangerous.

The Head fixed Loatheworthy with a look which suggested that however demented his behaviour might become, she was a Headteacher, and had seen it all before.

"Surely confectionery is still legal within the school system," she said. "Bad for the teeth, certainly, but one would have thought the possession of comfits unlikely to be a police matter."

Helen could almost hear the mental gears free-spinning in Loatheworthy's head as he struggled to the top of his confusion and disappointment, and she almost (but only almost) felt sorry for him.

"Jelly bean, anyone?" she asked.

After a brief pause Rowley reached over the Head's shoulder, and ensnared a bean. The Head scowled at him silently.

Helen raised an eyebrow at Loatheworthy, "If they're offending you, I can move them."

He blinked. "But," he said, "but they... "

He blinked again, this time more slowly, then brought his pointing hand sharply up to the side of his head and batted it by his ear as if shooing away something that only he could see.

Now both the Head and Rowley were looking at him as if he might be more than slightly crazy, as if he had just dropped his trousers, or uttered some dreadful profanity. It was just the look that Helen had been seeking. She fixed a demure, concerned smile.

"Perhaps you've been working too hard Mister Loatheworthy."

"Er," Loatheworthy stuttered. "Maybe I... I thought, I... Jelly beans. Yes, of course, no police, I just... don't like them."

Another slow blink, and at last he seemed to gain some measure of control, but he could not draw his eyes away from the sweets on Helen's desk.

"Yes. Yes, perhaps I am a little tired, but you... " He shook his head as if to dispel some recurrent mental image, then said in an undertone, "Really *don't* like them."

The playground door opened and the designated class two leader prepared to march his temporary charges to their tables. The Head put a hand on Loatheworthy's shoulder and began to guide him gingerly towards the corridor, now wearing the expression that she usually reserved for dealing with children afflicted with incontinence. He went willingly.

"Don't forget these," Helen called brightly, holding out the Special Needs files, but he ignored her, and the head piloted him away.

Rowley took the paperwork from her outstretched hand.

"I'm most dreadfully sorry about that," he said, finishing his jelly bean. "He's seemed a little overwrought all week. Odd chap. Excitable. You don't want to file some kind of, er... complaint do you?" He raised an eyebrow hopefully.

Helen thought for a moment.

"No," she said, eventually, sitting down again and putting the sweets back into her desk drawer, before locking it. "But I think you should keep an eye on him, don't you?"

School governors, Helen knew, were also audited by Ofsted, and evidence of strange behaviour by the leader of the inspection team could certainly be handy for Rowley. He nodded thoughtfully and headed for the door himself.

Then Helen could hear the Head's voice, low and almost gentle, disappearing away down the corridor as they continued their tour-

" ...Will this tough stance apply to all sugary treats Mister Loatheworthy? Or simply to candies? I mean, what *is* the Office's policy on sticky buns, for example?"

Helen looked down at the work on her desk, not seeing it, and allowed a great wave of anger and triumph and not a little relief to break over her. Instinctively, she closed her eyes, her hands balled into fists, and for the first time she actually allowed herself a daydream, welcoming it.

Suddenly, the classroom was dark, as it had been yesterday; shadowed and mysterious and threatening. She was sitting where she sat now, only her chair was twisted to face the windows. The door handle creaked and the door opened. Loatheworthy stole in, weasel-like in the shadows, and she swivelled on her chair to face him, a stout shotgun already up at her shoulder.

"Mister Loatheworthy," she said, and he jumped with great surprise, dropping whatever terrible cargo he had been expecting to deposit in her classroom this time with a great clatter. "I've been expecting you!"

Then, quite deliberately, as the children began to stream into the classroom around her, she let him have both barrels.

#

"Which one?"

"There… Do it quick… It's smaller than the others. There's Crodd's room, then count three windows in, ready?"

David nodded.

"Okay. Three, two, one… now!"

Helen pushed open her classroom door as quickly as she could, and as soon as there was enough space, David bobbed his head outwards in a shallow curve, furiously counting windows and blotting out the screams and cries of the children's lunchtime games. At the third window, down at the far end of the school, he could just make out the freckled, balding crown of a head. As he watched, it moved upwards, exposing small jowls and a neatly clipped red moustache, then turned directly towards him.

David ducked back inside, resisting the urge to press his back against the wall.

"See him?"

So that was the man he had unleashed the Presidents on; he almost felt sorry for him.

"Yes. God, yes. He looks like *Hitler*, only worse. And he definitely… " he flapped one hand towards Helen's desk.

"Oh yeah. Big time. First thing. He came straight to the desk. I wish you could have seen it; he looked as if he were coming completely unhinged. He accused me of moral insanity."

David nodded slowly. "That's not something you hear every day. But why? Why would he do something so… *extreme*?"

Helen shook her head impatiently. "God alone knows. Maybe he hears voices or something. I don't care. But it felt good, I can tell you that. It might be enough. I think he might just leave me alone now. Did you… you know?" She made a swirling motion with one hand.

David nodded. "Flushed it all. We'll have the mellowest rats in the country, unless they get together and go out for snacks, imagine being behind that in the queue at the all-night garage."

Helen was treated to a brief image of a large gang of rats standing on each other's shoulders circus-style beneath a grubby raincoat. The top rat was wearing outsized sunglasses and handing a note to the garage attendant which read 'Kurly-Wurlees Plees.' David was smiling faintly, as if seeing the same thing. She blinked the image away.

"I think that might really be the end of it, though," she repeated, as if trying to convince herself. "He looked beaten to me."

David had brought coffee in a cardboard caddy, and Helen watched him unload it onto her desk. Fragrant steam rose into the air. It must have been very hot, since he was careful to lift each tall carton only by the rim.

"Full-fat, no sugar," he said, sliding one towards her and absently reaching for a biscuit from a Tupperware container by the sink.

"Don't eat that," Helen said sharply, "a child made it."

It was the first rule a newly qualified teacher learned, and usually through horrible, horrible experience. Never ever, under any circumstances - even if the school had been mysteriously isolated from civilisation through the work of some evil scientific genius, and there is nothing else - *ever* eat anything that the children have cooked themselves.

Five-year-olds were the world's greatest and most creative unwitting poisoners. During her training, Helen had innocently accepted a fairy cake from a smiling child, which proved to contain an unwieldy glob of *Bluetack*, and a marble. Crodd had once almost eaten a piece of costume jewellery - an orange ring in the shape of a butterfly - cunningly secreted within a scone. He had handed the doughy item back to the child's mother with an apologetic request that she not be allowed to wear it to school again. The child's mother had told him sheepishly that she understood the difficulty well, since Jane, her younger child, had already done exactly the same thing at home and they had had to wait nearly fourteen hours to get the ring back *that* time.

In Helen's mind, Loatheworthy accepted a gently steaming fairy cake containing many items of jewellery that had already passed through at least three children. It was topped with black icing.

"They're not safe."

David stopped with the snack inches from his lips, then gingerly replaced it.

"So, what now?"

The question surprised her a little, and she thought carefully as she wandered to her desk and scooped up her coffee (not that hot) with her right hand.

"Nothing, I suppose. We can't go to the police, or to Ofsted, because now we have no proof. I say that, for now, we trust that Loatheworthy knows when he's beaten."

David was frowning impressively.

"Well? What do you suggest?"

He would like to have suggested that she hold her coffee cup with the other hand, but that wasn't possible.

"I don't know," he said. "This is all new ground to me. It just doesn't seem right that he should get away with it."

A gentle, almost dreamy smile surfaced on Helen's face, then disappeared as she took a sip of her coffee.

"Oh don't worry. He won't get away with it, not in the end. What we need is to find some way of... "

She was stalled by a knock on her classroom door.

"Co..."

Halfway through the word the door was pushed open to reveal Liz, the school secretary. Since the announcement of the inspection, Liz had been overworking wildly. She had three pens wedged in her hair, looking oddly like radio antennae, and wore her glasses on a chain around her neck. She lifted them and peered through them distractedly now, frowning over a bundle of yellow post-it notes. She glanced up, then did an exaggerated double take. She had not yet met David, though obviously he had been the subject of heated staffroom gossip (encouraged by Alison), and she stared for a moment. Her expression then modulated between her original frown of concern, and a lascivious grin, which suggested that she believed coital relations might break out between Helen and David at any moment.

"Yes?" Helen asked, a little irritated.

"Er, Helen," Liz said, shaking her head, as if dispelling an uncomfortable image, "do you know anybody with a lisp?"

Helen and David glanced at each other, then Helen answered carefully-

"I don't believe so. Why?"

"Ah… nothing. Nothing. It's just that we've had some weird phone calls to the school this morning, all from some guy with a lisp, asking us to 'lisht our shtaff.' Mean anything to you?"

Bewildered, Helen shook her head. Liz copied the movement-

"No. Okay. Good, good." She ticked something off on the top post-it. "Oh, and these two need to ask you something."

She strode off without further comment, and revealed two small boys, who now stepped forwards into the room. The taller of the two was wearing an outsized blue anorak with a hood which zipped up past his chin, and left only the tip of his nose and a large pair of horn-rimmed spectacles visible, making him resemble an ambulatory periscope. He also proffered a folded piece of paper.

"Gmph, ripf mumf dumf," he said from the depths of his coat. The tiny opening in his hood swung comically backwards and forwards between Miss Haversham and the strange man. Helen stood and took the piece of paper.

"It's a note, Miss," the other, smaller child explained.

"I can see that Adrian. Who is it from?"

"It's... from... " the child paused, one finger at his lips, as if calculating the remainder in a complex long-division sum, " ...erm. Eeeets frowom... Meees Greeen."

Helen unfolded the piece of paper, and read:

Dear Helen,

How goes the day for you? Everything here is foul and evil. Please could you give these two munchkins two packages of multi-coloured sugar paper for this afternoon's highly experimental art activity? Who's the guy? Is that David? Tell me later!

As payment for the sugar paper you may select and keep one *munchkin. They are loyal creatures, and will work hard for you and serve you well. Also, could you have a go at freeing Simon from his coat, as he is stuck, and is driving me mad!*

Alison.

Helen sighed and beckoned Simon towards her.

"How did you manage to get stuck this time Simon?"

"Unkf Mumf funf runf fuffmuff."

"Brilliant. And this is your space suit, is it?"

"Mumf mumf prumumumf."

After a certain amount of tugging and resisting the urge to swear (on both sides), the reluctant zip gave way and the small boy was set free.

"Okay you two; you know where the paper is. Mrs Green needs two parcels."

Helen took the cupboard key from her purse and unlocked the door, glanced nervously around inside, then, feigning impatience, ushered the boys through.

When they were safely out of sight, she wandered back over to the desk, and again picked up her coffee with her right hand.

David winced, then covered it with a question-

"You were saying?"

Helen continued in a lower tone-

"I think it's best if we just get tomorrow over first. Get the inspection completely out of the way with no more incidents." She sipped again. "I think we can do that - have a completely normal twenty-four hours, I mean - and if we *can* do that, then I can start to think clearly about what our next move should be. Whether we can… "

She didn't finish. There was a rustling and a whisper from the store cupboard, which made her fall silent, listening, her head cocked to one side. The whisper was followed by a giggle, a thump, and a metallic click. Helen shook her head impatiently and strode over to the cupboard doorway. David followed her, and it wasn't until they had arrived on the threshold of the cupboard that they heard Simon, the taller of the two boys, speak-

"Stick 'em up!" he said.

#

Mayhem and chaos in the mind are not always translated to the body, Loatheworthy had come to realise. Sitting in the tiny cubby-hole office which the school had provided for him, and staring at a cling film parcel of cheese and pickle sandwiches, he presented as normal an aspect as he ever did. Inside his head though, it seemed that something was on fire, and instead of progressing in an orderly fashion to whatever exits parts of the consciousness might use in such a situation, some of his mind was running round and round in tiny circles waving its hands and shrieking out some very awkward questions.

He had barely managed to ignore the noise during his session with Alison Green, and hoped that she had taken his stunned silence for icy disdain. Then, it had become louder still as the Head continued their tour through the school and tried to gain his opinion on a mind-boggling array of sweet treats. When she had asked him if he would recommend custodial sentencing for the possession of candyfloss, he had begun to suspect that she might be lampooning him in some way.

Now the noise was almost unbearable.

Pickle had oozed stickily from between his slices of white bread and was smeared across their plastic wrapping. This nettled him further. Once, he had overheard Barbara Willis, another member of his team, opining to an unseen colleague that Loatheworthy and his sandwiches were alike, because they were both always far too tightly wrapped. Perhaps she was right.

He gave in, and listened to the questions.

How had she done it? That was the first thing. Had Hall simply not held up his half of the bargain? Loatheworthy grimaced; he had supposed that Hall would, because he was being paid (which seemed naive now), and more importantly, because the Hall he had known as an adolescent had never missed an opportunity to make someone else miserable. Yet there had been nothing in her desk drawer.

He gazed blankly around at the office. He hated it, but he had refused to share the more spacious accommodation inhabited by the other members of the team (a fact for which they were eternally grateful). Originally, he had planned to have a Mobile Operations Unit set up next to the school playground, right in the centre of the staff car park. He saw it in his mind's eye, glorious, bristling with antennae and radiating his personality across the whole school district, its mere silhouette striking terror into the hearts of an entire industry. It would have been black and white, with an official logo, and perhaps a motto above the door, something subtle like 'Tremble! Ofsted Sees All.'

For some reason, the teachers had been opposed to this idea. He scribbled a reminder to himself to state in his final report that the staff car park might be an inefficient use of space; surely it should be reclaimed for purely educational purposes.

This made him feel slightly better, but only slightly.

He would have got his way on the M.O.U. anyway, were it not for budgetary considerations. He had had to bid fairly low in order to ensure that his team secured this inspection, and the money they had simply wouldn't stretch to it. He had been forced to forego some of his tools of repression in order to maintain a reasonable level of pay.

He blinked. It had been a mistake. Haversham remained apparently untroubled, and her desk drawer had not been *empty*, had it? Oh no, there were the jelly beans to consider.

Conspiracy!

She must have known what he was up to in advance.

The idea made him shudder slightly. She must have known, just as she seemed to have known that he would enter her classroom after dark on Friday. Just as her father had known what he was up to years before.

He began to pry at the sandwiches, picking at the edges of the cling film with his still-bruised fingers, trying to find a simple way in. Only the day before he had been sure that this was his chance - his bonus ball in the great karmic lottery. But now, in the distance, still far off but drawing ever closer, Loatheworthy thought that he could hear the buzzing of a fabulously large bluebottle, making its way towards him, laughing and squeaking his name with high-pitched glee.

He twitched, as if flapping at the insect; it seemed that some of the internal chaos was seeping through after all.

If Hall was part of some conspiracy and had told Haversham everything, then she had him.

Snap. Gotcha! She *had* built the better mousetrap.

But how could she have known what was going on? It was as if she could watch him at all times, as if she could see his every move.

Ofsted Sees All...

Loatheworthy sat up straighter in his chair and slowly turned his head first to one side, and then the other. There was nothing in the room apart from himself, his work, his chair, (his recalcitrant sandwiches), and this horrible desk. A rapid movement out through the tiny window caught his eyes, and he turned that way, but saw nothing except mangy children playing jump-rope and hopscotch, and light kicking off of Haversham's classroom door, which stood open. He drew the blind.

Behind him, a single framed photograph hung on the wall. It showed a whole school group, complete with teachers. Fashions and hairstyles dated the picture by at least half a decade, but, he noted with disapproval, most of the teachers were recognisable. He would suggest in his report that the staff were getting stale in their jobs, and perhaps they should be encouraged to move on.

Quelling his nerves, he stood and warily approached the photograph, looking carefully around the edges of its frame before reaching up and gently lifting it from the wall. He fully expected to see a tell-tale hole in the plaster and a tiny black lens hood protruding into the room, or at least the black grill of a listening device. He even set his face into an expression of world-weary scorn so that he wouldn't look foolish on this particular section of videotape, but there was nothing. No school-wide surveillance network informing on him.

He tapped the wall gently, still frowning. Even the other teachers were definitely hiding something from him. There was a room that they wouldn't let him see. It lay off the main staffroom. There was an alcove, and a door on the left-hand side that was kept locked. The Head had told him that it was simply the original staff toilet which, since the new ones had been added during the nineteen seventies, was used only in the most dire gastric emergencies. She had looked as if she were telling the truth, but then why keep it locked? And why not offer to open it? And why could no one produce a key? In his mind's eye Loatheworthy saw the small room opened, and it was filled with bugging equipment and evidence of widespread cheating in the SAT exams, presided over by Hall and Haversham. They were consuming the drugs that he had paid for, and they were all laughing at him.

He must reassert himself. He would *insist* that he be allowed to inspect that room. He was not absolutely sure that this fell within his power, but he would do it anyway. He would have a look tomorrow.

He placed the picture carefully on the desk, still unsure of it, turned, and almost pressed his nose against the wall, examining it for any signs of surveillance equipment, unable to shake-off the idea that he was being monitored somehow. Behind him there was the briefest of courtesy taps, and then the door opened and Barbara Willis entered the room. She paused in the doorway, looking at him curiously.

"George," she said, "what *are* you doing?"

Loatheworthy wished that she wouldn't call him George; he had asked her not to. He turned quickly from the wall, stuck for an answer.

"I was... I was, er... "

"Inspecting the *wall*?" Now the wretched woman looked amused.

"Well, I.... "

Her smile widened. "Does it come up to scratch?"

Loatheworthy recovered quickly, gave her his best scornful look, and then stalked, in what he hoped was a haughty manner, around the desk and sat on its edge. He folded his arms and angled his chin upwards. He was a professional again, in control, on top of the situation; there were no flies on... perhaps not.

"Is it connected to the school's jelly bean problem?" Willis asked.

Loatheworthy's eyes bulged slightly. So word had already spread. He *was* losing his authority.

"I thought there might be damp; I was looking for dilapidations."

"Uh huh," Willis said, carefully. "I just wanted to check this afternoon's schedule. Godfrey is in with the two classes on the far side of the school, that's Green and Crodd, I've left it up to him how long he spends in each, but it won't be more than ten minutes. Susan's in with Ewing, and we're covering Miss Fitzpatrick and Helen Haversham. I wondered which you'd prefer?"

Loatheworthy looked down at the photo, still on his desk. There was only one choice, he realised, a nasty thread of fear curling in his belly. He had to find out what Haversham knew, and what her plans might be.

"I'll take Haversham."

Willis sighed. "Are you sure? Only I thought you'd prefer Fitzpatrick, she seems more... jumpy, and I've already prepared the groundwork to go into Haversham's room."

"I'm sure."

Willis shrugged. "Okay George, whatever you say. Oh, and George,"

"Yes."

"I think you're sitting in your lunch."

She turned in the doorway and was gone.

Loatheworthy sprang up from the desk, looked behind himself, and saw the cling film package smeared across its surface. Scowling he brushed at the back of his trousers. Somehow he blamed Haversham even for this. Oh but he would regain the upper hand, and then she would pay.

Blobs of pickle dropped back onto the desk.

Oh yes, she would pay...

#

David looked into the cupboard over Helen's shoulder. It was actually a narrow corridor with a deep alcove to the left-hand side of its end. To David it seemed out of place in the airy classroom, as if it might have been an afterthought when the school was constructed in the heady psychedelic world of the late nineteen sixties.

'Hey man, we've like, got some bits man. Like - bits left over! They're makin' me paranoid, man. Man I'm freakin' out... '

'Be cool. Be cool Wavy Gravy, where's the fire? We'll just have us a nice snaky li'l ol' cupboard... '

The cupboard walls were lined with high, strong shelves stacked with bundles of paper. Some were open, spilling their brightly coloured contents around them in sheaves. In the far corner, David could see a collection of plastic hoops nestling against the wall. Stacked opposite them were a series of wooden trays filled with books and mysterious angular equipment. The trays were labelled in the round easy to follow script that all infants school teachers eventually seemed to adopt - 'Science', 'Maths', 'Music', and 'Misc.'.

In the foreground, two reams of paper forgotten at their feet, stood Simon and Adrian. They held the classic kiddie stick-up pose. Simon was pointing what seemed to be an elderly sawn-off shotgun at his classmate. He was grinning widely under his horn-rimmed glasses with one pudgy finger curled tightly around the double triggers. The shotgun's stock was not seated properly at his shoulder and the end of its barrel twitched left and right slightly as he struggled to hold it straight. That wouldn't matter though; at such close range David saw that any shot would likely turn the other child - Adrian - into soup. Adrian stood with his hands raised high in the air, but his expression had begun to change from one of indulgent fun to one of uncertainty as he perhaps sensed the danger that he was in.

David's mind seemed to race ahead of events, and he was treated to a vision of Simon tightening his grip on the trigger and recoiling violently. He saw a tongue of flame lick out to scorch the air before the gun's twin barrels, and he actually *felt* his own eardrums push in and pop out as the awful noise of the gun filled the air. Most terrible of all, he saw Adrian almost dissolve in a cloud of red droplets.

David had time to blink and the image left him. He raised one hand in warning and tried to get out some words, to tell Simon to drop the gun and back away, but it was too late. The boy's grin was widening as he prepared to bring his game to its logical conclusion.

Simon's fingers began to tighten on the triggers for real, the metal making indentations in his pudgy flesh. Adrian's face now definitely showed fear, his eyes wide, his mouth drawing down into a trembling bow. David braced himself for an explosion of sound.

In front of him, Helen said one word. She sounded calm, almost dreamy, and yet the word seemed very loud, as if it were borrowing the volume and the energy of the expected gunshot.

She said, "Toy." And Simon jerked the triggers inwards.

David closed his eyes tightly, but there was no shot. When he opened them again after an eternity, he saw that Helen was right. Of course the gun was a toy - what else had he expected to see in a classroom. Now he looked at the gun properly he could see the cheap sheen of plastic, and the edge of its moulding where some factory worker in Taiwan or China had glued its sides together unevenly. A splash of colour appeared from its barrels, but this was not the tongue of flame he had imagined, but a small red hand-lettered sign on a thin bamboo cane. It said, 'Bang!'

Helen collapsed backward, her own arm still extended, her finger still pointing upwards tracing an arc through the air. Since he had no time to think about the operation, David caught her neatly and gracefully at her waist, and with a small push returned her to her feet.

Then silence. Somehow David thought that he could still hear the echoes of the gunshot that never was, but that was just his heartbeat booming in his chest.

Inside the cupboard both children had turned towards them, and their looks of fear and satisfaction were fading as they took in the scene. Helen was looking at them with something like panic in her expression; the hand that had pointed out the gun's fakery was still aimed at them, the other was clapped over her mouth.

"Oh God," she said, very low between her fingers.

Helen's distress seemed to be instantly transmitted across the short space between her and the children. Seeing Miss Haversham, usually a figure of ultimate steadiness and near omnipotence, look so shaken acted upon the children like no cross word or promise of punishment could. Simon let the gun swing downward and the 'bang' flag scraped on the lino. Adrian's lip began to tremble, and his eyes began to close in a prelude to tears.

For a moment they all stood, an odd tableau, then behind the boys a single sheet of A4 paper quit a precarious hold on the edge of a shelf and seesawed lazily downwards to the floor. When it hit, Helen performed some internal miracle. She cleared her throat slightly and all trace of her previous expression was swept away and replaced by stern interest. Both hands were now planted firmly on her hips, though David could see that they still shook imperceptibly.

"Now boys," she said, a slight tremor working its way out of her voice as she spoke, "you know better than to play with the things you find in my cupboard, don't you?"

The boys stared, but this was familiar ground, a ritual of sorts. The storm of tears that had threatened began to pass away.

"Yes Miss Haversham," in chorus.

"If Mrs Green thinks that she can't trust you, she won't send you again now, will she?"

More confident, "No - Miss - Haver - sham."

Helen nodded a slow affirmation as Simon carefully, almost reverently, propped the gun against the cupboard wall.

"Right then. I won't mention this to her - this time, but from now on, you two do as you are told."

"Yes - Miss - Haver - sham."

"Come on then." And with that, she harried them to the classroom door. They went eagerly, each carrying a bundle of paper, welcoming this return from the brink of strangeness.

Frowning, David passed them, wandering into the shadows of the cupboard.

He stared at the gun. Odd enough to produce a toy shotgun, usually it was pistols or rifles, but a sawn-off? What was it, part of the junior bank-robber range?

It leant where Simon had left it, its ridiculous party favour message protruding like a tongue - a half-malicious caricature of a gun's true function. The end of the stock bore some initials - M. H., the plastic was dimpled and ridged to make this bit of moulding resemble untidy carving. David picked it up and put it to his shoulder, looked along the truncated barrel, and decided that even if it was a toy he didn't like it: it was too lifelike to be healthy, the proportions were too right, and why those initials? He propped it back up against the cupboard wall.

Helen had closed the classroom door and was leaning against it as if trying to keep something out. She still seemed distracted, and was unaware that David was watching her. She covered her eyes, then rubbed them with the heels of her hands, an act of denial, as if she were scrubbing away some internal vision, then she took in a deep breath and released it, and again seemed to recover.

"What just happened?"

Helen didn't answer, but instead strode to the cupboard door, and holding her hair away from her face, peered carefully at some scuff marks on the floor by the threshold. Frowning, she rose and pushed past him, then began methodically searching the highest shelves of the cupboard. Confused, David watched from the doorway.

"What are you..?"

Now she was looking lower. Nestling on a shelf, she found an old canvas shopping bag. It was obviously something that the children had once used for dressing up, one corner was wearing through, and as she snatched at it some play money fell through the hole and rolled towards David on its edges. He stood on a plastic penny and tried again.

"What are you doing?"

Now Helen had picked up the gun and was examining it, much as he had. She weighed it in both hands, her expression blank, unreadable.

She looked up now, agitated.

"Quickly. Help me." She held the gun away from her, as if it were something germy. "We have to get this out of here. I need something to wrap it in."

She began looking up and down the shelves again, and then turned back towards him, her movements rapid and panicky.

"Your jumper. Quickly, give it to me."

"Why?" He pointed at the gun. "That's yours, isn't it?"

"No. Yes. I don't know... Come *on*."

There was real urgency in her tone, and he saw nothing for it but to do as she asked. He took off his coat and peeled off his jumper, static crackling in his hair, and she snatched it from his hand, wrapped it around the gun, and tucked it into the bag.

There: a gift basket packed especially for your Mafia grandmother. Helen leaned against the wall, seemingly relieved.

"God," she muttered to herself. "I wished for it. *Wished* for it! And there it was. And I was imagining his *head*, on the *wall*." Then louder, "Could you... I need you to take this away from here."

They stood looking at each other. David replayed what she had just said in his mind to make sure that he had heard it right, and then struggled to find the right questions to ask her. He needed a delicate, subtle series of questions. Questions that would not raise doubts about her mental competency or excite her unduly. He settled on, "Have you gone mad? Whose head?"

Before she could answer, the classroom door handle dipped, drawing both their gazes, and the door was pushed open again, this time without a knock. A tall willowy woman stood on the threshold looking in at them.

The Headteacher looked from David to Helen and back again, and then eyed the open cupboard door and the shopping bag suspiciously. After a moment's reflection, Helen thrust the bag, complete with its plastic contents, at David, who caught it in his arms like a rugby ball.

This gave the Head pause. She looked at them both in turn again, eyebrows raised, expecting some explanation, but none was forthcoming.

"Right. Okay," she said, in the tones of a woman grown used to dealing with her staff's eccentricities. "Thought I'd let you know Helen, Mister Loatheworthy is on his way to you this afternoon."

"Of course he is," Helen said, then gave out a high-pitched giggle and clapped one hand over her mouth.

The Head showed no surprise, and her curious gaze came to rest on the bag once again. "Is everything okay?"

Helen was staring at her boss, wide-eyed, still covering her mouth with her hand as if she expected something dangerous to leap out. Then she seemed to realise the strangeness of her behaviour and slowly dropped it to her side.

"Yes. Everything is absolutely and completely fine."

To David's ear, she did not sound entirely convincing, but it seemed good enough to the Head.

"Good. Good," she said, turning her gaze to David.

"You must be Helen's young man, Mister... "

"Barclay, David Barclay." He reached around the bag to hold out one hand. The Head shook it once, smiling broadly.

"Excellent, excellent," she said, then wiped her palm carefully on her skirt.

David's expression fell.

"Sorry. Just left an emergency in the hall you see - all hands to the pumps so to speak. One of Kim's little ones has had an accident... actually more of a cataclysm... it was like a small lake." She shook her head in wonder. "One wouldn't have thought that so much liquid could emerge from a standard-sized child, but there it is."

David peered down warily at his own apparently blameless hand.

The Head's gaze was once again resting on the battered bag. "The things teachers must deal with these days. I almost expected some quaint fishing boats and a sunset. Anyway, I'll be off then, leave you two to whatever it was you were doing."

"David'll go with you," Helen said, still sounding shaky.

There was a short, awkward silence.

"Right," David said. "Of course. But I'll see you this evening, and we'll talk then?"

"Definitely. I'll be in after seven."

He took two steps forwards, and then the Head was upon him, taking his arm in a vice-like, bone-crushing grip, and leading him to the door. Helen gave a small wave and a look that might have indicated apology, and then the Head propelled him out into the corridor.

The woman was beaming again.

"Excellent. Known each other long, have you?"

They were striding down the corridor at breakneck speed, passing a blur of children's pictures and classroom bulletins. David didn't even have time to glance back at Helen's door.

"A few weeks."

"Marvellous. Perhaps you'd like to come to our Nativity, Mister Barclay?"

"Well, I... "

"I imagine it will be quite an unusual show this year... unique, and Miss Haversham will be there of course. You could walk her home," she added, nudging him gently in the ribs with one bony elbow and grinning a shark-like grin.

David thought it best to agree.

"Excellent, I have a spare ticket in my office."

They walked on towards the entrance hall, until they finally arrived outside a rosewood-veneer door, which was ajar, and bore a small plaque reading 'Rosemary Fairport - Headteacher'. On a chair by the side of the door there sat a very small boy. He was examining his shoes as if they fascinated him.

"Oh Wendell," the Head said, and the boy looked up mournfully. "Not *again*. What did you use this time?"

"Mash taters, Miss."

The Head turned to David. "Wendell is one of our repeat offenders, I'm afraid." David nodded sagely as if he understood.

With a long-suffering sigh, she pushed the office door open.

"If you'd like to wait in my office, Mister Barclay, I'll be five minutes."

She turned to the boy and took his hand. "Come on Wendell. I'm sure that little permanent damage was done. You can apologise, and then I'll take you back to class - we'll call it a Christmas amnesty."

The boy grinned, and she rushed off back down the corridor, using the same manner to propel the small boy that she had just used on David.

#

Once inside the office, David sat down with the bag on his knees. The sound of the Head's heels receded and he glanced around with the idle curiosity he always felt in someone else's place of work. There were pinboards and battered filing cabinets, the sound of children playing and someone typing, the smell of pledge, piles of photocopy paper, and a thumb-plate lock on the door. It all seemed quite comforting.

He re-played what had just happened in Helen's classroom, and looked for a simple way to interpret it, but found none. The image of Helen holding the plastic toy with such disgust came to him, and he heard Jonson say, ' ...that's one careful loony... is your girlfriend the careful type?'

With no more thought, David went to the door and looked both ways down the corridor. It was clear now, even of children, and the school was filling with a sense of expectation, of lessons in the offing. Inside again, he pushed the thumb-plate lock across and lifted the gun from its nest in the canvas bag, feeling the end of the stock and the barrel through his jumper.

It was still just as ugly and unexpected an object, and he held it up to the light slanting in through the Head's venetian blinds. Yes, there might be something there, and the Presidents' long envelope was still in his pocket.

Like almost everything with which they were connected, the Presidents' fingerprint kit was unexpectedly efficient, giving the impression that it was the result of years of honing a simple process. He read the instructions twice through, then dusted the bottom of the gun's plastic stock with a powder that was grey, rather than the black he had been led to expect by a thousand detective shows. Instantly it showed a series of shapes and swirls that reminded him of cloud formations. He replayed the image of Helen holding the gun again, yes- it was definitely a left palm print.

Next, he sprayed the print with some kind of adhesive that smelled like hairspray, and then applied one of the pieces of lifting paper. It felt plasticized and odd, moulding exactly to the gun's shape. He held it there for the required thirty seconds, counting under his breath and listening all the while for the Head's return. Towards the end of the count he grew nervous, and began to curse his own stupidity for not waiting to perform this process in the relative safety of his own rooms, but then it was finished, and the print was dried in his hand. He held it up, marvelling a little at its intricacy, then tucked it, and the kit, back into the Presidents' envelope. Now he was glad that it was over; he could rid himself of the whole idea by slipping the print under the Presidents' door.

He put the gun back in the bag, reached over, and flicked up the thumb-plate lock, then waited with it seated on his lap. He read fire-safety posters and a notice for last-year's summer fête, a list of staff-meetings, a poster for the local pool showing a frozen diver over the legend 'take the plunge at Hornby Leisure Centre', and a wanted poster for a suspicious-looking family of head lice. On the Head's desk there was a framed postcard which read *'I'd keep my job if I won the lottery. Of course I would. Aha ha ha ha ha ahahaha.'* As he was reading this, he noticed that the bag was suddenly heavier on his knees.

David continued glancing around for a few moments as his brain refused to process the information being sent to it by his senses. After a few moments more his senses side-tracked his brain by getting it to blink a few times and glance out through the window (look, look at the pretty winter picture) and then slipped the information in whilst it was distracted.

The bag was heavier.

David blinked once again for good measure, then looked down at it sharply, simultaneously shrinking away slightly, as if someone had just dumped a large and angry snake onto his lap.

His hands were drawn up near his shoulders, like a showy pianist waiting on a heavy chord. After an age he forced one hand to reach gingerly downwards into the bag and snag the edge of his jumper. He pulled; it didn't want to move. Gaining slightly in confidence, he pulled again, harder this time, and the jumper unrolled for a second time and came away in his hand, dropping the heavy something back onto his knees.

David looked down again and there it was: the gun, impossible, but staring back at him none-the-less.

It was different now. For one thing, the red flag no longer poked from its end, and for another it shone with a new deadliness. He looked at it for what seemed to be a very long time, hearing the echoing call of a crow drifting in from the field.

He looked around himself dazedly, beginning to sweat, then reached into the bag. He wrapped one hand around the truncated barrels and lifted slightly. It was not the plastic he had gripped only moments before, but metal; it struck cold beneath his fingers. The stock was close-grained, and the initials (M. H.) were now carved into it for real. He had an urge to look over his shoulder again, out through the office window, and see a candid camera and a grinning anchorman. Instead, keeping it out of sight, he inexpertly broke the gun and looked into the twin chambers.

Yep, there they were - the ends of two impossible cartridges. He tweezed them out with his fingertips and looked at them lying harmlessly on the palm of his hand. Their plastic coatings were a dull red, and their business ends a bright gold, catching a little of the light. He closed his fingers over them. He could feel tiny ridges in their plastic surface, and a kind of gentle shock creeping over him.

His mind replayed the vision of the gun going off, of their stored energy released, of the boy, Adrian, disappearing.

David sat in the Head's office for almost three minutes, looking down at the cartridges held in his fist and the gun lying forgotten in the bag, and his mind ran at lightning speed through various scenarios which might have brought him to this point. How could this impossibility have happened?

He had exhausted survivalist cults and space alien intervention, and was working on a scenario in which Helen was actually a Svengali-style mad genius, able to hypnotise hapless (but strangely attractive) graduate students at will and get them to do her foul bidding, when he heard heels clicking on the corridor floor again, approaching at great speed.

He dropped the cartridges back into the bag, scooped up his sweater and again used it to conceal the gun. As the Head pushed open the office door, he was rising from his chair.

The Head walked in shaking her head. "That Wendell," she said, "Expert recidivist. I've made him apologise to the caretaker, *and* his cat, but I don't think the poor animal forgave him."

All bustle, she opened a filing cabinet, produced a Nativity ticket, and handed it to David. It was photocopied on purple paper.

"Well - saved by the bell eh, Mister Barclay?"

David nodded. "Squink," he said, then cleared his throat and tried again.

"Thanks." He smiled a very sickly smile to cover his tracks. The Head simply nodded, still seemingly preoccupied with Wendell's mysterious crime, took his arm, and again (this time gratefully), he allowed her to guide him through the maze of corridors and out to the entrance hall. She opened one of the wide front doors, and ushered him through.

"We'll see you tomorrow evening, then?"

Dazed, and still holding the ticket, David nodded, then made his way up the path, leaning slightly to compensate for the new weight in the bag and walking carefully, as if he suspected that the school pathway might twist beneath him, and buck him from its surface.

After waving cheerily at him for a while, the Head stepped back into the shadows of the corridor, a stony expression replacing her smile. As David made the school gates she folded her arms and watched him carefully until he had moved out onto the street and disappeared from her sight.

#

By the time that Loatheworthy arrived in her classroom for the second time that day, Helen had begun to feel normal again. For two or three minutes after David and the Head had left her, she had had the shakes, unable to focus on anything but the open cupboard door and the image of Simon pointing a shotgun at his friend. Sitting alone at her desk, listening to her teeth chattering together, she had held one hand up before her face and stared wide-eyed at it as it trembled uncontrollably. This had been followed by a brief burst of hysterical giggling (as the image of Simon and Adrian was replaced by that of Loatheworthy's head, complete with rictus-like grin, mounted on her wall), and several hiccups. After that, her unconscious mind had gently taken her conscious mind aside, put a grandmotherly arm around its shoulders, offered it a boiled sweet, and told it that since she needed to appear to be normal for the children's lessons that afternoon, it should disregard the implications of what had just happened and file them away for later (this is more common than you might think).

When Loatheworthy appeared then, Helen was introduced to a wholly new experience in that she was actually slightly relieved to see him alive, and glad that for the first time in six weeks or so his presence did not immediately provoke a fantasy of his imminent demise.

They stared at one another across the space of the room for a few moments, and Helen was surprised that the air there did not crackle with suppressed tension.

"This is Mister Loatheworthy," she said to the class, sounding remarkable calm and wholly normal. "He is one of the inspectors that I told you about on Monday, just like Mister Godfrey. Say hello please class."

Dutifully the children chorused, "Good-after-noon-Mister-Loatheworthy."

Andrew Bailing always lagged behind the others with his chanting, and staring dreamily into space, he did so now, " ...noon Mister Love-Worty."

The inspector said nothing, but nodded, then peered around him with a pinched and pained expression. He seemed to be examining the walls carefully. He spotted Helen's chair, and without a word he went to it and dragged it into the corner of the room where he sat like a spider at the edge of its web, hunched over a clipboard.

With an amazing application of willpower, Helen ignored him and tried to lapse into the comforting rhythm of her work. The afternoon went surprisingly well, and Loatheworthy drew her attention only twice.

The first time was when, after she had ensured that each member of the class had had a reasonable stab at their number worksheet, and she had seen and commented on each one, she started them on some counting and singing games. Two completely tuneless run-throughs of those old classroom favourites 'more than twenty but less than twenty-nine little buns in a baker's shop', and 'above one-hundred but below one-hundred-and-nine little speckled frogs (sat in a speckled frog café, eating some most delicious flies, yum yum...)' followed. During the second song, Helen saw Loatheworthy twitch slightly, raising one hand up by his ear as he had earlier that day.

As she began to ask the children some number questions, she examined him more closely, and was pleased to see that Loatheworthy did not look good. He tracked her questioning through eyes that were slightly red-rimmed and feral, his hair and suit were rumpled, and there seemed to be a dark stain of some kind on his trousers. Helen found herself toying with the idea that he somehow knew how close to a real demise he had come, or perhaps it was simply that he did not appreciate their singing.

Then it was time to round off with some sorting and counting. The children already had the coloured block boxes on their desks, and each small group was set the task of sorting the blocks into lots, increasing in value from one to ten.

She set the groups going, knowing that it was almost hopeless. Five-to-six-year-old children, particularly tired five-to-six-year-old children, immediately before the Christmas break, have an attention span which runs on a scale from stunned hamster, through house-fly on speed, to lettuce leaf, and the class ably demonstrated this by forgetting what it was they were meant to be doing.

Outside the day's light began slowly to leech away as the children engaged in a variety of activities. These ranged from the arcane (a game in which you had to line up blocks of all colours and pretend that they were pasta), to the disgusting (I must make sure my nostril is *really* clean so that I can fit more than one block into it); and from the Zen (I will stare placidly at a block for the whole ten minute session), to the kleptomaniac (I like red red blocks, oh dear, they appear to have 'fallen' into my pocket). Few if any children played the counting game she had described, but circle group - most of whom could do this exercise standing on their heads - did use wonderful teamwork and communication skills in order to build a really *big* block tower.

Whilst the children didn't sort and count, Loatheworthy prowled the classroom looking over shoulders. When he reached circle group (their tower only half complete at this stage), he looked down at them and asked no one in particular- "How often do you do maths activities?"

The children looked up at him blankly. Helen watched with her arms folded, frowning, and ready to jump in. With luck, Andrew would answer. He was a dreamy boy, but bright as a button, gifted with language, and Loatheworthy wouldn't foozle him.

Tina answered, looking up at Loatheworthy slightly slack-jawed.

"What's mavs?" she asked.

Loatheworthy squinted at the child as if she had just offered him a personal insult, shot a boiling triumphant look at Helen, made some kind of note, and began to move on. Scowling mightily Andrew Bailing looked up at him through his round gold-rimmed glasses.

"She didn't understand what you meant. We don't often call it 'maths'. But we play counting games and do sum-sheets an' addin' up an' that every day." He nodded to himself. "*I* even add up on Saturdays."

Loatheworthy paused, obviously irritated.

"How often do *you* add things?" Andrew asked him.

Helen watched Loatheworthy narrowly, and the inspector seemed to consider not answering, but circle-group were all looking up at him expectantly, and with the barest (but nonetheless highly incriminating) flicker in his gaze back towards her desk, he drew himself up to his full height and cleared his throat.

"All the time," he said. Then, seeming to feel that more was required of him, he added- "I have several qualifications in Mathematics."

Andrew looked at him slyly. "Can you do four plus... " he thought hard, an expression of accomplished cunning dawning on his face, "...a hundred."

"Of course."

"What is it then?"

There was a pause. "Why don't you tell me?"

"I don't think he knows," Andrew stage whispered, sounding a little worried now. "Miss, he doesn't know - an' there's something brown on his trousers."

Loatheworthy gave that odd twitch again, half bringing his right hand up, as if he might be about to shoo away one of the snacks from the speckled frog song. "It's... it's sandwich pickle," he said, "and the answer is one hundred and four."

Andrew nodded approvingly. "Well done," he said, in eerie imitation of Helen. Loatheworthy withdrew.

Then at last, it was three o'clock: story time.

There was the usual tussle over who would sit closest to Miss Haversham, but generally the children were well behaved, sitting with their legs crossed and their hands in their laps: a perfect audience.

Each day the class voted for the kind of story that they would like to hear. Some days they preferred a book story, and Helen would turn the large pages slowly, so that they each had a good long look at the pictures; but two or three days a week they opted for one of Miss Haversham's special stories, and they did so today.

Helen laid out the options for them. They could have a story of valour on the high seas, or a fairy tale of woods and wolves. Or perhaps they would enjoy the story of Burglar Boris and his accomplice, horrible Horace... Helen picked a name out of the air... Hall, and how they fell foul of a policeman one fine day.

From the corner Loatheworthy let out a strangled cough, then juggled and dropped his pen. Helen ignored him.

Since she had made it sound by far the more interesting option, the children all voted for story number three, and Helen began. As the story grew, she saw the old magic overtake the children and smiled to herself, feeling calmer now. There were a few fidgets, a few children shooting furtive glances at the windows or at Loatheworthy, but mostly they were *in* the story to a depth that few adults seemed able to achieve. Helen knew that if she lowered her voice the children would unconsciously hunker down and make themselves smaller; at moments of triumph or tension they would sit up straighter, straining to listen; and when she added sound-effects, or the voices of characters, they heard them in glorious stereo, filtered through powerful imaginations.

The clock ticked on to three-fifteen, lights were lit and gloom dispelled, and Loatheworthy did not notice her hold on the classes' attention, it seemed. But curiously, as Helen's story progressed in leaps and bounds, and strayed far over into the world of the ridiculous. As her burglars - Boris and Horrible Horace Hall - skilfully pilfered the Queen's bejewelled nose-hair clippers and made their escape, only to be captured by Chief Inspector Lard of the Yard, Loatheworthy's body language became more and more defensive, and he crouched into his chair as if fending off some unseen attack. Finally, seemingly agitated, he rose from her chair, and began to wander around the classroom edge, inspecting the displays.

He seemed to be examining them in minute detail, his nose only inches from the wall, and with a terrible inevitability he eventually fetched up before some of the faked paintings. By the time the story was over, and the children were busy collecting their coats and scarves, he was staring, in fact, at the very work that Chloe had finished for Helen on Sunday afternoon. As Helen watched, he reached out with one hand and touched the lumpy paintwork, then withdrew his fingers quickly as if the surface of the image might be hot. Was he practised enough to tell that this was not wholly the work of a child?

She moved to intercept him, unsure of what to say.

"Imaginative, isn't it? For a five-year-old. Very detailed."

Loatheworthy did not turn to look at her; the painting seemed to claim all of his attention.

"How did you..? Yes, it is." He cleared his throat. "Is it copied from a photograph?"

Helen frowned and took in the image properly again. It showed a night-blasted field, a scarecrow, and a be-hatted and sinister moon. In the foreground were several grey, indeterminate blobs.

"I would say not. I think it came straight from the imagination."

"Yes... of course. You would say that... "

Again, Loatheworthy's shoulder rose involuntarily and his right hand made an abortive swatting motion. Helen backed off a step, and at last, he turned to face her.

They stared at each other under the odd image, almost toe to toe, again openly acknowledging that they were adversaries - sizing each other up like boxers before a bout. Helen struggled to keep images of some grotesque end for him from popping unbidden into her mind, and Loatheworthy searched her expression carefully. The noise of the children lining up by the door covered her words.

"I don't like you, Loatheworthy," Helen hissed. Strangely, it was the worst thing she could think of to say.

Loatheworthy blinked. He looked back at the strange image, then at Helen.

"What do you know?" he asked.

Helen could not help herself. She let the silence spin out for a few seconds before answering. It was a trick she had learned in dealing with the children. A bit of tension, then deliver your bluff. She leaned towards him slightly, almost whispering in his ear.

"I know everything," she said.

The inspector winced - a slight movement, but there, and immensely satisfying.

From the far corner of the classroom a short rattle from an old alarm clock sounded, sending Mister Tribble into a frenzy of cage climbing. Loatheworthy wheeled around, panicked, apparently expecting some treachery.

"Three-fifteen," Helen said, "home time."

And as if this were an order, Loatheworthy gathered his clipboard and fled the room.

#

And then the school day was ended. Those children who had not been persuaded to return and mangle carols in the final concert rehearsal at Hornby Infants that evening, made their way home for the day to their televisions, and video games, and well-worn Christmas wish-lists.

After the mad rush of the school-run, but before people began to arrive home from work, the few roads of Hornby were quiet for a time. A lonely figure, impressive and impassive, out on a hill to the south of the town, watched shop-lights come on, and myriad headlights flare and disappear. Eventually, it turned its back on the slowcoach firework display laid out below it, and set about its dark work. A ring of ancient oaks and chestnuts and a few hardy shrubs crowned the hill, and the figure left the rustling shadows there, and moved to the centre of the circle of trees.

It was the very crest of nightfall, coming winter-early here in what passed for the countryside. The sky had lost its colour, and the trees seemed to hunch together in pools of ground mist, as if they had witnessed something on Halloween that they had not yet quite managed to forget. As the figure waited, the old bells of St Peter's church chimed four solemn tones, rolling in on the faint breeze and echoing eerily on the hillside. As the last note died away, the figure began, as if it had been waiting for a cue.

A rope was produced from one trench coat pocket, and was measured out in arm-lengths. The dark figure stood between the trees and began to loop the rope around itself with terrible determination. Hands twisted the thick rope carefully, looping and looping, stopping at every third loop to make sure that they were tight and even and looked good. Slowly, a hangman's knot emerged from the plaiting, dangling, sinister, then pulled tight between outstretched arms to leave a perfectly formed noose. The figure looked upwards, surveying carefully, and an overhanging branch was selected.

Until this point, the air of intrigue and menace was complete. An observer would have been impressed by the ominous imagery and implacable determined movement. Now, however, the figure attempted to throw the rope over the bough. The first throw showed some panache. The rope was swung as a lasso might be, high into the air, then it completely missed the branch and crashed downwards, hitting the figure in the eye.

"Bugger!" Simon Dasch exclaimed.

Double vision did not help attempts two and three, and by the time
that he was readying himself for attempt number four the now not-so-
ominous figure, covered in leaves and mud, and something toxic that
he suspected a very unhealthy badger had left behind, decided that it
would probably be easier simply to shin up the tree and place the rope
over the bough manually. This he did, climbing inelegantly and
swearing quietly but very creatively under his breath.

Eventually things were set up, and the hangman's rope hung
impressively from the tree. Dasch took a plastic bag from his pocket
and began to arrange some objects on the ground beneath the noose.
Chief among them was a jar of supermarket apricot jam (for some
reason beyond his power to ascertain the pectin was necessary for the
success of what he was about to do), and he unscrewed the lid and laid
it carefully aside. He also had an unused five-year diary in which that
day's date had been circled in black marker pen, a hawthorn branch,
and a handful of red rose petals. He placed them all beneath the noose,
which swayed gently in the breeze, and, sitting cross-legged beside
them, uttered a few unintelligible syllables.

After perhaps two minutes, it became clear that nothing was
happening. Dasch huffed, rose, and strode over to the tree to which he
had attached the rope. He studied it carefully, and then gave it a sharp
blow to a smooth area on one side the trunk, uttering the arcane cry of
all those who use a technology the workings of which they simply
cannot be bothered to understand.

"Work!" he cried. "Work, you bastard!" (Thump) "Work!"

He glanced around himself. What was he doing wrong? This was
simple divination. He had the necessary symbolic objects, he was pure
of mind (...ish), what was it? Then it came to him. The *pentagram*, of
course, he hadn't drawn the pentagram.

On the outskirts of the copse, he found a sizeable branch which he
brought back and used to scrape a reasonable pentagram in the earth
beneath the rope and around the objects. Then he settled himself back
into position and began to concentrate again.

He lost himself in his work. Time passed. Eventually the rope,
already moving in the breeze, began to move with more apparent
purpose, swinging first in a circle and then in a small figure of eight.

When it had built up a decent rhythm and had begun to hum, Dasch began to ask his questions, starting with the simplest and ending with the most complex. For an eavesdropper hiding in the trees, the conversation would have sounded like one of those heard late at night on the radio bandwidths used by the police, in which only one side of a conversation can be received.

"Oh mighty essence of nature, invincible and omnipotent, all that there is, I bring thee questions," Dasch said in low tones. "These are questions of the future which are also questions of the past." He paused for emphasis. "Questions beyond the realm of mortal sight." He raised the palms of his hands skywards. "Tell me, what is it that I feel at work in this town, and how will its work be done?"

The trees rustled together conspiratorially. The branches rattled and whispered half-syllables into the darkness.

"Really? Dead? All dead? And you have seen this?"

Another rustle. The breeze flourished, lifting Dasch's hair from his forehead.

"But you cannot reveal the culprit's face?"

Leaves stirred. In the centre of the pot of apricot jam a tiny and impossible blue flame popped into existence and began to burn, flicking left and right.

"Oh benevolent and mysterious one, how might I prevent this tragedy?"

The trees shivered. At the edge of the copse a rotten branch collapsed, falling into the brown leaves below it. There was a long pause. Dasch's eyes rolled, trance-like, envisioning, then -

"Seven-twenty exactly... ball gowns... size twenty two... the Nativity... the enormous bottom... yes... Yes, I see it all... I understand."

The greedy flame now occupied almost half of the jam jar, and had begun to crackle and spit. The jar's label blackened, peeled away from the glass, and lay smouldering.

Dasch raised his hands again. "Oh puissant one... "

A crack like a gunshot overhead, and a chestnut, still in its green spiky casing, dropped at great speed from the canopy, and, with a noise which could only be described as 'boink', bounced neatly from Dasch's head.

"Ow! What'd you do that for?"

The trees muttered darkly.

"No *puissant*. It means potent and powerful."

Dasch raised one hand and gingerly began to rub his forehead.

"Yes. I know you prefer gooseberry, but they didn't have any whole-fruit gooseberry, and I won't buy you the cheap stuff any more, there's just too much sugar in it, it makes you crazy. Remember the hurricane, hmmm? 1987? Got a little fractious then didn't we? Anyway, I thought you might like to try apricot, it's something new."

The trees shivered in the wind in a way which evidently conveyed to the now crouching poet that although this particular incarnation of the power and eternal wisdom of nature wouldn't turn down any apricot jam, he'd better bring gooseberry next time, or wear a *very* hard hat.

The blue flame licked at the last of the jam and left. Cooling too quickly the jar shattered, and the poet knew that that would be the end of it. If he wanted to chat any more he'd have to go through the whole rigmarole again, *and* provide more jam. Anyway, he was tired, and the next twenty-four hours were not going to be easy.

He finished collecting up the pieces of broken glass, had retrieved his mobile phone from a pocket, and was preparing to ring his employer to give him the news, when his ears caught the faint sound of moaning and wailing on the breeze.

Half expecting some further terrible premonition of events to come, Dasch hunched his shoulders and tensed. After what seemed to be an eternity he cracked open an eye.

Nope. No dancing demons and pitiable tortured souls, but what..?

Then he caught the tune. It was 'Once in Royal David's City' sung by the massed ranks of tiny children down at the infants school. Wafted up to him on the night wind it sounded suspiciously like a large male ant-eater being very ill into a capacious and echoey tin bucket after a really good night out with all of his ant-eater friends.

Dasch sat down for a while on the cold grass, and listened to the noise (he could not think of it as singing). He wondered at its sheer unmitigated awfulness. And to think, the woman was down there right now, standing at ground zero, so to speak. He shook his head as a particularly awful ululating squeak reached him, and began to dial. Well, at least it proved one thing: she must have steady nerves.

The breeze muttered in the trees again - the ghost of a voice. The phone began to ring and he hunched into his coat to cut out the chill. Below him the town was in full dark, glimmering with Christmas cheer, and in the spaces between the lights, where freezing mist had begun to coalesce, things were beginning to happen.

Dasch nodded to himself. Yes; the woman had nerves of steel. That was good; soon she was going to need them.

#

By seven o'clock the night breeze had totally lost its battle with the mist and retreated, and when the bells of St. Peter's church chimed this new hour their sound spread out, and came clear and level to Helen's ears as she turned into her driveway. She did not see Loatheworthy's BMW neatly parked several houses away, but she felt tired and on-edge. She had tried to call David three times from the school, but he was not answering his phone, and this seemed to her some kind of betrayal; she needed to talk to him. Reaching into the pocket of her bag for her keys, she fumbled them with cold fingers, and they dropped to the asphalt. Stooping to pick them up, she froze.

A noise, coming from the back garden: a low grating squeak.

During that summer Helen had spent a lot of time in the long back garden, pruning and planting and slurping the odd glass of wine, and she had come to know most of the noises associated with it. This one was the swing-seat, now with its cushions bundled into the shed, moved gently backwards and forwards by unseen feet. It was far too heavy to be moved by a breeze, or by a fox or a cat out for a night prowl, and Marie was away staying with friends in Oxford.

Helen straightened up. What should she do? Head straight for the house and the phone, or investigate? Who would she call - the police? David? She felt indecision and the first stirrings of disquiet trying to take hold of her and root her to the spot. This was one unwelcome surprise too many. Up and down the street all was quiet. Sunday's light powdering of snow still lay like a light frost around a few of the gateposts, and the air was mistier now, as if the cold were fusing into a form.

Helen was heartily fed up with feeling anxious, watched, guilty, and slightly afraid, and her tiredness lent her courage. She selected her door-key and held it clenched in one fist as if it were a weapon, then looked at it thoughtfully and shook her head. What else was there?

She cast about the front garden, denuded by the winter - there must be something... yes. A year before, Marie's aunt had bought them a weird selection of garden ornaments, a little group of terra-cotta toadstools, and two of them had survived the frost and were still planted at the end of the long flower bed. Helen crept over and selected the smaller of the two, a long thin mushroom. She picked it up, brushed cold earth from its end, and hefted it, liking the weight; then she nodded to herself and began to inch her way silently around the side of the house, staying close to the wall.

The sideway was horribly dark. The tall back gate at its end blocked out any light from the moon or the neighbour's houses. She moved past her own side door and stopped to listen again with her hand on the gate, allowing her eyes to adjust as much as they could to the gloom.

There it was: a deliberate, almost stealthy squeak.

The seat was at least ten feet from the back gate, and she was sure that she had the element of surprise on her side.

Forwards... backwards... forwards... and then nothing.

Helen's eyes widened. Whoever it was had left the seat; she heard heavy grating footsteps on the patio. Without thinking she depressed the latched thumb-plate and pushed at the gate with all of her strength; a week of pent-up frustration and anger and guilt went into it.

The timing was perfect. The gate sprang quickly inwards and hit something satisfyingly hard. Whatever it was said, "Unk!" and doubled over. The gate rebounded, but Helen was ready for this, and when it reached her, she shoved it again. It bounced forward once more, catching the doubled-over figure a glancing blow to the side of the head and it dropped to its knees on the patio.

Helen stepped forwards, blood thumping in her ears, the mushroom raised high over her head, ready to fell the intruder again if he dared to rise; but then she recognised the coat, and the bag, and saw that it was David.

#

The central heating had come on through the timer, and so the kitchen, which was at the front of the house, was warm as well as light. Helen had switched on both the fluorescents and a lanky standard lamp, imported for the purpose from the living room, so that she could see what she was doing. She bent over David - who sat at the scarred oak table with his hands around a mug of coffee - gingerly dabbing at a good-sized graze on his forehead with some antiseptic and cotton wool. David was scowling, which didn't make her endeavours any easier. The stone mushroom stood on the table like a provocation, casting a menacing shadow.

Helen still felt shaky, but was trying to defend her actions.

"Look, I said I was sorry, *very* sorry. What were you doing skulking in the garden anyway?"

"I wasn't *skulking*, I was *waiting*, and I wasn't expecting to be charged by a madwoman armed with a giant ornamental fungus. Ow!"

He drew away from her, wincing and touching his own head. His fingers came away tacky with blood, and he looked at them as if it were a substance he had never seen before. "God, woman. You could have *killed* me."

She drew back.

"Firstly, don't ever, *ever* call me 'woman', and secondly how did you expect me to react? You know what's been going on."

David sighed, relaxing slightly, and she moved in with the cotton wool again.

"And another thing." Helen drew back, exasperated. "Did you know that you have a rabid hedgehog in your garden? The bloody thing kept butting at my foot. I tried to shoo it away but the sod wouldn't go."

She eyed him suspiciously. "I hope you didn't do anything cruel."

"Cruel. Cruel? You mean like bouncing it off of a gate and then threatening to cave its head in with an ornamental, but let's face it extremely phallic, toadstool?"

"Well Thwinn was probably just hungry, he's always hungry; he's more like a pet really."

"Tim! You mean you've named the bloody thing?"

"Thwinn, not Tim - it's an acronym: 'the-hedgehog-with-no-name,'" she said, looking sheepish. "Hold still. You're worse than a five-year-old."

"Your class you mean? I'm guessing that you have never forced any of them to the ground before trying to shitaké them to death."

She dabbed for the final time. "Don't get hysterical. Anyway, shitaké are a different shape, flat, I couldn't very well have brained you with one of those now could I?"

She leaned forward slightly and blew very gently on his forehead, drying the antiseptic before applying a sticking plaster. David kept very still. Helen eyed her job critically, "There."

"The perfect end to the perfect day," David said. "You know, last week was normal - well, relatively normal anyway, and I didn't even appreciate it. In the last two days I've broken and entered, I've disposed of large quantities of dope, and I've been menaced by a hedgehog and a woman with a lethally weighted truffle."

Helen went to the cupboard and retrieved an expensive-looking bottle of brandy. "Like some in your coffee?"

"Please."

Strangely, they had so far managed to avoid mentioning the object which waited on the kitchen floor by David's side of the table like a faithful dog. As Helen added a generous measure of brandy to each of their cups, David's eye now strayed to it, and he picked up the canvas shopping bag and plopped it onto the table. When Helen had taken the chair opposite him again, he asked the question he had been feverishly turning over in his mind for the previous three hours.

"What the hell is this?"

He reached into the bag, drew out the gun, and placed it on the table between them. It was plastic again, pointing blindly at the kitchen tiles, the party favour message again sticking from its end, the powder cleaned from its underside.

Helen surveyed it warily. "It's a toy gun."

"Earlier it was... different."

She looked at him intently, trying to gauge his expression, cradling her coffee cup tightly in her hands as if it might be anchoring her to the kitchen, and without it she might float away. After a long moment, she looked down at the gun again, as if it drew her gaze.

"It really was?" she asked. "I mean, I thought it was, and then I thought I might be dreaming it, but then... "

David nodded, "It was."

The kitchen blinds were not drawn, and darkness lapped at the glass of the windows, making reflections of them as they stared at one another. Then, in a low tone David described some of what had happened in the Head's office.

When he had finished speaking, Helen let out a pent-up breath. "There are some things I need to tell you," she said, "and they're going to sound a bit mad."

"A bit mad," David repeated.

"Yes. Loopy, deranged, out-to-lunch...   Mad enough for me to pretend that they've not been happening."

"Ow-kay."

Silence again, then- "Do you ever lose things?"

The question surprised him.

"What? Well I... "

Helen squinted with impatience, speaking more quickly now.

"You know - lose things: car keys, door keys, the TV remote?"

He nodded, frowning, "Of course I do, but - "

"Well, so do I. I've tried to ignore it, but recently, when I've lost something, and I really *really* want it, something happens."

David's eyes flicked down to the gun again. "Something mad?"

"Well, yes. The whatever-it-is turns up exactly where I expected it, even wanted it, to be. I'll show you, wait there."

She left the table and headed for the stairs. David sipped his brandy-laced coffee. Had he been expecting a confession? Yes, perhaps he had. There were footsteps and the sound of her rummaging around up there, and then she returned, coming down more slowly. Held out before her, tweezed reverently between finger and thumb as if it might be dangerous, she held a knitted grey and blue sock with a pattern of interrupted stripes and squares. She sat down again and placed it on the table between them. David chose not to comment.

"About a fortnight ago," Helen said, "I lost the remote control for the TV - you know? I turned the whole house over looking for it. I'd got to that point where you start to check for things in completely impossible places because you've looked everywhere else - like in the oven, or the grass box of the lawnmower, or even in Marie's Scuba gear. But then I found it on the arm of the sofa."

David eyed the sock carefully. The toe was turned in slightly, as if it were a puppet waiting for a hand to animate it. He had the uncomfortable impression that the sock was regarding him somehow. He cleared his throat, "So? That happens to everybody."

"Maybe. But then, when Marie came home from work that day, she told me that she had taken the remote to the office in her handbag. It looked a bit like her mobile, see?"

"Not really."

Helen sat back in her chair, and picked up the sock again, touching the blue pattern with one finger, as if it might represent buttons to press.

"When I checked, I'd actually been changing the channels all through breakfast with this."

A pause, then-

"With that?"

"Yep. And I kept it hidden in a drawer, because it changed, and changed back again. The pattern wasn't always like this, and I didn't want to see it any more. But then last week I did something else, I left a thing, a kind of charm... or trap, yes, a trap in my room at school, a stupid thing for Loatheworthy, to stop him poking around in my room, and I knew it would get him."

She dropped the sock back onto the table. David prodded it uncertainly with the tip of one finger; its pattern felt strangely lumpy and button-like.

"The gun *was* real," Helen continued. "It was real, and in a while it probably will be again."

She said the last few words in a hushed tone, as if the import of the phrase were only now sinking in.

David shook his head, but more to express the over-all impossibility of the idea, than to refute what she was saying. On the table between them there now sat a plastic gun, a large toadstool, and a dead sock-puppet, it was like the aftermath of some hallucinatory bank raid.

"So let me get this straight," he said, slowly and carefully, "you can do magic?"

"I suppose so, yes. Though I don't think it's like that. It's not deliberate; it's more like an instinct thing, a reaction, like catching a ball that's thrown at you or something. I can't do it on command." She thought of Loatheworthy and the mousetrap. "Well, not much anyway."

David shook his head. "And you're sure you're not a hypnotist, I thought you might be a hypnotist." He brightened suddenly, "Or perhaps you drugged me. Did you drug me?"

"No. I don't think so. You saw it happen, and it was real."

And so he had. It was irrefutable. He thought of himself holding the cartridges in his hand in the Head's office, lucid and fully aware. If this were some psychotic delusion, then it was one that he shared.

A question occurred to him, and he found that he almost did not want to ask it, since he was sure that it could not have a reassuring answer.

"How do you think it got into your room?"

Helen looked down at the table surface; clearly, this was a difficult subject.

"I think I put it there."

"Right. I take it you don't mean that you stashed it there after... after using it elsewhere?"

"No, no. I think I wished it there. It probably started life as something else. I've been having these little daydreams - harmless enough, you know, like I said, and a lot of them involved shooting Loatheworthy, but I never thought *this* would happen."

She repeated the movement he had seen earlier - covering her eyes with the heels of her hands. "I can't believe it. A *gun*, in a school. When I think of what might have happened. I'm so *stupid*."

David was watching her soberly and tracing the initials in the stock of the gun (now a plastic sham again) with one finger; he had spent a good deal of time that afternoon puzzling over those initials.

"There might be a more... ordinary explanation."

Helen looked up at him; tears had magnified her eyes slightly.

"Do you know who M.H. is? Does that mean anything to you?"

She thought. "No, nothing."

"Doesn't it seem a little odd that you would conjure up a gun and put initials on it which mean nothing to you?"

"Maybe it's something subconscious."

"Maybe. Or maybe the gun belongs to someone else who just happened to stash it in your classroom - maybe Loatheworthy himself? If he put the dope in the desk, why not a gun in the cupboard? Did he try to look there this afternoon? Did he behave strangely?"

"Well, yes, he was more twitchy than ever, I suppose. He asked me what I knew, but I put that down to the dope." She looked hopeful. "Maybe it was him, and I just turned the gun."

David sat back in his chair, also wanting to believe it.

"Saving one of those kids from a very nasty end." He regarded her gravely, indicating the toy with his coffee cup. "You think it will change back?"

"I don't know. The sock did, more than once, but it wears off eventually."

"We can't take it to the police for the moment then, even if we were sure that Loatheworthy did put it there. Not unless you want to end up in some secret Home-Office lab."

She scanned his expression for a sign of flippancy, and was disconcerted not to find it.

They sat in silence for a moment, then David took a deep breath. This was it, it was time; he was about to wade into some very deep water, but he had to know.

"Do you ever have blackouts?"

Helen looked genuinely bewildered- "Blackouts?"

"Lost time. Bits of days... or nights, that you don't really remember?"

She answered immediately, and with conviction-

"No. What... Why do you ask?"

David reached back into the bag that had contained the gun, and drew out his wall chart. It was curling at the edges, trying to roll up, and so Helen could not immediately see it; but she caught sight of her own image at its centre, and became very still as he managed to spread it on the table before her.

Her eyes roved across it, reading the text, following the red, accusatory lines. There was silence. David could hear the ponderous ticking of a clock, perhaps in an upstairs room.

Eventually she looked up and spoke.

"So you've been spying on me, from the start?"

"Yes. I mean no," he said miserably. "Not spying. Not from the start. I mean, only after a while, and I... It's the way my mind is. I couldn't help it."

"You *were*," she said, sounding surprised. "There's no magazine article, is there? You *were*. As if it's not bad enough being inspected at work, I'm being Ofsteded in my life. And you thought... you really thought that I killed those inspectors. You think I'm a killer."

David glanced down at the table. Pushed to one side, the sock seemed to be regarding him with open-mouthed shock and not a little disdain.

"Well what was I supposed to think?" He gestured towards the chart as if it were proof of some kind. "The Hoover pipe? The roses? And you could never tell me exactly where you were on those nights? And then you tell me that you fantasise about an inspector falling into an open sewer and *dying*? You admitted yourself, you've daydreamed about shooting him. What was I supposed to think?"

Her tone conveyed a gentle wonderment.

"Didn't you just *know*? Couldn't you just *tell* that I don't spend my spare time whacking civil servants?"

"Yes," David said in exasperation. "Think! At the school. Yesterday. Think what happened. I was just about to tell you what I'd been thinking... so we could laugh about it." Again, he glanced down at the chart. "Obviously I wasn't going to show you this, and that would have made it funnier. But then you suddenly insist that we break into the school, and inside we find trays of *Fermaxipan*. But I didn't call the police or anything. You needed help, and I believed you, but now… "

"Now?" she prompted, her tone leading and deadly.

David nodded at the plastic gun. "Well now things are even weirder still. What if you *are* doing it, without knowing it, say? Maybe you're leading a double life, a split personality thing? Or you block it out, or… something."

He ran out of steam before her increasingly icy stare, but didn't look away. Helen blinked first - the tiniest moment of confusion, of self-doubt, arrived and just as quickly dispatched. It seemed to fuel her anger-

"I trusted you, David."

"I know, but if you could just see it from my point of view, then you'd see."

"I don't have blackouts, or a split personality, and I didn't kill anyone. Our Hoover has always had missing parts; everyone's Hoover has missing parts. The roses probably ended up in a vase somewhere, and I couldn't give you alibis because I didn't know I was going to need them. You *lied* to me." There was a finality in her tone. "I'd like you to leave now, please."

David rolled his eyes. "God, talk about the pot calling the kettle black. You hid a few things from me too."

Her expression did not soften, and he saw that for now he was going to get nowhere. He found his coat, put it on with swift jerky motions then scooped up the plastic gun, and dumped it unceremoniously back into the canvas bag.

"Why are you taking that?"

"Because if Loatheworthy *did* plant it, it's not safe to leave it here, is it?" he said, scowling, and stepped into the hallway. Helen followed, matching his expression, and wrenched open the front door. Just past the threshold he half turned, perhaps making a conciliatory gesture.

"Calm down and then call me," he said. "We need to... " But that was too much, and she slammed the door and it cut his sentence in half.

Helen stood, breathing hard, staring at the infuriatingly featureless door, but the feeling of such a meagre victory piqued her anger once again. Calm down, *calm down!* He had admitted to suspecting her of being a murderer, had lied to her, gathered information on her. Worse still, he had made her wonder for the merest fraction of a second - *was it possible, could she have?* No, she had clear memories of Friday evening, and of the other crucial evenings, they did not involve murdering anything more sentient than a pizza - and now he wanted her to calm down.

With the comforting weight of the toadstool back in her palm she wrenched the front door open. David was a shadow out on the street.

"You're as bad as Loatheworthy," she shouted, "I'm *glad* I hit you with the gate."

There was little chance that it would reach him, so she heaved the toadstool at him with all of her might. It sailed high and wider than she meant, and she winced as it bounced off the bonnet of a car on the other side of the road.

David traced the toadstool's trajectory in surprise, watching it bounce and land on a grass verge. A streetlight flickered.

"We'll talk later," he said, and then moved off down the street. Helen watched him until he was out of sight, willing him to turn and come back, to give her a chance to say more, but his figure was soon soaked up by the tendrils of mist.

She looked up and down the street, unable to see far. She felt a building nervousness, as if she were facing a big examinations for which she had not prepared, a feeling that something was poised, ready to play out badly unless she could act to save the situation.

Across the road she could see a neighbour peering out at her from beneath the corner of a curtain; the toadstool would have to lie wherever it had fallen. She stared fiercely at the triangle of yellow light until it disappeared, and then went inside herself.

Loatheworthy sat in his car with the efficient climate control system switched off, enduring the cold, his face leant deep and ghoulish shadows by the green glow of dashboard readouts. He smelled of kerosene, his eyebrows and moustache were considerably smaller and slightly more charcoally than of late, there was soot on his cheeks and in his crow's-nest hair, and brown burned patches marked the shins of his trousers.

Late that afternoon, Loatheworthy had had himself an enormous bonfire in his back garden. He had burned any and all paperwork that might link him to events which could be considered even slightly questionable, including purloined school records bearing Martin Hall's name. For good measure he had also burned much paperwork which definitely did not link him to anything even slightly questionable, his tool shed, most of his garden fence on one side, and a picture of himself, his wife, and her mother, which usually hung in the dining room.

After that, he had begun to feel slightly more calm.

Now at least he was sure that he was unobserved, unless the teacher had managed to place a bug inside his car somewhere. He had put the car through the car wash earlier, eleven times, hoping that this might provide some protection, and it now gleamed reproachfully. He had also searched his clothes, his shoes, and his increasingly resentful wife for listening devices, but with no success. Then he had realised that the picture he had seen in Haversham's classroom was drawn from far away, not from the angle a tiny camera would provide; there must have been a watcher - someone tailing him and photographing him on Tuesday evening.

On Loatheworthy's knee sat his clipboard - his favourite and most faithful piece of equipment. On it sat a thin sheaf of teacher assessment forms which he was modifying as he sat and watched Haversham's kitchen, taking each, and rulering-in extra columns on one side.

He was grinning a sooty grin - he had some special categories to add to Haversham's teaching record. Oh yes.

As he drew his calming parallel lines, the scene in her classroom played out again and again in his mind.

The picture. It was the picture that bothered him most, for the picture implied proof of what he had done. Anyone but Loatheworthy would have walked past it without a second look - a child's (albeit a demented child's) pastoral: a field at night with a scarecrow, a jolly moon, a grey blob, and some stick figures. But Loatheworthy drove around in that particular grey blob; and he knew that one of those stick figures was standing almost ankle-deep in a heap of manure, and was about to hand the other a reasonably large sum of money.

Someone must have followed him into that field.

So, what was next?

Prison a voice in his head supplied with a worryingly insectile giggle, *and probably a man named Big Ron in the shower block.*

In the extremity of his feeling, Loatheworthy's fear seemed to have developed this voice of its own - a high-pitched, insane voice, which he associated with a certain winged insect ingested long ago. He rulered in another line; his ash-smeared fingers trembled slightly and the line wasn't quite straight.

I know everything...

She knows everything. Everything!..

'*How often do you add things?*' the child had asked. *Horrible Horace Hall... eating some most delicious flies, yum yum...*

Or was that coincidence? How could she know about Fly Day? Had she spoken to someone from Argle? Or was his penchant for consuming six-legged fauna far more widely known than he had anticipated?

And how does she know Hall's name? The voice asked in a helium-washed tone. *Name! How does she know his name if she's not in cahoots with him somehow?*

Twice Loatheworthy had tried to call Hall's rancid flat from Hornby's only payphone and got no answer. This was ominous. She must have turned Hall somehow, probably with money. But what did she want? If she sought to ruin him, she could have done that already. No, she must have something even more devious planned, something awful, something so grotesquely foul that he could not even imagine it. All he could do was wait. The intricacy of that afternoon's performance, of working each piece of knowledge so carefully into her teaching, suggested that Haversham possessed a profoundly disturbed and devious mind. Once again he was undone, thwarted, his situation all-but desperate.

At the end of another wobbly line, he caught his own red-rimmed, squinting gaze in the rear view mirror. He could not quite believe that he had been so utterly and completely outwitted by a primary school teacher, and so quickly. He had come here to try to bargain with her, or to learn something to his advantage, to gain *some* leverage that he could use. But there was nothing.

He had been sitting in the cold for too long now, and what he had taken as a gradual swell in the density of the mist outside - a Holmesian effect - was in fact his breath gently fogging the BMW's windows. Soon he would be completely closed in.

Loatheworthy reached out to open the passenger side window slightly, to clear things, and noticed there, scrawled in a hurried child-like hand, revealed by the building condensation, the words 'Loatheworthy is a Tosser!' He stared at the message, taken aback. It must have been one of those disgusting children, one of *her* class. He glanced at the house again, half expecting to see her looking at him and laughing, but all he saw was faint movement in the kitchen. He reached up impatiently to cuff the words away, and then drew his arm back, frowning.

The message had been written in the condensation - that meant it was on the *inside* of the window. Only he and his *wife* (and occasionally, when it was absolutely unavoidable, Barbara Willis) ever rode *in* the car.

Angrily he smeared the message away. Behind him Haversham's door opened and spilled light across her sideway and a thin young man was ejected into the night.

Who was he?

Drug squad mate. Waiting to take you to chokey. Hellooo Big Ron.

Loatheworthy reached for the ignition key, spilling his clipboard onto the floor as the man began to walk up the driveway towards him. The key felt slick beneath his fingers, impossible to turn. His breath stopped in his throat and the only movement in his chest now came from his heart, beating a thready, fear-soaked rhythm.

All was lost. Somehow Haversham knew his exact whereabouts at all times, and was now springing yet another trap. He hunched down further, fully expecting the man to approach, show him a concealed badge, and drag him from his car, but he simply turned right and began to walk away up the street.

Slowly, Loatheworthy relaxed, and let out a pent-up breath. Whoever he was, he hadn't even glanced in the BMW's direction. His earlier impression had been right. They had no idea that he was sitting here watching them. His paranoid fantasies of armies of watchers, hordes of listening devices, and the entire nation having access to detailed records of the minutiae of his life took one step backwards; perhaps she was just a teacher after all.

Haversham's front door opened again, and this time the woman herself stepped out onto the drive. She seemed to be saying something unintelligible to the man, and Loatheworthy finally did open his window slightly, to press his advantage and hear what she was saying.

The window motor hummed. He cocked his ear upwards.

" ...Loatheworthy!" Haversham bellowed, and then threw some kind of missile at him with a hefty overarm lob. Instinctively Loatheworthy covered his head with his arms, emitting a terrified squeak, as something long and grey (a grenade?) sailed through the cold night air and bounced from the car's bonnet, leaving a dent.

The street was quiet for a long time.

When Loatheworthy found that he could breathe again, and was sure that whatever Helen had thrown, it was not going to explode, he uncovered his head and peered around himself. The street was empty; the man was gone, Haversham was gone, and all the lights at the front of the house were extinguished.

He glanced around furtively, still sweating. A car turned the corner and begun slowly making its way towards him, careful in the frosty conditions, splashing light on the road from its fog lamps. Loatheworthy hunkered down again, hoping for concealment. It worked, and the car - a silver Jaguar filled with large dark shapes - passed by with barely a look at the BMW, and parked further up the street.

As quickly as he could, and with fingers that shook violently, Loatheworthy started his own car's engine, and abandoned Haversham's house to the night.

#

At the school the shadows were moving. Mister Tribble watched with great interest as a faint change in the light moved slowly past the closed door of Helen's class, and then on towards the staffroom. A definite shuffling sound could be heard (step - swish, step - swish), as if someone were determinedly dragging a sack, which was bulky but not heavy, towards some unknowable errand. Mister Tribble turned and wrinkled his nose at the room's only other halfway sentient being - the purple tyrannosaurus rex model which stared out into the dark and empty air with wide-eyed intensity - but it declined to comment.

Eventually the figure reached the staffroom again, unlocked the tiny room within and set to work, humming gently and cheerily under its breath. Within half an hour the job was done, the bag of equipment was empty, and the new thing sparkled and glittered, taking in even the tiniest traces of light in the dim room and throwing them back made wondrous with a hint of red, or green, or gold. It needed something else, a found thing, something random like the flip-flops, or the sink plunger. The figure quickly found what it was looking for, and there was the scrinch of sticky tape unrolled and deployed with enthusiasm and speed.

Following in the footsteps of a thousand people across Hornby decorating their homes over the last three weeks, the shadowy figure then stood back to admire its handiwork, and a sense of festive contentment dawned in its heart.

#

Helen awoke with jarring suddenness, half-sitting, leaving behind a thin and unsatisfying doze. She had dreamed that she *was* the killer, and had stalked through the darkened school with a shining weapon. Creeping up on some unsuspecting figure, with disconcerting deadliness, she had raised the weapon high, then woke. Disoriented, she glanced around her room, feeling that everything - her night-stand, the bulky wardrobe, her bookcases - might have jumped several inches into the air and landed with an unearthly crash. Her heart was beating fast.

Some noise had surely brought her from sleep. Was it the phone? Had Marie returned early? She listened, trying to pick it up again, then sank back onto her pillows. She was confused. Echoes of her dream played in her mind, and she felt great and absolving relief. The dream was absurd, and she knew it.

It was late, 1:10 by the ghostly green readout of her clock radio. The pillow was warm, her eyelids began to close, and so she was drowsing when she heard it again: a definite noise in the darkness. Downstairs, probably in the hallway, there was the discreet tinkle of someone carefully breaking glass.

Another noise now, more slight: an unpleasantly deliberate cracking sound. That could be someone picking glass shards out of a window frame before reaching through it. Helen sat up, fully awake now, the duvet pooling in her lap, and glanced at the nightstand again; her mobile phone was downstairs.

The noise went on, stealthy and deliberate, and she could feel panic trying to root her to the spot. To stave it off she slipped as quietly as possible out of bed and stood in the chilly room blinking owlishly. At least she had wakened quickly, forewarned, as if some internal radar had been set up and then tripped. Was there anything she could use as a weapon? Should she call out? No, that would confirm her presence.

Someone was fiddling with the front door lock now, twisting the handle from side to side. She could simply stand and scream, that would at least satisfy her panic, but it might not frighten whoever it was away, and she couldn't be sure that anyone would hear her, or if they did, whether they would respond.

On the back of her door hung her old brown playground-duty coat - faithful friend and trapper of Ofsted inspectors. She was shivering now, and its fur-lined hood had a friendly comforting look. From downstairs came the rattle of the safety chain - leaving only one bolt to be opened - then they would be able to simply push the door and walk straight in. She took the parka down from its peg and slid into it. It was at least a size too big for her, but somehow it gave her confidence, and, wishing that she had worn something more substantial to bed than PJ's (full combat dress, perhaps), she began to look around for something else. Under the bed she found her battered *Reeboks* and slipped them on, with no socks they felt cold and odd on her feet.

Someone, standing at the foot of her stairs, giggled: a high-pitched sound lacking merriment. There was someone *inside* her house, uninvited, a stranger (as the children would say), a strange laugh.

A deeper voice spoke now, indistinct, but something in the tone suggested that it was giving instructions. Helen put her hands in her pockets, searching for something useful, but her Swiss army knife was in her other coat, now hanging in the hallway. Here she found only tissues and an old glue-stick with glitter on the end. She imagined defending herself with this (*don't come near me, I'll use it... I'll glue you, don't think I won't*) then shook her head.

Silence from downstairs, a dangerous silence, tempting her to believe that they might have gone away. She stared at the bedroom door; there wasn't even a vanity lock. Why couldn't she have been out this evening?

An idea struck her, and if she had had more time to think it over she might have dismissed it as absurd, but even now the silence was broken as the kitchen floorboards began to creak. The next thing to try would be the stairs.

Helen moved quickly to the bed, almost on tiptoe, the ancient trainers helping to mask the sound of her footsteps across the room, re-spread the duvet and fluffed the pillows. She glanced around. There were a few things out of place, but nothing that mightn't have been left overnight. Other rooms in the house would probably look less tidy. She went to the window and slowly eased it open, knowing that the metal frame sometimes creaked.

She was greeted by the kind of still and intense cold that does not need the wind to spread it around, and her fingers instantly began to go numb. Her bedroom, the largest of the three, faced the back of the house, and there was nothing at the end of the garden except scrappy waste ground, then, higher up, a bank, the road, and fields. The garden was empty. Somewhere far off a dog barked twice and fell silent. The living room, which was also at the back of the house, had French doors and a large bay window with a gently sloping roof which jutted out before her. Looking at it now, it seemed further down and set at a steeper angle than she had remembered.

A noise on the stairs behind her forced her into action; they were coming.

She swung one leg over the sill and felt for the tiles of the bay with her foot. She had to lean out further than she would have liked, almost to the point of overbalancing, but then she felt the mossy roof under her toes, and managed to swing her other leg and body out, the parka rustling against the window frame.

She turned and crouched, hugging the freezing brickwork and saw a thin band of illumination appear at the bottom of her bedroom door - someone had switched on the hall light. Not a hallucination then, but a real break-in. Almost too late she realised that the window was still open.

The door handle rattled.

Helen reached up with her right hand, eyes wide, holding her breath, and in a single swift movement pushed the window closed, wincing as it creaked slightly. She ducked again, almost losing her footing as her bedroom door inched open.

Had the door opened quickly enough for the intruder to see her?

In the still air she could hear every sound clearly; footsteps moved into the room, four, five, a heavy tread, then stillness. She bit her lip. Would they sense that something was wrong in this room, its emptiness a sham? Other steps entered, lighter, but equally deliberate.

"Anything?"

"No Boss."

Helen didn't recognise either voice. Her mind, still teetering on the edge of panic, echoed the little interchange for her over and over at high speed. Neither voice was Loatheworthy's; could it be someone he had hired?

"Any shine of the shtuff?"

"No."

"What about the bag?"

"Nothing Boss, should we search?"

Now footsteps approached the window. Helen tried to get closer to the wall, to tuck herself in so that she would be hidden beneath the sill, but it was impossible.

"She'sh not in the other roomsh either. I thought you shaid she wash definitely here."

"She was. She must have left some time after that skinny bloke. Maybe by a back way?"

"Shearch. Make shure she's not hiding or shomething. And find that shtuff." The voice was much closer to Helen now, louder, obliterating her ability to think. She had the absurd urge to stand up, lean in through the window and tap the smaller man on the shoulder.

"When you've shearched the houshe, wait here for a couple of hoursh, she if you can shurprishe her."

A silence, then, "Now listen Bosh, er .. Boss, scum like Martin is one thing, but I ain't ruffin' up no primary school teacher, and that's that."

Helen froze, now not even breathing.

After another pause 'Boss' left the window's side and she had the impression that the figures had drawn together.

"*You* won't have to. Jusht keep her here until I arrive. I... I need to know what she'sh sheen."

The other man grunted noncommittally.

"She *shtole* from ush Bob, her and that moron Hall. I've... I've done shome thingsh... I'm working *hard* to be taken sheriously and I *will* be taken sheriously. How long do you think our bushinesh would lasht if word got out that you could shteal from ush and get away with it? You'd be unemployed in daysh. *Then* what would your mishesh do, eh, and the kidsh? How would you buy dreshesh?"

Another grunt, this one more committal.

"I thought sho. Shearch, and then wait."

Footsteps crossed the room and then her door closed. After a few moments there was a creak as her wardrobe was slowly opened. Helen breathed again, white vapour rising into the murky night air. What should she do? She couldn't stay here, one of them was sure to come out to the garden eventually and see her - the world's largest weirdest-dressed spider - clinging to the wall. Go to a neighbour? Yes, that was it - safety - go to a neighbour, lock the door, phone the police from there.

Bob's heavy tread moved to the centre of her room again. Had he seen her breath rising over the sill? If only she'd thought to re-close the curtains. She held her breath again, waiting for him to move away, but he didn't. What on earth was he doing? She started to get cramp in her calves and shifted her position slightly to ease the tension. Too late she felt a loose tile pop out from under her foot and she jerked forwards slightly, almost bumping her nose on the wall before her. Dislodged, the tile skidded down the angle of the roof, making a faint clattering sound. She looked over her shoulder, her view half-obscured by her hair, and followed its descent, hoping that it would stick somewhere. It didn't.

The tile hit the guttering rail and then turned end over end, falling into the night. Helen closed her eyes and hunched her shoulders, waiting for the crash as it shattered on the patio, bringing the intruders on the run; but it did not come.

When she was sure that gravity should have done its work, she craned further over her shoulder. One of the large patio containers, which in the summer held fuchsias and geraniums, and which she had been meaning to drag into the shed for weeks, had sprouted a small orange perennial roof-tile.

There was movement from her room again. Towards her? No, away, and then the sound of drawers opening. That meant that 'Bob' was on the opposite side of the bed, as far from the window as he was going to get. Helen looked over her shoulder again, it seemed a long way down, but it was now or never.

Wary of more loose tiles she turned around so that her back was to the house. It was maybe two or three feet to the edge, then ten feet straight past the window. Thankfully she *had* closed the living room curtains. It looked relatively easy, she was five-six tall, which meant a drop of a few feet if she did it right.

Behind her Bob closed one drawer and opened another; soon he would be finished.

Helen crawled to the edge of the roof, feeling slimy moss under her palms, turned again, and before she could lose her nerve, swung one leg and then the other over the edge. The parka caught on the guttering and she had to wriggle until it freed itself. She paused to get her breath, her upper body still on the roof, and then shifted her weight again and slid neatly out over the bay window. The parka ruffled and made enough friction to prevent a straight drop, saving her shoulders from damage. Her pointed toes bounced lightly against the living-room window glass and then, when she was at full stretch, the edge of the guttering came away in her fingers and she dropped to the patio below, landing badly on one knee and missing the plant container (complete with roof-tile) by inches.

Her fall was noisy, but no face appeared at the window above her, and she forced herself to get up and limp to the edge of the sideway. After her adventures that evening she had not closed the garden gate, and the small square of Mrs Grimmer's doorway that she could see over the fence seemed very inviting. The old woman's house was dark, though, and she was deaf, and her doorway (at the top of two steps) could be clearly seen over the fence from Helen's own. It was a risk.

She decided to try anyway and moved to the shoulder of the house, leaning there.

She had taken her first step into the sideway, her heart racing, preparing to run on her toes through to the front garden, when there was a sudden splash of light from her hallway: someone had switched on the downstairs light, and the door was open.

She struggled to halt her forward momentum, and her trainers crunched on the concrete. There was a long shadow now in the cone of light cast through the doorway. It was tall, gantry-like, growing ever larger. Helen stared at it, rapt, and then turned tale and fled back the way she had come, not caring now whether she made a noise or not.

The garden was a long one and sloped downhill. She pelted across the damp lawn, feeling water spray upwards with each footstep and soak her ankles. She ran towards the back fence, unable to hear what was happening behind her; unable to tell whether the thumping she could feel was simply her heartbeat, or heavy pursuing footsteps. She reached the back fence - a five-foot-high ageing monstrosity - and leapt at it, reaching for its top, gripping the damp, splintery wood. It was too high to boost herself over in one go, and so she placed her foot on a damaged slat, and hoped that it wouldn't give way. It didn't, and she gained enough height to swing one leg over and sit astride the fence, shooting a quick glance over her shoulder.

The lawn was empty. From the direction of the house, she heard a voice, indistinct - perhaps a reply to an unheard question. She thought she heard the word 'garden' and possibly 'cat', and that was enough to make her tumble unceremoniously from the fence and land, winded, amongst the matted grass and blackberry bushes on the other side.

She recovered and peered through the slats, strangely eager to glimpse her pursuer, oblivious to her scratches. Eventually he arrived, and again she could only see a shadow, an outline dimmed by the mist, standing on her tufted lawn with his hands in his jacket pockets looking from left to right.

She became morbidly certain that whoever it was, he was now staring straight at her, and he could somehow see her through the fence. When the figure began to stride across the lawn towards her, she again turned and fled.

Snoopy stood in the doorway of Helen's room, just before the jamb, seething with frustration at missing his quarry and watching Bob with interest. Unaware of his presence the larger man had taken a blue-green strappy summer dress from Helen's wardrobe and was standing in front of its mirrored door with a dreamy look in his eyes. He held the dress up before his considerable frame with one hand at its waist, so that when he moved left and right the skirt swished prettily.

Finally sensing someone at the door, but without turning his head, he said, "Whadya think Don? Oh sorry Boss, I was just, just... er... "

"What are you doing Robert?"

The larger man stood more to attention, the dress still held before him.

"Er, searching Boss."

"Shearching."

"Yes Boss. Thought there might be something important in the dress, y'know, hidden like."

Snoopy eyed his henchman. "Do I look shtupid Bob?"

Bob's colossal brow wrinkled as he paused for just longer than was necessary, considering the question carefully.

"No Boss?"

"No. No I do not. But you do Bob."

Bob looked slightly hurt.

"You do Bob, becaush you are a sicksh-foot four, eighteen shtone man wondering how he would look in a party frock. I've warned you about thish shtuff before." Snoopy drew closer. "You're a bloody *henchman*, you're meant to be frightening, terrifying, *not intriguing yet provocative IN AN OFF THE SHOULDER COCKTAIL DRESH!"*

Bob considered mentioning that the garment he held was actually casual wear, saw the spit shining on his boss's lips and the capillaries standing out in his cheeks, and decided against it. Instead he laid the dress almost reverently on Helen's bed and continued his search. When he judged that Snoopy had calmed down slightly, he said, "I don't know why you have a problem Boss. Shirley and the kids are fine about the whole thing. This *is* the twenty-first century." He paused, and then said, almost musingly, as if the thought had just occurred to him, "Perhaps you've got a bit o' that gender confusion yourself Boss?"

Suddenly Snoopy's face, almost glowing with rage, was very close to Bob's.

"I am in no way confewshed." He spat each word out through gritted teeth, then seemed to realise that he might just be protesting too much and backed off. "I jusht exshpect a little profeshionalishm." He lowered his tone. "When I go to the Cashino, all the other gangstersh *laugh* at me - they think I'm funny, and do you know *why*?" He didn't wait for an answer. "It'sh becaush you are alwaysh letting the shide down."

"That's not fair Boss, it's not always me. Remember when Donald contracted ergotism, got naked at the football match, and chased those people? Remember? That was embarrassing. And then he, y'know, he painted his er... painted his private parts blue and pushed them through the Chief Constable's letterbox? And we eventually found him in the main sewer? Said he was waiting for the Smurfs to clear the streets so that he could go up and take his rightful place as King?"

Snoopy's eyes had glazed. "Yesh," he said quietly, "I remember."

There was a noise at the top of the stairs and Donald bounded in. Bob tried to maintain his enthusiastic tone, hoping that it would be infectious. "Remember the Smurfs Don?"

The smile left Don's face. "Always. Always," he said. "I wait for their return, wait for the crowning glory... but they never come... They never come... "

Neither of the other men was sure whether or not Don was joking, until his smile beamed out again, though it never reached his eyes, tiny and bloodshot, perhaps marking them down on a list to be dealt with after the small blue revolution.

"Anything out there Don?"

"Nah. A noise. Probbly a cat." He eyed the frock on the bed and glanced up at Bob, who coughed and closed the wardrobe door. Don's faint smile resurfaced and he raised his eyebrows questioningly.

"That's never your colour Bobby. You need something lower-cut, frillier. Make a stronger statement."

"D'you think so. Even I wasn't sure about the colour... "

"Shut up! Shut up you pair of *barshtards*."

Snoopy reached down and picked up the dress, tried to tear it, found that he couldn't, and instead scrunched it into a ball and threw it into the corner. He turned back to them, about to say something, when a realisation dawned in his face.

He reached down to the bed again, his hand caressed the pillow, then slowly reached under the duvet.

"Have you been in thish bed Bob?"

"No Boss, who'd you think I am Goldilocks?"

"Well shomeone hash, becaush it's shtill warm."

"Well she's definitely not in the house Boss, been everywhere."

Snoopy moved to the window and pushed at the glass - it swung open easily - and he looked out and down, towards the back fence, his gaze almost feral.

"A cat, eh? If you two don't buck your ideash up, I will have to kill you. Do you undershtand?"

Any jocularity departed. Both men nodded.

"You followed that bloke thish evening?"

"Yeah," Bob replied meekly. "He went to a house in Woodcroft Road."

"Right. Get the car. Thatsh where we're going."

Helen reached Horseshoe Road and allowed herself to stop by a lamp-post, her breath rasping, a stitch flaring in her side. She leant against the cold concrete and steel, her vision clouding, and she wondered vaguely if she were about to throw up. Eventually she recovered, and still breathing hard, turned to look behind her.

Was that a figure in the mist, a shape?

She squinted, cold sweat ran into her eyes; it was almost impossible to tell, but the urge to flee was strong. She obeyed it, walking now, quickly, almost trotting. She was trying to remember where there might be a phone-box, but such information was denied to her tired mind, and she kept moving; her feet seemed to have already plotted a course.

When she arrived at the next corner, that of Elm and Woodcroft, she realised where she was going: David's house, it was closest.

The houses on Woodcroft were Victorian, built for a grander age when commuting to the University from Hornby had been the preserve of the don with country pretensions, rather than that of the poorer students. The houses were twisted and gabled, four and five stories if you counted rooms in cellars and attics, and they seemed to loom over her. She reached number seven and tried to decide what to do. Should she ring the bell this late? No, that would bring unwelcome questions.

The house was tall with a high-peaked roof and a facade of sandy coloured brick which showed as a livid yellow under the streetlights. White-painted window frames surrounded high imposing rectangles of glass which grew into arches at the attic level. One of these was opaque, perhaps a bathroom window, and it gave the house an elderly, suspicious aspect, as if it peered at her with only one uncataracted eye.

She listened; the night was no longer quiet. Somewhere out in the mist, and drawing closer, she could hear a car moving at low speed, creeping towards her along the kerbside.

David sat at his desk, his head resting on Helen's picture, caught in the central web of his outspread and now crumpled wall chart. It was late and he drifted gently in the hypnotic shallows of pre-sleep.

Strange images chased each other through his mind:

Helen, pointing at the gun and saying, 'toy'; the cartridges, real in his hand...

He found that he accepted what he had seen as an established, solid and undeniable fact. This was strange in itself, miraculous but comforting. It was as if a knowledge of Helen's alchemical ability was as commonplace as knowing that she had brown eyes, or liked jelly beans. It seemed in some way natural, as if he had always known it. Perhaps, he reflected lazily, at some base level, everyone already believed his or her partner to be in some way magical.

Helen, glancing away from him, a flicker of uncertainty in her expression. The picture of the diving inspector, with the sink-plunger securely stuck on the top of his head...

Did this new information make it more or less likely that she was a fiendish killer? That was the thing. Could she wish up a syringe brim-full of fermented *Fermaxipan* at just the right moment? Again, his mind went around in a loop, pitting evidence against his belief that she couldn't have done such a thing. She was innocent, she had told him so, and that should be enough.

These thoughts chased each other around and around his head, slowing and speeding, darting and suddenly halting like the fake fish in his tank. He was tired of them and fascinated by them at once. There was something important about the diving inspector with the plunger, some odd link to this image that would not come to him, and so his thoughts circled it, looping and swimming on then looping again. They stopped abruptly when a percussive noise roused him.

He sat up as it happened again. Something rattled on his window frame. What was that? A crazed bat? A stone? Really small hard rain?

It happened for a third time, hitting the glass with a dull and dangerous-sounding thud, then someone hissed his name. Still not seeing straight, he made his way over to the window; the fake fish eyed him nervously.

There appeared to be a dishevelled talking womble out on the pavement.

"David," it hissed, peering up at him, "wake *up*. David!" Its voice was horribly loud in the soundless mist.

David grabbed his glasses from the desk and put them on. It was Helen, bundled up in her ridiculously oversized coat. He felt absurdly pleased to see her. As he watched she took a step backwards and looked to her right, ducking, trying to see through the mist, as if she were being pursued. He pushed the window open and leaned out.

"Shhhh," he said. She looked at him blankly from under the fur of the coat's hood.

"I'm not going to murder you. Let me in."

David shook his head in gentle exasperation-

"Wait for me in the porch."

A large car turned into Woodcroft Road and David saw the fuzzy outline of headlights way off in the distance. Helen also seemed to have seen this, and moved quickly up the short garden path. David closed his window again, then stood very still and listened.

Nothing inside; not a creak. Hopefully Gibble was also sleeping; her bedroom was at the back of the house, so perhaps they had gotten away with it.

He looked around at his room, his eye lighting on his pile of Ofsted murders research. On top of it there now lay the remnants of a two-day-old toasted cheese sandwich sitting forlornly on its plate. He scooped up notes and sandwich and shoved both into his wardrobe, then moved to his door and listened again: still nothing. The house was deathly quiet; even the ancient central heating system had stopped its infernal ticking and clunking for the night. He felt an urge to hurry.

David had lived in the house for three years, and thought that he knew where all of the creaky floorboards and springy stair risers lay, yet his progress to the door sounded like the strings section of an orchestra tuning up for the Proms. Finally he reached the long hallway, and he could see Helen waiting behind the coloured glass of the worst test of all: the vintage front door.

He slid back three bolts, painfully aware that from her second floor eyrie Gibble could be on them in seconds, then turned the door handle cautiously and pulled, moving the huge door through its creak-zone as quickly as possible. When he had a gap of perhaps eighteen inches, he peered through.

Helen stood on the doorstep looking worried and bedraggled. The mist had soaked into her hair, muddying its colour and plastering it to her forehead, and in the darkness her face seemed pale, her eyes wide and bright. There was a tiny scratch below her right eye and a small tear in the knee of her trousers (which, he noticed with surprise, were decorated with small teddy bears wearing nightshirts and nightcaps).

"David, for God's sake let me in there's... mmp MMP!"

He had reached out through the doorway and laid his palm across her mouth.

"We have to be quiet. You know my landlady's a... a difficult woman." He peered over his shoulder down the long hallway. "I think she's one of those Nazis who escaped to Brazil for a while after the war."

Helen glared at him over his hand and he took it away, "Sorry." He pulled her inside and went through the ritual of re-closing the door.

Helen tried again, "In my house, there were these "

From above them, there sounded a long and ominously stealthy creak. David winced, and they both stood, listening. No clamour arose, no sound of footsteps, and no shrewish voice called. Behind them a car pulled into the kerb-side, cruising past, and moonish headlights slowly washed a diffused silvery light about the hall.

They stared at each other in the glow. A car door slammed and there were muted voices, then nothing. David pointed once to the stairway and began to move towards it through intricate, stained-glass shadows. After a few moments of silence, Helen went to the front door, nervous of it, unwilling to stand in the light for too long, and tried to rattle it. With its three bolts drawn again, the door did not move; it was far sturdier than her own.

A little heartened, Helen followed David upstairs.

#

The only alcohol David had in his rooms turned out to be a bottle of Strega that he had brought back from Italy two summers before. Some of the liquor had evaporated, leaving delicious sugary peaks around the neck of the bottle, but it was still over half full, and Helen sat on his bed, sipping from a coffee mug. She had locked herself in his bathroom, cleaned up slightly, and changed her womble-coat and soggy P.J.'s for a pair of David's jeans (which she had had to roll up) and a sweatshirt, once red, now faded pink which said 'Doctoral students do it with a meticulous eye for detail.' Both were warm and smelled comfortingly of fabric softener. Slowly, as she told her story, the alcohol and the warmth of the room had calmed her, melting away her post-adrenaline aches and pains and fusing them into a background hum that felt like tiredness.

David was standing in the middle of the room, pointing the handset of a telephone at her. Even at this distance, she could hear the metallic purr of the dial tone.

"But we have to call them, don't you see?" he hissed. "I mean, these people broke into your *house*. We don't have to tell them about... about anything else, but this... this is serious!"

Looking at him now, pale and worried, no longer telling her to calm down, she felt her anger at him melting away. She could even see how he had come to suspect... what he had come to suspect; her behaviour had been odd, and all of the pieces (looked at from the right direction) seemed to fit.

The wall chart was on his desk, and she followed its lines with a fingertip, then giggled a little hysterically. It was absurd, too absurd to take seriously now, characteristically boyish and academic - researching, making a wall-chart - the work of an overactive imagination.

She thought of him taking the plastic gun with him, and before that the bag of mysterious foliage, even though *this* was in his mind. He *had* had her best interests at heart then, even when some part of him suspected that she was a psychotic killing machine.

"What if they arrest me for slaying public servants in highly exotic ways?"

"Well, I er... I. But they... "

"No. No police," she said, calmly, glancing around at the rest of his rooms. There were bean bags, a desk, and an enormous wardrobe. Everywhere there were untidy piles of paperwork and one entire wall was taken up by cheap bookcases, filled and filled again with an eclectic mix of reading, from Kant and Ovid to several *Beano* annuals, and something intriguingly entitled *Miller's Endless Sea of Fuzz*. Retelling what had happened at her house had kindled a certain excitement in her. Loatheworthy, it seemed, had at last made an error that they would be able to exploit.

"But they were obviously dangerous. Really dangerous." David gestured at her with the phone as if something had just struck him. "What if they burglarise you? They could be emptying the entire contents of your house into a big van even as we speak."

Helen considered this. "No. I don't think so. They only seemed interested in me, and in getting their hands on the dope."

"But they, but... "

"Think about it," she said. "I heard them talking, they knew I had it. And they knew that I was a teacher. You and me, and Loatheworthy should be the only ones who *know* about the dope, so he must have sent them."

"Yes, but... "

"Well - if he sent them, if he was willing to risk that, then he *really* wants it back, and believes that he's in trouble somehow, and we've finally got something to bargain with. Maybe he handled it, or it can be traced to him or something. He doesn't know that we've got rid of it, does he?" Her eyes glittered, "You should have seen him yesterday when I said I knew everything... I understand now; and now I finally have something real to threaten him with."

David wondered if her bravado was genuine, or inspired by adrenaline or Strega, or something else... The dial tone clicked off, and was replaced by an automated voice telling him in the slow and calm tones usually reserved for delicate hostage negotiations to please hang-up now.

Helen glanced around herself again. "Anyway, if we call the police now your landlady is sure to be involved, and you'll end up getting evicted."

David's frown deepened. "Now you're just clouding the issue."

"Oh go on - let me threaten him, please? Just verbally. I really want to."

After a further moment's hesitation, during which the automated voice urged him in slightly more firm tones to hang up, he did so and moved back to the window.

"One odd thing though," Helen said, "they seemed to think that I was in league with someone called 'Hall'."

Gingerly David pushed one curtain (now drawn) aside slightly, and peered around it. Outside all he could see was mist and a bright halo of headlights from slightly further up the street, diffused, and fading as it reached the pathways. It looked like a scene from *The Exorcist* out there. He thought he could see shapes - figures - moving, hunched over, but then they were gone. He cupped one palm over his eyes, and tried to see around the light, but the car with its headlights on stayed hidden from his view.

"Do you know who that is?"

When Helen didn't answer, he turned back from the window. She seemed thunderstruck.

"They called him Martin," she said, in a still lower tone. "Martin Hall. *M.H.* That despicable troll *did* put the gun in my room. And I thought that I'd... I can't believe it, a gun with children. I will kill him. Kill him or at least hurt him a lot, that heinous repulsive little stain."

David was looking at her, wide-eyed.

"Oh for God's sake, not *really* kill him. You know, sooner or later they're going to catch the actual Ofsted murderer, and then you're going to owe me a really big apology."

He had the good grace to flush slightly, and looked back through the window to cover it, frowning at his restricted view. "I still think this is far too dangerous. I know how this works. I've read a lot of detective fiction. Drugs and guns, and hired goons. The next thing is more dead bodies. You know? I'm against dead bodies in general, but either of *us* becoming dead - I'd really like to avoid that."

"Me too," Helen replied. "What about this? What if I agree that we phone the police tomorrow - once we're clear of your Brazilian ex-Nazi - and report an ordinary break-in? I mean we can't connect it to Loatheworthy, can we? And as you said, we certainly can't tell them the whole story - toy guns aren't even illegal. Then, in the meantime, I can still get him alone somewhere tomorrow, threaten him, and see what I can get him to say."

David could at least see some sense in that. As he absently dropped the curtain again, there was a long stealthy creak from the hallway. He had time to hold up one hand to signal for quiet, and then three loud raps sounded on the door, which jumped and rattled slightly in its frame. They looked at each other, startled.

Helen glanced at the window - they were three stories up - this time there would be no daredevil escape.

The knock sounded again, then Mrs Gibble hissed righteously from the hallway, "Mister Barclay, open this door at once."

Relieved, David rolled his eyes. He mouthed the word 'landlady' and pointed to the bathroom. Helen nodded and made for the door. Too late, David remembered his bath mitts shaped like Sooty and Sweep and then dismissed them with a mental shrug.

When the bathroom door was safely closed behind him, he put his hands in his hair and messed it up, took off his glasses again and wandered, over-clumsily, to the door.

"What is it?"

"Open the door."

Behind him Helen dived out of the bathroom, grabbed her pile of clothes and the womble coat, and disappeared again.

"Mrs Gibble, it's late, can't we talk in the morning?"

"Open up now, or I'm calling Peter. He has a screwdriver you know."

David backed off, horrified. A screwdriver? He had always thought of Peter as a Stanley-knife man. Then he realised that she meant that he would use it to remove the lock-plate. He looked over his shoulder again, checking the room one last time, then he opened the door a tiny amount, bracing it with his foot, and peeked through at her.

"Mister Barclay, you are aware, I take it, of my rules on visitors, especially of the opposite sex, after seven PM?"

David yawned exaggeratedly. She really was from the dark ages. Did she think that sex was impossible before seven? He looked at her again, his head on one side, and she met his gaze with a sour glare. She looked determined, and that was inconvenient. The last thing they needed was to be turned out onto the street into the waiting arms of whoever it was that Loatheworthy was using to do his dirty work.

"Yes. I know all of your rules Mrs Gibble, but it's late. I need to sleep. What do you want?"

"I want to come in and inspect your rooms."

"There's no one here but me. Now let me sleep."

Her stare increased in intensity and the corners of her mouth turned upwards in what might have been a smile; there was a meagre triumph in her eyes. He suddenly very much regretted his Internet jape.

"I *heard* you talking!" She nodded, as if this proved some heinous crime. Mentally David rolled his eyes. This was going to be difficult.

"I talk in my sleep."

"I suppose you answer in your sleep as well, do you?"

"Yes."

She looked confused, then- "I heard *two* people moving around." Get out of *that* one and play fair, her expression said.

"Probably, er... mice."

"Mice?"

"Well, er... rats actually, huge sods. Size of an Alsatian I'd say. I sometimes think they might drag me off in the night, you know, as a hostage: *bring us cheese or the skinny one gets it.* I left a trap out for them, but they ate it."

Gibble goggled at him. "There are *no* rats in my house! Now let me in or I'm phoning for Peter."

Behind him there was a faint creak. *Oh for God's sake,* David thought, *keep still woman. This is difficult enough without you* confirming *her suspicions.* Then an idea hit him. Quickly, he pulled the door open and Gibble instinctively took a step backwards as he moved through it, then he closed the door securely behind him, and leaned against it. He smiled benevolently. "Oh *bugger*," he said. "What a tragedy, and I've locked my keys inside."

Mrs Gibble's smile widened, and she dipped into the pocket of the horrible housecoat and drew out a large and well-populated key ring. It jingled merrily in her hand.

"Never mind. I have a spare."

She bent towards the lock.

David tried one last time. "Mrs Gibble, I must protest at this intrusion."

"Protest all you like, I'm still coming in."

She turned the key and opened the door with a flourish and a very nasty grin. She had been waiting for this moment for a long time. Down the hall, David could see Geraldine looking up at him resentfully through sleep-clouded eyes. He mouthed 'help me' at her, and she disappeared.

Once inside Gibble moved straight to the bathroom door and rapped on it with her knuckles. So she had known all along, but she couldn't have seen them come in, or he would already be out on the street.

"Hello in there. Let me in."

No answer.

She reached down for the handle.

"Er, Mrs Gibble, we're both adults, is there really any need for... "

She turned it and walked confidently in. "Ah ha!" she said. David closed his eyes, preparing to tell Mrs Gibble that Helen was actually his long lost cousin, or sister. No that would never wash.

When no angry accusations were launched, he opened his eyes, one at a time. Gibble stood in an empty bathroom. He managed to camouflage his own look of surprise as outrage when she turned to him, her finger raised again. "I *know* there's something going on here."

From down the hall there came the sound of rapid and rhythmic squeaking: Geraldine jumping up and down on her bed, David hoped. He suppressed his own grin as Mrs Gibble's shone forth, convinced now that she had misheard, that it was *Geraldine* who was going to end up out on her ear tonight. She feigned disgust. "Young people," she said, "have the morals of alley cats."

David nodded sympathetically. She moved back to the door.

"You have no shame." She passed out into the hallway and he felt almost giddy with relief.

"I know," he said. "We could learn a lot from you. You have... piles of it."

Gibble turned, catlike in the hallway, pointing at him again. "I'll be watching you Mister Barclay."

He nodded, "Good. Goodnight." Then he closed the door and locked it.

David leaned against the door for a while, determined that if she came back, he would ignore her and pretend to snore loudly. From down the hall he heard Geraldine's door open and the same performance began there. He would have to thank her in the morning.

Presently his eyes came to rest on the chair by his desk, and he dragged it over to the door and wedged its straight back beneath the handle. That would keep anyone out for a while. Then he crouched slightly and peered under the bed. The dust and the small pile of socks he saw made him grateful that Helen hadn't chosen to hide there. That left only one place.

He walked to the enormous wardrobe and stood hesitantly in front of it, feeling an absurd urge to knock. Instead he reached out, grasped the left handle, and pulled the door wide open. Helen stood facing him, wearing her huge coat again. She was holding what appeared to be a glue-stick menacingly in front of her, as if it were a weapon. Startled, David took a step backwards, hit the back of his knees on the bed, and sat down hard. From inside the wardrobe Helen solemnly handed him what she was balancing on her left hand: the plate with its sad cheese sandwich remains still clinging to its centre, part of which had gone green. She stepped out, and then sat down beside him.

"This," she said in a shaky voice, "has been a very odd day."

#

By three AM, around and about, the night had settled, and was waiting for morning.

Helen and David slept deeply at last, curled together in David's narrow bed...

In the wardrobe beside them, Martin Hall's shotgun was real again, oiled and glinting. Secreted earlier in a shoebox inside a plastic carrier bag, it waited...

On the street below, out of sight of David's window, Bob, Snoopy's henchman, sat on cold leather in the now dark Jaguar. He waited and watched the house-front with intermittent intensity, day-dreaming that Stella McCartney would one day make plus sizes...

Two miles to the north of Bob, in a hastily rented but tasteful flat in the centre of the town, Simon Dasch also sat in darkness. Looking out at the mist, he listened to a particularly tricksy bit of Bach and drank a good supermarket Shiraz from the most ostentatiously large goblet he could find. He let the music calm him as he rehearsed his plans for the morning...

Almost a mile to the east of Simon Dasch, the killer of six, alone again in the gloomy school, contemplated a stage set and smiled; things were ready at last...

All of these things waited, like silverware tucked in a cutlery drawer, ready for the next day's banquet. Unaware of them, but nevertheless feeling their weight, Helen and David slept on.

VI - Thursday

The phone was ringing: a harsh tone in the early morning which catapulted David from an uneasy star-lit dream. This one had begun with the regulation malevolent chain-smoking duck, which asked him (in his mother's voice) when she could expect the patter of little webbed feet. Then it had progressed to piles of spent shotgun shells scattered on the floor like rose petals by a brace of lisping gangsters, all of whom had climbed - like circus clowns from a tiny car - out of Dr Love's opened valise. With his eyes still closed he reached out a hand to where the phone should be and grabbed a handful of extra pillow. Weird.

He was warm, comfortable, and slightly hung over, and so his mind moved slowly, working over parts of yesterday as if his memories were cryptic crossword clues. Six across: when is a gun not a gun? Nineteen down: who's hiding in the school today? Twenty-four across: why does the bed seem so crowded?

He opened his eyes and found himself looking at a vaguely female form and a lock of fine blonde hair sticking out from beneath the duvet. He smiled, and wedged his head back into his pillow until the phone rang again, and, almost in self-defence, this time he managed to snag it. An unrecognised female voice said-

"Hello David. Good night, was it?"

Helen was also awake now, prizing open eyes that felt as if they had been gummed shut. She had just decided to ignore all external events - including a small Strega headache - and concentrate only on the most important matters at hand (such as the pillows, and the duvet, the warm, warm duvet), when David appeared before her again, red-eyed and corkscrew-haired, looking like a down-and-out with his own telephone.

"It's for you," he said.

Helen blinked, took the phone, remembered yesterday in a rush, and woke up quickly. The plastic was cold on her ear.

"Hello?"

"My God! You *are* there. You absolute strumpet - and with David! I never would have *believed* it. Was I right? *Was* he an animal? A sex machine? Was he? Was he? I bet he was! It *is* always the quiet ones. Tell me everything in the most perverse and clinically accurate detail."

"Hello Marie. What's going on?"

A silence, a deep breath, then-

"Well, actually, whilst you were out last night, doing the wild thang with you know who..."

"We did not do the wild thang."

She glanced up. David was sitting on the edge of his bed, looking at her wide-eyed. She gave him a brief smile.

"Well, whilst you were doing *whatever* you were doing, we had a break-in."

Helen sat up straighter. "Are you calling from home?"

"Yes. Don't worry. The police are here, well, *a* policeman is here, and there's another one in the garden. He's quite good looking actually."

The colour had drained from Helen's face. David mouthed, "What's going on?" at her, and she shrugged her shoulders at him.

"Are you okay?"

"I'm fine. I decided to pop back early to pick up a few things and found a big hole in our front door. I called the police from Mrs Grimmer's."

"Was everything... okay in there?"

Marie was suddenly careful- "How do you mean?"

"I mean, did the police find anything... anything out of the ordinary?"

"Well, after I'd called them I went over there with my badminton racquet, to see if you were there. I mean, I didn't think you *were,* but I had to check. Mrs Grimmer came with me. I think it was the most exciting thing that had happened to her since the war."

"What did you find?"

"Just that we'd had some mondo-weirdo burglar. Took nothing of mine," she sounded vaguely affronted, as if this might be a criticism, "and I don't think he took much of yours either, just left a dress out on your floor. Weird! The police think he might've been one of those underwear freaks. They'd like to speak to you."

"To *me*, why?"

The mild hysteria in her voice must have been accurately transmitted down the phone lines.

"Whoa there. Don't panic. They just want a statement." A pause, then in a lower tone, "Is there anything I should know about, Helen?"

"No, of course not, what would there be?" She didn't wait for an answer. "Does it have to be this morning?"

"Hang on, I'll ask."

Helen heard the phone slam down on the hall table, and then almost immediately the faint sound of voices from the living room; the unmistakable tones of Marie flirting mercilessly. She covered the receiver with her hand.

"Marie's at the house. We haven't been burglarised, but I think I'm going to have to talk to the police."

Unwilling to risk creeping to the second floor kitchen, David was rootling in his tiny refrigerator, his face appeared above it, worried.

"What will you tell them?"

She sat up, and the duvet pooled in her lap.

"Nothing, for now. We've nothing *to* tell them, at least not until I can get to Loatheworthy."

At the mention of the inspector's name, her expression darkened considerably.

A crackle and Marie was back. "They want you to come and confirm that nothing of yours has been taken, but you can go and make a statement later on, after school."

Helen bit her lip, thinking it over. "What's the time now?"

"About," a pause, Marie's voice grew more faint as she craned around to see the clock, "ten to seven."

"Okay, well I'll see you in half an hour."

Whilst Helen retired to the bathroom, David found a solitary and forlorn bagel hiding at the back of the bread bin, stuffed it into the toaster and put on coffee.

He went to the window, lifted the curtain carefully with one hand, and looked out onto the blue gloom of the street below. He could make out a van, a few parked cars, and nothing out of the ordinary. Still, it made him nervous. Somehow he felt the scene had potential, a stored energy. The phone rang again, and he jumped, then warily retrieved it from its cradle.

"The owl hoots twice in the moonlight. The vole sharpens a tiny spear and waits... I file down my teeth, and lie in wait for the postman "

"Hello Jonson."

"Barclay. It's you. Good, good. There's been a development. We have something... something interesting for you. Very interesting. You will meet us in the library."

It was an order, rather than a request. He managed to say-

"Jonson, what...?" before there was a clunk, and then the hum of the dial tone.

He gazed at the purring receiver in his hand. Something interesting? What did that mean? Did he really want to know? Helen came out through the bathroom door.

"Who was that?"

"No-one," he replied through a sickly grin. "No-one important. I have to go to the library today is all, for some work."

He offered her half of the bagel, and she took it and sat down opposite him, then glanced at the window.

"Do you think it's safe out there?"

He shrugged. "I don't know. I feel... nervous."

Helen nodded.

"Me too. Here's what I think we should do," she said, gesturing with the bagel. She had developed a new, almost manic determination this morning, he noticed.

"I say we sneak out of here. I'm going home so I can change and check out my room. Then I'm going to school, as normal, where I'm going to seek out Loatheworthy, and fake him out." She nodded to herself. "I can do that, I know I can, I'm a teacher by God. If I can fake out a determined and utterly conscienceless six-year-old, I can do it to Loatheworthy. He was jumpy enough yesterday, practically wet himself when he thought I had something on him. You go and do what you need to do in Oxford." A new idea hit her. "I don't know, maybe you could do some research on Loatheworthy - perhaps he's been in trouble before?"

David nodded as if the idea were also only just occurring to him.

"Then, after school, after the Nativity, we go to the police station and tell them as much of what we know as we dare. What do you think?"

David took a bite of his own half of the bagel. By then, by late afternoon, he would know whether it was entirely wise for Helen to go to the police, he would know what Jonson's 'something interesting' was.

"It sounds like a plan," he said.

#

Bob the henchman had left the tinted confines of Snoopy's Jag, where he had kept a lonely all-night vigil, and was leaning back against the car's curving flank, not enjoying his cup of lukewarm morning tea. He had made it with an attachment that plugged into the car's cigarette lighter and a crumpled tea bag, but there was neither milk nor sugar. He was simultaneously watching David's front door and the man in the van.

Bob had been in the henchman business long enough to know that unmarked and mysterious vans could mean trouble, and trouble was what he was anxious to avoid this morning. The van had arrived about fifteen minutes before and parked opposite the house (or the row of houses) that he had been left to watch. He was fairly sure that he should be watching number seven, but numbers nine and fifteen also looked shifty to him.

"Which one?" Snoopy had hissed at him as they cruised the street late last night.

"That one. No, *that* one. It had a door, anyway."

"A door? They've all got doorsh you pointlesh moron."

"Well, it's this mist, it's confusin' me."

Snoopy had fumed silently. In the rear-view mirror, Bob had seen his face turn purple. "But you followed him to thish shtreet?"

"Oh yes. Definitely," he had said, though he was only about seventy percent certain.

Now, as a thin morning light prodded the mist away as if it were an over-friendly but suspiciously damp dog, he felt more sure of himself; it was definitely this street.

Five minutes ago, the bloke in the white van had left the cab, putting down a copy of the *Sunday Mirror* (though it was Thursday), and strolled around to its side (where Bob could not see him). Bob had heard the side door slide open, and something rattle, as if it were being checked, and then the door close again.

This made him very nervous indeed.

In Bob's mind, the van was full of Special Branch officers, armed to the teeth and ready to pounce.

The bloke didn't look like a copper, though. His hair was too long, swept up from his forehead and carelessly shaggy, contrasting neatly with a moustache that was waxed into points. Also, he was wearing a white boiler suit that seemed slightly bulky, as if it were covering other clothes. It was possible that he was a plumber or an electrician waiting to start a job, though there was no logo either on the van, or on the boiler suit itself.

Bob glanced at the bloke again. It was a nonchalant glance that he had developed over years of following people. The trick was to make it look as if he just happened to have turned his head that way.

The bloke in the cab was staring straight at him. He smiled a cheery, welcoming smile and waved his fingers over the top of the van's steering wheel. Bob looked away in confusion. What should he do? His instinct was to climb into the Jag and drive away. It would be difficult to snatch the teacher with the bloke watching him, even if he was just a plumber. Come to that, he didn't even *want* to snatch the teacher - God alone knew what the Boss wanted to do with her, but Snoopy's sweating furious expression in the rear-view mirror came back to him, and held him in place. The Boss really wanted this one, *really* wanted it, for reasons which were difficult for Bob to fathom (though, he was quite prepared to admit, he would never win a ribbon in any fathoming contests), and to disappoint him a second time might be extremely hazardous.

The bloke put down his out-of-date paper, shot a boiler-suit cuff, and peered down at his watch as if he were timing something very carefully, then he left his cab and went around to its side again. Bob tensed, reached behind himself, and put his hand on the Jag's door handle. This was it. The keys were in the car's ignition, and if he needed to get out of here, he could do it reasonably quickly - more quickly than the unmarked van, anyway.

There was that rattling sound again.

Hardly daring to look, Bob braced himself, and then he was assailed by wonder.

Such colour! Such choice! And they were all sized for the larger lady!

The sound was tiny plastic wheels passing over the uneven road-surface. The wheels belonged to a large dress-rack which the bloke, whistling tunelessly between his teeth, was wheeling down the street towards him. Hanging from the rack, swaying gently like ripe fruit on some fantastic tree, were a series of garments in a rainbow of colours. Wrapped in plastic they ranged from the most abbreviated club-wear, to something in which you might glide about a forest glade, holding the powder-blue silk skirt out prettily with one hand, opposite a prince (or in Bob's case, a princess). All of the apparel looked to be just about in Bob's size. He swallowed hard, his hand leaving the car door handle, his eyes following the rack intently. When it was almost in front of him, the bloke appeared from behind it.

"Nice eh?" he said, and Bob, captivated by lustrous fabrics, completely failed to see the door to number seven open just enough for a person to slip through.

Shielded by swathes of satin and silk (and just a little acrylic and leather), David stuck his head out onto the street and looked around. It was exactly seven-twenty. The night mist had faded and the sky had lightened. He stared at the bizarre spectacle of a tall man in a white boiler suit standing with his back to them and holding up a shimmering blue full-length ball gown (complete with matching clutch bag and elbow gloves) before the eyes of another, more stoutly built man. These two could not be dangerous, David decided, and so he and Helen slipped out silently, hand-in-hand.

As they made the street, neither of them saw the kitchen curtains twitch behind them, perhaps no more than an inch to the left; they were too absorbed by the soundlessness of their escape.

"It's the shoes though, isn't it?" Boiler-suit was saying as they made the corner of Woodcroft road, embraced and parted, "You just can't get strappy sandals in an eleven without paying through the nose."

#

When Helen reached the house, she found that there was a policeman at the front door dusting for fingerprints. He was wearing a rumpled grey suit that matched his hair, a blue tie, cream coloured latex gloves, and was obviously in a big hurry. As she walked up the sideway he dipped into an open briefcase laid out on the concrete and took out a small brush. Without looking up at her he said, "Miss Haversham? Sorry about the mess. Nearly done. Go right in. Touch whatever you like, except this door."

She had found walking back to the house, retracing yesterday's panicky steps, soothing, and the familiar hallway with all the lights on, and with Marie's voice coming from the living room, completed the effect. Any last vestiges of coaly fear were pressed into hard, slightly angry diamonds.

Her room was as she had left it. Nothing had been taken, except, as Marie had said, a dress lay crumpled in the corner. She went to it, frowning, unable to guess its meaning.

Those diamonds shone a little. Sending people to her *house*! Loatheworthy was going to regret that.

She showered and prepared for her day, deliberately running through her lesson plans in her mind so that she would not see visions of the inspector dispatched in a gruesome yet picturesque manner.

Downstairs, Marie was sitting on the sofa, nodding as a constable Abbot read her statement aloud. She had reached out and placed a hand on the constable's knee, perhaps to offer him moral support. Over Marie's shoulder, Helen could see out through the patio doors. Part-way down the glass, she could see two marks left by the toes of her trainers.

"Here's one of our security leaflets. Obvious stuff really," Abbot was saying. "Have your locks changed. Fit a mortise if you can, then even if someone breaks a window and reaches through to the handle, they can't get in as long as they don't have key." He stood and pointed to the French doors. "And it would be wise to get some kind of deadlock fitted there, too."

Marie batted her eyelashes.

"Thank you officer, so much. We'll do that. I've left a message with a glazier, and he should be here by ten. Lucky in a way - it's my day off." Now she turned to Helen. "So I'll be at the carol thing later, we can... talk, then. Actually, we'll both be there. Dominic here also has a contact at the school."

Abbot glanced up at Helen.

"Melanie Blake, my niece. She's an animal. By the manger, I think. She'll be five in January."

Helen nodded. A face came to her: a short bob haircut and a tendency towards lollipops. There was a strong familial resemblance.

"It's a nice age."

"Nice? God no, she's like Caligula."

Marie nodded encouragingly. "Fabulous. Well I'll call a locksmith and get things underway." She dropped Helen a wink, then grasped Abbot's elbow and led him off towards the kitchen.

"Can I make you coffee, or some breakfast constable? It's a shame that you can't stay for a while longer, I'd feel so much more safe with a man around."

Helen was left alone in the living room. The mantle-clock ticked, and through the marked windows, she thought she could see footprints snaking away across the lawn.

Yes. Loatheworthy was going to be very, very sorry.

#

In the library it was not-quite cold and not-quite quiet. Amidst the morning hum of pages turning and people thinking very hard, David became aware of the regular squeaking sound only gradually. After a few moments of listening, he looked out from the curving pile of ancient copies of the *Athenaeum* behind which he was hiding, and glanced around himself. The undergraduates were gone, and only tutors and pale hard-core research students remained, scattered around the rows of desks, surrounded by their own piles of obscure books and periodicals.

Though most works had to be retrieved from a series of vast underground book-caves, diligently hollowed out beneath the Bodleian library by a savage horde of warrior-librarians sometime in the dim past, students were trusted (just) to retrieve reference works and suchlike themselves. The reading room shelves were high and students not very energetic, and so they were provided with an assortment of ladders to help them to reach the books at the very top. Some were rickety Victorian affairs - insanely dangerous mini spiral staircases worked around a central pole. These would begin to creak and sway alarmingly, like the mast of a doomed ship, once a student was halfway to the top. The result was always the same: some unwary (but hopeful) reader would reach this point of no return, then clutch the treacherous wood, and begin emitting a series of high-pitched and unearthly gurgles and screams, before hurling themselves, with unaccountable enthusiasm, at the hard library floor.

These ladders had survived into the twenty-first century purely for their entertainment value.

Other more modern appliances resembled miniature versions of the moveable stairways used to board aircraft. The more experienced (or less suicidal) students preferred these, and one of them was making its way towards David now, one wheel squeaking intermittently as it rolled.

He watched its creeping approach, entranced. Eventually the ambulatory staircase drew level with his eyes, a small door in its wood-panelled side popped open, and he could see two eyes staring out at him from the darkness within. There was also a hand.

As David watched, an index finger was extended, and pointed over his shoulder.

"Barclay!" a voice hissed not two inches from his left ear.

David wheeled around, his heart in his throat, to face an apparition in a long black raincoat.

The figure looked shiftily from side to side and then leaned over him. The coat was buttoned from top to bottom and its collar was turned up, meeting the lowered brim of a large black hat. Added to this, the figure wore enormous dark glasses, and a drooping (and quite obviously fake) Zapata moustache. David squinted.

It was Jonson.

Jonson wiggled an eyebrow at him. "Don't attract attention to yourself Barclay," he hissed sternly.

David looked around. Without exception, everyone in the sparsely populated library, even the librarian, was looking in their direction.

"Follow me. Ask no questions, and don't look behind you!"

They had come! David felt absurdly honoured. The Presidents rarely left their underground lair.

Jonson was already striding away, his hands in his pockets, and David began to follow him to the main doors. He could see the ragged ends of Jonson's horrible brown jeans swishing below the hem of his raincoat.

The staircase, which David now assumed contained Kennedy, followed on behind, emitting its squeak at increasingly regular intervals as it struggled to keep up. As this strange parade exited the reading room all eyes turned to follow their retreat.

Jonson led David to one of the many mysterious oak-panelled doors that were liberally dispersed around the library and stood outside it. He withdrew a gadget from his coat pocket and pointed it at the door. It was about the size of a pocket calculator, and as David watched, two implements, which looked suspiciously like transistor radio aerials, extended from its top edge. It began to emit a repetitive beeping sound as Jonson swept it over the surface of the door.

"Jonson, just tell me what..?"

Jonson simply held up one hand and waited. Eventually the machine beeped in a different tone, and a green light lit up on its surface. Then Jonson retrieved a huge bundle of jangling keys from his pocket, selected one, and turned it in the heavy lock.

"Where did you get those?"

"Oh," he said, airily, "we have keys to almost everywhere. After you."

From behind them came the 'squeak... squeak' of Kennedy approaching the doors to the reading room in his staircase. David rolled his eyes, "This had better be good."

Jonson opened the door just enough for David to slip through and he found himself in total darkness. Instinctively he adjusted his glasses on his nose and then held one hand up before them. Nothing. He could see nothing.

From outside the darkness he heard Kennedy, muffled now by two sets of wooden panelling, stiffly thanking someone (they had probably held the enormous reading room doors open for him), and then the squeaking approached the cupboard and ceased. David supposed that Kennedy had parked his staircase immediately outside the door, hiding it from the casual observer.

There was a click as Jonson flicked on a small torch and held it immediately beneath his fake moustache, casting Halloween shadows over what could be seen of his face. The huge dark glasses were gone, replaced by the more customary rose-tints. David glanced around himself, and saw some familiar shapes: they were standing in a broom cupboard.

"Hello Barclay," Jonson intoned. "Stay perfectly still please."

David scowled as Jonson swept the black instrument up and down his body and then waited. After what seemed to be a very long time it beeped again, and showed the green light.

"Is he clean?" Kennedy's voice hissed from outside the door.

"Electronically - yes. In absolute terms - it's doubtful," Jonson replied.

"Tell him then. Be quick."

Jonson regarded David solemnly.

"Are you sure you wouldn't prefer it if we left you alone," he said, "left you with your suspicions… kept you in the dark, so to speak?"

David took a deep breath. He could feel something fist-sized and unyielding, knocking rhythmically in his chest, and with some dim awareness realised that it was his heart.

"No," he said, weakly, "just tell me. I've had enough dark thank-you."

"Sure?"

David nodded. This was it: crunch time. His future would be determined here. Was it to be a shamefaced grin and an *hilarious* story for the grandchildren? Or would it be months on the run, changing their names to Carlos and Murgatroid, being chased across deserted twilit moorland by men with dogs and torches. Perhaps a spot of extensive cosmetic surgery followed by a move to Columbia, and always, always waiting for Helen to arrive home spattered with some unidentifiable liquid, or reeking of petrol, and say- "Oh dear, I think I've done it again."

"Surely sure?"

"Oh for God's sake, tell me."

Jonson sighed and drew a piece of paper out of his coat, then made a business of straightening it and examining it carefully. Before he could speak, Kennedy's voice wafted in through the wooden panelling.

"There is no match between the prints you supplied yesterday, and those on the Ofsted murders' suspect file."

Jonson closed his mouth with a snap (dislodging one side of his moustache, which dangled ferretoriously).

"I was going to say that!"

David slumped against the ancient woodwork and was prodded gently by a mop. Blessed, warming, calming relief flooded through him in a great golden wave. He let out a sigh in the darkness, and saw not two ragged figures chased and harried by bloodhounds across a blasted heath, but he and Helen sunning themselves on the white sands of a beautiful, gently curving bay. He saw a future where he would not sweat when Helen drew near to sharp objects, a future where the question 'and what do you do in your spare time?' would not have be handled with unusual care.

"So Helen did not wield the plunger?"

"Definitely not," Kennedy replied. "Still, don't be too disappointed."

"I'm not disappointed, I'm… "

What was he? Ashamed? Feeling foolish? Surprised? Embarrassed?

"I'm relieved."

Jonson frowned-

"Well, hold that thought. Did you know that you actually slid two sets of prints under our door yesterday, Barclay - well, three, if you count your own."

David nodded, "I did?"

"Yes. The left palm print - very nicely taken, by the way - belongs to one Helen Jane Haversham. We looked her up - she's nice. There was also a single right index finger belonging to one Martin - believe it or not - Albert Hall, esquire. We looked him up too; he's not very nice."

That cut through the fog of David's reverie-

"Hall… M.H. Who is he?"

From behind the panelling, Kennedy spoke again-

"Small time thug. Local ASBO king who moved on to some nastier stuff. I don't know how you got his print - hopefully by accident - but I'd keep away from him if I were you, Barclay. He might bite you."

So, it was all true. The rose and the vacuum-cleaner attachment were simple coincidence. An inspector *had* invaded Helen's classroom and planted enough dope there to choke an elephant, or at least make it hungry and sleepy. He must be working with this 'Hall', and had also left behind a firearm.

David's feelings of chagrin morphed quickly into righteous indignation, tinged with a little fear.

"I gave you a name… did you find anything out about him?"

Jonson shifted the torch he was holding down to something which lay on the dusty floor between them. David stooped to pick it up. It was a bundle of papers, perhaps four inches thick.

The torch shone on Jonson's face again.

"That's all we could find, I'm afraid." He sounded genuinely sorry. David wondered briefly if the Presidents had a file like this on him, then shook the uncomfortable thought away.

Jonson was now stroking his stricken moustache as if it were a treasured pet. "It makes fascinating reading."

David looked up again- "It does? Why? How? I need to know quickly, if you can tell me anything, I'd be… "

"Forever in our debt? You're there already Barclay. No. It's a cumulative effect. Read the file, you'll see what we mean, or not."

Kennedy's voice drifted in again-

"It's time."

Solemnly, Jonson took a small Dictaphone from his pocket, and placed it on the floor in the darkness and pushed play. His own voice began to emerge from the speaker.

"If you are hearing this message, Barclay, then it means that you are still alive." In the background of the tape, David could hear stifled laughter. "Please remain still for the time being." Jonson flicked off his torch and they were plunged into total darkness again.

"You are not afraid of the dark, and that is good. Soon Kennedy and I will be gone. We do not wish our exit strategy to be observed, and would instruct you to wait at least two minutes before leaving this cupboard."

Jonson flicked on the torch again. His moustache, hat, and raincoat were gone, wrapped up and bundled into a corner. He stood before

David wearing a dinner jacket and a white bow tie over his T-shirt and foul jeans. He was holding a large hessian sack, and now dropped David another wink.

"We are off to lie in wait at the party next door at All Souls, in order to find Doctor Love," the recording said. Jonson waggled the sack provocatively. "Have fun now, won't you."

And with that he opened the heavy oak door, and in a brief flash of light from the outside, was gone.

"Wait Jonson, what should I..?"

"As we said," the tape continued, "you should wait for at least two minutes."

And then there seemed to be no more. From outside David could hear the slowly retreating 'squeak... squeak' of the staircase as the Presidents made their retreat.

The ream of paperwork was heavy in his hands; it would take some reading. Would there be anything truly incriminating? Anything to take to the police station that evening?

"We don't know," the recording of Jonson's voice said from the darkness.

David stared down at where he thought the tape machine might be for a long moment. Eventually relief dawned in his mind as he reached the conclusion that the Presidents had simply spooled the tape ahead for a while, and recorded a generic response at the end of their message - knowing that he would be there, thinking things over - just to mess with his head.

The light on his digital watch showed him that it was past eleven o'clock now. He ought to start reading.

He smiled ruefully to himself. It was so easy to be taken in by the Presidents' act, even when you knew them. They were not mind readers. The tape was a classic Presidents' twist.

"No," Jonson's taped voice said quietly from the darkness, "*This* is a classic Presidents' twist."

Another silence, and then clutching the big file David left the broom cupboard.

#

At breaktime Helen stomped into the staffroom and found it empty. She stood at the counter for a while, hoping that the familiar instant coffee ritual would calm her, and looked out over the field where the children were once again screaming at each other like psychotic killers under Crodd's benign gaze. Loatheworthy was nowhere to be seen.

She had at last undergone her final inspection period of the week, and in her disappointment and frustration that Loatheworthy had not shown himself, had barely noticed Barbara Willis sitting at the edge of her class. In fact she had not realised until later that it was finally all over. All of the planning, the sleepless nights, the sense of invasion and worry over slights and injustices real or imagined, was over, for a few years at least - unless she moved schools. And even then, the new system: shorter inspections, less time to prepare (or run around in tiny circles screaming and waving your hands in the air) seemed better, easier to cope with. Beneath her fury, Helen felt the ghost of relief. This was not the sudden and complete wash of solace which accompanies the discovery of lost keys, or the realisation that you have miscounted and there are not two children missing at the end of school excursion day, it was a slow thing, weak and ebbing.

She was bringing her cup to her lips, scanning the play yard, and anticipating a caffeine rush, when she heard the whimper. It came from low down, close to the floor. Helen glanced around, seeing only the staffroom's sparseness: timetables, memos, an advertisement for the Nativity pinned to the cork-boards, and an old Department of Education information poster in which someone had mercilessly highlighted all of the grammatical errors. The whimper came again, and she rolled her eyes, reluctantly placing her cup on the counter.

"Hello Miriam," she said, moving to close the staffroom door.

The older woman was crouched under one of the desks, her arms and legs crossed, completely swathed in black.

She smiled uncertainly, "Hello dear."

Helen crouched, coming down to Miriam's level. "What are you doing under there then?"

"I'm taking a leaf out of the children's book, actually dear." She smiled dreamily. "Such directness, the smallest ones. When they feel threatened they go and hide somewhere; it makes you feel better. Eventually, of course, it's socialised out of most of them, but still... "

Helen thought about this- "Mind if I join you?"

Miriam's eyes twinkled behind her black-rimmed glasses, "The more the merrier, dear."

Helen retrieved her blessed coffee and wedged herself under the desk next to Miriam's, backing in and wriggling until she was leaning against the wall. Miriam was right; it was comforting - shrinking the world down to a manageable size. She felt better.

"Helps you to think, doesn't it?" she said.

Miriam nodded, pleased. "Yes. It helps you to plot... " her eyes glowed, and she stared into the middle distance, " ...to plot a wicked, *wicked* revenge. Death throes, rivers of blood, terrible agony, that sort of thing."

Helen nodded as if she understood.

"How's it going, really though?"

"Oh, not so bad. You?"

"It could be worse."

Miriam studied her expression carefully. "That's not the point though, is it?"

Helen sighed, "No. No I suppose it isn't."

They sat in silence for a while.

"It was all very different when I started dear."

"Hmmm?"

Miriam smiled a brittle smile. "Oh I know what you think. You think I'm going to say that children - and parents - had more respect for you then. Well they did." She nodded to herself. "They did, and if you asked them to do something, they jolly well did it. More or less unquestioningly, no matter how mind-bogglingly pointless and stupid the request might be. What teacher said was important."

"It still is Miriam. Everyone likes to pretend that we're useless, but we just keep turning out kids who can read and write and count and build weird, *weird* stuff out of household junk."

Miriam nodded. "I know that dear. It's not being told how to do my job by parents, or even by the children that bothers me - its being treated like an idiot by those upstairs." She pointed upwards and the tip of her finger grazed the underside of the table.

"When I joined up it was a profession worth considering - not much money, never much money - but a profession none the less. Now they refuse to treat any of us like professionals. They treat us more like... like those things, oh you know... " she flapped her hands impatiently, "vacant stare... horrible smell, oh you *do* know! No table manners!"

"Students?"

"No... *zombies*. It's as if we're not qualified to make decisions, or... or evaluate the children, or give a lesson off-the-cuff any more. Everything is directed from *above* and judged from *above*, we're only here to transmit their signal. I tell you, I'm going to retire as soon as I can."

Helen was wondering whether she should try to talk Miriam out of this when the staffroom door was pushed open and they heard footsteps approach. They looked at each other, eyebrows raised, until grey trouser-cuffs and a pair of highly polished loafers with stepped-up heels came into view.

Loatheworthy.

Miriam clutched Helen's elbow painfully, stopping her from moving. He couldn't find them crouching under the tables, her expression said, he'd have them sectioned. Helen had to agree, this was not the confrontation she had wished for.

Loatheworthy stopped, three feet from their hiding place. They watched the trouser-cuffs twitch as he surveyed the staffroom. Slowly, Helen began to draw her feet towards her, further out of his line of sight. Why had he turned up now? What was he doing in here?

Loatheworthy walked to the old toilet door and rattled the handle. It didn't give. Then he depressed it and pulled as hard as he could. Helen could see him rocking back on his heels, but the door held firm.

He surveyed the room again, then spotted Helen's handbag on the counter-top by the sink. Her eyes widened as she remembered that she had left it there.

Loatheworthy paused by the counter for a few moments, then walked to the staffroom door and closed it. He made a circuit of the room, very close to the walls, as if he were inspecting them for something, then fetched up by the counter again. They heard the unmistakable sound of him taking things out of Helen's bag and placing them on the counter-top. Helen made as if to leave the shelter of the tables, but Miriam's grip did not lessen on her arm. The older woman looked at her imploringly, and she subsided, trying to remember what was in her bag anyway - a lipstick, her keys, her address book, some screwed up notes and tissues, her phone, and anything she had confiscated from the children during the morning. She gritted her teeth as Loatheworthy painstakingly turned everything out, replaced it, then stood, drumming his fingers on the counter.

Helen had just decided to challenge him anyway, when they heard his footsteps retreat to the door. He paused, listening, and then disappeared through it. They waited in silence, then:

"See. No respect at all!"

"I think he's a special case Miriam," Helen said. She began to climb out from under the desk. "I'm going to check on my classroom, in case he decides to have another prowl there whilst I'm absent. Coming?"

Miriam shook her head. "No. I think I'll wait for the bell here dear, think about retirement."

"Well, I'll see you at the carol concert then?"

Miriam nodded, a meditative smile already settling on her features.

#

When Helen arrived back at her classroom, her handbag (with nothing missing, and more importantly nothing added) slung over her shoulder, she found that the door was almost, but not quite closed. She stood at the jamb in the empty corridor, listening. From inside she could hear the sound of papers being shifted, and a low-grade mumbling, a kind of mantra from which she could detect a few words.

"Watched," the voice said. "Always. Followed. Everywhere. Prison... oh *yes* prison, that'll be nice George. Could've been *king* of waste treatment... could've been best man... but oh *no* George, not you."

Helen pushed the door open silently. Loatheworthy was at her desk, rapidly going through a pile of paperwork that she had left lying there and dropping it onto a less tidy pile on the floor, all the while muttering to himself. Her desk drawers were open; she had left them shut and locked; the inspector must have forced them, again.

Helen glanced around her classroom. Everything else seemed to be where she had left it. The store cupboard door was shut, and the children's trays were lined up, but that meant very little. Her eyes were drawn again to the far wall, to the art display. There, one image, the one that was mostly by Chloe Green, was missing. It had been ripped from the wall hard enough to leave scraps of sugar paper behind, held there by staples.

Helen cleared her throat, still standing on the threshold of the room. Loatheworthy jumped, emitted a wheezy squeak, juggled those papers he was holding, and then dropped them to the floor. He turned to face her slowly, his hands half raised as if she had burst in upon him carrying a revolver, and ordered him to turn around.

Loatheworthy looked terrible, as if he had last slept a week ago. He was weasel-eyed and wearing a shirt and suit so new that Helen could see the shop creases in them. She wondered idly what had happened to the one he had worn yesterday. His moustache had been inexpertly trimmed, and he seemed to be missing part of one eyebrow; this gave him an eerie, permanently surprised look.

"New technique is it, Mister Loatheworthy? Government sanctioned petty larceny? Not satisfied with going through my handbag?"

Loatheworthy's mouth fell open, and he actually stamped one foot in utter frustration. It was something that Helen had seen the more theatrically-minded five-year-olds do, but never a grown man.

"But I was *alone*. How do you *do* that?" he asked, his tone petulant.

Helen shrugged, as if to imply that omniscience was a talent that all primary school teachers were expected to cultivate.

Loatheworthy made an effort to collect himself, to restore their roles as teacher and inspector in his mind.

"I... I want to make a deal, Miss Haversham."

A deal? Interesting. Still, she lingered in the doorway, trying not to appear too eager to hear what he would say.

"What kind of deal?"

"You have something that I want."

Helen tried to keep any glee from creeping into her expression.

"I do?"

"Oh Yes. You do."

He perched on the edge of her desk and tried for an expression of businesslike efficiency. Unfortunately, because of the missing eyebrow he overshot and landed squarely in zealous loony territory.

"You have an item which I find inconvenient." He scratched the missing half of his moustache. "The fact that you haven't already involved the authorities suggests to me that you wish to make a deal of some kind. Now I am not a rich man, and I don't think you want money, but I may have something that you *do* want." Here he tapped the outer cover of his clipboard, which was lying on Helen's desk.

Helen stepped fully into the room at last and closed the door behind her with a click, still trying to keep her poker face. Was he talking about the dope, or the gun? Both were more than inconvenient, surely. Still, her reasoning had been sound: Loatheworthy did not know that she now had neither of these items; it seemed that she *could* bluff him.

"I don't think that you have anything that I want."

"Nonsense. Of course I do. I have what all teachers want."

"And what's that? Classrooms free of guns and dope?"

That was too much for him, and his arm shot into the air and swatted an apparently imaginary fly hovering above him. Helen stared, and then moved towards him, pressing her advantage.

"What do we all want, Loatheworthy?"

A crafty smile.

"You want a good inspection report. You want to be graded well and told that you are good at your job. You want Ofsted to say 'Oh yes! This school is a good school! We won't come back for a long long long time.'" The smile welled up into an idiot giggle. He patted the clipboard again, as if it were a pet, "I can give you that."

Helen had thought that she was angry with the inspector when she stepped into the room. Now she realised that that had been a shallow, surface thing; now she could hear her own pulse in her ears, a monstrous thud, like a neighbour banging on the wall for quiet. An ember of the deepest, hottest resentment that she had ever felt glowed within her, fanned by the sickening realisation that he was right, she *did* want that. These thoughts blossomed into a gentle, dangerous smile.

"Okay, let's talk about what *you* want."

"I want *this!*"

Now he was holding Chloe Green's picture out before him slightly, at chest level, as if it were a shield. It was upside down and the sun/moon's grin - her own work - had become a dangerous leer.

Helen blinked at him. "You can have that. I'll get the class to paint you more if you like."

"But I want the original. The photograph."

"The photograph? I... " Helen stopped herself in time. "Oh, *the* photograph. I see. And that would show..?"

"*This!*" Loatheworthy shook the image before her. "Is it a deal?"

Unable to fathom what he might mean, she changed tack-

"Only if you tell me *why*. I need to know why. Why did you pick on me? Why this school, in this town? What did you think was going to happen? Did you even *think* about it? A child with a *gun*, and those idiots last night, at my house. Why *me*? Why *this* school? Do you understand what could have happened?"

Without thinking she reached forward and tapped with her index finger on the centre of his forehead, emphasising her words, "Someone - could - have - been - killed."

Loatheworthy's face flushed with guilt or confusion, it was difficult to tell which, and he took a step away from her, his expression hardening, cunning returning.

"I could do the other thing too, you know. The other thing, oh yes. Special Measures. You must have heard of that. Special Measures... Every teacher's nightmare, I should think. I've seen it. *Seen* it. Inspections once a month. Press attention. The school's reputation in the toilet. Rolls drop, the younger teachers leave in exasperation for other schools or careers in insurance, the older ones give up. Of course it's the children who *really* suffer."

That was it. Helen thought of the dope sitting plumply on her desk, of Simon and the gun, of that giggle coming from her hallway in the middle of the night, and finally of Miriam, a perfectly competent teacher cowering under the staffroom tables, and something inside - her self-control, she supposed - finally gave way. She took another step towards him, seeming to tower over him, and his expression of cunning began to fade.

"Now Miss Haversham... Helen, I really think... "

Helen's hand shot out towards her desk, and seized the stapler. Loatheworthy recoiled as if she had hit him. Without thinking she stapled the end of his tie to her desk and then pointed the business end of the implement at him.

Loatheworthy tried to stand, found that he could not, and then reflexively put both hands in the air, stick-up style. Chloe Green's picture lay on the floor between them. Helen jabbed the stapler through the air, and he backed up. The staple pulled out of her desk, releasing his tie, and he stumbled backwards slightly. She felt a queasy kind of joy.

"See! You don't like having things pointed at *you*, do you?"

He scrambled to get away from her desk, almost fell because his hands were still in the air, saved himself, and then managed to back up. He wore an expression of almost comical amazement. Helen followed him, closing in on him.

"I... I don't know what you... "

"You've made a mistake, Loatheworthy," she said. "An error. We know all about you, and we can connect you to the dope *and* the gun - so how about putting *that* in your report."

Loatheworthy backed around the corner of the room, and began to totter towards the door. He looked genuinely surprised.

"*Gun*? I... " he spluttered.

"So here's your *deal*," Helen said, each word now vibrating with fury. "I don't know what the other inspectors will find. They seem like a reasonably fair bunch to me so we'll leave them out of it. But if I read that report and find out that you have said anything, *anything* unfair or untrue, then we go to the police. If anyone else comes to my house, we go to the police. In fact, if I have to *look* at you ever again, we go to the police."

Loatheworthy's mouth worked silently, as if someone had turned down his volume control. From the corner of his eye, he seemed to notice that his own hands were still in the air. He dropped them warily to almost waist height, but still held the palms out towards her.

"Keep those up," Helen barked. "And get out of my classroom."

In her fury she could not see that to open the door and escape Loatheworthy would have to actually get closer to her (and the stapler), something he was unwilling to do.

"Get out!" she commanded. The stapler wobbled in her vision, "I'm going to count to three... One... "

Grimacing Loatheworthy reached falteringly behind him and began to edge the classroom door open.

"Two... "

Now he was leaning backward almost limbo-style, simultaneously trying to keep his face away from the stapler, and open the door. At last, he got it open; unfortunately, Helen had reached the end of her countdown.

"Three!"

Without thinking, she squeezed the body of the stapler. Loatheworthy saw her fingers move, and flinched further, his mouth drawn downwards in a sudden panicky bow.

"What are you..? Please, I... "

She squeezed. Twice. Again.

Backing through the doorway Loatheworthy winced, his eyes closed tight. Silver staples flew through the air and bounced harmlessly from the fabric of his tie. He opened one eye and looked down at it.

Helen, breathing heavily, beyond all self-control now, gestured with the stapler again. The violence of her expression was enough for Loatheworthy, and he turned tail and fled. She watched him retreat quickly down the corridor like the white rabbit, and felt curiously empty. *Oh my ears and whiskers*, she thought, not yet calm enough to wonder what she had just done.

She glanced behind her and saw Alison peeping out of her classroom door. Alison beamed at her encouragingly, and gave her an exaggerated double-thumbs-up sign.

"That's the spirit," she said. "Don't let the buggers grind you down. And if they do, kill them with a stapler."

Helen blinked, and looked down at the implement in her hand as if seeing it for the first time.

Well, it had not gone *exactly* to plan, but she had certainly threatened him.

#

Loatheworthy fled through a maze of corridors, a fleeting shadow passing quickly, half-perceived from within classrooms, the office, and eventually the almost empty school hall. There, a head turned by slow degrees to watch his progress from deep within the shadows of the stage, and there was the sudden blooming of a smile of anticipation.

The hall echoed this pleasant sense of emptiness to be filled, of something ready to be made. Chairs were stacked along its walls, ready to be put out for tonight's audience. On the piano sat three neat stacks of photocopied programs so that proud parents could wonder over their child's name in print. The stage was dressed (or almost...) and held in readiness. A thick orange curtain hung before the painted scene of a stable in the small town of Bethlehem. All around there was evidence of a tired old magic ready to be brought out, paraded, made new and enjoyed.

A hand trailed across the curtain from behind, disturbing it in a languid swirl that quickly crossed the stage, and sent down a fine rain of dust from the rail above.

Now fingers on the piano: one note only, played very softly, dropping into the silence. Still smiling, the figure looked upwards, and saw the hole cut in the scenery from which would shine the spotlight star, and perceived the room beyond, where the spotlight was housed. The size of the hole was perfect, and the figure let out a happy sigh. This would be the best display yet.

It was time to gather materials.

#

Still in the drone and mutter of the library, David turned the pages of yet another yellowing copy of the *Hornby Recorder*, a local newspaper which had ceased publication late in the nineteen nineties.

Now he could see what the Presidents had meant by a cumulative effect; the contents of their file lay spread out around him.

On page four of this particular issue of the *Recorder*, there was a black and white photograph, accompanying a two-column story of the 'man bites dog' variety. Except in this one, the dog had definitely bitten the man.

The image showed a small figure, just identifiable as Loatheworthy, running past the photographer at some speed, arms flying, knees pumping, as if just making the tape in a strange record-breaking one-hundred-metre dash. Apart from the sense of motion it conveyed, what rendered the image remarkable (perhaps even unforgettable) was Loatheworthy's trouserlessness. The trousers in question, the text revealed, had been effectively shredded and removed by the family pet: a pedigree Chihuahua of unusual cunning and aptitude for destruction, who rejoiced in the name of Dweezil-firecat-snipkiss III. Dweezil-firecat-snipkiss III, could be seen in the background of the shot, a tiny blur of fur-in-motion, giving spirited chase, mysteriously dedicated to the task of fully exposing his owner's sock-suspenders and royal blue Y-fronts to the nation.

Reading through the Presidents' careful research, David realised that the pattern that they wanted him to see revolved around a strange partnership between Loatheworthy's essentially unpleasant nature, and a series of bizarre accidents. For example, during August of nineteen-eighty-two, Loatheworthy had sweated beneath the yoke of a full Inland Revenue tax audit. Though the Revenue had found nothing irregular in his accounts, during this period they did also investigated eleven of his colleagues, working through them in turn, and at his recommendation. Loatheworthy had apparently used his opportunity of access to the authorities to spread his misery around.

In October of nineteen-eighty-two, Loatheworthy was rescued by the fire services from beneath his own garden. The unusually warm weather had caused the voluminous septic tank secreted there to rupture, and during the inspector's evening stroll, his perfectly manicured lawn had collapsed beneath his feet and spilled him into the stygian depths below. Since he had been unaccompanied on his walk, Loatheworthy's weak cries for aid went unanswered, and he spent four hours alone there. Eventually, just after midnight, a disoriented squirrel fell in after him. The furry creature's tiny mind, it seemed, was so deranged by its experience that it became hopelessly enraged, and Loatheworthy was forced to spend the next several hours, before his rescue was finally affected, fending off increasingly fiendish and frenzied attacks from the chattering creature.

The incident with Dweezil-firecat had happened immediately after Loatheworthy had instituted a round of redundancies at the water company where he had once worked.

When he moved into the world of education, and then Ofsted, Loatheworthy's opportunity to commit minor transgressions obviously increased, and during these years his house flooded, his car was impounded, and on and on. It was Karma in action. It was satisfying in its own way, but of little use to David.

He turned to the next item. The Presidents had been thorough. He had already read through the inspector's financial and credit history, and this section, which had been headed 'press' in Kennedy's neat rounded hand. He still had the bulk of the file, including sections labelled 'work' and 'home' to read, perhaps there would be something more useful there.

Gradually the idea was dawning in David's mind that it might be dangerous just to be *around* Loatheworthy at the moment. The inspector, they knew, had been behaving *very* badly recently, and if the pattern he saw in this folder were followed, some redress, at once awful and absurd, surely lay just around the corner.

#

At just past midday Loatheworthy left the unnerving glacial calm of Crodd's room. Since he had spent the entire session cowering down beneath the classroom windowsills, muttering incoherently and hoping that Haversham would not see him, he had had little effect on Hornby's only male educator, and Crodd had simply ignored him completely. In the last few hours, Loatheworthy's mind had travelled through the gaudy land of quivering and puzzled shock (what *gun*?) He had passed the out-of-town shopping centre of petty relief (perhaps Haversham would not act against him now, unless provoked); and now - as he crept in near silence with his back pressed to the wall through the maze of school corridors - he had fetched up in the roadside café of growing indignation, where the buns were bewildering, and the coffee was bitter.

The woman was clearly not just a wily and devious opponent, she was also quite mad. What had she meant? He was sure that he had not handled a gun. Was it some new dope slang that he was not aware of, or had Hall done something *truly* stupid?

His back was against the wall now, both literally and figuratively. He should cut his losses, leave the school and not come back. Despite his threats, it would be difficult for him to make any trouble for Haversham. He could knock the lessons that he had personally observed, but neither Willis nor Godfrey would be driven from their opinions. At best, he could deliver a mixed report on her personally, and what good was that? What leverage was there in that? Maybe he should give up, quit while he was only behind on points and follow her instructions; perhaps that would be the smart move.

The thought stopped him in his tracks. Around him, the school was lunchtime quiet. The teachers were either in the dining hall, or working in their classrooms. The children were once again outside, and he could hear their noise, faint and seemingly far away. It was an attractive idea. Let it all go now, move on, let the past be the past.

But then she would own him for the rest of his life, always dangling his misdemeanours over his head. An image of Helen's face flashed before him - furious, pointing the staple gun - and he felt humiliated and bewildered rage seize him again. How could she have seen through all of his carefully laid plans so easily, as if he were one of her pupils whose motivations and schemes were obvious to adult eyes; as if he were the teacher, and Haversham the inspector? Could he be threatened in such a manner and let it go?

He stood slightly straighter in the corridor.

No. He could not allow himself to be bested by both father and daughter. There must be something further he could do, some way to turn the tables. She had attacked him with a *stapler* for God's sake, evidence of mental incompetence, hostility, obstructionism, and misuse of school property.

There *must* be something he could do.

Loatheworthy found himself approaching the staffroom once again, and hearing the hum of slightly hushed voices, he quietened his tread.

He stood, clipboard in hand, ready to pretend to be reading from it if anyone should leave the room and see him lurking. The door was open perhaps three or four inches, not enough for him to see through, but enough to hear.

" ...going to do?"

The older teacher, the nervous one who played the piano and always dressed in black. There was a shrillness in her voice, a tremor suggesting the onset of hysteria. This could be interesting.

"Is he, er..?" A fascinated tone - it was Ewing, the one with the big hair and the disconcertingly peaceful gaze.

"Yes, I think he *is* dear, but I'm not in charge of first aid any more, Crodd is, so I can't be sure." A sudden brightness to the voice. "He might be hibernating!"

"People don't hibernate Miriam."

"Yes. They do. I saw it on television. Cryogenics it's called. You can have your head frozen. And people fall into lakes in winter and thaw out ten days later. Until then everyone thinks they're, well, y'know... like him. And the only way to tell is with a rectal thermometer."

A meditative pause, then- "Nope. No, I'm not doing that. Anyway, it's not even very cold in here. You don't think the fact that he's gone *green* is any indication?"

"Doesn't mean a thing dear. Might just be being festive. I had a great uncle who could go green on command."

"Really?"

"Oh yes. He used to make money on the side with a *very* unsavoury cabaret act. *The Human Courgette*, they called him."

"Did *he* go stiff as well?"

"Oh, you saw it then."

Another long fascinated pause. Loatheworthy could hear himself breathing.

"No. I mean *he* seems rather stiff. Unmoving."

"Hmmm... Well let's be scientific about it. Poke him with something."

"Nope. I'm not doing that either." Ewing giggled, a brittle sound, frightening rather than jolly. "What do you think the inspectors will make of this?"

"Oh, I don't know. Probably say it's a poor use of school space, at least."

A noise, like the shuffling of feet, then the older one spoke again.

"It's *just* the sort of thing they look for. We must keep it from them. Something like this could sour their opinion of everything else we do at the school."

Loatheworthy had heard enough. It was time to make an entrance.

Clearing his throat, he swept through the door and into the staffroom. On hearing him, both teachers turned quickly to face him, wearing expressions of exaggerated guilt and surprise. Loatheworthy was gratified to hear what might have been a gasp from the older woman.

He perceived his problem immediately. Including her hair Kimberly Ewing stood five foot five inches tall, and in her black heels Miriam was barely an inch taller than that, yet standing shoulder to shoulder they were still tall enough to effectively block most of Loatheworthy's sight through the open door of the mystery room.

They faced one another.

"Good afternoon," Loatheworthy said, rising slightly up onto his toes, trying to see over them. Instinctively they both also rose slightly.

"I thought the staffroom was out of bounds," the older one squeaked.

Loatheworthy frowned mightily. "Nowhere," he said, "is out of bounds for the Inspectorate." He followed this with what he hoped was a weighty stare, then feinted to the right, but they were too quick for him.

He tried the direct approach, "What's in there?"

"Nothing!" Both women replied.

He put on his most friendly and conciliatory expression. "This is routine," he said. "I have arranged it with the Head, and I know it's a little inconvenient, but we do have to inspect *every* part of the school."

Miriam smiled back. "We'd like to show you, really we would," she said. Her smile twitched slightly and her eyes were far too bright. "But we think it might give you the wrong impression."

Loatheworthy nodded, feinted to the right again and both teachers followed him, leaning slightly in that direction. Too late, they realised his ruse, and he managed to dart to his left and at last look into what used to be the staff toilet.

The image that greeted him there was so bizarre that at first his mind refused to take it in, then details began to seep through.

The room was small and almost square, perhaps nine feet on an edge. There were no windows, and only a single grimy and shadeless light-fitting, bringing weak highlights to dull grey tiles, and giving the impression of a prison cell. On the far wall there stood a small wash-basin, and to his right a single lavatory, complete with a plastic seat, high cistern, and a long rusting chain.

Horrible though this example of Armitage Shanks chic was, it was as nothing when compared with the apparition perched on top of it.

There, in a posture that suggested a bird about to fly, sat Martin Hall, or more correctly, what had once *been* Martin Hall. His feet were together, his knees bent, and his arms were outstretched by his sides, pointing at a rakish angle towards the floor. He stared out into the bathroom, holding forever a look of exaggerated surprise or expectation. Someone had wound a large amount of green tinsel around him, carefully covering arms and legs and, with his triangular posture, this made him resemble a short, squat Christmas tree which someone with an unusually extreme sense of festive cheer had rooted in a disused WC.

As the teachers had said, Hall had begun to turn a delicate shade of green. He was decorated with baubles, and twinkly fairy lights were spun across him, flashing on and off with a faint but cheery glow. Though even this wasn't the most disturbing detail. Oh no. The most disturbing detail, Loatheworthy discovered, was that, instead of a fairy atop this tree, there was a bright yellow plastic bottle of Toilet Duck, neatly Sellotaped to the front of Hall's head, so that the crooked spout pointed accusingly outwards.

Loatheworthy turned to the teachers, his eyes wide with shock, seeking and finding some confirmation that he wasn't hallucinating. He seemed to take in every detail with extra clarity; now everything he saw was in Technicolor. Miriam and Kimberly had drawn away from him, mimicking the children they sometimes taught. The curious pocket of shocked calm in which he had found them had begun to melt away. Miriam's heavy black glasses rested crookedly on her nose, and as one hand moved slowly upwards to correct them, he saw that her nails were bitten to the quick. Kim was silent, as if what she had seen was at last sinking in.

Miriam spoke in a high, almost strident voice-

"Does this mean we'll fail? I suppose we'll fail."

When he made no move to answer she twitched again, and plunged onwards. "It's hardly fair. I mean, this isn't really reflective of our school ethos. It doesn't happen every day, you know. Usually we're so tidy."

At last, Loatheworthy felt that he could speak. "The Ofsted murderer!" he croaked.

" ...And you must know, from watching us that we're all *far* too dedicated and busy for ritual homicide... " The woman was babbling, he pointed towards the door.

"Go," he said. "Go and get someone."

Miriam blinked, and looked at him resentfully. He flapped at her with his hands, "Go. Quickly!"

She took Kimberly by the arm, and led her from the room. When they were gone, Loatheworthy turned slowly back towards the bathroom, hoping that the view there had improved; it had not.

His initial shock was now ebbing away, drawing back to reveal a stark shoreline peppered with the discarded ice-cream wrappers and beer cans of self-interest, and the half-buried cigarette ends of self-doubt and fear. Though seemingly mesmerised by the scene before him, he felt no guilt at Hall's apparent demise, only creeping shock and a feeling of exposure: an increase in his now near-cosmic paranoia.

The Ofsted murderer! Here! Where he had been working and sneaking around all week! If he hadn't been cautious enough to send Hall that night it might've been *him* there, a sickly green, decorated, and spreading festive cheer from the pan.

Loatheworthy took a deep breath, realising that the full impact of this thought had not yet reached him; he might have to wait days for that.

Hall's decorations blinked and glittered and put pastel shadows of themselves all around. Slowly, Loatheworthy's shock began to transmute into a gentle wonder, a sense of opportunity. At last! Perhaps things were going to go his way; perhaps luck had swung behind him. He had wished fervently for some solution to present itself, and here it was.

He began to glance around the staffroom, looking for anything that belonged to Helen Haversham. Eventually he saw what he wanted standing by the sink. Drawing his handkerchief from the top pocket of his suit, he tiptoed heavily across the room, picked up what he was sure was Haversham's cup from beside the sink, and emptied a residue of coffee. He held the chipped cup up before his nose then closed his eyes, thinking.

Yes. If it wasn't her cup then she had definitely drunk from it, he had seen her, and therefore bits of her would be on it, DNA and suchlike.

Yes officer... she was behaving most strangely, ranting about weapons and drugs... and she tried to kill me with a stapler...

It might be enough.

He crept back to the bathroom door holding the cup, wrapped in the thin material of his handkerchief, by the tip of its handle, as if it were made of explosives. He looked at Hall's corpse. Whoever had decorated him had a great sense of balance and drama for the lighting. Perhaps Hall would have been consoled by the idea that even though he had been a second, perhaps even a third-rate human being, he had made a first-rate Yuletide ornament; or perhaps not.

Loatheworthy stepped inside the small room and, turning his face away squeamishly, wiped the edges of the cup on the corpse, hoping to leave some trace of Haversham there. Then, wondering about the detecting abilities of the average policeman, he placed the cup at Hall's feet, at the base of the toilet, turning it on its side so that a final trickle of coffee ran from it.

Then, still ignoring Hall, Loatheworthy stepped back to admire his handiwork.

That would certainly wipe the smile from her face.

An image of her popped into his mind again, as he had seen her earlier - furious, almost snarling with rage - and a truly uncomfortable surety crept over him, and he wondered why it hadn't occurred to him immediately.

Perhaps she actually *was* the Ofsted murderer.

Yes, she had found Hall somehow about his business, extracted the information she needed, and done this... this *weird* thing. He suddenly became acutely aware that he was alone at this end of the school.

Loatheworthy heard the faintest of noises behind him, perhaps the buzz of a bluebottle escaping the winter and coming home to roost, or perhaps it was the light scuff of a shoe on the floor. He began to turn, expecting to see that Ewing or Fitzpatrick had doubled back, but he never completed the movement. He felt something heavy but seemingly very soft connect with his shoulder and the right side of his head. His eyes closed, and he felt as if he were falling, falling from some great black height, clutching with both hands at the greasy rope of consciousness.

He missed it and tumbled headlong into the dark.

#

A little while after Loatheworthy's already lightly battered head had connected heavily with the staffroom floor (a spectacle which both women thought they would happily have paid to see, but which in reality they would not have enjoyed at all), Helen and Alison sat in Alison's classroom with their feet propped up on tiny chairs, staring out at the playing children.

"What were you *thinking*? I mean, I once heard of a teacher who *swore* at an inspector, but he taught secondary school English, so it was practically compulsory, but *attacking* him with a *stapler*?"

"I know. I *know*. I... I just snapped." Gloom descended upon them.

There was a noise at the firmly closed and locked classroom door - more of a scratching than a knock - and both teachers rolled their eyes exasperatedly. In the excitable run up to the Christmas break the children's tolerance of each other was wearing thin, and the practice of coming to teachers in the lunch hour to tattle on some imaginary but hideous crime was a growing fad. Both women were loath to punish such behaviour since they might then one day miss a genuine grievance, but the complaints were becoming increasingly bizarre. Helen's class had taken to seemingly random accusations that they were being 'followed' or 'stared at' by a classmate. As far as Helen could tell, what either accusation actually meant was that they had spotted the offending person standing near to them in the playground. Alison could top this, since yesterday one of her boys had come to her in tears complaining that Jordan had deliberately eaten his Power Ranger.

Sighing, Helen rose and turned the key in the door and was surprised to find not a pupil, but Kim standing in the doorway, one hand still limply raised, ready to scratch again.

"Hello Kim, what is it?"

The woman said nothing, but simply stood there, staring up at her imploringly. Her eyes were very round, her face doughy and white; she looked shocked. Alison appeared at Helen's shoulder. "What is it?" she said. "You look awful."

Kim ignored the question, raised her hand further, and made as if to scratch at the door again. Her hand landed on Alison's shoulder with a small plopping sound. Alison and Helen looked at each other frowning, worried by this new complication. Alison raised her eyebrows, put her thumb and forefinger up to her lips, and mimed drawing on a small but incredibly satisfying cigarette.

Helen shook her head. "I don't think so," she replied. Gently, she took Kim's hand and led her, uncomplaining, into the room, closing the door behind them.

"What is it?" Helen asked again, "Is it bad news from home?"

After a short pause, Kim shook her head slowly from side to side.

"Is it one of the children, has something happened?"

An agonising hesitation, and then again the slow shake from side to side.

Helen thought, then, excitedly, "Have you won the lottery?"

A more definite shake this time, then Kim whispered a single word- "Green." Both women leaned in to hear her, then drew back.

"What's green?" Alison asked, "Me? Do you mean me?"

They waited, but again there was no answer. Alison huffed-

"This is ridiculous. It's like dealing with Skippy."

She took Kim's hand and patted it gently, then, peering at her earnestly, asked in a terrible Australian accent-

"Is it Timmy, Skip? Is he trapped in the abandoned Plutonium mine with a rabid albino koala who's in rut and decided that Timmy's his best bet for procreation?"

Kim simply stared.

"Is it Loatheworthy?" Helen asked, "What'd he do now?"

At this, Kim's eyes grew even wider, and she said more insistently- "Green. Green! In the toilet!"

Working with small children provided an astounding variety of things that you might, if you were unlucky or unwary, be surprised by in the toilet, but this still flummoxed them. Luckily, at that moment there was another knock at the classroom door, and without waiting, in strode the Head with a martial bearing, followed by Miriam. She surveyed them with a steely gaze.

"Miriam says we have a problem," she said. "This is training scenario D4 - A corpse in the toilet, and the inspectors are already appraised."

She clapped her hands together once, smartly, as if she needed to gain their attention.

"This is it, people. This is what we prepared for. It's damage limitation time. I'll be damned if I'm going to let one little corpse in the toilet tarnish this school's reputation. Tell them Miriam." And with that she swept back out of the classroom again, and away down the corridor.

The teachers stood for a few seconds of stunned silence, then there seemed nothing for it but to follow her. Helen and Alison propelled Kim between them, whilst Miriam excitedly told her story, her gaze darting around the corridor walls as she walked.

They had bowled into the staffroom before any of them had had time to wonder over what they might find there, and Helen felt a ridiculous urge to close her eyes, to not see whatever it was that had disturbed the other teachers so. The sight that met her was perfectly ordinary: tables and chairs, her coffee cup standing in the centre of the counter, posters and reminders. It was horrible, certainly, but only in the way that every staffroom she had ever been in was horrible, filled with ancient gripes and lessons in waiting.

The door to what used to be the staff toilets was firmly closed.

"Mister Loatheworthy?" the Head called. When there was no answer she stepped diffidently up to the toilet door and knocked gently; there was no reply.

"Damn. He's probably sloped off somewhere to call the police."

They gathered around the door, Miriam and Kim hanging back slightly. The Head raised one hand towards the handle, then dropped it back to her side.

Seemingly unaware that she was speaking aloud, she said quietly- "Delegation. Del-e-gation is the secret of good leadership." Then, in a slightly louder tone, "Alison, perhaps you'd like to..?" She gestured invitingly towards the door handle.

Alison looked alarmed. "What? Why me?"

The Head glanced around, seeking another option, but all except Kim refused to meet her gaze. She reached for the handle again. As she was about to grasp the cold steel, Alison said from behind her-

"How do we know *he's* not in there?"

The Head stopped again, "Who?"

"The murderer!"

Again, except for Kim, everyone took two paces away from the door. After a moment's thought, Miriam reached forward, grasped Kim by the shoulders, and pulled her back in line.

The Head considered this for a moment.

"Okay," she said, in a voice low enough to be inaudible from inside the toilet. "How about this? Alison, you go and get one of those chairs," she pointed to some children's chairs stacked in the corner, "and hold it up. Helen, you swing the door open, and if anyone's in there clobber them."

"What if it's Loatheworthy?" Alison asked.

Again, the Head thought for a moment.

"Do it anyway,' she said. "We'll call it an accident."

Alison turned, but Miriam was already there ahead of her.

"I'll do it!" she said, bright-eyed and smiling. "I like the sound of that. Oh yes." Helen shrugged, and the others backed away from the door, seeming to shelter behind her.

Once again, Helen found herself reaching for a door that she did not wish to open. She grasped the handle, looked up at Miriam - who stood with the chair raised to chest height, legs pointing outwards, making tiny aggressive jabbing movements - and began to count softly out loud.

"One... Two... Three."

She whipped the door open with far too much force, half expecting it to be locked, and then her vision was confused by a blur of motion. It was Miriam, charging into the room, moving faster than anyone would have believed possible, brandishing the tiny chair before her as if she were a lion tamer.

"Neyaaargh!" she screamed, Kamikaze style, her hair and clothes flying crazily behind her. "Die!... Die foul scum!... Die!... Dieeee!"

Momentum carried her to the end of the room, where she turned on her heel, still brandishing the chair, breathing hard.

The room was more or less empty.

The other teachers peered in; a row of heads craning around the door. Miriam jabbed at them with the chair once more, for show, and then put it down.

The room, unused for as long as any of them could remember, was not particularly wholesome, but it certainly did not contain anything more unspeakable than limescale.

Miriam shook her head slowly, seeming to search every available space with her eyes. Eventually she tip-toed over to the toilet, lifted the seat, and peaked gingerly over the rim.

There was nothing there, no sign of any tinsel, baubles or fairy lights, and most importantly, no sign of any corpse. Leaving her trusty chair behind her, she retreated to join the others.

"Oh very funny," Alison said. "As if our lives aren't complicated enough we've got to put up with a weird 'corpse-in-the-toilet' hoax." She looked at Miriam.

"Did Ofsted put you up to this?"

"But he was *here*." Miriam indicated the space above the pan, "Standing like *this!*" She mimed the pose. "Kim saw it too!"

They turned to the younger teacher who was still staring blankly ahead of herself. "Green," she said, without conviction. "Green."

From the playground there came the unmistakable sound of Crodd once again ringing the hand-bell to announce the end of lunchtime; the children would soon be returning.

The Head cleared her throat-

"I see. Well I suppose we're all reacting to the stress of the inspection in our own ways. Thank you Miriam, Kim. Very good. Very entertaining. Excitement over, I think, everyone. Let's make our way back to our rooms, shall we?"

"But... but... " Miriam stuttered on, more quietly. The head ignored her.

"We've much to do. Classrooms to tidy. Rehearsals to be endured. I'll see you all in the Hall at three fifteen, and not before."

Muttering and grumbling, the teachers retreated, leaving Helen behind. Something caught her eye, a flash of dull colour leaning against the wall behind the toilet, and she reached in and snagged it, instantly recognising Loatheworthy's beloved clipboard. Without hesitation, she flipped the cover open for a look at the paperwork within.

The top page was divided up in a format with which all teachers had become horribly familiar – it was a small tick-list table with columns used to record verdicts of 'Excellent', 'Good', 'Satisfactory', or 'Unsatisfactory' on various aspects of their teaching. The table bore Loatheworthy's name as inspector and Helen's as inspectee, and had been specially widened to include three further columns; all of Helen's ticks lay in the additional 'Useless', 'Wretched,' and 'Execrable/Possible Evil?' columns.

Helen stared at that for a good long time. From down the corridor the sound of young voices was becoming insistent. Was it a threat? An admission of defeat? Evidence of some profound unhingement? Or all three?

She could not decide, and with no idea of what it could possibly mean, she simply took the clipboard back to her classroom, and began her afternoon.

#

Oxford was showing one of its most pleasing aspects, and as the afternoon darkened, it became a frosted picture-postcard. David looked out over Radcliffe Square at the floodlit buildings. Lights glowed in the Radcliffe Camera, and its silvered dome glinted, winking indecipherable signals towards the roofs of All-Souls where a few people in evening dresses and ostentatious academic gowns were already arriving. If Dr Love did turn up, David wondered, would he be foolish enough to accept a sandwich from the Presidents?

He shifted in the uncomfortable wooden chair, unconsciously trying to catch sight of his breath as frosty vapour. He had now worked his way through three-quarters of the Loatheworthy file, and knew more than he wanted to about the little inspector.

To his right lay a pile of photocopies of school rolls stretching back for a decade. One name was highlighted in pink: Martin (believe it or not) Albert Hall. He had been a pupil of Loatheworthy's for three years before achieving expulsion. Next to that was a printout of Loatheworthy's telephone records for the last month. Hall's name appeared twice. It was all beginning to add up nicely; if only he could find some motive.

Now David turned to an envelope at the back of the file and found a spool of microfilm in a cardboard case. Kennedy had pencilled 'Ref-6.iii?' on the outside.

David found himself an unoccupied reader, and began to thread the film in. Quickly, he realised his problem. This cartridge of film contained almost the entire print run of an irregularly published society magazine called *Chrysalis*. It had run between nineteen seventy-one and nineteen ninety, and whoever had used the film last (probably Kennedy) had wound it to its end - he would have to work backwards.

The reader's viewing lens had warped over its years of service making it always slightly out of focus, and by the time he had reached March of 1986, David had developed a slight headache. He carried on anyway, winding past discussions of the miners' strike and the Falklands conflict, of the winter of discontent and the emergence of punk rock. He surveyed television reviews of long-dead and hopelessly quaint sitcoms and cutting-edge documentaries examining social changes that never were.

Finally, he reached 1977, winding through now at a speed that made a librarian favour him with a hard stare. The first two issues of winter passed him in a blur, and then he reached volume six, issue three, and began to read.

It was on page six. He sat back frowning and then slowly leaned forward, peering at it carefully. The photo processing and reduction had rendered the image sinister, like the police photo-fit attached to some dark, long-ago crime. The image was stark, showing three men holding up wineglasses. It accompanied a brief article about lavish City parties, and showed the inside of a very swanky dining room - all chandeliers and wood panelling. The caption read: 'Reclusive Millionaire Maximilian Watt, CEO of HCH entertains guests at the infamous summer bash, c1976 (L-R: J Haversham, Watt, and G Loatheworthy).'

Watt was a small man, sitting at the image's centre, leaning towards the camera and grinning. To his left, a taller man was folded into the same sofa. The family resemblance was immediately apparent. There was something in the expression, some depth to his gaze discernible even from the grainy print that made it clear: it was Helen's father. Loatheworthy sat to Watt's right. The inspector had had more hair then, and improbable lamb-chop sideburns, but the moustache remained. He was facing the camera, but, David noticed, his eyes were narrowed, and showed an expression not of good cheer, but of fear and spite. This was directed over Watt's head, towards Helen's father. Behind Loatheworthy's head, unseen, Watt had raised his fingers and bent them, making a pair of absurd rabbit ears; he grinned at the camera impishly.

David sat back again, and let this new information settle in his imagination. So Loatheworthy nurtured some ancient grudge, not simply against Helen, but against her entire family. He had employed Hall (an ex-pupil), to somehow further his ends, framing Helen as the Ofsted murderer. Once the gun settled down into one form or another, they would even be able to prove this.

That was enough. He should check that the gun was still safely stored in his wardrobe and then break the good news to Helen at the school.

#

David made it back to Woodcroft Road by ten past four. The journey in from Oxford had seemed to take an age, and now he felt the urge to hurry. A car passed, bathing him briefly in light, and he moved on up the pathway, paying no heed to the silver Jaguar again parked four spaces away from number seven. He did not look upwards, and so he did not see that the curtains were drawn in his room, leaking light from around their edges. He had left them open that morning.

Inside, the hallway was filling with foul-smelling steam issuing from the kitchen. He wrinkled his nose: Mrs Gibble's famed poisonous vegetables, boiled for over an hour and served with every meal (for which her boarders paid extra). They had a texture and consistency somewhere between fermented seaweed and swamp gas, and should have been classified as a chemical weapon.

As he neared the kitchen, the lady herself appeared in the doorway, satanic in a giant cloud of steam, clutching a blackened wooden spoon.

"Mister Barclay, there's a... " she said, in a frosty tone, but she had made the mistake of not blocking his path, and so he slipped past her.

"Sorry Mrs Gibble, can't stop, I've got piles and *piles* of things to do."

Gibble didn't follow, and he didn't look back, bounding up the stairs three at a time.

He had his own door almost a quarter open before he realised that the light was on and drew back. Had he left it on that morning? He ran through events in his mind; no, he didn't think so. This was it then: a visit from Peter, eviction. Mrs Gibble certainly knew how to pick her times.

There was a movement to his left: the barest shift of toe on carpet coming from behind the door. David regarded his side of the door levelly, then placed both hands at its centre; he would take a leaf from Helen's book. With no further thought he pushed the door open as hard as he could and it flew inwards and hit something with a satisfying thud. When it bounced back at him, he sidestepped it neatly and swept into the room, a look of theatrical surprise on his face.

"Hello Peter," he said, beginning to remove his coat. "Sorry about that, didn't see you lurking there." He reached up and touched the graze on his head. "The same thing happened to me yesterday. Hurts, doesn't it?" Then he glanced up, and immediately realised something was wrong.

There was the size, for a start. This man was more slender than Peter, a couple of inches shorter, had less hair, and appeared to be wearing a rather sharp suit. David could not imagine Peter in a suit; he surely would not have been able to manage all of those buttons.

"Shon of a *bitsh*!" the figure exclaimed, standing at last, and David saw why one hand had been concealed. He shot a glance towards the wardrobe: open.

Snoopy blinked hard, trying to clear his vision, ran his fingers through his hair, looked at them in disbelief, then raised the sawn-off, heavy with reality, to chest height. Instinctively David put his hands in the air.

"Sorry," he said, only realising how weak that would sound as he was half way through saying it. "I thought you were someone else."

Snoopy advanced on him.

"Who do you work for?"

He punctuated his questions by jabbing the air with the gun, now clutched in both hands.

"Where'sh Hall? How did you get hish gun. Thish ish hish ishn't it!"

David cocked one ear towards the man, his expression somewhere between apology and panic. "Sorry," he said, "I didn't quite catch that last bit."

"Thish," Snoopy waved the gun slightly, "Thish ish hish!"

A pause. "Sorry, maybe if you slow it down a bit, all I'm getting is a hissing sound."

Snoopy jabbed him hard in the chest with the gun, and David sat down on the bed.

"Shtop jerking me around. I know you're working with that teacher. You've shtolen from me, and I can't have that. Now, I'm not an unreashonable man... " He cocked his head to one side, smiling faintly, as if hearing something out of David's earshot.

"Acshually, you know what? I *am* an unreashonable man, *very* unreashonable." His smile widened horribly. "And I'd quite like to shoot you today, undershtand?"

David nodded.

"Okay. We are going to the shcool to have a little talk with Mish Haversham." Snoopy giggled. "Shcools. I *like* shcools."

David thought as quickly as he could whilst staring down the barrel of a gun, and this turned out to be not very quick at all.

"Helen doesn't know anything." Snoopy raised his eyebrows, and David thought again. "Actually Helen knows *everything*, all about you and Loatheworthy, and I'm sure she's told everyone. The police have been to her house, and they'll be staking out the school, so you may as well give this up now."

The nose of the gun rose until it was pointing at David's face.

"I don't care who she's told, or what she knows, and the *plodsh* aren't at the shcool." He twitched the gun barrel towards the door. "Letsh go."

David trudged back down the hallway, sure that he could feel a hot spot in the centre of his back exactly where the gun, now secreted inside Snoopy's coat, was aimed. As they drew close to the kitchen, he began to hope that Mrs Gibble would step out to berate him and complicate things, but the door was closed. Hideous greenish vegetable steam crept from the kitchen and stuck close to the carpet like a special effect in a cheap horror movie. David tried to linger by the door, but Snoopy moved him onwards.

Once they were outside, he was prodded towards a silver Jaguar. In the car, behind a screen of condensation, he could make out a huge figure hunched over something. Snoopy rapped on the window, a back door popped open, and David slid onto a cream-coloured leather seat. The man behind the wheel was watching a hand-held television set. Snoopy slid in after David, the shotgun pointing towards him unerringly.

"Letsh go Bob, the shcool."

"Oh but Boss, are you sure? I mean it's *Blue Peter*, they're lighting the advent crown… couldn't we just... "

Snoopy leaned forward in his seat; the leather creaked.

"You have teshted my patiensh *enough* today. Drive."

#

They reached the front of the school with horrible speed, just as the Nativity was about to begin. The foyer had been hastily decorated with paper chains and lights which glowed blithely in the semi-darkness. Parents' cars were parked (illegally) all around the school entrance, and separate from them, parked inside the gates and also decorated with tinsel and fake snow on its tinted windows, there stood a brand new black Bentley. Both men glanced twice as they walked past.

Snoopy carried the gun in a way that suggested that he was practised in this sort of thing. It was held out of sight in one of the pockets of his long coat, but he did not allow David to forget its presence. Even when they had been getting out of the car, leaving Bob in the front seat to go back to his mini-television and the mental composition of a letter of resignation, David had felt the sharp edge of the truncated barrel pressing just above his kidneys.

As he reached to open one of the school doors, feeling the cold metal under his hand, the unreality of the situation washed over him. Seemingly distant, he could hear the Headteacher giving a pre-ordeal speech over the quietening rustle of uncomfortable parents folding coats and programs, yet he was being marched into the school, at gun point, by an underworld hit man, who was probably in the pay (unofficially at least) of Ofsted. Amazing.

More amazing still, he realised, he was going to have to do something soon, make some move, before fear rendered him completely helpless.

He tried one more time.

"This is crazy! Why has Loatheworthy got it in for the Havershams?" he asked. "I'm sure Helen hasn't stolen anything from you, and she doesn't know who Martin Hall is."

Snoopy simply smiled unpleasantly. "Where ish she?"

"She might be in her classroom."

Another jab with the gun. "Okay, let'sh go there then."

Though they probably would not have been challenged with the school hosting so many strange adults, they moved quietly, and with caution; Snoopy seemed to know where he was going. The corridors were empty and dim, half of their life drained away by the late hour, their daytime buoyancy reflected only in the bizarre wall displays. From the corner of his eye, David viewed what seemed to be miles and miles of snow-scenes, reindeer, Santas and Christmas trees, and in one memorable scene Santa being stuffed into a chimney by an Action-Man commando unit.

As they drew near to a classroom door (not Helen's, David was sure, but his idea of the school's layout was still slightly hazy), he decided to make his move.

He stopped just outside the classroom door, pointed into it, and said in the most astonished-sounding voice he could muster, "What the hell is that?"

He expected some lapse in concentration, a glance into the doorway, perhaps a chance to run, or at least to strike out in some way - that's how it always worked on the television - but Snoopy's alert yet muddy gaze never left him. The half-smile became a sneer.

"You'll have to do better than... "

At that moment, ahead of them, two Dickensian urchins, complete with caps and ragged scarves and trousers, erupted into the corridor, shrieking and fighting as they passed. The smaller of the two, giggling maniacally, seemed intent on beating the larger one to death with a complicated paper lantern.

As they approached, Snoopy took a half-step backwards, and they passed between the two men. It was all David needed, and he bolted through the classroom door, slamming it behind him.

Hoping that the layout of this room was similar to Helen's, David ran for the front windows, seeking the door that would lead out to the play yard, knocking over chairs and jars of mysterious unseen equipment. He ran the length of the room, seeing a ragged time-line display slip past on his right. He ran past Confucius and Buddha, Henry the Eighth and Shakespeare, Ghandi and Hitler, Elvis and Nixon, and by some miracle, reached the door and found that it was unlocked.

Helen watched the Nativity with a growing sense of existential dread that a school production alone could not explain. She had not seen Loatheworthy since lunchtime. Perhaps he had taken her threats to heart and she would never have to see him again, but the inspector's absence was ominous, and waiting for David to arrive was maddening.

Here everything *seemed* to be going to plan. The first three carols had now been 'sung'. The customary matching pair of troublemakers from the back row of the choir had been ejected, and the children, she had to admit, replete in their purpose-made costumes, looked wonderful. Those of her class who were not involved in the short Nativity which would make up the production's central sections (interrupted by carols at appropriate places) formed the second two rows of singers grouped on either side of the stage. Each was made up to look like a Victorian urchin, with fake dirt on their faces. The two children on the end of each row held lanterns on sticks which they waved about mercilessly in time to the music, occasionally causing those before them to duck and scowl.

It seemed to be doing the trick for the parents. So far it was certainly better than last year, when the Archangel Gabriel, who was also narrating the early stages of the Nativity, had managed to knock over a large Christmas tree with his trumpet, had said "bugger" quite audibly, and then haughtily enlisted two donkeys (after all, he was an *Arch*angel) to help him pick up all of the spilled baubles.

Helen was sitting on the corner of the front row, her chair turned sideways, ready to leap up and assist should this be necessary. Alison had drawn the short straw to be 'prompter' this year, and she sat hidden from most of the audience at the extreme edge of the stage, pretending to be slightly bored, but actually enraptured as always by the magic of school theatre.

Seeing Helen glance at her, Alison pointed out into the crowd and mouthed something. Helen shot her a quizzical look, and she did it again. It looked like- 'That's him.'

Instead of watching the door for David, Helen began to glance around the audience. She did not see Simon Dasch, lounging unobtrusively at the opposite end of row one, but instead caught Marie's eye. She was sitting next to constable Abbot in row five, and smiled and offered a tiny wave.

This was probably the biggest crowd the school would draw all year. All of the chairs were taken, and parents lurked along the back wall like lost souls. The hall was well designed, making dramatic use of a gently sloping roof space, so that the stage end was much higher than the audience end. It was a trick of perspective that worked well, making any production, even the school's 'sharing assemblies', seem more spectacular. Now Helen could almost feel the pride washing in from the audience in waves as each parent slowly became convinced that *their* child, no matter how small their part in the proceedings, was actually the star.

She glanced at Alison again and followed the line of her surreptitiously pointing finger more carefully, then finally caught on. It was their mysterious patron. He sat, almost in the far corner of the room, in a very modern-looking motorised wheelchair, a checked blanket over his knees. So much for her theory that he might have been an ex-pupil - this man was far too old. He wore a cardigan over an open-throated shirt, and he was thin, painfully so. He seemed otherwise unburdened by his age, however, sitting straight and tall in the chair, smiling at the production with all of the pride that she saw in the faces of the parents sitting around him. Two men in dark suits flanked him, men so large they looked as if they might break the chairs on which they perched: security. Was he somebody's grandfather? *Did* they have a secret heir to a fortune in the school?

Her eyes were drawn back to the double doors at the hall's end. Where was David?

Behind him, David heard an adult voice call out sharply - someone in pursuit of the children no doubt - and then, as that faded, there was the lethal sound of the classroom door handle being depressed.

He made it outside onto the gravel, scrambled to his left, and disoriented, ducked left again. Aided by the playground furniture he got his bearings. He was facing the window he had helped Helen to climb through only two days before. If he had gone to the right there would have been more classroom doors, more places to hide, but it was too late now.

He stopped to listen, his back pressed against the school, but he could hear nothing. If he made a run for it he would surely present an easy target, disappearing across school grounds, and if...

His breath caught in his throat. Was that a classroom door opening?

Suddenly all he could hear was his own heartbeat. Was the gunman even now walking stealthily towards him, under cover of all that noise?

There was only one way out. He turned and looked upwards. The window he had watched Helen disappear through still wasn't properly closed. He was a good six inches taller than Helen, yet still the distance seemed forbidding; would he fit through? He listened again - all was quiet. Knowing that further debate would only weaken his resolve he grasped the sill and boosted himself upwards. Nudging the window open with his body, he slid between it and the frame.

It was only when he was almost completely through, expecting to hear Snoopy behind him at any moment, that David realised what he was diving into - at least it seemed to be unoccupied. He missed his grip on the cistern and almost put his foot straight into the toilet bowl, then landed heavily, banging one shin. He moaned and rubbed it furiously, muttering incoherent imprecations under his breath until the pain began to ebb away.

As David opened his eyes someone tapped lightly on the door of the stall, it was unlocked and moved slightly, and a female voice said, "Hello? Is everything okay in there?"

David glanced around himself in superstitious awe, realisation dawned, and mortal dread gripped him once more.

He was in the Ladies.

Another voice, from further down the row of stalls said, "Sounds nasty. More fibre in the diet, that's what you need, or senna."

David's mind reached overload for a few moments, and he envisaged himself reaching out and locking the door, and never, ever, coming out again, *ever*, no matter what. But there was a maniac loose in the school; he had to alert Helen, the other teachers, and eventually the police.

He pulled the door open just as the woman outside (a parent, he supposed) was about to knock again. Seeing him, she took a step backwards, her hand still raised.

Should he tell her what was going on? Would she believe a strange man who had mysteriously appeared in the Ladies? He decided that she probably wouldn't.

"How do I get to the hall from here?" he asked.

She looked at him with the same lack of comprehension and dawning disgust that she might have shown if he had been standing there wearing nothing but his woolly socks.

He ignored this. "The hall, which way?"

From inside one of the stalls the other woman called out indignantly, "Is that a *man*?"

David raised his hands in a placating gesture. "It's okay, I'm nearly a doctor," he said. Strangely, this did not seem to help, and he pointed to the window.

"There's another man... he's dangerous. Just try to stay in the toilet for as long as you can."

He would not have believed it possible, but the woman's expression darkened.

"Agnes," she said, with studied fascination, "I think it's one of them there *deviants*."

There was the sound of hurrying from the stall, and David decided it was time to leave.

Beyond the heavy bathroom door there was another dim corridor festooned with children's work and echoing to the sound of carols being savaged. No not savaged, David decided being fair, just bounded up to, knocked over, and given a light mock mauling with plenty of dribble.

He crept into the corridor, staying close to the wall, planning to follow the sound of the singing, which should, in theory, lead him to rational people. As he approached the corner, he heard voices by the bathroom door. He strained to hear and thought he caught the words "pervert", and "get him", and then, as he began to turn back towards the corner, he felt the gun - returning like a particularly annoying acquaintance - jab him just beneath his rib cage on the left side.

He froze, not turning, and Snoopy leant upwards and whispered gently in his ear, "Shtupid."

Another sharp jab. David did not know whether to hope that the women would or would not come out of the bathroom.

"Sho Shtupid."

Finally he turned to face his captor again.

Snoopy was grinning at him furiously.

"I'd *like* to shoot you," he said. "*Like* it. Hmm mmm. Only not jusht yet." Again he prodded David with the gun. "Thish way. She's in the hall. They're *all* in the hall."

Mary and Joseph (both from Alison's class this year) shuffled uncertainly onto the stage and were told by a less than kindly innkeeper that there was a rush on in Bethlehem this year, it being Christmas and all, and there was no room at his inn - had they not thought of booking ahead? As the couple turned away, comically weary, two lumpy younger siblings seized their chance for stardom, and executed a cunning plan. Easily slipping the grip of their parents, they began to mount a mini pitch-invasion, waddling up the stage steps. The first child provided a distraction by making a 'nee-nah' noise, whilst the second made a spirited attempt to reach the Christmas tree and its fake presents. He ran - as fast as his training pants would allow - towards the tree, which, following last year's debacle, had been relegated to a far corner of the stage and anchored to the wall with twine.

Helen rose in her chair, but the rotten kids' parents, grinning sheepishly, were there ahead of her. A Dad grabbed the first miscreant and bundled it, complaining, out of sight. A Mum proceeded to crouch by the stage's corner and attempt to persuade the other child to leave voluntarily. The child, whose name was apparently Mark, had spied brightly coloured wrapping paper, and was not about to be pried away from it with words alone. Helen looked at Alison again, and the older woman rolled her eyes theatrically, then, noticing something, pointed again, this time towards the back doors of the hall.

Helen glanced that way, shielding her eyes until eventually they became used to the dimness. Then she made out a gangly figure standing by the hall door. At last!

With most of the audience still distracted by the tense drama unfolding at the stage's edge ("Don't be silly now Marky, come to Mummy." ... "Pwesents." ... "Come to Mummy." ... "Pwesents *nice*." ... "Look! Mummy has ready cash... ") Helen was able to leave her seat and make her way along the side of the audience to the door. Only one pair of eyes followed her progress, those of the school's patron, turning in his chair and whispering something to one of the hulking security men.

Irritated by David's lateness, but pleased to see him none-the-less, Helen reached the door, planning to invite him in and show off the last ten minutes of their hard work. Then she caught his expression: anxious, slightly pained, and her own anxiety deepened. What had he learned today? He seemed to be motioning for her to stay where she was with one hand, and then abruptly he stopped. Frowning, Helen hurried to the door.

When she was out into the foyer the door swung shut silently behind her, cutting off a truly impressive amount of lowing from the stable animals, and the first few bars of 'Oh Little Town of Bethlehem'.

"What is it?" She asked.

David only shook his head and stepped sideways into the corridor; then she saw the smaller figure standing behind him.

"You!"

"Shut up."

She pointed, "You. You were in my house. You're working for that despicable little miscreant aren't you? Where is he? Well he's gone too far now. This is the end. I'm going to... "

Suddenly the barrel of the shotgun was mere centimetres from Helen's face. She could smell gun oil, heavy and threatening. Involuntarily, she backed into the corridor wall. Snoopy giggled; a faint sound, barely heard, but chilling.

"Be quiet!" he said. "Teachers! You all talk too much. Chatter, chatter. All the time, yap, yap, yap. I shupposh you're jusht not shcared enough yet, are you?"

David took half a step towards him, but without taking his eyes from Helen, Snoopy said, "Don't even think about it."

He rested the gun-barrel on the tip of Helen's nose; it was cold.

"That wash shome very shpeshial shtuff you shtole from me. Very shpeshial. Very valuable."

Through the wall Helen could hear the production continuing, the animals still lowing in the background of the carol. She could see tiny flecks of silver way down deep in Snoopy's irises.

"You are going to tell me where it ish."

"Do it!" David hissed. "Zap him. Do it to him. Now!"

Having the gun that close to her made Helen feel cross-eyed and dizzy. She scrunched her eyes shut and tried to knock Snoopy over with a thought-bolt. She felt nothing though, a slack rubber band, all the tension dispelled. It seemed her talent *was* out of her control, an involuntary thing. She couldn't remember actually willing the gun, or any of the other things to change, it had just happened, like a reflex. She could remember thinking the word 'toy', and it had just happened. Maybe that was it. What should she think?

It came to her, and she thought the word 'DUCK' at Snoopy as hard as she could, hoping to drop him straight to the floor so that he could be disarmed.

She felt something this time, something leave her, and she opened her eyes expectantly, and met Snoopy's cool, seemingly amused (and fully upright) gaze.

He blinked. "What the nwayack wash that?" he asked, backing the shotgun away slightly. "What did you..? I felt... " He shook his head.

"No matter. Nwaaaaak." Sudden confusion showed on his face and he leaned in towards Helen again, his eyes narrowing-

"What did he mean? What did you do?"

"Nothing, I... " She glanced at David, who was now looking at them both as if they were lunatics engaged in a double act. Behind her, she could hear the production going awry. The animals - always one of the most militant groups in any school play because of their lowly status - had given up softly mooing and braying, and were all making strangulated quacking sounds. Within seconds it had spread to the choir and even to a few rows of the audience, and 'Oh Little Town of Bethlehem' ground to a halt.

Snoopy looked nervously both ways along the corridor. "Thish ish a madhoush." He seemed to make up his mind about something. "We're going to my car, and then we'll find ush shomewhere a little more private to talk, a warehoush." Then, almost to himself, "Or a river. Shomewhere with shome niyshe reed-beds... Have to get me some *crushty* bread."

He recovered himself. "You'll like thish, being a teacher," he said. "I might make an *exshample* of you two, oh yesh. People will *learn* from what happensh to you."

Snoopy nudged David in the ribs and pointed down the corridor with the stunted gun barrel; they began to move.

The Headteacher's clear tones rang out in the hall. "Now children," she said, "you know what I've told you about quacking on school time!" The quacking subsided, the piano sounded again, and the audience quietened. 'Oh Little Town of Bethlehem' was restored.

"What happened there?" David asked.

Helen shook her head, "I'll explain later."

As they approached a door on the right hand side of the corridor, they heard excited voices up ahead, lots of them, and without a second look Snoopy tried the handle of the door, found it open, and began to usher them through.

"But this is... " Helen protested.

"Shut up." Snoopy said again, and they all squashed into what David assumed was yet another store cupboard. They stood in near-complete darkness, and Snoopy pulled the door almost closed behind them.

David looked around himself. This was an odd space, perhaps fifteen feet long and three feet wide, but taller than the other school rooms he had seen, with a higher false ceiling. Up above him he could see something round, like a basketball, gently glowing in the darkness. Was it some kind of light globe? He could hear it creaking gently, as if it were heavy and swaying, though he could see no movement. To his extreme left, he could see the shape of another Christmas tree, short and squat, its lights unlit. He thought that the room must be next to the hall, since he could hear the production still more clearly.

'Oh Little Town of Bethlehem' had come to a ragged end, and the children were now singing a brief song David didn't know about shepherds. He looked towards the door, and saw faint light glinting on the gun barrel and in Snoopy's eyes. Snoopy was holding the sawn-off up almost at his shoulder, and his finger was curled around the triggers. David reached out, and Helen grasped his hand firmly.

The excited voices reached them and stopped directly outside the door. Snoopy did not flinch; his finger simply stroked the triggers.

"Where'd he go then?" A woman's voice, high and excited. "Who'd have thought it? Our very own lurking *toilet* pervert!"

"Shut up Marjorie, this is important, we *have* to find him."

This one David recognised: it was the woman who had knocked on his stall door a few minutes earlier.

"String him up!" It was the other woman, the one who'd recommended fibre. Even in the darkness, David could see Helen frowning at this new irregularity in her school.

"What'd he look like then?" Marjorie asked.

"Ooo, evil. Evil he was. Tall and evil, and his eyes were too close together, and he had a twitch, and one of them goaty beards."

"You didn't even see him!"

"Well, I'm extrapolatin'."

"You're making it up. He didn't have a beard. *Was* a bit lanky though. Brown hair, dark eyes, wearing jeans and a brown jacket. And he looked a bit, you know, wild-eyed - and he *was* making the most alarming grunting noises."

Helen looked at David quizzically, he could think of nothing else to do, so he simply shrugged his shoulders. Beyond her, he thought he could see Snoopy smirking. He gestured with the gun and they moved further into the room, and the excited voices drifted away.

Next door the production wound on, and they were treated to the sound of an improvised scene in which three six-year-old shepherds, complete with tea-towel headdresses, robes, crooks and bushy grey cotton-wool beards, discussed the arrival of this year's Archangel Gabriel. In the interests of sexual equality, the head shepherd this year was a small girl named Emily.

"What's that over there?" Emily asked.

"Thassa sheep," chorused the shepherds.

"What's that over there then?" Emily asked again.

"It's a *sheep*," the other shepherds replied, with a hint of exasperation.

"Yeah? What's *that* over *there* then?" Emily sounded annoyed herself now.

"Where?"

"Right over there, in the corner of the sta... er, sky?"

"Oh *there*. That'll be the Archangel Gabriel!"

Another child spoke, in the mock deep voice that only the smallest rising-fives could manage.

"Behold," he said. "I am the Narkmangel Remedial, and I... I am allowed to tell you stuff!"

In the closet Helen winced involuntarily, knowing how long Kim had spent coaching the Archangel. When she opened her eyes again, against all reason, Snoopy was still there, holding the gun.

"What do you want?" she whispered. "I didn't *steal* anything of yours; I *found* it in my classroom. I didn't even know it *was* yours. I don't know anything about you. I thought it belonged to Loatheworthy."

At the sound of the name, a commotion began above them. The creaking sound intensified, joined now by a series of intermittent muffled squeaks, as if someone were attempting Morse code using only a guinea pig. Snoopy's eyes and the tip of the gun jerked upwards fractionally.

"Whatsh that?"

He pressed forward with the gun. Helen took a compensating step away from him, both hands now in the air. Behind the wall, the production was faltering again. The children were, for the moment, silent, the audience more restless, and above the polite coughing and shuffling David clearly heard Alison hiss the words - "Behold! Our Saviour!"

Snoopy turned to look at David. "Nwaak. Who *ish* Loatheworthy?" He demanded, "Ish he your bosh?"

"I don't... "

Above them there was a thump, a louder creak, and more strangulated squeaking. Totally unnerved now, Snoopy raised the gun higher and backed Helen into a corner with it.

Then time seemed to slow down for David.

The gun was still held up near Snoopy's shoulder, so that the barrels were almost level with Helen's face. As David watched, something happened: the shotgun changed beneath Snoopy's hands, and once again the sheen of metal left it to be replaced by flat, unreflective plastic. The barrel moved upwards, and David moved with it.

He dove towards Snoopy, arms outstretched ready to bring him down. The gun had lost its weight, and Snoopy's body jerked backwards slightly as he tried to compensate, to re-balance himself. David hit him from the side with as much force as a standing start could give. Twice surprised, unbalanced, Snoopy fell, taking the hand that had been bracing the barrels of the gun away to catch himself. He landed heavily with David half on top of him, and immediately began to struggle and curse.

David had surprise on his side, but Snoopy - an ex-physics teacher - was the more experienced in dirty fighting and disproportionately extreme violence. As David reached up to try to pin his arms, he bucked and rolled over, pushing David to the floor, and - grinning with the effort - he brought the gun upwards, wedged it under David's jaw, and began to choke off his air supply.

Large black flowers began to bloom and die in David's sight as he struggled hard to push Snoopy away. He could feel the gun pressed against his throat, and then it changed again, not plastic now, but cold gunmetal again. After what seemed like hours, he managed to curl one hand around the short barrel and release the pressure slightly. There was a blur of movement in the distance of his vision as Helen grabbed Snoopy by the shoulders, and tried to pull him away from behind. Snoopy simply ducked, and Helen lost her grip and fell backwards.

Free again, Snoopy drew the gun away from David's neck, and as he began to rise, struck out with stock and caught him a glancing blow to the nose.

Knocked back to the floorboards, David heard one of the children say something to a now silent audience, and he heard Helen shout his name. Snoopy began to reverse the gun, to point the barrels at him again, and at the same time push his fingers through the trigger-guard, ready to take a shot.

Then the world became a blinding white light.

#

To the Nativity audience, it looked like this...

Something had gone drastically wrong with the production. Everybody knew what was to come now, it was a familiar story: the Archangel should be telling the Shepherds of the miracle in the stable at Bethlehem; but the children had been distracted by something going on behind the stage, some commotion. When Miriam left the piano to hoist up the huge starry sky backdrop in order to reveal the hand-painted scene of peace and joy and harmony at the stable, lit by a beautiful spotlight star shining through the scenery, they were greeted with the sight of Miss Haversham standing over two men wrestling with a gun. Instead of the powerful spotlight poking through the carefully cut hole in the black sky above them, distributing God's largess over the scene, there was something quite *quite* different.

"Behold!" Gabriel said, bravely battling on, reiterating what was written on a small chalkboard, hanging incongruously in the stable's entrance, "A star!"

From the front row, in a clear, carrying voice, slowed by entranced realisation, one of the parents said-

"That looks more like a moon to *me*!"

Another voice said, "It's very *avant-garde* isn't it? For a school play?"

There was complete silence, and then, from almost the back row, one person began to clap. It was a startling, solid sound, a repetitive beat.

Less stunned than most by the sight of Loatheworthy's posterior, gently glowing under a coat of luminescent paint, the school's patron - Mr Maximilian Watt - was applauding enthusiastically.

"Oh well done!" he called. "Encore! *Encore!*"

Constable Abbot, sitting in the second row, leapt into action. He had a better view of the stage than those at the back, had quickly noticed the oddly shaped Christmas tree at the extreme right of the backdrop, and had judged that the blood on David's face was not make-up. He made for the stage. Simon Dasch stepped on to the boards ahead of him. Coming in like an over-dressed arrow, he put one knee in Snoopy's back and neatly scooped the gun from his grip before the gangster's fingers could tighten. Then he turned and mugged shamelessly at the crowd. Abbot ignored him, hauled Snoopy from David's prone form, and pinned him to the stage with practised ease.

#

In Helen's classroom Mister Tribble was showing off, running from one end of his cage to the other, before doing some bar acrobatics and making a truly spectacular dive into his bedding. Helen, David, Max Watt in his gleaming wheelchair, Simon Dasch, Marie and the Head, were waiting nervously to be interviewed by the police. They watched Mister Tribble in exhausted silence as he crawled from the cotton wadding and went to sit in his food bowl in order properly to enjoy their amazed adoration.

David and Helen sat together, hand-in-hand, David still clutching a bloodied handkerchief, which one of Max Watt's security men had given him, to his nose. A police doctor had told him, in a way which implied he should stop being such a wretched malingerer, that his nose wasn't broken, merely bruised, and the swelling would go down in two or three days. He had dry swallowed two painkillers, and along with the adrenaline they had left him with a nasty taste in his mouth.

From down the corridor they could hear the whine and click of a police camera, a sound punctuated by the occasional powerful flash which seemed to bleach the corridor for a fraction of a second, making them all blink. The police had photographed the staffroom already, and were now working on the school hall, fingerprinting and documenting everything.

The parents had mostly dissipated, fleeing towards Christmas with their tired and excited offspring, leaving their names and addresses with a constable on the way out. The human need to process things through gossip was strong, however, and the school seemed to posses a peculiar type of gravity for some families, pulling them in and holding them in orbit, talking for hours at a time. One such group was slowly walking past the outside of the classroom now.

"You know," Helen heard a man's voice say, "as an expression of *pure* theatre I think it was startling - but I'm not sure I understood it."

"Hmmm... hmmm..," another male voice replied. "I think it was really about consumerism gone mad, you know? All the greed that we go in for at this time of year. I mean, the corpse Christmas tree with the toilet duck, and replacing the star, the *sign* of Christmas past with an enormous naked bottom. That was pure genius; inspired social satire."

Inside the classroom the small group of people gazed at each other helplessly. Only Watt smiled a gentle, satisfied smile.

"Now you see that's interesting." The voices were moving away now, growing more faint. "Because with the guns and everything, you know, the armed struggle beneath the gigantic oppressive bottom, I thought it might have been a protest - about big government, say, or carbon emissions."

Constable Abbot, still out of uniform and flushed with success, arrived in the doorway and knocked politely on the frame. They all looked towards him.

"I thought you'd like to know," he said, "That *was* the body of Martin Hall on stage. It looks as if the killer stashed it in the school overnight, and that confirms the statements given by Miss Ewing, and Miss Fitzpatrick."

The Head nodded with apparent relief. At least her staff were not utterly insane.

Abbot seemed to brighten-

"Apart from that, it all turned out rather well," he said. "I may as well tell you, since you'll probably see it on the news later anyway, although the blackout's holding for now, but he's a match!"

"A match?" Helen asked.

"Yes. The Met. had a print from one of the earlier crime scenes, and it turns out, it's his. He left a hand-print on the plunger that he left on that inspector's head at one of the other crime scenes. He *is* the Ofsted murderer! Didn't seem the type to me at first, but it all checks out with our profile."

Abbot counted the evidence off excitedly on his fingers. "He used to be a physics teacher, and it was a short hop from that to gangsterism. In 1998 he had a psychotic episode in a classroom, and was fired on the instructions of - wait for it - a schools' inspector. This Hall seems to have been minding a consignment of various drugs for him, and some of his personal stash - the *Fermaxipan* - was mixed up in it. Open and shut case really. Looks like he killed Hall, he thought he had killed Loatheworthy, then he was going to get you two in place somehow, and have you revealed in the final scene of the Nativity."

"What *about* Loatheworthy?" Helen asked.

"Well, he's confirmed your story. Apparently, he *hired* Hall to plant some incriminating stuff in your classroom, and it backfired horribly. They took him to the hospital, and he's got suspected concussion from the crack he took on the back of the head, and a few bruises from being tied up, and apparently that paint was indelible, so it'll take months for it to wear off... But he's basically okay; shiny and glowing, but okay. In one way he had a very lucky escape."

They were silent for a moment, as if picturing the gentle stable scene once more, and then Abbot shook his head, perhaps to dispel the image. "You've given your statement haven't you Mar... er, Miss?" he asked, directing the question at Marie.

"Oh yes. I was only here to watch the play, and I gave my name and address at the door."

"Well, you could go. If you like I could arrange a ride in a squad car for you, or call a taxi?"

Marie nodded, turning to Helen. "If you don't mind, I think I will be off. Things to do at home. This is why I left education - far too much excitement." She made towards the door.

Abbot glanced up at the Head. "Mrs Fairport," he said, "you're next."

The Head took a deep breath and also rose to follow him. Abbot glanced over at Watt questioningly, as if the two of them had some unspoken understanding; Watt nodded to him, and as Marie and the Head left the room, the constable closed the door firmly behind them.

Abbot led Marie and the Head out into the corridor.

"Okay," he said, "they'll be ready for you soon Mrs Fairport, they're set up in the school offices, and if you just give me a second Miss, I'll get you that taxi."

Marie smiled and nodded, and she and the Head, who still seemed rather dazed by the whole affair, began to make their way slowly up the now bright corridor. As they passed the entry to the school hall they looked in, over the now empty rows of chairs, the scattered programs and discarded costumes, to the stage. There, a police photographer was still at work, kneeling, and pointing his camera upwards, recording the remnants of the crime scene. The Head sighed.

"Who'd have thought it," she said. "I mean, when Ofsted turn up, it's the kind of thing you pray for, *wish* for, anything to get rid of them; but when it actually happens... incredible."

Marie peered at the stage, then closed one eye and sighted the scenery, complete with the policeman, through a frame made of her forefingers and thumbs. She measured distances and angles and imagined what the scene *would* have looked like if that horrible little man with the gun hadn't turned up and spoiled it.

Under the cold artificial light of evening, the whole idea seemed mundane and dull; not true art at all. She could barely understand why the idea, why the *scene*, why any of the scenes had seemed so compelling to her, so vital, things that needed to be made - it was inexplicable.

She nodded to herself; it was over now, fading like a dream upon waking. It was quite fortuitous that she had picked up that plunger in the *Duke of Wellington*. The little man with the lisp and the gun would be able to claim it all for himself now; the scenes would be his.

How lovely for him!

Now she would move on, and find a new way to express herself. She had heard good things about the flower-arranging classes at the adult education centre, and there was always mime.

The Head continued her musing.

"That whole bottom thing was a bit of a bonus really... No more than that inspector deserved - a true spectacle. I wonder where the murderer found all that day-glow yellow, I've been looking for it for weeks."

"It was locked in your secretary's desk," Marie said.

Abbot appeared in the corridor behind them. "On its way now," he called. "It'll meet you at the front gates."

Marie looked through her fingers for a few seconds more, then gave him a cheery wave, winked at the Head, and strode off towards the school entrance.

The Head watched her go, various expressions warring on her features. Had she not been turned away from Abbot, he might well have asked her what was wrong. But she was turned away, he did not see, and with the tiniest, dismissive shake of her head, she entered the school offices to give her statement unchallenged.

Back in her classroom, Helen had waited almost a full minute, listening to Abbot's shoes tap-tapping on the corridor floor as he bustled around collecting and dismissing witnesses, before she turned to Watt and Dasch.

"Okay. What is going on?"

Dasch was silent, and simply peered out through the darkened window. Watt still smiled his gentle smile, as if considering the question on many levels and choosing his answer carefully. Eventually, having made his choice, he took a deep breath and spoke. His voice was low and mellow and did not seem to fit his frame, but it was pleasant to listen to.

"As Mister Barclay here will tell you," he said, "after his work in the library today, I became involved because I knew your father - your mother too, actually - a long time ago."

Watt studied their faces, looking for some reaction, then laughed gently at their puzzlement.

"It's true. All children seem to believe that their parents did not exist before they were born. Well yours did, Helen. Your father was a junior partner in an excellent and very lucrative business of mine, many years ago. It was my first business, in fact, and I've always felt something of a debt to him." He sighed, almost wistfully. "He was a uniquely talented man in those days, your father... uniquely talented, as you are yourself."

Helen and David exchanged a dark glance, and then Helen looked back, her eyes narrowing with suspicion. "Dad's never mentioned you."

"No. No reason why he would have. It was a long time ago, and when he left we... we just dropped from each other's radar. We send cards at Christmas, and on each other's birthday and so on, but no more than that."

"I've never seen one."

That quelled the old man's smile.

"I see. Well perhaps our rift ran deeper than I had supposed. We had a... a disagreement of sorts, you see, over company policy."

Helen's suspicion remained.

"Why are you here then, tonight of all nights? Is that coincidence?"

David thought that he saw an almost predatory expression pass over the old man's face.

"Not exactly, no. I knew that your parents were in Australia, of course, and then I happened to read in the local press that George was leading the team that had tendered to inspect your," he gestured to the room around him with one hand, "lovely school. That made me realise that I would have to watch things carefully."

"What about Loatheworthy?" David asked thickly, withdrawing the bloodied handkerchief from his nose, peering at it warily. "How does he figure in this? You knew him too. Did you know what he was up to?"

Watt laughed, but to David it seemed mirthless.

"Caught me, David - can I call you David?" He did not wait for a reply. "Okay, I didn't just *read* about the school inspection, it was brought to my attention because since he left my employ I've maintained an interest in George. You've researched him a little, I believe; perhaps you understand his nature. He did something that he shouldn't have, once. Almost ruined everything, and his actions still live with him."

Watt nodded towards Helen-

"Your father forgave him, of course, almost immediately, but I... well I didn't." Watt's mood darkened. "I kept up with George for years. I needed to see that his story followed a certain... pattern. Obviously I hoped that one day he would learn, or grow, or something, but I have to admit, it's so much fun that he never did. A terrible irony for him that he should become an inspector - one who makes his living looking over others' shoulders."

Before Helen could jump in with another question, he continued-

"But none of that is relevant. What *is* relevant is that George obviously bore a grudge against your father, and saw you as his chance to get even, so I called in Simon to help things turn out right. Simon has certain talents, again unique. Sometimes when I offer him enough money, he acts for me."

Dasch did not acknowledge him, and still gazed moodily out through the window.

David looked down sorrowfully at the bloodied handkerchief in his hand-

"Turn out *right*. We were almost killed, there was a *shotgun*."

Watt frowned. "You were in no danger," he said. "Simon had made sure of that."

David scowled. "You mean you *knew*. You knew about that guy... Snoopy, about the Ofsted murderer, that he would come *here*?"

Watt and Dasch exchanged a glance, and then Watt shook his head.

"No. Not precisely. We thought there might be... repercussions of one sort or another, but you must understand there are always variables, always things that you cannot see, cannot fully anticipate."

Helen's voice was steady, but low.

"I'm sure you think that you have the best of intentions Mister Watt," she said, "but *I'd* prefer not to be 'kept up with'."

Watt held up one hand to quieten her, and then leant forward in his chair. The fabric of his seat creaked; the predatory look that David had seen so fleetingly, returned. Now the old man reminded David of a bird of prey, watching, calculating, ready to spring from its perch,

"Helen," Watt said, his voice now so low that it was almost an undertone, "I know that you understand that my motives were not entirely pure. Though Simon here is a useful ally, he has a set of scruples which sometimes baffle me, and refuses to advise me in the way that your father once did."

Now Dasch simply watched them, his expression unreadable.

"So I am always on the lookout for new staff." Watt rocked in his chair, as if he would escape it. "Those early days were so *right*, so *powerful*. The business I did then was insignificant when compared to the business I do now." He clenched a fist, struggling to express himself, truly animated at last. "But *then* it was better. *Knowing* - being *sure* how things would be - that was *perfect*, flawless." He recovered himself somewhat, the passion draining from his voice.

"Your career so far, Helen, has led me to believe that you are the right person for the job I have in mind. You can *make* things... *shape* them, just like your father, if you know what I mean? The job pays well, certainly better than teaching... there would be no need to mention this to your parents."

Helen stared, and David wondered if she was actually considering the offer, then she too leant forward so that her face was only inches from Watt's. The eagerness never left his features, but David thought that he could also see a certain amount of fear now.

"No," she said, her words given more force by their softness. "I know you've watched me Mister Watt, and now that will stop. I won't shape things for you. This is the end of it for me. It stops now."

It was a simple statement of fact. Watt did not argue. David glanced at Dasch, and thought he could see approval in his expression, a faint smile perhaps.

There was the merest of raps, and then the classroom door opened again to reveal Constable Abbot. Helen sat back and smiled. Abbot seemed surprised to see them sitting so close.

"Sorry. Am I interrupting?"

Helen replied, "Not at all Constable, we've said what we needed to say."

Watt nodded slowly to himself. If he was disappointed, it did not show. He looked up. "If you don't mind Constable," he said, "I'm getting rather tired, and Simon and I would like to give our statements now."

There was a low hum as Watt began to pilot his chair over to the door before the policeman could answer. Dasch also got up, favouring Helen, David thought, with a look that one gunslinger might give to another. Then he cracked a smile, warming his expression, and held out a hand. Helen shook it.

"Good deal," he said, then turned on his heel, and stalked off after Watt, his boot heels sounding on the linoleum.

#

Later, when they had both given lightly edited statements and David had finally managed to stop his nosebleed, he and Helen walked home through the chilly streets. They escaped a gaggle of press at the school, and were both secretly sure that they were walking the other one to their door in order to guarantee their safety. Bundled up and numbed by the cold they felt an odd sense of peace. They were too tired, it seemed, to ask or answer any more questions for the moment.

They left the orbit of the school and the few groups of parents still hanging around the streets chatting. Helen waved once or twice, eliciting squeaks of delight from a couple of her class members who were always astonished to find out that she existed outside of the school gates, and then they passed on, again hand-in-hand.

David turned their strange interview with Watt over in his mind as they walked, as if something about it bothered him, a shadow there, hiding something.

A few streets away from David's house they paused by a road-sign. The stars, seemingly magnified by the cold, were vacant and pitiless. Around them the houses were decorated with gaudy good wishes. Three houses up Helen could see a plastic moulded Santa, bright red and white, complete with a sack of toys, glowing steadily on someone's roof, like the world's most jolly burglar. She wondered what the town would look like from above now, what an alien visitor swooping over, making holiday movies for his friends and relations would see: twinkling lights, apparent cheer.

"I'll take the image of those eight policemen pulling Loatheworthy out of that scenery to my grave," she said.

David nodded, "Who'd have thought he could be wedged in so tightly. But still, to have one's buttocks as the lead story on three separate news shows - he must be very proud."

There had been so many parents taping the carol concert that the television networks had been spoiled for images. In the end, most of them had selected footage taken by Robin Green - his camera had had the most powerful and steady zoom. Helen giggled, but as they walked on, became more serious again.

"Of course, we haven't escaped Ofsted," she said.

David was astonished. "Really? They'll be back then?"

"Oh yes. The Head told me, they're going to give us a term to recover, and then re-inspect." She deepened her tone, sounding suddenly like the voice-over on a movie trailer. "There is no escape, from Ofsted." Her mood did not darken, however, and she shrugged. "After this one," she said, "I figure the next inspection will be a breeze - I'll stay cool - no more panic and daydreaming exotic demises for petty officials for me. Nope, I'm on the wagon."

David stopped by a street lamp.

That was it. Now he understood what had bothered him.

You can make things... shape them, just like your father... Watt had said to Helen, and she could.

Earlier in the week, Helen, sitting opposite him in the pub: *daydreams really... Loatheworthy gets caught in a mantrap, Loatheworthy falls into an open sewer and dies, Loatheworthy's head is mounted on the wall in my bathroom...*

Could she have..?

But it was bigger than that. A parade of images ran through his mind, things that he had seen very recently, but which had remained unconnected until now...

The children's Christmas drawings and the red riding hood display - all woodcutters and wolves in bed...

The inspector as Santa... The inspector as Grandma... The poster in the Headteacher's office showing the diver...

Yes! That was what he had been trying and failing to see yesterday night - it was the same pose as the inspector with the sink plunger on his head.

Hitler, and Nixon, and the Statue of Liberty...

Yes. They were all there on the walls of the school. All things that Helen had seen, day after day as she worked there and her enmity towards inspection - no, towards *inspectors* - grew.

Standing in the lamp's glow he asked himself the scary question - the question which could lead to enlightenment or the abyss - *What if..?*

What if fantasy was a virus that the real world could catch? What if wishes *could* be broadcast and manifested? Could you murder by proxy? Be guilty of dreaming unknown homicides; moving the protagonists, murderer and victims, like a blindfolded chess player?

Could an untold grudge spread out and shape the world?

No. Of course not. His mind rebelled. He had been too full of such suspicions lately, and they had all proved absurd.

Realising that she was now walking on alone, Helen turned to him, frowning slightly; the streetlight shone in her hair and made it an angel's cap of light. For an instant she seemed young enough to have starred in the Nativity.

David was looking at her; he seemed almost solemn.

"Do you think that's really the end of it?" he asked. It was a serious question.

Helen searched inside and found that, almost to her own surprise, she *did* believe that the strangest period of her own life (so far), and certainly the weirdest few months for teachers generally, had reached their conclusion together. Unsmiling, picking up his solemnity, she nodded. That seemed to be enough for David. He joined her and they walked on, falling into step, a slow lulling rhythm that pleased them both.

When they reached David's house Helen asked him what his plans were for tomorrow and he didn't answer. He had spied the odd shapes heaped up in the garden. As they drew closer, David could see that it was as if someone (probably Peter) had attempted to re-create his rooms on the chilly lawn. There were piles of books and boxes, packed suitcases, his computer and Hi-fi, and as a centrepiece, his desk and office chair set out as they had been upstairs.

On the desk sat his tank of fake fish, swimming merrily backwards and forwards. On the chair sat Dr Love wearing a camel-hair coat and a grey fur hat with earflaps, his feet propped on the desk and his fabled brown valise leaning beside him. Love was reading the last few pages of David's thesis, frowning deeply, and as they approached, he looked up at them.

"Excellent Barclay... excellent," he said. "Finished I'd say, and on time."

He reached down beside him, and without ceremony snapped open the valise.

"Narg!" David said, dropping away from Helen's side almost into a crouch, and covering his eyes with one arm.

Love dropped the thick bundle of papers into the case and snapped it shut.

"Overwrought, is he?" he asked Helen mildly.

She glanced down at David, now returning to his feet. "Yes. It's been a difficult week."

Love shot out one gloved hand. "Bernard Love," he said, smiling warmly. "Don't think we've met." He glanced at David again. "I'll have this bound *for* you, shall I Barclay, then we can start arranging examiners."

Still wide-eyed, David said nothing.

A frown crept over Love's features.

"It *is* finished isn't Barclay? I mean, you're done with crime fiction for now, aren't you?"

David considered, his mind casting back over the previous days.

"Oh absolutely," he said.

Love nodded, clapping his hands together in the cold. "Excellent," he repeated. "I noticed that you hadn't put in a final full-stop, that's all. Obviously a typo. Took the liberty of biro-ing one in for you." He picked up the valise. "Seen the scholarship committee by the way, recommended you for a junior fellowship - It should go your way - I've got these photographs of some of the committee members at a hotel in Woodstock - disgraceful business." He glanced around himself, as if noticing the furniture and piles of belongings for the first time.

"You'll be able to move into the college soon I'd've thought. Anyway," he shook Helen's hand again, "It was delightful to meet you Miss..? "

"Haversham."

"Miss Haversham. Of course. I shall bid you both good-day; I have some half-witted computer scientists to enrage."

He wandered off. David and Helen stared after him.

"Who..? " Helen asked, "What..?"

"Don't ask," David said. Above them a second floor casement drew up, they gazed upwards, and the sharp form of Mrs Gibble could be clearly seen.

"You!" she cried, shrill in the still air, leaning far out. "You Are *Evicted*. You can bring your key back in the morning. All of your disgusting belongings are there." She pointed down towards the door. "And I've already re-let your room."

David said nothing, gaping up at her, he was too tired to be angry or argue.

"See your stuff!" Mrs Gibble continued, her voice building to a crescendo of pride and recrimination, and finally triumph, "...there's *piles* of it. Do you hear me? *Piles* of it!"

The window slammed shut on her staccato laugh. It was a very definite sound; then the light in the window died. David sat down on his suitcase and propped his chin forlornly on one hand.

Looking at him Helen felt suddenly suffused by a perverse Christmas cheer which stole over her like wakefulness. Suddenly she felt good, really good, happy and ready for a holiday. The balance of things *was* somehow re-established, she thought. The inspection was over, the Ofsted murderer was caught, and they had survived. She was sure that there would be more snow this Christmas, that it would fall heavily in the next few days, blotting out the details of the town, cleaning it up, making it all white - and she couldn't wait; it was time for a holiday.

She held out her hand to David.

"Why don't you come and spend Christmas with me? With us, I mean?" she asked, "Marie and me. All the shopping's more or less done, the decorations are ready to go up - we're set. It'll be great."

David gazed around at the strewn lawn. "What about all this?"

She shrugged. "Get what we can carry, what you really need, and we'll pick up the rest later. Alison's hubby has a van."

David thought, his breath visible in the faint light from the house, then he looked up and down the street as if he expected some other solution to present itself there. It didn't, and at last he stood.

"Are you *sure* this is a good idea?" he asked, "I mean, our history together has been... eventful."

Helen smiled. "Of course. What could possibly go wrong?"

"Okay," David said, taking her hand again and hefting the suitcase, "It's a deal."

Together they walked away, closing the gate firmly behind them.

THE END.

Printed in Great Britain
by Amazon.co.uk, Ltd.,
Marston Gate.